"Already regarded as one of ... the last decade for his stirring Golden Age ... Wright proves he has the right stuff to write exciting modern day epic fantasy with the terrific *The Last Guardian of Everness*." —*Midwest Book Review*

"*The Last Guardian of Everness* is the first part of the *War of the Dreaming* and looks to be a wonderful epic fantasy. Unlike other epic fantasies, Wright blends the very real world of today with his rich dream world, the two meeting in the myths of central Europe. The background of the dream world unfolds intriguingly, with a wealth of characters and settings. For fans of fantasy who enjoy a rich and textured story that unfolds in twists and turns, *The Last Guardian of Everness* will be a wonderful read." —*SFRevu*

"*Mists of Everness* rips along at the same manic pace as the first half, veering between high-toned mysticism and farce, lashings of derring-do and moments of hilarious absurdity.... Wright gives us adults permission to sit back and let that inner child behave badly and bravely by turns, while speaking in tongues and remembering forgotten mythologies." —*Locus*

"The second volume of Wright's War of the Dreaming series dives headlong into the action that ended the first.... Wright blends our everyday world with the dark world of nightmares." —*Romantic Times Bookclub*

"Making appearances in no particular order of appearance are figures out of Greek and Celtic mythology, Arthurian romance, Masonic iconography, American history, Shakespeare, children's parables, J. M. Barrie, nuclear physics, the classic movie Casablanca, and a sex scene in the White House ... Just enjoy it." —*Sfsite.com*

"Engrossing fantasy fueled with high imagination and memorable action sequences ... You really get the sense that Everness and the land of dreaming are magical places.... Throughout the whole book, Wright's writing style is clear, descriptive, engrossing and sometimes lyrical." —*SFSignal.com*

MISTS
of
EVERNESS

BEING THE SECOND PART OF
THE WAR OF THE DREAMING

John C. Wright

A TOM DOHERTY ASSOCIATES BOOK
NEW YORK

MISTS OF EVERNESS

Edited by David G. Hartwell

A Tor book
Published by Tom Doherty Associates, LLC
175 Fifth Avenue
New York, NY 10010

www.tor.com

Tor® is a registered trademark of Tom Doherty Associates, LLC.

ISBN 0-765-35179-X
EAN 978-0-765-35179-1

First edition: March 2005
First mass market edition: June 2006

Printed in the United States of America

0 9 8 7 6 5 4 3 2 1

Dedicated with
affection and respect
to the sailors, officers, and aviators
of the SS Donald Cook,
SS Hawes, SS Mitscher, SS Oscar Austin,
SS San Jacinto, USNS Kanahwa,
and the Fighter-Attack Squadron 105:
We all know this tale is a fantasy;
in reality, evil forces could not
and will not prevail against you.

❧

Contents

MISTS
of
EVERNESS

I

The
Amaranthine
Fields

I

Once there lived a shining field where amaranth and
moly grew. Bright with color, the amaranth blossoms
swayed, and tall grasses bowed when soft winds blew.

The field was in a valley surrounded on all sides by
Iron Mountains, and no creature could come over them
without wings. Birds and butterflies of all types lived
in the shining field and played and sang and flew
among the trees and flowers, but no cat, no fox, not
even a squirrel.

Only two creatures in that valley lacked wings. One
was Meadow Mouse. (But even Meadow Mouse and
all his kin claimed descent from a mother mouse
who'd escaped by a trick from the dreary house of
Horned Owl before suppertime. She had been carried
on her wedding night in Horned Owl's claws over the
Iron Mountains, and Meadow Mouse's people have an
interesting tale to tell over the episode.)

The other was the Sad Princess, who lived in a Tower in the center of the valley, atop tall Willow Hill, in the middle of a ring of Weeping Willow trees.

The Tower was made of sunset colors, stones of scarlet and pink and cerise, with many wide windows of deep purple glass. It was a Tower without doors, for every creature in the valley flew (except, of course, for Meadow Mouse; but he was so clever at getting into places that the lack of doors did not hinder him).

Some of the folk in the valley told the tale that the Tower had once been part of a castle in the clouds, but which had foundered against the peaks of the Iron Mountains one day when it flew too low and sank down to rest on the valley floor. Whether this was true or not, only the Willows knew, for their memories stretch back far indeed, but, like most trees, they were secretive and would not say.

One bright spring day Meadow Mouse walked up to Horned Owl's house and knocked on the door with his walking stick.

"Hello, Owl?" he called out. "I've come on a quest for the Sad Princess. It seems she has lost her name. Can you help me find it for her? For you are known to be wise."

"Who?" came a voice from the house.

"It is I, Meadow Mouse."

The door swung open, but it was only Mrs. Owl. "I'm sorry, but my husband is away at Parliament."

"Parliament?"

"It's something owls do when they get together, dear; it's boring at best, but it's not as bad as what crows do. But please come in; I was sitting down to tea."

"Thank you, no," said Meadow Mouse, suppressing a shiver. His tribe and the Owl family had made peace long ago, when the Sad Princess first came (although she had a different name back then), but the Mouses still did not like to watch the Owls dine. It brought back unpleasant memories.

Mrs. Owl blinked behind her huge, round spectacles (her eyes were round and yellow and alarmingly large), and she said, "I'm sorry. But I was going to nibble on some cheese and biscuits with my tea, and I'd hoped to have some company."

"Cheese?" Meadow Mouse's whiskers stood up at the merest mention. "But I thought Owls did not eat such stuffs."

"Well," said Mrs. Owl, "we keep it for our guests. Now that the war is over, sometimes mice stop by; and I know how particular you vegetarians are about what you eat." And so she bustled into the kitchen, and Meadow Mouse followed after, trying not to look timid.

But the Owl's house was not so dark nor so dismal after all, but nice and tidy. Nor were there bones of mice coughed up in balls lying across the floor, as the nursery stories Meadow Mouse heard in his youth had said. Meadow Mouse reflected that Owl had married, after all, and Mrs. Owl perhaps had reformed his untidy bachelor habits.

And when Meadow Mouse was settled down with his tea and biscuits, and they had talked about the weather (an easy topic to discuss in Shining Valley, where it was always spring), Mrs. Owl asked, "What's all this about the Princess, then?"

"Shall I tell you the story?" asked Meadow Mouse.

"Please do! I love stories!"

"As who in this valley does not, my dear Mrs. Owl?"

"My favorite is the one Gray Goose tells, about fields of endless ice far to the south, which her people used to visit once a year, back in the days when Winter still invaded this valley each December. You always knew his terrible white armies were on the march, she said, because they hung their battle pennants on every branch and overhang. But, dear me! Tell me your story, do. We hear so few good ones from mice. Er—I mean. Well, at least my husband is in the one story you always tell," her voice trailed off lamely. Mrs. Owl hoped she had not hurt Meadow Mouse's feelings. She knew his people did not have many stories at all, since they could never fly out of the valley to the outside world. But Meadow Mouse pretended not to have noticed but began his tale without further ado.

II

"The Weeping Willows were weeping again," Meadow Mouse began. "And I heard Bright Starling singing to them. 'Why do you weep?' she sang. 'We live here in a vale of Amaranth, flowers unfading forever, where winter never comes, and those who breathe of their perfume know ageless youth and beauty evermore. Why, therefore, do you weep?'

"And I heard the wind walk among the willows and carry this message back to Bright Starling: 'We weep because the Sad Princess has forgotten how to fly.'

" 'And how has she forgotten this?' I heard Bright Starling ask. 'The secret is so clear. Every fledgling learns it when they leave the nest; joy is the answer. Joy and freedom carry us aloft.'

"The willows let the wind carry this message back: 'Her joy is gone because she has forgotten her name.' "

III

Mrs. Owl clucked her tongue. "My, doesn't that Starling have a way with words!"

"The point is," said Meadow Mouse (perhaps a touch impatiently), "What are we to do about it?"

"Do?" Mrs. Owl blinked. "One doesn't 'do' anything about melancholy; it's like the weather. It comes and goes."

"But my dear Mrs. Owl," and now a touch of sharpness entered Meadow Mouse's voice, "this goes deeper than melancholy, deeper than sorrow. This goes right to the root! She has forgotten her name, and we must find it for her."

"Exactly so!" came a new voice, deep and low, and Meadow Mouse jumped, spilling his tea all over his brown coat.

It was Horned Owl himself. Despite his portly girth, he always moved quite silently. (And perhaps he had come into the kitchen from behind just to make poor Meadow Mouse jump. Not that Owl was particularly malicious, but Meadow Mouse had been speaking sharply to his wife, after all.)

"How was Parliament, dear?" asked Mrs. Owl.

"Stuff and nonsense," rumbled Horned Owl in his deep voice, waddling over to the teapot. He turned his head entirely around and spoke back over his shoulder. "We were debating (ah! Hello, Mouse) the same issue Mouse here spoke of, but with all the motions and points of order, writs and resolutions, it will take us all month and well into the next to decide what our good Mouse here has already pointed out so clearly. We must find the Sad Princess her name again."

"Oh, she'll get over it, dear," said Mrs. Owl.

Horned Owl threw out his chest and puffed out his cheeks in a sign of great displeasure. "This is not something one gets over, like the sniffles! The Princess might be in danger!" (He did not mind speaking sharply to his wife; he only minded when other people did it.)

"Don't get your feathers all mussed, dear," said Mrs. Owl. "No one in Shining Valley can be in danger."

Meadow Mouse was more than a little intimidated by Horned Owl, but his love for the Princess made him speak up: "Mr. Owl, sir, please excuse me! Tell me what this danger is, sir! Please do!"

Owl cocked his head and stared down at Meadow Mouse with one eye. "I heard it from Cardinal. You haven't heard the tale?"

Meadow Mouse swallowed and looked up at the huge, imposing figure of Horned Owl. "I love stories."

And to his great surprise, Horned Owl became jovial and sat down with his tea. "And who in this valley doesn't!"

IV

"I had gone to consult with Cardinal on certain consequential church matters, which, while of some importance, don't come into this tale. His secretary, Secretary Bird, had just left, and we were discussing certain small matters as I was preparing to depart, when, all of a sudden, who should come in (without being announced, mind you) but Mrs. Crow. She was all a-flutter.

"'It's all my fault! It's all my fault!' she kept squawking. Now Mrs. Crow is a delightful woman, you know I think the world of her, but that voice of hers! Well, she sounds like a crow. It took Cardinal more than a moment to calm her down and get the story out of her.

"It seems her husband had taken their egg to the Princess to ask for her blessing before the baptism. Now then, you know Crow used to be our undertaker, back in the days when winter still came here, and he's been quite put out ever since the war ended. And so he didn't want to burden (that was Mrs. Crow's word for it, mind you) didn't want to burden their young son with the family name of Crow."

Mrs. Owl exclaimed, "Whyever not? I think Crow, son of Crow, would be a fine name."

"Don't interrupt, dear. Well, I thought Crow, son of Crow, would be a fine name . . ."

"Didn't I just say that?"

"Ahem! A fine name, but no, Mr. Crow would have none of that. He wanted to name his son after his cousin the raven. Well, according to Mrs. Crow, the Princess positively drooped when she heard this name. Drooped over like a flower. Almost fell out her window, if Mrs. Crow is to be believed (and, while I think the world of her, I do know the woman has a tendency to exaggerate). Ah . . . Where was I?"

"Raven," chirped Meadow Mouse.

"Ah, yes. Crow said that when the Princess heard that name, she wept. Water came out of her eyes! Frightened poor Mrs. Crow half out of her wits when she saw that. Crying! It's something owls never do, I can assure you, and I've never seen crows do it either. What about you, Mouse?"

"Mice don't weep." Meadow Mouse shook his head. "When I'm sad, I eat."

"Wise policy," commented Owl.

Mrs. Owl said, "And is that how Sad Princess forgot her name? Because of Mrs. Crow's little boy? Maybe we should speak to the Crows about the trouble they're causing."

Horned Owl said, "You may not recall what her name used to be."

Meadow Mouse said eagerly, "What? What?"

"Happy Princess."

V

Meadow Mouse was overjoyed. "You mean you knew her name all along? I can go back and tell her straightaway!"

"It's not so easy, Mouse!" Horned Owl said ostentatiously. "I haven't told you yet what Cardinal told me."

Meadow Mouse cocked an ear forward. "You have my full attention, sir, I assure you."

"Cardinal told me, and he is very learned in matters of doctrine, mind you! Cardinal told me the following story."

VI

"In the beginning, the Happy Princess was brought into the shining fields surrounded by mountains to keep her enemy the Wizard and his nightmares away. And the Princess walked along the tiptops of the tall grasses and plucked flowers from her scepter, dropping them where she walked. It is from these flowers moly springs up, which is why no one in the valley here can use stories for wicked purposes."

"How can a story be used for a wicked purpose?" asked Mrs. Owl.

"My dear, I really wish you would not interrupt. I lose sight of my target. Yes, wicked purposes. Cardinal said it was something called 'fibbing,' sort of a complex, metaphysical idea. I can't say I quite followed him, but you know how these church doctrines are. Anyway . . .

"The Princess was brought by her mother to the secret place where Oberon and the Fairy-Court had been celebrating a May Day feast and saw where certain gods, while drunk, had spilled the ambrosia and nectar from their goblets onto the grass. There was a little puddle left. The Princess planted seeds there, and the flowers drank the nectar, and from them all the flowers of amaranth spring forth. And it was those flowers that drove back Old Man Winter when he came next with his armies over the northern mountains, for he cannot abide their sweet perfume. And it was this, more than any other cause, which put an end to our old wars, your people and mine, Mouse; for we may eat when we choose, not when we need to, and can go without food forever and live happily upon the scent alone while the amaranth blooms, for it is the scent of Life.

"Because of this great service, of ending Winter's reign and ending the War, and because of the other happiness she brought, she was crowned Happy Princess; but her true name is older than this, older, so Cardinal assures me, than this valley itself."

Meadow Mouse said, "I see why the Cardinal told you the tale! Now we can find the Princess's lost name."

"I don't quite follow," said Mrs. Owl, blinking.

Meadow Mouse hopped up. "We need only find the mother! The Princess's mother must have been present at her christening!" But then he sat down again. "But where in the world can we find her? Can we send a messenger to Oberon, the Emperor?"

Horned Owl shook his great head gravely. "Not even mighty Eagle, the king of all winged things, can fly so high as the Autumn Stars, where legend tells the castle of the hibernating warriors awaits. Do you know the story? They lay curled up in a tree or something, dreaming of the end of Universal Winter, when they shall wake and bring in Universal Spring, and the world shall be fully alive again."

"You are wise, Owl," said Meadow Mouse. "Who else might know the Princess's name, or know the pathway to the stars?"

Owl shook his head again. "They say Phoenix has gone so high as the Sun and learned from him the secret of descending in fire to rise again; but Phoenix lives far to the south, outside the Iron Mountains. And even the Sun is not so high as the stars."

Then Owl drew himself up, blinking. "But, wait! Pigeonhawk might know. They say he once flew to the Moon, for he is a secret and mysterious old bird."

Mrs. Owl blanched. "I heard he is a sorcerer! That he built his nest in the World Tree once and slept for a thousand years beneath the roots of an oak! Even if he does know where to find the Princess's name, who would go ask him?"

Meadow Mouse shivered in terror at the mere mention of Pigeonhawk's name. Even Horned Owl hunched up his shoulders, shrugging. "I certainly wouldn't go. Not that I'm afraid, mind you. But sorcerers and crackpots just aren't received in polite society."

But Meadow Mouse was thinking about the Princess. He dearly wanted to help her, and for a special reason he had never told anyone else. It was simply that, in a valley where everyone had wings, the Princess was the only other creature who walked afoot; and he always felt particularly close to her for that.

And she had once told him not to worry that he could not fly, and whispered to him that she also had once not been able to do it, but that later she had learned the secret. And this gave him hope.

It was that hope, more than any courage, that caused Meadow Mouse to straighten up in his chair and put down his tea. "I'll go," he said, in a firm, quiet voice, "if you will tell me the way."

VII

It took Meadow Mouse all day and all night and all the next day again to climb rock after rock and slope after slope of the frowning mountain to the north where Pigeonhawk lived. And just as he was faint with hunger, fatigue, and despair (for the refreshing scent of amaranth had been left far behind), he came suddenly upon the barren aerie of Pigeonhawk.

And here was Pigeonhawk himself, grim and solemn, wrapped in a blue robe tinged with gray, standing on a crag overlooking the valley. "Come forward, Meadow Mouse: I will not harm you. But do not step within my charmed circle, for I have drawn the rune *Algiz,* the rune of protection, all about me here with my foot."

Meadow Mouse crept forward meekly. He saw the marks clawed into the rock all around where Pigeon-hawk stood, but he could not tell if it were a secret magical system of writing or not. Frankly, it looked like bird scratches to him.

"Do not speak!" said Pigeonhawk. "I know what has sent you to me. The Princess has lost her name. I know the emptiness such loss entails, for I myself once had another name, a name I carried for another. I shall not return his old name to him till he learns contrition, repentance, and remorse. Likewise, the Princess shall not regain her name until she learns forgiveness.

"Listen, and I shall tell you the secret of our world. Our world is a false one, a copy or image of the true world, which is beyond the reach of our senses. It is from that true world our Princess comes, a place and condition that I cannot describe nor can you imagine. I will, however, attempt to tell you one mystery of that world.

"There is a thing there called Death. I do not know what color this thing can be, nor shape, but certain mystics envision it as something like a great evil king, tall as a mountain and black as night. When Death strikes, all your limbs go numb, and your body falls and rots away, and your thoughts depart and do not return. It is like Forgetfulness, but deeper. It is like being eaten by an owl, yet you do not get up again. It is a horror beyond any thing we know.

"In the true world, certain spirits living there are under the curse that they do not know whence fly their thoughts after death strikes. If one spirit puts Death upon another, that is a great unkindness and evil: it is called murder.

"In that other world, the Princess fell in love with a

raven-spirit who was under such a curse and who committed this unkindness to Galen Amadeus Waylock, whose secret name is Parzifal. I see you know of whom I speak.

"For a day and a night of the true world, which is equal to an age here, the raven-spirit kept his crime a secret from his love; and when she discovered it, she fled here to our world, using the Silver Key of Everness. But she was as innocent of the mysteries of our world as we are of theirs; and when Forgetfulness, summoned by her weeping, came upon her, she did not know the Three Signs to raise in her defense.

"And so our Princess dances on the meadow-grass, and dances in the moonlight, her eyes bright with unshed tears. Nor can she go home again, nor use the Key of Everness, for she has forgotten why she sorrows, why she dances, or what is her name.

"Many ages of our world have passed, and time in that world also; days, or weeks.

"Now you may ask me three questions. Speak, but choose with care. For we shall one day be brought to a high place and judged on the prudence of our actions."

VIII

Meadow Mouse nervously brushed his whiskers with his paw, staring up at the gold-eyed bird of prey. Meadow Mouse thought carefully, then asked, "If Parzifal were brought back from the dead, and the Raven bridegroom brought here to remind her of her name, would our Princess remember and forgive him?"

"Only if the Raven did the deed himself, with none to aid him, could she forgive—if he repented his fear of death, which led him to the crime, and healed all harms that fear had caused."

And because he had been cautioned to be wise,

Meadow Mouse thought carefully and asked, "Is there any price for this?"

The Pigeonhawk said, "Yes; the Princess will meet Death that day, and Death will reach out his great talon to carry her away."

Meadow Mouse's alarm made him ask, "Can I save her?"

"No."

And for a time, the great Pigeonhawk was silent, but then he spoke, as if to elaborate upon that answer. "Only one might save her; but he is trapped below the sea; and only one might free that one; but he is wounded and paralyzed and ensnared in evil sorcery and held prisoner in a dungeon by a Warlock."

Now Meadow Mouse was silent, his thoughts all scampering. He turned his beady, bright little eyes away from Pigeonhawk out to where the shining valley lay in the light. His eyes roamed the valley, and his gaze traveled from the Tower (which had perhaps once been a castle in the clouds) past the Weeping Willows, to the Old Oak, the Rushing Brook, and the Brook's solemn older brother, Wandering Stream, and thence to Shadowy Lake where Gray Goose lived. Here was High Hill, and Flowering Dale, Hidden Coomb, and, next to Shadowy Lake, lay Wild Marsh where Stork's nest was.

A great love for the valley and all who lay within came into Meadow Mouse's heart then, and so he said, "Pigeonhawk, now you must take me up in your dreadfully sharp claws and fly me over these mountains, I beg you, to wherever this man lies, whomever he is, so that I can do my part to save the Princess. I am only one small mouse, and I can only do what one small mouse can do, but that is more than if I do nothing, or wait for others to do my tasks."

"I will take you," said Pigeonhawk. "I will bear you from this kingdom to that other place, a place so terrible and strange that all words fail. Nor can I tell you what you must do, nor can I warn you of the dangers there, for you have foolishly wasted your final question, and I may not speak beyond what is allowed."

Pigeonhawk opened up his terrible sharp talons, sharper than the sharpest thorns, crueler and larger even than Owl's, and reached toward Meadow Mouse.

"Wait!" said Meadow Mouse, shrinking back. "I want to tell my mother and my seven hundred brothers where I am going."

"You may not."

"But she'll worry so! And I should pack something . . ."

"If you hesitate, or look backward, the enchantment of this valley will make you forget your courage and resolve, and your delay will last forever; you will be trapped here, eternally resolved to go, eternally delayed by some further scruple. Come! Already it may be too late!"

But he did not move his claws forward. The cruel talons hung in the air, half-open, poised above Meadow Mouse; and Pigeonhawk cocked his head aside, to glare down at Meadow Mouse with a large, fierce, yellow eye.

Meadow Mouse plucked up his courage, and jumped up into the talons with a flourish of his tail. "Let's be off, then!" he said, with only the smallest quiver in his voice.

Pigeonhawk fell off the cliff, snapped out his wings, caught the wind, and soared. All the while, Meadow Mouse shrieked with terror. Then the glory of flight overcame him and his squeaks became squeaks of joy.

Pigeonhawk flapped his wings, found rising air. The Valley fell away below. Meadow Mouse saw the Iron Mountains pass beneath him, peak and chasm, crag and cleft. And then, in a break between two mountains, a dark green glint of trees unknown, unnamed waterfalls plunging to alien rivers, and strange new fields beyond the fields he knew.

"Pigeonhawk," said Meadow Mouse, "if I encounter Death there, in that land, will I be permitted to come back here?"

Pigeonhawk did not look down but kept his beak pointed at the far horizon. "That question, I truly wish I were allowed to answer. The knowledge is mine; I may not speak."

Strange lands and seas were below them, and a moon like none Meadow Mouse had ever seen rose up pale and full in the east.

In the distance, where the sunset was spreading along great ranges of cloud, broader than any horizon Meadow Mouse's valley had ever let him see, the Towers of Dusk rose up, gold minarets draped with purple, rose, and red, with the setting sun a fiery ball between them. Faint and far in the distance, Meadow Mouse's ear caught hints of the music sung by the Hours and Seasons, and the harmonies of flute and lute and clash of cymbals that rose to greet the descending sun.

Meadow Mouse said, "I say, I've just had a thought. Shouldn't there be a way I can also get you your old name back, while I am out there trying to get the name of the Princess?"

Pigeonhawk did not look down, but stared with his fierce eyes into the sunset. "That question, also, I truly wish I were allowed to answer."

Meadow Mouse thought about that for a while. "Well, I'll try to get it if I run across it."

"That is kind of you," said Pigeonhawk solemnly.

2

The Nemesis
of Evil

Emily slowly came awake, her mind still drugged and dimmed by nightmare-images of her son, leaning over her, fire in his hand. And later, when the other men had come . . .

Memories slowly came back to her. Her son, Galen Waylock, had been in a coma for months. The doctors had given up hope. But then, unexpectedly, he had woken. But his eyes were strange: dark and magnetic. His voice had been like the voice from another world, majestic and inhuman.

Galen came back to life with someone else inside him, some strange and archaic phantom from the Dark Ages. A man with strange knowledge, strange powers—why not use the word?—a warlock.

The Warlock served a darker power yet, something he feared and hated and feared to disobey; something the world had forgotten, or had been made to forget. He had spoken of this power briefly to his minions, briefly, while Emily lay paralyzed at his feet. The

Black City called Acheron was rising from the waves, he said; and when it rose, darkness would cover all. Emily made a small, strangled noise from paralyzed lips, for she had heard the name of Acheron before, in the nightmares her son described to her. The Warlock, glancing darkly down, made the merest gesture, whispered a name of power: there had come a smothering pressure inside her brain that drove her into sleep.

She dreamed of a dark and windowless city drowned beneath the waves, seven towers of imperishable metal rising into the sunless gloom of the abyss, while blind and transparent fish sported among the tombs and monuments, or shapeless squid, mute and grown to monstrous size in the eternal night, floated near the barbicans and gates, their pale hides trickling with firefly light, their eyes like lamps.

From the city rose a dim and broken sobbing, and she was terrified to recognize it. It was the voice of her ex-husband's father, Lemuel, that odd old man who lived alone in a deserted mansion on the coast. Lemuel had been calling out to her, telling her to warn someone, something. What was it?

The memory was gone. Only the sick, sharp sense of overmastering terror remained.

Only a dream. Now she was awake. Or was she?

Blearily, she looked about her. She was lying where the horrible person who was impersonating her son had dropped her, on the carpet before the fireplace. It still was dark in the house, but the first rays of red sunlight were streaming through the upper branches of the trees outside, wreathed in mist.

She was still benumbed and could not move her arms or legs, but there was a tingling sensation, as if her limbs were returning slowly to life.

Emily heard snoring from down the hall; she recognized it as belonging to Wil, having heard it for many nights these past few years.

After Peter, her first husband, had returned from his

post overseas wounded, unable to stand or walk, Emily had remarried, as was only sensible. It was sensible to avoid a life as a crippled man's nursemaid, wasn't it? Sending Galen off to live with Lemuel had also been sensible. The old man, odd as he was, was rich and could afford to see to the boy's education.

Heaven knows, Wil, her second husband, had not wanted Galen around. He'd made that plain enough.

But now, paralyzed, she wished Peter were here. He always knew what to do in a moment of danger. Usually it was something brutal, involving gunfire and broken bones, but he knew. Many evenings, back when they were first married, Peter had spent showing her his knife collection, showing her how to give an attacker a scalp wound to send blood into his eyes, how to cut the tendons in the wrist with one stroke. (She remembered Peter had been so disappointed that no mugger had molested them during their New York trip.) He knew how to handle emergencies, back when he had been whole. He always knew. If Peter had stayed here . . . where had he gone? She did not remember him leaving the house tonight.

If only Galen were here. Galen, her little angel, was so bright, was so good at everything he tried to do. If only Galen had returned alive and sane from the dark place you go when you go into a coma, whatever Land of Darkness lay beyond the world of men . . .

Instead, there was no one. No one but Wil, snoring away.

From where she lay, Emily started shouting and shouting, then screaming, for Wil to wake up.

The front door swung open without noise. Beyond it was darkness.

There was something in the darkness. Emily made her eyes into slits and pretended to be asleep.

The silhouette of a tall man glided forward into the room. He was draped in a long cape of unrelieved black. His head was bowed, and the crown of a wide-brimmed black hat shadowed his features. In the gloom Emily could not distinguish the hat from the cloak, and the whole apparition seemed one eye-defeating mass of inky blackness. With the silence of a specter, the man flowed into the room, silently shutting the door behind. The hat tilted left and right, as if he were carefully and quickly examining each detail of the room.

Now he raised his head, and Emily saw the brim of the hat rising like the rim of an eclipsing planet to reveal his features. His cheeks and chin were hidden in the high collar of his cloak, wrapped in the long scarf he wore. As the hat brim tilted farther up, Emily caught a hint of strong, high cheekbones; then, a hawk nose; and finally, eyes as greenish gray as the eyes of a cat, perceptive, daring, with a frightening look of forceful intelligence. The man was not young; there were wrinkles around those startling eyes, and his eyebrows were silver.

For a moment the man stared down at her, his gaze traveling over her with the cold, swift precision of a trained doctor making a diagnosis. Emily kept her eyes as slits, wishing she could move.

His head jerked up when the noise of Wil's snore came again. A black-gloved hand, bearing a ring with a strange, gleaming gemstone, came into view from beneath the cloak. In that fist was a .45 automatic; the gray metal was lined with black, nonreflective tape the same dark hue as the gloves and cape.

Then, with a rustle of fabric, he stepped beyond her range of vision down into the hall.

She tried to move and found she could curl her fingers slightly.

A moment or two later the dark man returned. Emily caught a glimpse of the man returning the gun to some unseen holster beneath his cloak, and also pocketing a miniaturized camera with some sort of special lens attachment.

The figure turned its back to Emily and bent over the coffee table where half empty cups lay next to an unemptied ashtray. The black figure spoke in a calm, clear voice. "The fact that you can see me indicates you've been exposed to magic. Do not fear."

As he stepped around the coffee table, Emily could see what he was doing. One black glove was brushing powder onto the coffee cups. The other held a strip of cellophane that he carefully applied to the fingerprints, which became visible.

"Who—who are you—?" Emily choked out.

"I am the enemy of the men who came to your house tonight and of their leader, who is a master-criminal and super-hypnotist who calls himself Azrael de Gray. He is an archfiend whom I intend to bring to justice. I am one whose life he has tried to destroy. I am his nemesis."

"I can't move . . . ," she said.

"I can release you from Azrael's hypnotic charm. But before I do, you must answer my questions."

The black gloves now held tweezers and small plastic bags. With the steady hands of a surgeon, without a wasted motion, the figure began picking up flakes of cigarette ash and tiny threads of fabric lying on the table and the couch.

"Let me up first!" Emily panted.

"The mesmeric forces involved do not allow for that." Now the figure paused in his work and turned the force of his gaze upon her. She stared in alarm into those green eyes, but something she saw in their depths seemed to calm and reassure her. He said, "You must decide to help me."

"Yes . . . ," she said.

"The men who came here. Describe them."

"An old man in a purple robe, with a squint. The second man was dressed in a nice business suit. Gray hair. He talked like he was educated. The third man was dressed in leather. He had a shaved head, tattoos, and an earring."

The black glove fanned out three photographs before her eyes.

She said, "Yes, those are the men!"

"These are the minions of Azrael. The man with gray hair, the one in the business suit, is the dangerous one." The dark finger touched the second photograph. "He's Guy Wentworth, regional director of the Bureau of Alcohol, Tobacco, Firearms and Explosives. He is one of the most powerful members of the Justice Department, and his family connections link him to underworld crime bosses and to influential political figures in Washington. Two years ago he began training a special squadron of assault agents, answerable only to him. Congress and the press have been blocked from making any investigations into his actions. Two of his political enemies have died recently; one by suicide; the other died in his sleep, apparently by a heart attack."

Emily said, "And the others?"

"This man is Kyle Coldgrave, who calls himself Father Malignus; he is the leader of a Satanist group called the Church of the Dark Eschaton. The tattooed man is Angelo Cassello. He had been in a state institution. An insomniac and drug addict. It seems he took drugs to drive off nightmares. A small-time crook, he robbed to get drug money."

Emily said, "Why those three?"

"They are each men who can reach or send another into the state of consciousness you are in now. Guy Wentworth controls a dream-research center, where secret and illegal experiments are carried out, whose true purpose is hidden from those who fund them— experiments on human subjects. Kyle Coldgrave practices Eastern meditation and ecstatic rituals. Angelo Cassello is insane. They each entered the Dream

Realm. Something within that realm found them, called them, and is using them."

Now the man in black moved around the room, spraying some chemical from a black aerosol spray can at spots on the walls and floor. He took out a complex-looking pair of goggles, bent to examine the results. Next, he attached a special lens arrangement to his tiny camera and directed it at those places. He asked her who had arrived first and in what order, where they had stood, what they had touched, what they had said.

She answered the questions as best she could, but said, "Galen—or whoever was impersonating him— wouldn't tell them much. But he told them there was going to be a battle, at the mansion of Everness, and that they were not to loot, even the smallest thing. What is within may not be changed."

"Mansion?"

"My husband's family's mansion. Ex-husband, I mean. My father-in-law lives there. Lemuel Waylock. A huge place, number fourteen out on route AA, on the shore near the Bay."

"What is this mansion? What is Azrael's interest in it?"

Emily answered, "You're not a human being, are you? You are a dream-figment. Made out of hopes and fears and children's stories. Old radio plays. Comic books. A dark avenger. You cannot be real."

"I am human. I adopt this guise while I continue to exist within this halfway state between waking and sleeping. There are archtypes, patterns, mythic images in the human racial subconsciousness, and anything that lives up to the standards of those myths, who acts out those archtypes, is not forgotten by the natural universe, and does not drown in the Mist. I am a man. I have a wife and a child. Sometimes my daughter can see me, and sometimes she forgets. No one can remember me when awake. Azrael did this to me. The man who killed your son did this to me. While I play the part of the avenger, all the hidden, buried psychological forces in man that dream of vengeance will assist me. I ask you to trust me. I will avenge your son, who is possessed by the ghost of Azrael. Tell me your secret."

"The mansion controls the gate between waking and dreaming. I thought my father-in-law was crazy. I mean, eccentric. I thought it was a cult. My son spends a lot of time with him. He practices dreaming. He knows old-fashioned fighting, like in Robin Hood movies, you know, swords and lances and bows and arrows and all that stuff. He has recurring nightmares, and he fights them. I mean, he thinks he fights them, but he's just dreaming. It's not really happening. I wanted to take him to a psychiatrist, but it did not seem to be hurting him. . . ."

A hot tear slid down her cheek. She sniffed. "D-do you mind? I mean, I can't move my hand. . . ."

The black figure reached down with his gloved finger and wiped the tear. The cold voice issuing from beneath the shadowed hat brim spoke again, but this time it sounded almost human. "Raising children is hard. We must not blame ourselves for every evil that befalls them."

"I could have stopped it. If I had only . . ."

"You can stop it now. Tell me of the mansion."

"The real world and the dream-world are the same there. Everything in the house is reflected in the dreams you dream when you are in the house. So, if there is, like, a candlestick on a table in real life, if you take a nap in the house, you dream about a candlestick, and it looks the same. I slept there once. I don't remember what I dreamed, mostly, but I remember that much, and it scared me. I never quite believed it though."

"And your son?"

"Practices memory techniques, so when he wakes up, he remembers."

"Why?"

"He's a guard. A watchman. When the attack comes from the nightmare-world, he's supposed to stop it. Somehow. There are all these secrets."

"He told you?"

"I'm his mother. You think I can't figure out his secrets?"

"Azrael wants to control the mansion, to control entrance and egress from the dream-world?" He did not wait for an answer but stood and moved to the phone. He drew an electronic instrument out from beneath his cloak and attached it to the wires. He spoke into a microphone jacked into the telephone. "Calling Burbank! I want the last ten numbers dialed into this phone. I am sending the signal through now."

He made an adjustment to his machine. Then he said, "Also, send all available information concerning this address, number fourteen, rural route AA, Sagadahoc County, Maine—also known as Everness Mansion—into the electronic file in the armored limousine. Out." He took the jack out. Then he turned toward the door, as if ready to rush away.

Emily stopped him by saying; "They'll be gone."

The dark figure turned toward her. She could see no face, for he was silhouetted against the dim red light of dawn painted against the window behind him. But she could see two points of light reflected in his eyes, shining from beneath the brim of his hat.

Maybe he thought he was human. Emily wondered how long this being had been in the dream-world and what that environment might do to a person, how it might mutate him.

"Explain," the cold voice commanded.

"It's dawn. The powers of the night retreat. Whatever the Warlock wanted from the house, he's got it by now, or he's gone back into the shadows. Night-magic doesn't work in the daylight. My son told me that. I didn't believe his stories, but I listened."

"What does he want in the house?"

"A key. A silver key."

"What does it open?"

"I don't know. Something that needs to be kept shut. Peter's family has been guarding it since forever. I wonder if Peter changed his mind and believes in this stuff now. Do you think he went to the mansion and got involved in the battle? They'd capture him, right? They wouldn't kill him, would they? He's a cripple, for God's sake! They wouldn't kill him!"

The dark figure did not answer.

Then she said, "Is my son really dead? Really?"

The man in black said, "There are those who count me dead, yet I live. Do not despair. The world is more strange than first it seems, and there are many things hidden. Yet the rules of logic cannot change. If Azrael is a ghost, and is yet a conscious being, able to act and move, this means death is not final."

Emily said, "If death is not final, then you can't kill him. The Warlock; you cannot defeat him!"

The voice spoke softly, perhaps with a hint of cool humor: "Ma'am, I was not planning to step out into the open and shoot him in the head."

"There is no way to fight him. No human power can touch him. You didn't see his eyes. Staring out from my little boy's face! I can't move! *He* did this! All *he* has to do is look at you."

"He will not see me."

"How can you fight him, then? You can't!"

"Evil acts toward its own defeat. There is a force in the universe, a selective amnesia that hates magic and tries to hide it from men. A mist. It clouds men's minds. Every man the Warlock confounds with magic is sent into the mist, and from the mist I recruit my allies: my organization grows larger the farther the Warlock's power reaches. When the time is right, we forgotten men will come forth from the mists, and strike."

He held up his black glove once more before her eyes, and the mysterious stone in his ring seemed to pulse and writhe with crimson, rose, and scarlet gleams. "Stare into the burning eye of my fire opal. See into its utmost depth! It is the color of the rising Sun, of approaching day. The numbness that possesses you is an illusion; your limbs are whole and full of vigor! As you wake, you will realize that whatever hypnotic spell you are under has ended with the suddenness of a dream!"

And she did wake up then, yawning and stretching in the middle of the floor.

"Oh, thank you!" she started to say. But then she noticed that no one was in the room with her. She blinked, rubbing her head. "Strange. I could have sworn I was talking to some . . . but it must have been a dream. Must have been . . . ?" Because the strange conversation was already becoming vague and shadowy in her memory.

But when she woke up Wil a few moments later, and he told her that he had almost jumped off the side of the reservoir last night, she started to pack.

It was less than fifteen minutes later, they were in the car, speeding down the road. Wil was still arguing.

"But where are we going?" asked Wil. "This is crazy!"

"On vacation," she snapped. "Anywhere. We'll decide when we get to the airport."

"This is so crazy!"

"This is perfectly sensible," she said. "Something we can't explain and we can't fight has tried to kill you once. They—whoever they are—know where the house is. If you can't explain it, and you can't fight it, and it's trying to kill you, you run. You run the hell away. It's just common sense."

Wil stared off behind him into the rising Sun. Then he said the last thing she'd have ever expected. "But, if we do this, we'll never find out what happens . . ."

Something in the sadness of his tone touched her heart, too. Almost, she felt the impulse to turn around, to join whatever mysterious supernatural struggle was going on between her family and the forces of darkness. Almost.

"Be practical!" she snapped angrily. And she pressed down on the accelerator.

3

Duress
of the
Warlock

I

Peter had been in hospitals before, after he stepped on a land mine in a swamp and lost the use of both his legs. And he had spent months and weeks on his back before, peeing in a tube and drinking from a straw, so this was not so bad.

Of course, he had had the use of his arms back then, so this was worse.

Peter had been in the stockade before, back before his marriage, when he was young and full of beans and stupid and picked a fight with the corporal on guard. God, that had messed up his record for so many years. One-week confinement in stockade; pack drill and two-week CB after that.

But then it had been friendlies who had him, not the enemy, so maybe this was much worse. And this was an enemy from some nightmare-land, mumbo-jumbo hell beyond the edge of sanity, who—thanks to the fact that Peter had lost the fight at the old mansion—were about to fry up the Earth with an apple in its mouth, or something. Good going, Peter.

World about to end. And he was here. There was nothing to do but lie on his back and think about his life.

That land mine had been defective and poorly placed. It had not had enough punch even to blow his foot off, so he was lucky. Shrapnel broke vertebrae in his spine, so he'd never walk again, so maybe he was not so lucky. Got him shipped back home, so maybe that was lucky. His wife dumped him, so maybe unlucky. But she was a cruel bitch, so maybe lucky. Then his son, Galen, went crazy and went into a coma. Unlucky. Galen woke up again. Lucky. But he woke up even crazier. Unlucky.

Then things in Peter's life started taking a turn for the weird. His son turned out not to be crazy after all, but dead. Sort of. His flesh still walked the Earth, possessed by an evil ghost, a wizard from the Dark Ages named Azrael de Gray.

Galen had never been crazy. His son had been a soldier in a war against the mumbo-jumbo freaks from magic-land, some sort of hell inhabited by shapechangers and rotting corpses and all sorts of shit that'd turn your hair on your balls white. Very unlucky.

So, he was kinda glad his son had been in his right mind all these years, but it would have been easier on the rest of the world if Galen had been hallucinating, and the things he thought were coming had not been real after all.

Galen had died in the line of service. He had died a soldier's death, died still thinking his old man thought he was nuts. Peter had never gotten a chance to talk to him, never gotten a chance to set things straight.

Because that big Russian fellow, Raven Varovitch, had made a deal with the Devil and killed Galen in order to save the life of his little wife. Wendy was her name. Unlucky for the both of them, because when

Peter got out of here, the girl was going to be a widow
and the guy was going to be a corpse.

What hurt is that he'd liked the Russian guy from
the moment he'd seen him. Nice guy. And what man
wouldn't kill someone for his wife? If you had a wife
worth killing someone for. But when Peter got out of
here . . .

When who got out of where? Peter was going
nowhere. Because his son had been right and magic
had been real and monsters had come up out of the sea
and stormed the old mansion. And Peter got caught in
the cross fire. Of all places, in that spooky old mansion
where he had been born and raised. Azrael de Gray
had come up out of the night-world with a squad of
men and an army of horrors.

There had been magic weapons hidden in the house
all this time, just like his dad had always told him.
Wendy found a way to summon the weapons the mansion had been guarding since King Arthur's time. One
of those weapons, the Rod of Mollner, came into Peter's hands so that he could slay the two giants,
Surtvitnir and whatshisname, Argle-bargle. Something
like that. But the Rod was cursed. He threw it, and it
returned to the hand of the thrower, and the impact paralyzed his arm. The damn thing was meant to be
thrown by some Viking god or something, not by a
middle-aged, hard-ass jarhead in a wheelchair with
two bad legs, whose bright idea was to use a weapon
he didn't know how the hell worked.

And it was really dumb to throw it the second time.

So the black hats won. Azrael de Gray was in control of the mansion, which meant—as far as Peter understood this mumbo jumbo—that he ruled the world.

There was something worse than Azrael coming,
something big and bad.

And Peter was down for the count. And never getting up again. Arms and legs out of commission. World
about to end. Very, very unlucky.

If Peter had done his job right, if he had only done his job right, Azrael would have been the one flat on his back, paralyzed in all four limbs, and peeing in a tube.

Peter replayed the battle in his head.

There had to be some way for a little mortal man to use that damned god-hammer properly. If only he could have figured it right. If only these nightmares about the beast would stop. If only Raven had used the ring when he'd had the chance.

If only, if only. Crap. Peter wished he could just go crazy all at once and get it over with.

Bergelmir. The other giant had been called Bergelmir.

II

Peter, from where he lay, could view the bleak, gray metal slab of the door, often left hanging open, and a bit of the drab olive corridor beyond. And why bother to close and lock it? Peter wasn't going anywhere . . . . and his captors knew it.

He could usually see the guard stationed in the corridor.

It was not the same man every day, but he always had the same expression on his face: dull-eyed, drowsy, harsh.

The guards never spoke nor laughed; they never fidgeted nor smoked, but stood in postures stiff as a Queen's Own Beefeater at Buckingham Palace. Peter would have admired the military discipline, if it had been military discipline.

Peter might have felt sorry for them, if he had not seen, where their collars were not buttoned tight, a witch-mark of a shape he knew. Whatever enchantment these men were under now, the original vow that had put them in the Warlock's power had been sworn voluntarily.

Whenever he turned his head (and all he could turn
was his head), Peter could see the security camera
clinging to the ceiling above the head of his bed. The
large-wheeled cart on which his medical equipment
was kept was to the right of the bed. Farther right was
the small, dusty square, crisscrossed by bars and thick
wires, of the tiny window. That window was his only
source of happiness. Some days he would lie for hours
staring at the dusty square, hoping for a glimpse of
clear blue sky. Once, to his great delight, he saw a bird
fly by.

The window was his entertainment. If he got bored
with the view, he could always turn his head and stare
back at the guard or at the medical equipment on the
cart.

They didn't bother to feed him; an intravenous drip
led from the cart to his arm, with nutrients to keep him
hungry, always hungry, but alive. A catheter led from
his diapers to a pump on the cart, to carry his wastes
away. For his thirst, they had hung above the headboard one of those little sipping bottles bicyclists
sometimes used, with a straw and nipple for him to
suck on.

Also on the medical cart was the EEG machine that
monitored his brain waves for REM sleep patterns. Peter sometimes entertained himself by banging against
his pillow with violent yanks of his head, to see if he
could dislodge the little metal tabs taped to his skull.

The only other thing to look at was the drawing
chalked on the wall. But the sketch was of a hideous
beast, a shaggy, hunched shape with snarling fangs
and dripping claws, biting at the chains that bound it.
The Beast looked something like a bear, with the arms
of a gorilla and the head of a saber-toothed tiger.

Peter saw enough of the creature at night, in his
nightmares, when the Beast stepped out from the wall,
and prowled around the outside of whatever dungeon

or oubliette he was in that night. He had seen more than enough of the beast and did not care to look at it.

No, he'd rather look out the window. Once he had, after all, seen a bird fly by.

The Beast had not always been there. On the first night there had been nine candles surrounding his bed, which, in his nightmare that night, became an encircling wall of fire imprisoning him.

The next day Azrael de Gray had come, tall, imposing, with the cold, dispassionate eyes Peter remembered from the sitting room portrait he'd been afraid of as a child. Azrael wore a large cloak woven with cabalistic signs and zodiacal symbols. When he had drawn out and put on a conical wizard's cap with stars on it and moons of different phase around the brim, Peter had laughed out loud. The get-up looked like Mickey Mouse as the Sorcerer's Apprentice in Disney's *Fantasia*.

Azrael silenced Peter with a curt gesture. The voice in his throat had simply dried up immediately. It was a day before he could talk again.

Then Azrael had drawn the picture of the Beast in chalk upon the wall. Around it he had inscribed circles and triangles, with phrases written in Latin and Arabic script along each border. Azrael had said nothing at the time, except a brief prayer to the angelic intelligence governing the planet Mars. And then he had left.

Peter enjoyed staring out the window. Every now and then he saw a passing cloud. Once he saw a bird.

On the fourth day Peter's hunger pangs had diminished to a tolerable level, as if his body were forgetting how to crave food.

It was on the seventh day Azrael de Gray came once again, this time to speak with him.

III

Azrael de Gray was perfectly dressed in a handsome blue pinstripe suit and a dark blue overcoat of the most expensive cut—but the effect was made absurd by the several necklaces of heavy gold chain he wore; the half a dozen diamond studs at his wrists and collar; and the bracelets, rings, and a woman's belt of gold links.

There were three men in business suits behind him, one carrying a chair. One man looked normal in his poise and expression; one walked with a swaggering, rolling gait, as if he were not used to human feet, and he said, "Stow 'er there, mate!" to the third, who put down the chair. This third man had the glassy stare of hypnosis or enchantment.

Azrael waved them away out of earshot, down the corridor. He took a can of Morton's salt from beneath his coat and traced a circle all the way around the room, squeezing to walk into the gap between the headboard and the wall. Then he faced the wall and made a gesture—middle and ring finger curled, forefinger and pinky straight—in four directions, murmuring, "Depart! Depart! Depart!" Then he hung his overcoat on a hook on the wall so as to cover the chalked face of the Beast.

Evidently the Wizard wanted privacy. Peter noticed wryly that Azrael did not think to turn off the security camera, however.

Azrael sat.

"Hope you didn't get all dolled up on my account," grunted Peter.

Azrael ran his beringed fingers through the many chains of jewels he wore. "These stones, grown in the womb of Earth to that perfection which mirrors Heaven, are possessed of double virtue, being, here, emblems of wealth; there, as amulets of infused power. Yet I see by your curled lip you disdain my finery as gaudy show; so, too, have my advisors condemned my appearance. You mock me for a peacock; yet I would not be a peahen. This generation of man is more strange and fabulous than any land of Orient or Hyperboria. Why would your people cherish drabness over splendor in garb, wearing denim and dark stuffs, they, whose wealth makes seem Solomon and Croesus unto paupers? Your bounty expands beyond the riches of the immortals who dance upon Mount Cytheron and cloud-dark Olympos, but your dress is soberer than monks at penance. Observe this sleeve seam, stitched with finer hand and more evenly than any fairy seamstress of the court of Finn Finbarra could do! La! Do I dress too much? I wore but rags and scabs in Tirion."

"You sure as hell talk too much," said Peter.

Azrael stiffened.

Peter said, "It's getting to you, ain't it?"

Tiny lines appeared around the edges of Azrael's eyes.

Peter said, "You're just dying for someone to talk to. You come back to earth after all those years, and nothing's the same as you remember. No one here even knows or cares who you are." Now Peter laughed bitterly. "Yeah, I know what it must feel like. Welcome home, veteran."

A look of cold majesty darkened Azrael's features. He stood abruptly, his hand lightly resting on the chair back, as if strongly urged to leave, strongly impelled to stay. He turned toward the door. Then, as if drawn against his will, he turned again toward Peter.

"I have come to plead with you," he said in a hushed tone, his eyes aglow with strange emotion.

IV

"I must have the Silver Key again, to bar the Gates of Everness; for dreams escape into the daylit world, now, before mankind has been made ready and equipped to conquer them."

"Ain't working out the way you planned, is it?"

Azrael said nothing. His face grew cold and haughty.

Peter said, "The planetarium in the attic—if it still works and ain't burnt—that'd tell you right where she was if she was on Earth. So she's in the dream-land. But you—ain't so easy to get around now, is it? How many gateways closed when so many paintings and tapestries went up in smoke? Or maybe the dream-colts don't have to come anymore when you call? Well, well. Who the hell's fault could that be?"

Azrael gripped the chair back with his fist and his knuckles whitened, but his grim face showed no change of expression.

Peter said, "Sure, I'll help you, seeing as how you're family and all. Mind if I call you 'Dad' while my dad is laid up?"

Azrael pursed his lips and narrowed his eyes.

Peter said, "And you made me so comfy here. You know I'm hungry all the time and my muscles are rotting? You know how much having this tube up my ass hurts?"

"Where were you, sir, when I was in Tirion?" answered Azrael, lowering.

"Where were you when I was young and hated my father for being a liar, when the only thing I wanted to do was meet the wizards he was always talking about?"

Azrael's dark eyes took on a sardonic glitter. "Forgive me, I was detained."

"And why the hell should I forgive you anything?" uttered Peter, a note of anger trembling in his low voice.

Azrael's face grew stern again, like a stone door closing. "Everness can be healed with the Silver Key and this world defended from the hordes of dream. Defended and more."

Peter squinted. "Out with it. What more?"

V

Azrael leaned forward, his face, for once, not a mask, but showing deep and animated passion. "This world, and man, are mightiest things; yet they have not yet pulled down the stars to do them homage. The thousand worlds and far-flung golden realms beyond, with all their majesty and twilight-haunted splendor, are as nothing to this iron world and its dreadful, daylight strength. It shall all be ours.

"The prophecy reports the next King lives, even now, somewhere upon the Earth; now, even now; the King destined to restore the Empire and knit up the sundered universe. His bloodline shall rule both gods and men; his sway shall reach unbound beyond Heaven, Earth, and Hell, to compass all cosmos entire. No less than the cosmos shall the kingdom be; nations shall be subjects as much as constellations.

"The last King, I lost to Oberon and Nimue, and the promised Empire was stillborn, slain by Cupid's bow and fairy-scheming.

"Now again he comes, the King; and the gods themselves tremble on their onyx thrones, and the plumes of their wide wings all tremble, for they know the conquests of High Heaven cannot be stopped, if my wit can unwind their spirit-snares; and this world shall be the throne and capital of all creation!"

VI

"New king, eh?" said Peter. "Forgive me if I don't stand up and clap. I vote Republican."

Azrael leaned back, his face impassive once more, but his eyes still burning and glittering. "The promised King shall reign a thousand years, his scepter close the gulf between this world and the next; and peace and justice shall issue from his hand."

Peter said, "Oh? So that's why you're doing all this?"

"Indeed." Azrael spoke in a hushed whisper.

"For peace and justice? Well, well, well. You got a funny way of showing it. I guess the 'peace' is attacking and burning your own house. And the 'justice' must be throwing your own family in jail without a trial for no reason. Right?"

Peter laughed harshly and continued, "No, Azrael, old boy, I guess things are pretty rough for you right now. You would not even be here talking to me, trying to get me to help you find Wendy Varovitch, if her husband hadn't already proved to be more trouble than you figured."

There was a slight glimmer of fear in Azrael's eye.

Peter said, "He's escaped! Raven escaped."

Azrael let go of the chair and took a step backward toward the door. It was fear. Peter realized Azrael was superstitious. Maybe magicians had to be. And he was facing something he did not understand.

Peter spoke in a quiet, calm, relentless tone: "You're scared. You thought you had it all figured, but it's coming apart in your hands. Falling apart right before your eyes. You thought you could betray your nightmare-friends the same way you betrayed your family. You thought you could use the Key to shut the Gates of Everness before Acheron came up from the bottom of the sea. You can't. Silver Key is gone. You wonder what Morningstar is going to see in your soul when he looks you in the eye. You wonder if Morningstar has a special chamber in his black tower set aside just for you. How did you let that Silver Key just slip between your fingers like that? You don't know what you're up against, do you, pal? You don't know who we're working for."

Azrael's face was immobile, but he had gone pale and he was backing up toward the door.

"You are so pathetic, having to come beg your victims for help! But I guess you magician types can't do anything if we don't help you hurt us. If we don't consent. But you! You don't need to help the ones coming to hurt you. You've already consented. You signed a contract in blood."

Azrael whispered, "By what prophetic art can you know this? How can you know of my contract? Or that the ink was blood? I was warded . . ."

Peter said, "What are you going to do if the trumpet blows and wakes all the sleeper guys to the Last Battle? Think your tricks and charms can stop the likes of *them?* On the other hand, what are you going to do if the trumpet doesn't blow and Acheron comes up out of the sea? Maybe Morningstar will let you be his court jester. But how you going to juggle for him, if he doesn't let you keep your eyeballs and hands?"

Peter continued sarcastically: "But, no, wait! You got this brilliant plan. This King guy is going to stop all that, right? But if he's so just and fair, what's he going to think when he looks at the likes of you? You were hoping he'd admire you, right? But what's he really going to do to you, once he runs the universe? Maybe he'll just do to you what you did to my dad."

Peter paused to let that comment sink in.

Then he said in a soft voice. "You're going to Hell, pal. Down into stinking Hell. You're already falling down the pit; you just don't know it 'cause you ain't splattered on the bottom yet. Going to get out of it somehow? Try flapping your arms. Need my help? Happy landings."

Azrael turned and fled from the room, holding one hand before his face, middle fingers curled, thumb and pinkie extended, as if warding off a curse.

Peter's laughter chased him out the door.

VII

Peter stared at the overcoat for what seemed a long time, thinking.

When the orderly came in, as he did every day, to check on Peter, turn him over, and sponge him off, the orderly did not, of course, remove the overcoat. He checked to see that the security camera was still operating; but no one had told him, nor would he have believed, that a graffiti monster chalked on the wall was part of the security.

When the orderly left, Peter was suddenly overcome by a sense of alarm and anger. "How could I miss it!" he asked himself. "How could I be so stupid! Got to go to sleep right now before Azrael realizes what he's done! Morpheus, Somnus, ah, whatever the hell your name is, Hypnos, and you other guys, knock me out!"

VIII

Immediately he was asleep. In his dream he was once more in the barren dungeon of some grim tower, whose barred window slit looked out upon a lonely moor. Peter was on a narrow plank, and in the dream he was tied down hand and foot by many winding yards of cable.

The Beast still prowled outside the tower, roaring in rage, growling, slavering, and rattling its massive chains. Every now and again, it scratched at the tower doors, or smote, and the tower trembled from the blows of its paw. In the far distance, across the windy moonlit moor, Peter could hear a lonely churchbell ringing. Six times it rang.

But when the Beast prowled out to the far end of its chain, Peter could see through the window that the Beast wore an overcoat draped over its head. The Beast stumbled, batting at the coat hem with its massive claws, but it could not dislodge the fabric.

Peter strained at the ropes that bound him, but this was one of those dreams where one is trapped and cannot escape.

"Great," grunted Peter. "Now what the hell do I do? Wish for a magic mouse to come by and nibble away these ropes?"

And he sighed because he realized that Galen would know what to do. Moody, dreamy Galen, who couldn't stand up to the kids who picked on him at school, and who couldn't keep his job as a paperboy because he overslept; Galen knew all the magic words and mumbo jumbo that made this dream-stuff operate.

"Maybe I was too hard on the kid," Peter said.

A large brown mouse, walking upright, wearing a vest with a pocketwatch and carrying a walking stick, hopped up on Peter's chest. The mouse was puffing and brushed his little furry forehead with a hanky.

"Good day, sir," said the mouse. "It'll take me a while to get through these ropes, but not to worry! I have strong teeth!" And he bent down and began gnawing at the knots on Peter's wrist.

It looked just like something out of a Beatrix Potter illustration. "Well, the God-damned cavalry comes riding over the hill, and it's God-damned Mighty Mouse."

"Begging your pardon, sir, but that's 'Meadow.'" The words were slightly mumbled, as if his mouth were full. "Sorry I took so long, but I could not get by the Hatred Beast until the Wizard blinkered it with his cloak."

"Who sent you? The good fairy?"

The mouse scampered back up across Peter's chest, and Peter could feel the little paws tapping on him. The mouse looked up with beady little black eyes as bright as buttons. "Fairies? Oh no, sir. Don't be ridiculous."

"Sorry. Don't know what came over me."

"The fairies work for Oberon and Titania, King and

Queen of the Seelie Court in Mommur, the City Nev-
erending. The Knights of Oberon sleep among the Autumn Stars. I am merely a humble mouse from Shining
Valley, trying to do my part to help."

"Well, keep nibbling. Every little bit helps."

The mouse scampered away out of sight down to the
left wrist, commenting, "Exactly our philosophy, sir,
except that we say every little *bite* counts. There! Pull
up your arms!"

"Can't. They're still stuck."

"Not if you don't wish them to be, you big baby. It
makes me sick to see a great hulking man like you
turned coward. Turns my stomach!"

"What! No stinking little rodent is going to . . ."
And he pulled his right hand up. The ropes spun up
into the air and fell away, disintegrating into dust and
cobwebs.

Peter pulled up his left hand and rubbed at his
wrists. "What does this mean? My arms going to be
working when I wake up?"

"That, I cannot say, sir, seeing as how I am not a magician. But I hope that if you remember this dream,
you may well be whole when you wake. That rope was
woven out of your own hair, so it could bind you."

"Hair?" Peter rubbed his hand over his crew cut.

"Perhaps you call it by another name in the waking
world. When your hair stands on end? Fear. That rope
was woven out of your own fear. Only magicians can
do spider-work like that."

"But what if I can't remember this when I wake up?
Damn. My dad taught me this exercise I was supposed
to do when I was a kid, but I never bothered . . ."

"Come now, sir! Every mouse pup and nesting bird
knows how to build the Keep to keep Forgetting away!
It's easy! Picture a circle inscribed within a square.
The circle is the Tower of Ever, and the square is the
four seasons of the High House of Time. Imagine the

square now as a door, guarded by a man with two faces, forward and past, and in his hand, a wand that divides."

"That's the front door of the house where I grew up."

"Then this should be child's play for you, sir. Imagine the door opens, and you are in a tower with four doors. Each door has a guard. The lion carries the golden orb that shows his majesty; the angel has the sword of the four winds; the bull comes from the sea; the eagle carries the torch to reignite the rising Sun. Down each corridor is a season . . ."

"You don't even have to say anymore," said Peter. "You're describing the very house where I grew up. I remember all those decorations. Dad made me used to repeat every object in every room with my eyes closed."

"Very good, sir. If you want to remember a new thing, put it somewhere in the mansion of your memory."

"Uh . . . Okay. There're two little brass rat statues in the hall behind the marble Apollo."

"Mice, sir. The Smynthian is the god of mice."

"Whatever. From that statue, you go down two flights of stairs, there's the kitchen in the west wing next to the bonfire room. There's a table in the pantry where I used to hide when I was a kid. Sometimes we kept a wedge of cheese on top of that table in a box. Let's say there's a mouse there, and he's got a key dangling from his watch chain. The key unlocks my hands. Yeah. Sound good? I think I'll remember that."

Meadow Mouse, still standing on Peter's chest, spoke up. "Did you say you actually lived in the High House of Ever? Then—I suppose you must know Galen Amadeus Waylock!"

"Sure. He's my son."

"Oh my! This is a singular honor, I must say! An honor! The father of Galen Waylock! You must be so proud of him, sir, so very proud. The echoes of his

name ring everywhere! And, ahem, and what did you
say your name was again?"

"Pete."

"Oh. What dreams have you made?"

"Who cares about that? You got to tell me what to do
next. What's the plan?"

Meadow Mouse twitched his whiskers. "Plan? I
haven't the foggiest notion, actually."

"What? I thought you magic animal types always
knew what to do. You know, Puss in Boots, shaman
totem animals, witch familiars, that sort of garbage."

Meadow Mouse's whiskers drooped. "Well, I am
very sorry about that. Didn't really get good instructions, you know. My fault, really. All I know is that
there is someone who can rescue the Princess; and that
someone must be rescued by you."

"Any idea who that someone is?"

"Well, frankly, er . . . no."

"Race? Color? What country they live in? What
planet they live on? Maybe I should just rescue everyone in the universe till they're all safe."

"He's trapped somewhere underwater."

"Oh, that's a big help. I'll call the Coast Guard and
find out every rowboat and yacht that's capsized. This
is after I walk down the corridor on my hands and beat
up all the guards with my teeth."

Meadow Mouse shrugged. "Sorry."

"Your commanding officer didn't bother to give you
a briefing before they sent you out?"

"Actually, no. Our commanding officer, as you call
her, is dancing in the moonlight, weeping, because she
can't remember her name. You see, we do things differently where I come from."

"So I gathered." Peter sighed and looked around the
dungeon. He saw nothing to give him any ideas. Besides,
it was a dream, so the shape of the stones and position of
the chains and cobwebs changed from time to time.

He glared at Meadow Mouse, who still stood on Peter's chest. Mouse fingered his whiskers nervously.

"So how the hell would you do things in fairy-land?"

Meadow Mouse blinked his little black eyes. "Well, sir, we do things more spontaneously. More naturally. By instinct."

"Instinct. Great."

"Well, I am a mouse, you know. Instinct works fine for us."

"Give me an example."

"Well, now . . ." Meadow Mouse looked thoughtful. Then he asked, "Of all the people on Earth, whom would you most like to rescue?"

"Me? My dad, of course. . . ." Peter's voice turned glum. "Hate to see him kick off before I got a chance to say . . . well, you know. To tell him what's on my mind."

"And where is your father now?"

"Sick. In a coma."

"Where have his thoughts flown?"

"Raven said he was in Acheron . . ."

"Don't say that name!" Meadow Mouse dropped his walking stick in alarm, clapping his paws over his round ears.

Peter had sat up, and Meadow Mouse tumbled into his lap. Peter was saying excitedly, "Hey! He *is* the guy I'm supposed to rescue! He's in Acheron, and Acheron is underwater!"

A hideous great voice called out. "Three times you called the name of blackest woe! In service to that name, I come! With each time I am released, I grow! And I shall grow to swallow all the Earth when time is done!"

The door of the dungeon was flung down from it hinges. There, in the doorframe, loomed the Beast, rearing upright on hind legs; and somehow the overcoat had fallen from its face to come around its shoulders, so that the Beast seemed a vast, cloaked being, larger than all things around it, larger than all outer space. Darkness and smoke seethed from its black fur and blood dripped from its terrible, huge claws. Its fangs and eyes were glittering white against the dark mass of its triangular and shaggy, bestial head.

A distant bell rang six times as it stepped into the room.

4

The Face
of the
Beast

I

As the dark creature lumbered into the room, Meadow Mouse leapt from Peter's chest to the pallet near his shoulder, whispering into Peter's ear, "Say its name!"

"I don't know its God-damned name!" Peter hissed back.

"We don't recognize people by what they look like where I come from. Looks change."

The monster stepped closer, its yellow eyes gleaming like mirrors in the gloom. Peter had heard that animals cannot tolerate to look a man in the eye, so he stared at the huge, black beast.

The creature straightened, throwing back its shoulders and raising its blood-stained chin. Its eyes were wiser and deeper than any human eyes and so filled with majesty and terror that it was Peter who had to struggle to keep from lowering his gaze, not the Beast. In some way he could not define, Peter had the sense that the creature looked like a beast, not because it came from a level below humanity, but from above.

And, as he looked, Peter's stomach knotted with an old, old fear, and bile rose in the back of his throat. The creature's fur stank of napalm and of burnt vegetation from some lush, rotten, and overripe dank jungle. Here, too, was the scent of burnt gunpowder, of gasoline, hot metal, human sweat, blood, and charred meat.

"I know you," said Peter, for he recognized and remembered those smells; the knot of fear that slithered in his stomach came only at those times. "I know you . . ."

"Not many look into my naked face without panic," the creature spoke in a purring voice, but the echoes of its voice from the wall sounded faintly as if thousands of distant men were screaming, some in triumph, some in terror. "But I see my claw marks still in you." And it raised a great hooked talon to point at the scars and seams of surgery that twisted along Peter's legs and belly.

"War," said Peter. "You and I go way back. Stay the hell away from me."

Suddenly Peter saw a wall of white brick circling his bed, and he smelled the smell of salt.

On the other side of the salt brick wall, he heard the Beast prowl, sniffing, and he heard the rasp of claws against the stones.

"Mortal man," came the purr of the terrible voice, "your kind, throughout all time, has sacrificed your fine young men upon my altars. The arms and legs and eyes, the innocence, the hopes, and the lives of those young men they freely heap upon the bloody altarstone to me. You, too, have given me your blood, your legs. You have no hope ever to walk again. I am pleased with you. Ask of me a boon."

"You work for the enemy," said Peter. "Why should you offer me anything?"

The Beast said, "Listen," and it rattled the massive

links of the heavy chain it bore. Then it said, "The fallen archseraphim I serve is like all other monarchs. Each king and each republic who calls me forth lets slip my chain a little ways, and always promise to their folk to bind me up again when time is done, and wreath the land in olive leaves, not flames. No promise is more often forsworn. For each man to defend himself must sacrifice to me as well and loose me from my chain a little ways. One day the chain shall break, and I shall be as I once was when all men worshipped me, when no men dreamed of peace, and every stranger was an enemy. Even the angels will fear me on that day; for all the cosmos shall shake when the final horn-call sounds the battle of the end of time." The voice of the Beast was melodic and beautiful, but the echoes from the wall were a thousand thin wails of the dying in pain.

"So what? What the hell is all that supposed to mean?" barked Peter.

Meadow Mouse whispered softly in his ear, "Ah, sir, it may not be my place to say, but I don't think it's such a good idea to talk with this creature . . ."

The Beast said, "Observe! Here is my meaning!"

The dream changed. Peter now lay on withered grass, fettered to the roots of a tall and leafless tree. The Beast's chain was pinned to the crown of the tree, so that it could pace all the ground every way around it but could not approach the roots, lest its chain get tangled and snagged in the outflung branches and the Beast be brought up short.

"See where your weapon is," snarled the Beast, pointing upward.

The chain was pinned between two branches at the crown of the tree by Mollner, the magic hammer. Mollner lay across the two branches, its haft threaded through a link in such a way that if the haft were dislodged, the chain would slip free.

"Call and the weapon will fall into your hand, mor-

tal man," said the Beast, "There will be power in your
hand to slay your captors, perhaps, and to spill their
blood upon the ground."

"This is a trick of Azrael's!"

"Indeed. But who is its victim, you or I? Why does
he hide my eyes when he would speak with you? He
thinks my might will serve his ends alone, he is a fool;
for I am an impartial god, most equitable of humor,
and accept sacrifice as well from those who hate as
those who honor me." Peter heard the faint scream of
multitudes dying in pain behind the Beast's voice as it
spoke.

"That damned rod will paralyze my hands again!"

"Cowards' hands, afraid to face the wages of war!"
Now the Beast fell to all fours again and began to pace
back and forth before and behind the tree, restless, as a
lion in a cage paces. "Come! Will weak and whining
words win your freedom from your foes? I will grant
you this, that with my own hand I will slay the first
man you engage in battle. And then . . ."

"Then?"

"I will wed you to one of my daughters. Hear me
tell of them.

"One dresses in rags and is beaten and scarred, for
her house has been burnt, and she has been raped by
soldiers, and she saw the brains of her lovely babies
dashed out against the breached walls of her city, while
she wept for her lost husband, who lies in an unmarked
grave in an unknown spot in foreign lands.

"The other daughter is dressed in gold, a crown of
oak upon her head, and all the world waits upon her
nod. Children of slain enemies are her slaves and pull
her chariot. She holds an olive branch in one hand and
a scepter of iron in the other, and none dare speak
against her or disturb her peace.

"But these daughters are twins, and you will be wed
to one of them if you unleash me, they are twins, and
all kings fondly conceive they will wed the second

when they open the gates to the temple of Janus, but most must wed the first."

Now Meadow Mouse ran out toward the Beast, scampering quickly, his thin, high voice an angry squeak. "You were banished from our lands! Banished!"

The gigantic Beast snarled and rose up on its hindpaws as the mouse leapt at it, and the eyes of the Beast were like two balls of yellow fire, and its great claw shimmered like lightning; but even though this great Beast faced nothing but a small mouse, for some reason, there was fear in those terrible eyes and hesitation as the paw rose up . . .

Then the dream ended, and Peter was awake.

II

Peter lay in the bed, and his hands tingled. Slowly, he began to flex his fingers.

For a long time he lay there, breathing through his open mouth, eyes closed, letting the feelings of victory and relief wash through his body. His hands. He had his hands again.

Suddenly he realized he could scratch. With a great effort, Peter forced his arms to stay immobile at his side. How best to use this advantage? He might not have much time . . .

He looked around the room. Nothing had changed. Security camera overhead; small, barred window; wheeled cart of medical instruments, some on a top shelf, some on the bottom. And outside the door, the dull-eyed guard.

Call the hammer? Not likely. Not if he could do something else instead.

Peter crossed his middle and ring finger. Slowly he inched his wrist to the left so that it was pointed at the guard. "Apollo, Hyperion, Helion, Day!" Peter whispered, without moving his lips.

Immediately the glassy stare left the man's face. He looked alive again, as if there were a soul behind those eyes.

But, aside from that, there was no other reaction.

"Hey, soldier, come here!" Peter called.

The guard turned his head, looked his way, looked away again. That was all.

Peter muttered, "Morpheus! Somnus! Hypnos! Take him out!"

But nothing happened.

Peter said, "Soldier, did I ever tell you I was in the Tet offensive? We had been in the field over a year, and it was all mud, blood, and dirty water. Hadn't seen a warm meal or a cigarette in months. Orders came down we were suppose to cross twenty-five miles of bad terrain in two days to meet up with units from Khesanh. So there it was, four in the morning, and four hundred degrees at least, and the only thing you could hear was the water dripping off the leaves. Drip, drip, drip, sounding like footsteps . . ."

It took less than half an hour to get the guard down the corridor and at the door.

". . . our own fucking artillery shells. 'Friendly fire,' they call it. So Jefferson stands up with that idiotic flag he's been carrying all this time and starts waving it over his head. Shouting. 'Hey, we're Americans.' That sort of thing. As if anyone could hear him. Bang. Piece of shrapnel catches him in the head, and we drag him back down into the muddy water, 'cause we can't tell if he's alive or not. Ramirez gets the radio going just at this point . . ." Peter paused.

The guard asked, "So what happened?"

"You got a cigarette on you?"

The boy looked uncertain. "We're not supposed to give you anything or hand you anything. Orders." But he stepped in the room.

"What's your name, soldier?"

Again the boy shrugged uncomfortably. "Can't say.

Orders. Don't give you anything, don't apologize, don't give your name."

"They tell you I was here without any trial? No arrest warrant? No nothing?"

Now the boy shrugged again, but, this time, with a look of blank indifference. "What do I care about that?" he said.

"It's unconstitutional, soldier."

"What do I care about that?" the boy said again.

"You swore to support and defend the Constitution," said Peter softly.

The young man grinned as if Peter were a simple-minded child who still believed in Santa Claus. "Fuck that," he said.

"I didn't quite hear you, soldier," said Peter, even more softly.

"This isn't 1776 anymore, you know. This is the new millennium. Get with the program. We're running things now. Some of the Pentagon, some of the Congress, they're our boys now, and they make sure we get to do whatever the mission requires."

"Your mission is attacking American civilians on American soil?"

"No. They're just little people. Just in the way."

All this time Peter had been hoping that Azrael had enchanted these people, like Wil had been enchanted, to make them do stuff they did not want to do. But no; it looked like these fellows knew what they were doing and were neck deep in it.

Why the hypnosis, then? Peter had a guess. His father had warned him what happened to mortal men when they saw too many things from the Other World, touched them, trafficked with them. People tended to forget and to be forgotten. Azrael might have enchanted his henchmen, done something to their minds, to allow them to work alongside supernatural monsters like Kelpie and Selkie, without forgetting their names and their lives.

Or he might have enchanted them to shut up and stand still when on guard duty, so that they would not say or do something accidentally to mess up Azrael's plans.

The soldier was still chatting on about the little people. "Civilians get in the way, we can shoot 'em, gas 'em, burn 'em: no one is going to look into it. Not the papers, not the press. They get switched, if they do."

"Switched?"

"Switched for one of our side. Skin 'em alive, throw the skins in the water. An hour later, someone who looks like him is walking around. Something."

"So that's your side, is it? You must be fucking proud to look in the mirror in the morning."

The boy shrugged again. "The world turned out to be a weird, fucked-up place. UFO-type weird, you know? Voodoo weird. And there're things in the water, coming. Nightmare things. Things people can't fight. Invisible things."

"You don't know jack, soldier," said Peter, grimacing. "My family's been fighting against the night-world for centuries. We got it under control. We got—"

"You got nothing, old man!"

"You swore to them, didn't you? Azrael and his crew."

A hushed whisper. "We don't say his name. The Warlock. He's got the Power."

"So. The U.S. government you swore to protect and defend when you put on that uniform has got one whup-ass monster-truck shitload of power too, seems to me."

The boy snorted. Evidently that did not seem worth answering.

Peter said thoughtfully. "Now, let me get this straight. When you joined up, did you swear to fight for the flag of your country, or did you swear to cut and run when some freak in a pointy hat doing card tricks managed to give you the willies and turn your sissy-ass spine all yellow? You love your country, soldier?"

"Don't make me laugh. What's to love? Compared to what's coming up out of the sea, this country is about as crippled and paralyzed and worthless as . . . well, as you, old man. Everything will be swept away when the Darkness covers all. But not me. No sir. I ain't getting swept away. I'm a survivor. You either do or get done to in this life, you know? Victim or victor. And its not like anyone leaves this outfit alive. Everybody's got to sleep sometime. That's our motto."

"Swell. Some motto."

The other man shrugged. "What the heck. At least it's easier to say than *semper fidelis*."

Peter would never have been able to kill a man in the uniform of his country—until now. The young man's craven words, whether he knew it or not, had just put the signature on his death warrant.

"Well, you're most likely right. Gotta go along to get along, I always say, and what's this damn country ever done for me?" Peter tried to smile. It was certainly the worst acting job he had ever done in his life.

The idiot actually grinned at him. "Yeah, now you're getting it, old man."

"Hey, be a pal and adjust this baby-bottle thing over my head here. Just move it closer to my head so I can reach it."

The young man nodded, slung his rifle, and stepped forward toward the bed. He reached out his hand . . .

III

Peter flung himself upright, one fist driving into the young man's groin, the other hand grabbing for the pistol holstered at his belt.

The young soldier staggered back, doubled over, and

the hammer of the pistol, as it was coming out of the holster, caught on a belt loop. Because the soldier was bent over, the holster was pushed up at an odd angle. Peter had his hand on the pistol, and he could feel the cross-hatching of the grip slipping through his fingers.

The soldier was staggering backward. Then the pistol was spinning in midair, inches beyond Peter's outflung arm.

The soldier's shoulder knocked the overcoat off the hook as he fell back. At the same moment, he shrugged his slung rifle down into his hand.

The pistol clattered to the floor. Peter was throwing himself out of the bed, also falling, needles ripping painfully out of his arm, numb legs pulling on the bedsheet, EEG machine yanked up off the cart and across the pillows.

The soldier raised his rifle. Peter lay with one shoulder on the floor, the pistol far outside his arm's reach, legs still on the bed, tangled.

Peter raised his hands as if surrendering. "Don't shoot!" The soldier sighted down the length of the barrel. Peter could see down the muzzle of the weapon. There was no mistaking the look in the young soldier's eye. Peter had tricked and humiliated the young man; he would accept no surrender. Peter was about to die.

"Mollner! To my hand!" shouted Peter; and immediately there was a loud explosion from somewhere in the distance behind the soldier, as if a wall had fallen.

The soldier's finger began to tighten on the trigger.

A mouse jumped out from beneath the bed, scampered up the soldier's boot.

The soldier shouted in pain; his arm jerked; aim spoiled, the round flew wide.

The noise of the rifle fire in an enclosed space was shockingly loud, despite this, Peter heard the slug fly by his ear, buzzing like a bee, and smack into the wall behind him.

There was a second explosion, as if a second and

nearer wall had been smashed by a wrecking ball; then a third, even louder still, as if the source of the terrible explosions were approaching through the building, shattering walls as it came.

The soldier shook his leg; the mouse fell out of his pants leg, teeth bloody; the soldier stepped on the mouse with his boot, crushing it.

At the fourth explosion, the lights went out; the only illumination came from the dusty window.

The soldier raised his rifle again, and the wall behind him exploded.

Concrete blocks erupted into the room in a shower of dust. The soldier turned, eyes wide, just in time to see the bricks painted with the shape of a hideous beast falling on him. The bricks separated as they toppled, making the beast seem to swell in size and disintegrate as it toppled.

From the midst of the shattering, scattering brick, an iron hammer flew. It struck the soldier in the skull, sending brains and blood flying over all parts of the room. Two halves of his helmet rebounded from the ceiling, ringing.

The mouse was twitching feebly amidst the rain of falling dust and pebbles. And, because Peter was staring at the mouse, he hardly noticed the strong jar that shook his arm when the hammer, still smoking from the heat of its flight, and dripping warm blood, came to rest in his hand.

It came to him suddenly, like a memory from a dream, that the mouse who used to eat the cheese in the pantry in the west wing, where Peter used to play as a boy, had somehow (and this part wasn't quite clear) removed the paralysis from his arms . . .

Then he remembered the dream, each word.

Peter crawled on his elbows over the rubble to where the tiny brown mouse lay.

It was a small, ordinary-looking little thing, and it had been mauled by the blow from the soldier's boot.

It lay on the floor, limbs still, its little sides heaving with labored breath.

Peter picked it up in his palm. "Don't worry, pal." He whispered, "I'll get you to a—well, to a vet, I guess. I'll get you to someone . . ."

But how? Peter heard shouts in the distance, booted feet running, sounding far away, perhaps in a stairwell.

He slipped the mouse into his shirt pocket. Now what?

He looked around, and saw an amazing sight. The wall in front of him had a hole several yards wide blasted through it. The room beyond was a wreckage of broken pipes and wiring, with a hole in the far wall; beyond that, a wrecked room with a hole in its wall, then another toppled wall, and another. All the holes were perfectly concentric, making a corridor of destruction all leading to Peter's hand.

Peter looked at the small iron hammer in his fist. His hand tingled slightly, as if he had slapped it against a stone, but he had suffered no damage beyond that.

"Just like the damn magicians," muttered Peter, "you don't consent, show no fear, they can't hurt you . . ."

Experimentally, he flung the hammer at the window. The whole wall exploded outward and chunks of masonry, twisted steel beams, and sheets of insulation were sent spinning out into the air. He was on the fourth floor of a building in some sort of small base or compound. Below, he could see a service yard, and in front of him a low, squat, gray building; a water tower atop that; and beyond, twin rows of barbed wire. Beyond the fence was flat, brown scrub, patches of grass leading into dry, empty lands.

He heard shouts in the distance, the hooting of an alarm.

The hammer came whistling back through space toward him. He held up his hand, face calm and stern.

The hammer struck his palm a solid blow and stung like a fastball slapping into a catcher's mitt.

"Knock the legs off the water tower," he told the hammer, and flung it.

Like a meteor, the hammer flew. In the distance Peter saw the water tower slowly sway and crumple, and several tons of water pour out and flood the building's roof. The tower tore off part of the roof as it fell; water poured from upper-story windows.

A whistling shriek announced the approach of the hammer.

At that moment, a young guard came around the corner and through the door. His face was flushed pink, panicky. He raised his rifle, even though Peter, lying on the floor, held up his hands, shouting, "Don't shoot! I'm unarmed!"

The kid put his rifle to his shoulder. Then his eyes jerked up to look at something behind Peter. Peter heard it from behind him, whistling through the air, singing like a dropping bomb, a sustained note dopplering down the scale.

Peter jerked his hand aside; the hammer missed his hand and flew past, struck the boy in the chest, smashing him against the far wall and breaking all his ribs with a horrifying noise. An astonishing amount of blood spurted from the gaping chest wounds.

The young man gasped out a girl's name (surely it was his sweetheart or wife) his hands clutching feebly at his beating heart and pumping lungs, which were exposed to air amidst the sheaths of torn muscle and the splintered wreckage of his ribs. He slid down into a pool of blood and viscera.

The hammer jumped back into Peter's hand.

"Shit!" said Peter, staring in horrified pleasure at the hammer. He looked at the two dead men, shook his head. He almost felt sorry for them. Almost.

Either one of them could have pegged him, if they

had remembered their training. Whatever unit these losers had come from, they must have been the bottom of the barrel, where the rotten apples were.

What about the mouse? Peter scooped the little creature out of his pocket.

The mouse had stopped breathing. Peter didn't know what to do. Putting down the hammer, he rubbed the mouse's belly with his finger. "Come on, pal. Don't give up yet." The mouse was still warm.

He put it back in his pocket when he heard soldiers in the corridor. He looked for cover. The bottom shelf of the medical cart might hold him, and it had blue plastic drapes that could be drawn. It took only a moment to throw the machine from the cart's bottom across the room and out through the hole into the air. Then he hid on the lower shelf, pulling his knees in with his hands. He jerked the blue plastic drapes shut.

Men ran into the room. He heard voices.

"You and you, stay in the corridor!" "Jeez, Sarge, what a mess . . ." "Look at what he did to Kilmer! He's all over the place!" "Holy Mary Mother of God, what the hell could do a thing like that . . ." "Sarge—looks like he bashed a hole in the wall and walked out." "He weren't paralyzed." "You three, through the hole with me. Buddy, stay here. Keep contact with Vazquez and Ebersol. Move it, people, move it!"

More footsteps. Men clambering over fallen block and brick.

Peter crossed his middle fingers, whispered, "Morpheus, knock out Vazquez, Ebersol, and Buddy." Then he inched the sheet up.

To the left, he could see two soldiers in the corridor, sitting down, yawning. To the right, another soldier stood with his back to the room, staring out the gaping hole toward the fallen water tower.

Peter wondered if this were "Buddy." Maybe a nickname was not enough for spirits to work with to zap someone.

The hammer was lying several feet away, among the scattered brick and splattered blood coating the floor.

Peter stealthily put out his hand, whispering, "Psst! Mollner! Come to Papa!"

IV

Buddy heard a scraping slither. He turned. He saw a muscular, scarred arm reach out from underneath the equipment cart, and the hammer hopped up into the hand.

Peter flung aside the blue sheet as the soldier, too late, raised his rifle. Peter flung the hammer with a backhand horizontal sweep of his arm, shouting, "Only the gun!"

It was like being hit by a truck.

Buddy's next clear memory was of lying on his back, staring up at the blue sky, and seeing the broken pieces of his rifle, barrel bent, spinning slowly through the air.

It took him a moment to realize that he was draped over the rubble of the hole in the wall, his head hanging in the air, sliding.

A pair of strong hands grabbed him. There was a haze of pain as he was drawn inside.

"My arm's broke!" he screamed.

"Shut up," came a calm, hard-edged voice. When the soldier's vision cleared, he could see the huge-shouldered, scarred man lying next to him, one beefy hand twined around the soldier's shirtfront. The other hand was up in the air, fingers spread, right up above the young soldier's face.

Buddy saw the man's features. There was something in that face, those eyes, that looked just like the boss' boss, the crazy guy in pimp jewelry who told Wentworth what to do.

"Tell me where they're keeping Lemuel Waylock. Old man, tall; bald, big white eyebrows."

"I ain't telling you shit!"

There was a whistling roar, rushing from high pitch to low, and the iron hammer flew into the room and smacked into Peter's palm. The hammerhead was still smoking and steaming, and a drop of the gore that coated it fell from the hammerhead and lightly touched the soldier's cheek.

"Second floor! Room 201! Corner room on the far side!"

"Now tell me how sorry you are for pissing me off."

"I'm sorry, sir!" the young soldier barked.

"I'll accept how and when I damn well please. Morpheus! Knock 'im out!"

A blanket of warm numbness stole through the young soldier's body and closed his eyes. The pain in his broken arm receded, and he fell into a profound, deep sleep.

5

The
World of Mists
and Shadows

I

Two men stood where the slabs of concrete and macadam were buckled and torn. The roof overhead was a mass of splintered steel girders, swaying remnants of lighting fixtures, torn wires. In the middle of the garage, past where the heavy steel doors that had once covered the truck bay lay, rested a huge, crumpled wreck. Several machine-gun barrels protruded from the mass, twisted at strange angles. One tread of the vehicle was unwound.

"Tell me what I'm looking at, Van Dam." The first man was dressed in a well-tailored business suit, a yellow slicker over that. On his head he wore a hard hat.

The second man had a thin, gray moustache, and wore a transparent plastic coat over his uniform. "That was our armored personnel carrier. Mr. Wentworth. Three inches of titanium alloy armor. The weapon struck only into the engine block. You can see where the prow is caved in? Those big triangular shards?"

"Yes."

"See how they are bent backward at the tips? That was caused by the backward passage of the weapon as it ripped itself out of the impact area."

"And that?" Wentworth pointed upward.

"When the men tried to come out of the vehicle, he knocked over the columns and brought down those chunks of concrete on top of the hatch, trapping them inside. It was pretty clear he was trying not to hurt the men."

"Fourteen dead? And that's not trying to hurt them?"

"Mostly from friendly fire. He was pulling his punches," said Van Dam.

"Hm. Looks like he knew just where to hit the vehicle."

"It was Gus Waylock, after all."

Wentworth seemed surprised. "You've heard of him?"

"Yes, sir. Captain Peter Augustus Waylock, Twenty-eighth Infantry, Medal of Honor, several Purple Hearts. Very highly decorated. Some places, his name is legend."

"Well. I wonder if that helped him. Show me the cross corridor."

"Careful here."

They walked.

Van Dam said, "This hole here led us astray for a while. We thought he had gone out of the building here, because of this hole. Here's the stairwell. Look out for that door."

"I'm okay. I can step over it. What happened here?"

"We think he threw the weapon directly down the stairwell to collapse the stairs. Lost two men here. See where the supports are shorn? The lab boys say they can estimate the kinetic energy of the weapon in motion from that. The weapon strikes with something equivalent to a heavy antitank round."

"What happened down that way?"

"Sonic boom blew out the windows all along that corridor. The weapon can fly faster than Mach One."

"But why did you think he was in this corridor at this point? Wasn't he still traveling in a medical equipment cart by then?"

Van Dan said, "At this point we think he was giving false orders over our radios. He had Kilmer's walkie-talkie. When we found out, he ordered a radio silence."

"He ordered?"

"Yes, sir."

"And that's what caused the thing at the cross corridor?"

"Yes. This way. Look out for that broken glass."

"I see it. Now, how did he get onto this level if he didn't actually come down the stairwell?"

"We found some cable looped around the roof braces. Either he had a confederate on the roof with a winch, or . . ."

"Or what?"

"We don't know yet how much control he has over the weapon in flight. He may have tied the cable to the hammer, and ordered it to fly up and through the braces. If so, the hammer has a lifting weight capacity we estimate at nine hundred pounds."

"Was this while he was carrying his father?"

"We're not sure. Personally, I think the cable was just another false trail. I think he slid down the garbage chute into the dumpster."

"Any idea why he destroyed the pay phone on the fourth floor?"

"Something strange there, sir. The coinbox was exploded outward from the inside; there was no entry damage. It may have been the first thing damaged. Here we are. Look here. Uh. This is pretty messy, sir. The medical examiner isn't quite done yet . . ."

"I've seen worse. Well, Maybe not. Where was he standing?"

"Lying, sir. He was here, where he had carved out a niche in the wall. We think it took three blows of the weapon. You see here where the wall is shorn away? There are three layers of melted rock; the rock momentarily liquefies under the impact."

"Okay. He was here. There were two squads, one coming down each of these corridors. They can't see each other. What happened next?"

"Remember, they're not coordinated because of the radio silence . . ."

"Even so, how do you explain this?"

"Well, sir, it was also dark. One of the first things he did was knock out the generators and the backup generators. Also, the weapon had already struck among both squads several times."

"How? Was he throwing it through the wall at them?"

"No, sir, he only did that the one time on the third floor. The men say the weapon was turning the corner each time, changing direction as it flew."

"He can throw the thing around corners?"

"With English, I suppose, sir."

"Is that supposed to be a joke, Van Dam?"

"I wish it were, sir."

"So all our men shoot each other to pieces in the cross corridor. And that's how he got away? I don't understand. How did he get out?"

"We think it was at that point he threw the weapon through the fence."

"How far away would you say the fence was from here?"

"Half a mile, sir. The alarm went off. Naturally, the men converged toward the breach."

"And he was here all the time?"

"Yes, sir. He and his father were dressed in our uniforms at this point. He just lay among the wounded.

You see where he got the idea; the father was still un-conscious. When the ambulance crew came, naturally they just assumed . . ."

Wentworth shook his head. "I don't want to hear any more."

II

Miss MacCodam smiled as she walked, for she loved the library. It had been built in a day and age when the local contributors had been generous and showed proper respect to learning. The main desk was in an atrium surrounded by tall Greek columns, and the light from the setting sun shined through the tall, green glass windows.

Behind the desk quiet aisles led back among tower-ing stacks. Miss MacCodam imagined, in that pro-found silence, the deep wisdom of the ages meditated. In her mind's eye, these stacks of book were erected to the memory of the geniuses long dead, the monuments to the giants who had built civilization, or, if not mon-uments, then walls—walls holding back the tides of ig-norance, barbarism, and decay, that each generation, rose up in new forms to pull down the pillars of society.

She breathed in satisfaction. When the library was closed, it was so solemn and quiet here. The silence of a thousand sleeping stories, dreams, records, experi-ments, accomplishments . . .

A slight snore rippled across the silence.

Miss MacCodam halted in shock. She swung her eyes about. There, in the small room set aside for chil-dren, she saw a figure slumped over the tiny table. It was a shaggy-headed bulk in a long, black coat, now faded, torn, and stained. Because the table and chair were small, child-sized, he seemed huge.

As she stepped into the room, she smelled a rank smell, as if the man had been sleeping among garbage.

How could she have missed seeing him here before? She had checked this little room twice before locking the main front doors.

She wondered if she should call the police.

"Sir! Sir!" she said, in a stern voice.

The shoulders jerked. The man snorted. Then he raised his shaggy head.

It was not just the small size of the chairs that made him seem huge. The man was huge.

His beard and hair were black. His face was pale and streaked with tears and dirt. He clearly had not eaten in days. And his eyes were the saddest eyes Miss MacCodam had ever seen in a human face.

He spoke in a hopeless, lost, small voice. "You see me then, eh? You are mad then, or a poet. You are daydreaming." He spoke in a thick, Russian accent.

"It's after closing time, sir."

The man nodded sadly. "There are no closing times for me. Turn your back. You will see me no more. I am ghost. But I cannot die, you see?"

Miss MacCodam stepped backward.

The man spoke in a sober, slow voice. "There is another world alongside the world you know. Men of shadow live there, wrapped in mist. They fade; they die. People cannot see them, cannot remember them. Invisible people, wrapped in mist. Wrapped in sorrow. Wrapped in loneliness. You see me; the mists have parted. Soon mists swirl shut again. You will forget. Go away." And he put his head back down on his folded arms, which lay on the tabletop.

He muttered, "Library is only place to go; can talk with the dead here. No one else can talk to me. Great minds. Fables . . ."

She said softly, "Do you need something to eat? Do you need some money?"

A laugh, or perhaps it was a sob, came from beneath the lowered head. "I need one hundred dollar bill of Ben Franklin."

She said, "There is a can of soup in the librarian's lounge. I can microwave it for you . . ."

The man slowly raised his head. "Why would you help me?"

"Because, well . . ." She couldn't tell him that his eyes reminded her of a picture she once liked when she was small. "Well, you're not drunk or anything . . ."

"Tell me. What do you see here?" And she saw he had taken several days' worth of newspapers off the rack from the main room. "Look at this picture."

"It's the flooding. Terrible, isn't it? The government is going to ship them relief aid . . ."

"Here."

"Fires in the Southwest. Terrible how many people died. They say it may have been arson . . ."

"Here."

"This? Protestors in front of a hospital. They want more money to study the epidemic . . ."

"Here."

"Hurricane Clement. The National Guard is giving tent space to people whose houses were blown down."

"Brain in your head, it is shrouded by mist. Look at where my finger is pointing. Right here. Look."

"It's . . . I . . . I'm sorry, what was I saying? It's after closing time, sir. . . ."

"There is a giant wading down the river, stirring up floods. He made heavy snows in the mountains, you see? Is why coldest winter on record. Footprint of fire-giant there, in ashes investigator standing next to. Arson, yes! Can't you see it? And storms! Man dancing in air above wreckage of flattened houses. Right there in picture. Look right here where my finger is touching. Man on rotting horse at door to hospital. The pro-testors are next to him, he kills them with his poison, he smiles, they cannot see him. Photograph does not lie." The man had stood and now loomed over her, pointing down at the scattered newspapers.

"Sir, the library is . . . what was I saying? What . . ."

"Look. You see I have piece of paper here with a hole it?"

"Sir . . ."

"You see hole, no?"

Miss MacCodam spoke in a small voice. "Yes, I see it."

"I put it atop the picture of the flood. I cover everything but the giant. Where is hole now?"

"I . . . the whole picture is covered, I suppose . . ."

"Hole cannot disappear. Where is hole?"

"I . . ."

"Use logic. Use reason. Magic cannot deceive logic."

Miss MacCodam screamed. "Oh, my God!! There's a giant monster wading in the river! His face is covered with ice!"

"Ah!" The man sat down with a smile. "Was hoping that would work. Interesting test, no?" He sat there, nodding to himself.

III

Then he said, "Did you say was some soup I could have?"

She was pulling up the piece of construction paper and putting it back down again, staring at the newspaper photograph over and over again. "Oh, my God . . . oh, my goodness . . ."

Miss MacCodam looked up. "What . . . who are you?"

"My name is Raven, the son of Raven. I am one of the people in the Mist. One of the forgotten. One of the unforgiven."

Then he put his hand out to cover up the photograph. "Do not look too long, or you will fall into the Mist as well, perhaps. Do not tell anyone else what you have seen in the photograph or they will push you into the Mist. Do not look for the horrors in the pictures; you may see them. Do not watch the news on television this evening. Once you forget me, you are safe again . . . I think."

Miss MacCodam said, "Tell me."

He shook his head. "You might fall into Mist. Dangerous. And it is so lonely. So lonely. Did you ever have anyone you used to tell everything to? Someone who, unless they had heard the story yet, the thing didn't seem like it really happened?"

"Your wife?"

He nodded sadly.

"What happened? Did she . . . did she die?"

"No. I did."

It was not until she persuaded him to come to the lounge and she started feeding him tomato soup (his hands shook, and he could not hold the spoon), that he began to tell his story.

IV

"Was in prison. Not real, legal prison, but was like prison in Russia. Soldiers, not guards. 'Protective custody,' they call it. Was put there by wizard. But wizard is from old times, and does not understand our modern American constitutional system of rights and rule of law, not like I understand, I who must study this for citizenship. So I confess, you see?

"I killed Galen Waylock.

"But he is not killed on federal territory. Is not federal case.

"Is like with me; I am park police. Crime on park grounds, is federal land. Federal land, federal case. But I have no jurisdiction I see crime off park grounds, yes? So with them.

"Wizard think is like old days. He think his friends can throw me in dungeon like a king throw man in dungeon. No explanation. No warrant. But, aha! Cannot do in America. Perhaps wizard is gone that day. Perhaps his friends make mistake or are not so hypnotized as he think. Someone make mistake, perhaps. They send me to real prison.

"Real prison, I have rights. Right to a lawyer. But I have no lawyer. I only have one call; only lawyer I know is Wendy's father, who does not exist. I call her house. Leave message for make-believe lawyer.

"Next day, mistake corrected; federal men come to take me back. Now is federal case; very secret, very high level. Have papers saying they can take me. Signed papers. Signed in triplicate.

"So I hit a guard with the leg from the cot. Maybe they think cot leg too thick to rip out of floor. Are wrong. I think I kill him. Maybe not. I thought they would shoot me. I tried to make them shoot me.

"Now they move me to stronger cell. Different place. Bars everywhere. Real prison. Maybe is mistake again, or maybe wizard no longer care about me.

"There was weight room. I work out. Make myself stronger. Other prisoners are bad men. One man, I broke his fingers, five fingers, when he say I must act like his woman for him; they leave me be after that.

"There was television there. I could see the things on television. The Princes in the hurricane. The Kelpie with the sick and dying. The giant in the snowstorms. The giant in the fires. All my fault. So many people dead. My fault.

"No one else can see them. All call me crazy.

"Guards start to not see me. They leave me in cell sometimes at mealtimes or leave me in exercise yard when we should go in.

"The news say the hurricane has killed many people; thousands have no homes, no food, many dying every day.

"It is my anniversary. I decide to kill myself.

"I hang myself with twisted pants leg from the light.

Is no high place to jump from, so I must hang and choke myself. My eyesight goes dim. Darkness fills vision.

"I see a light, surrounded by ring of light. It is like moon on evening of mist, with ring of silver around. Light hangs from the smallest finger of most beautiful lady I have ever seen, and she is walking through the jail cells, and her slippers make no noise at all. There is wind blowing her hair, and her long skirts of green and silver. Hair is black as midnight. And long, all the way to her knees, it goes. Eyes are green as the eyes of a cat. Wind touches nothing else. Wind makes no noise. The lamp is the elf-lamp I have seen before.

"She speaks. Her voice is like silver. Like music. And I am terribly afraid of her.

" 'There is hope,' she says. 'There is always hope.'

"I tell her I can see no hope. Perhaps I only think I tell her, since, you know, I am choked.

"She says, 'There are always stars, though you cannot see them by day. And they are larger and older than all your world and all its troubles.'

"I tell her I care nothing for stars; how can they help me?

"And she smiled so sweetly. 'And you, a sailor, can say that? You cannot see my star with your eye, but it is there. It will guide you safe to port. To home, to your wife again, if you let it. But you must raise your eyes to see it. My husband comes to save you, but he must travel across the man's world with man's steps and cannot come with the speed of dreams.' And she looks at me between the bars of my cage, and her light is shining like a star.

"I tell her my wife will never forgive me.

"And she laughs again, and she says, 'If you kill yourself, she'll never speak to you again!'

"But I killed a man.

"And she tells me there is no death.

"So I lift my hands and part the rope holding me to

the lamp bracket. I fall. I breathe again. I see clearly again. She is gone.

"I tell my cell mate this thing. He tell me a story. My cell mate, he tell me there is a man who is the foe of evil. Invisible man, who clouds men's minds. A figment, a specter, a shadow. All criminals fear this man. Many stories of this man; but they are foolish tales, meant for children. Like funny book hero, you know? But criminals are frightened of him. Cell mate, he tell me the man of darkness is coming for me tonight.

"I ask about this man to others when we are at mess hall. They look at me with fear. You are crazy, says one of them, only crazy people hear stories of this man; no one else can hear them.

"That night, a black shadow came to cell door. He wear long, black cape, black hat, face hidden in scarf. But his eyes. His eyes stab through things like knives. Like the eyes of a genius. Like the eyes of a judge in a court of law. Like the eyes of a king!"

V

Raven had rolled off the bunk and stood up. His cell mate, on the rack above, had not stirred, but lay sleeping, mouth open, grizzled cheeks looking pale and sickly in the dim light from the cell block corridor. Evidently his cell mate had not heard the man speak.

"Of course I can see you," Raven answered the man in black. A black-gloved hand rose up. Redder than a spot of blood, redder than the planet Mars at night, a cool fire seemed to burn and flicker on his ring finger. It was a scarlet opal.

The dark man said, "Then you are farther gone than I suspected. We must have you out of there."

The man took a length a wire from beneath his cape and connected the alligator clips to contact points on the cell door and wall. Then he took out what looked like a thin, metal instrument, painted with a nonglossy black paint. He turned the instrument in the lock, and there was a click.

The door he opened only as far as the wire would allow.

"Come!"

"But I am criminal. Murderer. I belong in cage."

"Galen Waylock is not dead."

"What?"

"He is only under a spell. You can save him. You can save yourself. Come! I have no time."

Raven slipped carefully out through the partly open door. The man in black shut it, relocked it, removed the clips, wiped the bars. Raven admired the swift, certain precision of his motions.

"Follow me. I know how little noise you can make when you try. Try now."

With a whispering rustle of cape, the figure turned and glided off down the walkway.

The cells rose tall to either side. There were men sleeping, turning on their bunks; one or two were awake. If any of them saw the pair, they did not cry out.

The man in black took out a thin, telescopic length of rod from his cloak. When they arrived at the corner of the cell block, the man in black reached up with the rod and plucked away the Polaroid photograph that had been taped across a wire in front of the lens of the security camera. Raven saw it was a photograph of the walkway where they stood, a picture taken from the height and angle of the security camera.

The man in black whispered, "Guard station at the end of the walk. I will spread my cape. Stay exactly behind me. You must always keep me between yourself and them. Understand?" And he held up his ring and stepped forward.

When they had finally climbed down and were outside the last wall, and the man in black was winding the cable of the grapnel back into the silent, air-powered catapult beneath his cloak, Raven asked in a voice of awe, "Who—Who are you?"

The man pulled aside the scarf he wore doffed his hat. His features were dark and harshly handsome, hook nosed, high of cheekbone. His hair was silver.

"You don't remember me? That's a good sign. Think of me as your attorney. I am a man of law; I bring justice where no justice is otherwise possible. Come. I arranged to have a cab waiting this way. The cabbie is a friend. He's insane enough to be able to see us, but stable enough to fake sanity, at least to the degree as will satisfy New Yorkers."

They began walking in the tall grass along the side of the road. The night was crisp and cold, and the starlight glinted from frost along the roadside.

"Don't walk in the road. Motorists won't see you."

Raven said, "Tell me what is happening."

"I arrived too late to stop Azrael from taking the mansion. Gwendolyn had flown away by then; and you and the Waylocks were in custody. I suppose you noticed how normal men could not see the mythical beings? That's a phenomenon of the so-called mist."

"Mist?"

"Think of it as a psychological barrier. You are familiar with hysterical blindness? No? Men who are hypnotized into thinking they are blind will still move to avoid objects placed in their path. They react to those objects but do not consciously remember them. There is a state of being whose objects are to normal men as normal objects are to men suffering hysterical blindness. I am one such object in that state. The mythical beings are other such objects, which, unlike me, are native to that state. You may soon be another, if you do not take steps immediately to prevent it."

"You must say more."

"Listen. Sometimes men, through despair, or madness, fall into this condition. It's rare. People can't see them. If they do, they can't remember later. Most Men of the Mist start stealing to live. They can't keep jobs, because their employers forget they are there. Relatives can't feed them, because the relatives forget."

"What about pictures? Documents?"

"The phenomenon is psychological, not physical. Normal people simply cannot see any object that would remind them of the affected person."

"How is this possible?"

"Unknown."

"What about touching? Hitting?"

"If you try to attract too much attention, you start fading. You go blind, or maybe you turn transparent. You go numb, maybe insubstantial. I have limited data on this point. Maybe legends about incubi are based on this. The point is: once you are in the Mist World, if you start to steal from the normal world, or hit people, or wreck their belongings, the Mist gets thicker around you until you lose all contact with the real world altogether."

Now they were cutting across a field. They went over a split-rail fence and down through a copse of trees. The tangled branches were like a net overhead.

Raven was shivering, and his breath came in clouds. The man in black handed Raven his cape. Beneath, the man wore a black jumpsuit with a harness to which dozens of tools, weapons, and pieces of equipment were attached.

"Why do you dress in this way?" asked Raven.

"Childhood hero of mine. Ever listen to old radio programs? 'The weed of crime bears bitter fruit'? No? I thought it was particularly apt, considering how I'm turning this curse to my benefit.

"Second reason: if the universe can explain any action as if there is no mist, then the mist doesn't get any thicker. If I dress in black, and hide, then maybe the reason why a person doesn't remember me is because he didn't see me.

"Third reason: did you notice how Azrael de Gray

was dressed? Even when there was nothing but a bed-sheet, he had to have a cape. Magic works by impressing an image on the racial subconsciousness of mankind. Simple images, old images, work best. Capes are impressive; sweatshirts are not. Swords are quaint and poetic; machine guns are not. Imagine a blindfolded statue of Justice with a balance in one hand and a machine gun in the other. Absurd image. It is the impressive, poetical things that have magic in them."

"You carry guns."

"Half the things in the Mist World are immune to gunfire. Guns, as a symbol, have not percolated down into the racial subconsciousness."

"But you carry guns!"

"There's always the other half."

"Other half?"

"Evil men who use the Mist to hide their crimes. Police cannot see them. But I can. Some crimes are subtle, and it takes a while before the mists thicken around such criminals, thick enough to eject them from the universe. If I reach them, I eject them first."

"But how do you live? Without stealing?"

The man in black answered, "In the old days, people left food out for fairies. Must have been easier then. Now there are several ways. If you take up a new identity, a new life, sometimes the universe will let you back in, if the new person is sufficiently different from the old. I have many such false identities: a wealthy playboy, a fighter pilot, a janitor, a newspaperman.

"Some jobs you can keep without having to see people face to face. Stockbrokers, accountants, certain types of news writers. I have several of such men in my employ. Others can live on the fringes, seen, but not looked at: cab drivers, street bums.

"I have set up a network of such men, to combat the network I found in place among the maniacs and madmen serving Azrael de Gray. By keeping these men away from crime, I can keep the mist from closing over them.

"For example, my cabbie here; he still lives in his old house, and sometimes the mist gets thin enough that his wife, who thinks he is dead, can have a reunion, which, the next day, she thinks was an erotic dream.

"And my broker, he just does his old job entirely by phone, making sure he never gets to know his clients personally; lonely, yes, but he is the only one in the mist who has been able to keep open a bank account that the tellers don't forget about. He's the only one of us who is overweight, since he can actually order food delivered and pay for it."

In the distance, Raven could see an automobile, sitting, lights off, by the shoulder of a dirt road.

Raven asked, "Who is Azrael de Gray?"

The man in black said, "I was hoping you could tell me. Back when I was in the real world, I was a rather important figure. You would not believe how important. There just aren't that many inventors and engineers who are also attorneys, financiers, and who own their own newspapers. Without my consent, I had become sort of a political figure, a standard-bearer, a focal point for those who wanted to work hard, be free, and keep the money they earned for themselves. My editorials made quite a stir; but they also brought me to the attention of Azrael.

"Let me tell you something of my past: My greatest joy in life was solving problems; I made quite a bit of money solving other people's problems for them. Then the government regulators did their best to take away as much of that money as possible; people who did not know my business tried to tell me how to run my business, whom I could hire, when, where, how, and why. That was why I became a lawyer, you know; I wanted to be able to defend the wealth my inventions had brought me. But when the people vote in unfair laws, knowing those laws does not help; the only way to defend yourself then, is by molding public opinion. I bought a newspaper. I made it successful. I hired private detectives for some of my staff to help me track down a conspiracy I had noticed in the halls of power. Politicians, media bosses, criminals were showing a peculiar degree of cooperation. I tried to find why, tried to find how to solve the problem.

"They found me first.

"Azrael's people approached me with an ultimatum: join them or else. They said they could strip away my family, my wealth, my position, all my accomplishments, my fame, everything—make it as if I had never existed. They showed me clear evidence of their supernatural power. Naturally, I defied them."

"And Azrael cursed you."

"Yes. This was four and a half years before he came to Earth."

"What?!"

"Azrael's scheme has been long in formulating. He has been communicating with his recruits here for years, in their sleep. His coming to this world was the culmination, not the first step, of long-laid plans."

"And the curse?"

"I admit it was difficult, at first, to have all one's accomplishments and life stripped away and forgotten. But my mind, my discipline and dedication, are what created those accomplishments, and nothing and no one can strip me of them. So I keep telling myself."

They approached the cab. The man in black continued. "At the outset, I estimated it would take five years to overthrow Azrael's plans and, after that, about ten years to get back to the same wealth and status as I had had before. One advantage, of course, is I wouldn't have to go back through law school if I sit for the bar in a state that allows open examinations. Also, certain applications of the magic I've learned might lead to new scientific developments that will be widely marketable. Just the use of hypnosis as a safe anesthetic has immense potential. I can't wait to get this Azrael problem out of the way so I can get back to work!" He rubbed his hands together and smiled.

VI

Raven had eaten the two cans of soup in the little kitchenette and the box of crackers the librarian kept there.

Miss MacCodam asked, "And what happened next? Did you become part of this vigilante hero's secret organization?"

"No. His first order, even before I got into cab, was to seek out the Gold Ring of the Niflungar, and stop the hurricane. Magic ring. But to use it, you must forswear love. I cannot forswear love. But, yet . . ."

"People are dying in those storms, their homes destroyed, their lives destroyed. Some of them are losing loved ones, too."

"Is what he said. We argued. I left."

"How have you lived? You look so hungry . . ."

Raven drew himself up. "I would not steal. Even when it is so easy. Invisible men can steal anything. So I must starve, even with food in front of me. Sometimes I eat what restaurants throw away, or what people leave behind on their plates . . ."

"And what now?" asked Miss MacCodam.

"Now I am wrong. Now I must find magic ring. All I need to do is get hundred dollar bill, go to sleep, have dream about Franklin."

She said, "That's impossible. No one can have a dream about something just by wishing they could."

"I think Galen could do this. I do not have his training. Maybe if I went to Everness; all dreams there are true. But how can man like me, without job, without life, find hundred dollar bill? If I steal, the mist will close over me, and no one see me ever again. Now I am willing to give up love, and I cannot."

He put his head down on the kitchenette counter, infinitely weary, sad, hopeless. Miss MacCodam reached forward and stroked his tousled hair.

He jerked his head up, eyes staring blearily.

She pulled her hand back. Her face felt warm; she was blushing. "Uh. Is it stealing if I get you a bus ticket? The bus driver might not see you, of course, but if the ticket has already been bought, you'll have a perfect right to be there."

"Bus ticket? To where?"

"Everplace. Whatever you called it. I assume there is a Gate of Ivory and a Gate of Horn; that's the way Virgil describes it in the *Aenead*. It's in the U.S., isn't it? On this planet? Good. Because they're having a supersaver special for anywhere in the United States. . . ."

"Why?"

Miss MacCodam leaned forward. "I don't think forswearing love means what you think it means. The ring you're talking about, it's the same as the ring in Wagner's opera cycle, isn't it? Well, if you remember from the *Götterdämmerung,* Sigfried is married to Brünnhilde, and later to Gunther's sister, I can't remember her name. Obviously, he didn't foreswear love."

"What? What do you talk about?"

"If it's like what Campbell describes in his *Occidental Mythology,* then the ring is a symbol of self-image, a Jungian archetype. Like a signet ring, it symbolizes self-identity, and the fact that it's gold, which the ancient alchemists took to be the metal of refined virtue . . ."

Raven held up his hand. "You are scholar. Learned woman. I see this now. I will follow your advice. What do you think I must forswear, if not love?"

"Passion. Reckless love."

"You mean, the kind of love that makes man kill other man, a stranger, to save his wife?"

"I really don't know," she said, suddenly uncertain. "I'm only guessing . . ."

"No. You are scholar. I hear the wisdom in your words. Even if you are wrong, I have hope now. I am thinking, I can maybe use this ring without it destroys my life. I will take your bus to Everness. But why do you help me?"

She smiled. "Haven't you ever helped anyone before? A big, strong man like you?"

"Sometimes."

"Well, maybe little mousy librarians like to feel big and strong too, you know. Besides, I saw the thing in the photograph."

Raven stood, and now he stood with his back straight. "Last question. How can I get a hundred dollars? You are not rich woman, no?"

She smiled again. "I'm richer than you know." She pointed out the door toward the stacks of books. "Rich in priceless treasure. There is a book on how to spot counterfeiting in the 300 section with plates showing all types of bills. If you don't need a real bill, just a picture, you can photocopy the proper pages out of that book. I'll call the bus company . . ."

Raven stooped over the sink and washed the stains of dirt and tears from his face.

6

The
Messenger
of Darkness

I

"How long do we have to stay here, Hal? This is humiliating."

"Be quiet, Mr. President. I'm not going to ask you again." In the steel and concrete bunker two levels beneath the Pentagon, the carpet had been taken up from the center of the room and a pentagram in gold wire had been inscribed into the floor.

Surrounding this on three sides were computer banks on raised daises; on higher banks, behind them, stood radar screens, information terminals, telecommunications nexuses. The high ceiling was in shadow. Giant map screens hanging from overhead displayed, in green glowing lines and dots, weather patterns, troop positions, satellite telemetry, phone lines, highways, railheads.

On the fourth side, where two computer banks had been moved, stood an empty throne. One arm was carved with a red dragon, the other with a white; a Roman eagle stood on a pole behind the throne; over the seat was flung a bear skin, with skull and claws still attached.

On the fifth side, where the fire-control alert stations had been, was now an altar surrounded by candles. A dead lion cub lay on the altar stone, blood draining through channels in the stone into a silver chalice.

The president, three members of his cabinet, the White House chief of staff, and twelve high-ranking members of various bureaus, whose budgets and activities appeared on no public record, were there. Nine law clerks who wrote opinions for the Supreme Court were here, dressed in black robes.

In front of them, nearer the altar, was the man the president had called Hal. He was the chairman of the Federal Reserve Board, and over his blue pin-striped suit, he wore a cloak of white lamb's wool.

Behind them, and nearer to the center of the room, were men in the uniforms of generals and admirals of the Joint Chiefs of Staff. Strangely, these men's faces were young, and they had the tense, calm look of security officers and bodyguards.

All these men were kneeling.

Between two urns, one of lilies and one of red roses, Azrael de Gray was behind the altar, dressed in resplendent robes of pigeon blue, dark blue, and black, with silver trim. Seven necklaces of seven precious metals hung from his epaulettes, all connected to the huge diamond he wore in the midst of a pentagram of magnetized steel in the center of his chest. His shoulderboards and puffy sleeves exaggerated his size. His tall, pointed hat was sewn with diamond chips in the shape of constellations; around the brim floated moons of various phase.

Azrael dipped an aspergillum into the chalice, and, with a flick of his wrist, sprinkled blood to the carpet, calling out in a great voice, "Phaleg! Bethor! Aratron! I call upon the Outer Gods, who are dimmer than great Morningstar, whom we call Hagith, Eophoros, and Phosphoros, though are allowed to mount the zenith, an honor denied to their master. By that master's secret name, Bringer of Light, Teleos, come forth. I charge you; I compel you; I conjure you. Come forth from the mist, Aratron! Aratron! Aratron! Thrice called by your secret name, and I have brought the king's blood for your sup!"

A column of darkness began to form in the middle of the gold pentagram, shot through with black flickers of a darker hue, as if a dark counterpart to lightning were dancing around the column of a tornado.

The president, still kneeling, palms clasped together, sneaked a glance over his shoulder at the manifestation, his eyes white with terror, his face beaded with sweat.

Hal, the chairman of the Federal Reserve, reached back and jerked on the president's tie. "Eyes front!" he hissed.

The president jerked his eyes back toward the altar but shivered in the cold wind that began to blow through the chamber.

Some people coughed. One or two of the men in back, pretending to be praying, bent their noses forward toward their clasped hands and tried to pinch their nostrils with their fingertips.

Azrael raised the bloody chalice on high, head thrown back, garments whipped by cold and stinking winds, proud face illuminated by the strange lightnings radiating from the manifestation. With burning eyes he stared into the heart of the darkness.

II

In a darkened room not far away was a bank of television screens, each monitor showing the scene from different viewpoints and angles.

The top left monitor showed the tornado of darkness forming into the image of an iron-faced goddess, draped in black and armed with a flail of chains and shackles.

Van Dam put down his cigarette and toyed with a control on his chair arm. "Depth seems funny on that camera. Woman looks bigger than the room she's standing in."

Wentworth took a sip from his soda bottle. "Don't worry about it. Must be supernatural. Are we getting a reading from microwave detectors?"

"Like you said, sir, all four detectors report the woman manifestation is farther away than the opposite wall, even the detectors facing each other. It's impossible, but there it is." Van Dam pulled a banknote out of his wallet and handed it to Wentworth.

"Impossible in three dimensions. Thanks."

Van Dam took a puff on his cigarette. "Heard anything lately about the Coldgrave problem?"

"I tried to talk to Azrael about him. Coldgrave is useless at this point. Why do we need a handful of religious fanatics when we have practically the entire might of the U.S. military at our disposal? But Azrael wouldn't hear of it. Maybe he still intends to make the man Pope, like he promised." Wentworth shook his head in dismay. "We might have to eliminate Coldgrave. Blame his death on the missing Waylocks or the Russian fellow."

"Are you so good at telling lies in your sleep, sir?"

Wentworth shrugged. "Well, it's just an idea."

Van Dam suddenly straightened up in his chair, biting through his cigarette, so that the burning tip fell across his chin to the floor. "Holy Jesus God! Ah— Uh—"

Wentworth nodded. "Azrael said she'd show up in a bad mood. That's why we put the security men nearer to the pentagram, dressed up as top brass. He was pretty sure she wouldn't kill Azrael at this point, but that she'd have to do something to someone to show she means business. Hm. Look at that. Azrael said she'd get two or three guys; and she took out two. He knows his business. Ah . . . you all right?"

"I don't know, sir. All that blood. We used to do something like that to frogs we caught when I was a kid. . . . I . . ."

"Here; just put your head between your knees for a moment."

"Okay. I'm Okay."

"Poor Bob's got splatter all over him."

Wentworth took another sip from his soda. Then he said, "What language is that?"

"Babylonian. We should be getting a translation text over screen six in just a moment. Those CIA guys are pretty good at real-time translation. Wonder what's keeping them."

"Her accent?" said Wentworth.

"Maybe the roaring noise is interfering with the equipment. Say, what did you tell the National Zoo people about the lion cub?"

"National security. Accidentally killed in transit. What did you tell the Smithsonian people about the Hope diamond?"

"Terrorist threat. That we'll swap back the real diamond once we catch the terrorists."

"Mm. Good line."

"Did Azrael actually need the biggest diamond in the world for his ritual here, sir?"

Wentworth shrugged. "I guess. Spirits are impressed by that sort of thing."

"Hey. She flinched backward. What's he got in his hand?"

"Moon rock from the Apollo shots. Guess the spirits are really impressed with that one, too."

"Terrorist threat again, sir?"

"Naw. We just took it and reported it missing. Our man got caught, but by the time any hearing rolls around, it'll be past the Ides of March. Speaking of which, are your men ready?"

"Sir, we can have major riots in all the target cities of any size you specify. Declare a national emergency and martial law within the hour. We already have the press editorials written calling on the president to assume emergency powers and the congressional mandate authorizing it was passed as an amendment to another piece of legislation. I'm just worried about the funding. Not all the rioters will do it just for loot."

"Don't worry about that. I'll give you Hal's special number. You phone him up; they'll roll that amount of money off the printing presses. Doesn't appear on budget, no congressional meddling, nothing."

"Congress doesn't know about it?"

"Anyone who doesn't take bribes doesn't have enough funds to run. Anyone who does, we can blackmail and shut them up. They all know about it."

"What about the bomb?"

Wentworth put down his empty soda bottle. "I still say riots are enough. And even if they aren't, let's bomb an empty military base. Maybe the one that Peter Waylock just trashed. Any atmospheric ignition of a nuclear weapon will scare the pants off everyone in the world. The American people will let us issue universal identity cards, track everyone's movements, search houses without warrants, and suspend habeus corpus if they think we're looking for terrorists with a nuke."

"And Azrael?"

"He told me once he talked a king into killing every single baby born on May Day in the whole kingdom, putting them all into a ship and drowning them all."

"So? What does Azrael say?"

"Azrael says do Los Angeles."

Both men were silent for a while.

"Some of my favorite film stars live there . . ." Van Dam started to say.

Wentworth pounded his fist on the chair controls. "Where's my goddamned translation on screen six! I want to hear what they're goddamned saying!"

III

". . . Step not again from the circle, I charge you and compel you, by this; behold, I hold in hand a stone from the floor of Heaven, which is nothing of Earth. All beneath the circle of the Moon I therefore put beneath my authority, for the Moon is in my hand. Even you, Great Princess, Noble Duchess, Great and Mighty Queen, here, in my place of power, must obey the ancient laws. I charge you speak your message in human words henceforward, in a fashion neither deadly nor dangerous to men, swiftly and without error."

GHOSTS WEEP ABOVE THE CORPSES. THE MESSAGE HERE IS PLAIN, MORTAL MAN. THE DISPLEASURE OF GREAT MORNINGSTAR COMES LIKE A BEHEMOTH TO TRAMPLE YOU.

"Speak. Here is the adamantium stone, called Hope, which I wear within the figure of Solomon, and by it again I compel and conjure you."

GREAT MORNINGSTAR REMINDS YOU OF YOUR VOWS AND REMINDS YOU OF THE PENALTIES AND CURSES YOU HAVE UTTERED TO CALL DOWN UPON YOURSELF IF THOSE VOWS ARE FORSWORN. GREAT MORNINGSTAR REQUIRES THAT YOU AT ONCE EMPLOY THE SILVER KEY TO OPEN THE GATES OF NIGHTMARE, AND ALLOW THE CITY OF IMPERISHABLE TOWERS OF PAIN, WHICH IS CALLED DIS, AND CALLED ALSO ACHERON, TO COME FORWARD INTO THE WORLD OF MEN.

GREAT MORNINGSTAR REMINDS YOU THAT A PLACE HAS BEEN PREPARED FOR YOU IN HIS KINGDOM, WHICH SHALL BE FILLED WITH AS MUCH PLEASURE OR PAIN AS GREAT MORNINGSTAR'S PLEASURE OR DISPLEASURE SHALL MEASURE.

"Ah! Peter knew . . . Aratron! By the Rivers of Hell

I charge you, by Phlegethon, by Cocytus, by Lethe, by Acheron, by Styx, bear the message to Great Morningstar, who is the lantern of the night, adding no word and taking none away, that the Silver Key is stolen but shall be swiftly recovered; and that, once the Silver Key is mine once more, the Gates of Horn and Ivory shall open, and a mighty army shall march through, conquering and to conquer; and that all Earth and the world beyond shall be ruled by him who holds the scepter of Morningstar."

I AM CHARGED BY GREAT MORNINGSTAR, THAT, SHOULD YOU SAY SUCH A THING, TO REPLY; HOW IS IT THAT HE WHO STOLE THE SILVER KEY HAS NOW HAD IT STOLEN FROM HIM?

THE WOUND OF THAT KEY IN HIS HEART GREAT MORNINGSTAR STILL BEARS, AND WHAT PASSIONS, OTHERWISE UNKNOWN TO HIS PURE KIND, WHICH WERE UNLOCKED THERE, OF THEM HE REMINDS YOU, WHICH PASSIONS MAY TURN TO MALICE AND WRATH, WITH WHAT RESULTS YOU WELL KNOW. HE REMINDS YOU WHO FIRST SO WOUNDED HIM.

"Tell Morningstar that I recall each word of what we spoke to each other on the day the Unicorn was slain, and ask of him whether or not my promise made that day was kept? Require of him to reflect upon whether the passions and desires of a living man, which beat now within his breast, have not made him greater than the sterile and dutiful purity of angels, as I had promised?"

WHEN DARKNESS COVERS ALL, ONLY THEN SHALL OUR DOINGS BE HIDDEN FROM THE GAZE OF HEAVEN.

"What is your meaning? Do you accuse me of deception, spirit? I charge you by the four rivers of Paradise, Pison, Gihon, Euphrates, and Hiddekel, to

answer clearly, presently, in a fashion neither dangerous nor uncomfortable to man, in speech."

GREAT MORNINGSTAR WONDERS AT YOUR
FAILURES. WHY HAVE NOT THE HOLY THINGS
OF THIS LAND, ITS BISHOPS AND ARCHBISH-
OPS BEEN BROUGHT HERE TO THIS ALTAR?
ONCE THE CHURCH OF THIS LAND IS WITHIN
THE SHADOW OF THE SERAPHIM OF ACHERON,
WITH THAT SINGLE SPELL, ALL THE DREAMS
OF ALL THE FOLK OF THIS LAND BECOME
OURS. WHY HAS THIS NOT BEEN ACCOM-
PLISHED?

"The folk of this land have no state church. There
are many bishops of many churches, and their power
over their flocks is no more than what those congrega-
tions freely and voluntarily bestow."

HOW IS THIS POSSIBLE?

"I do not know, Great and Mighty Queen, I suspect it
was done to prevent just such a spell as we had intended. Nonetheless, the folk of this land fall swiftly
under my spreading cloak. Each leader who bows to me
puts the dreams of all his followers into my command."

SHOULD THEIR KING TAKE UP THE SWORD,
ALL THOSE DREAMS SHALL ONCE AGAIN BE
FREE, WITH SUCH SWIFT EASE AS THE PART-
ING OF A COBWEB.

"They have no king, Great Spirit."

NO KING? NO KING?

"Hence there is none with authority enough to oppose the spread of my dream-web."

THIS VICTORY DOES NOT AMEND YOUR
FAILURES. IF THE SILVER KEY FALLS INTO
THE HAND OF OBERON, MANKIND SHALL BE
TAKEN BACK INTO THE FIRST GARDENS OF
YOUTH, TO LIVE WITHOUT WANT OR MISERY,
SUSTAINED BY THE PERFECT BOUNTY OF
THE FRUIT OF EARTH, TO LIVE IN PEACE
EVERMORE.

"Say also that they shall live without liberty, without thought, without effort, victory, dignity, or pride."

THESE WORDS MEAN NOTHING TO SUCH AS I AM.

"Spirit, answer me this: Is the Silver Key in any danger of falling into the hands of Oberon? Answer in a fashion not hurtful to men, I charge you by Leviathan, Typhon, Tiamat, Ladon, the dragons of the four quarters, who are not bound by fate."

FOUR DRAGONS, FOUR QUESTIONS I ANSWER, PLUS A FIFTH FOR THE HONOR OF LORD MORNINGSTAR. LISTEN: THE SILVER KEY IS IN THE VALLEY OF NEVERDALE IN THE MOUNTAINS OF IRON NORTH OF ZIMIAMVIA, IN THE SECOND CIRCLE OF THE DREAMLAND, IN THE QUADRANT OF THE AIR BENEATH THE CRESCENT MOON. IT IS IN THE REGION OF THE SEPHIROTH BINAH, CALLED ARCADIA, LAND OF THE YOUNG, THIRD OF THE TWELVE PLACES WHERE THE SEELIE COURT OF OBERON THE FAIRY-KING PAUSES IN ITS ROUNDS, TO FEAST. NO CREATURE SAVE THE WINGED MAY GO THERE.

"Who has the Key? Why can my amulet of North Star's Blood not reach there?"

THE DAUGHTER OF TITANIA THE FAIRY-QUEEN HAS THE SILVER KEY. THE VALE OF NEVERDALE HAS MOUNTAIN WALLS SO HIGH THAT THE NORTH STAR IS BELOW THEIR PEAKS, AND THE LIVING CREATURE OF ARALIM, WHO LIVES IN THAT STAR, CANNOT BEHOLD HER.

"Who is this daughter, and why has she not rendered the Key to her father Oberon?"

AMONG MEN SHE IS CALLED GWENDOLYN MOTH VAROVITCH. OBERON IS NOT HER FATHER. THE FAIRY-QUEEN AND FAIRY-KING HAVE PARTED WAYS, FOR REASONS YOU UN-

DERSTAND BETTER THAN ANY OTHER MAN,
SAVE THAT ONE WHO HAS TAKEN YOUR
PLACE.

"Ah! No! How could she!"

IS THAT YOUR FIFTH QUESTION, NAMER OF
NAMES? I NEED BUT ANSWER ONE QUESTION
MORE.

"I wish to know the name of the bridegroom of Titania. . . . No. No, my vengeance must wait. Spirit! Tell
me the true name of Gwendolyn Varovitch."

YOU KNOW THE PRICE TO BE PAID FOR
TRUE NAMES. KNOWLEDGE IS BORN IN PAIN.

"I will pay it. Speak!"

HER TRUE NAME IS LITTLE BIRD, FOR SO
SHE IS CALLED BY HER BELOVED.

IV

"Of these gathered men, you may take the first one
who coughs or fidgets, moves or stands or speaks. That
one shall satisfy you, and thereafter you shall depart.
Gentlemen, I suggest you remain still; I shall presently
return.

"Spirit! Your master placed ninety legions of the fell
creatures of Acheron at my disposal, darkling elves,
fallen cherubim, and demons, the whole of the Un-
seelie Court; I call upon them now in the names of the
four kings whom they have served in times past: Ozy-
mandias the Damned, Solomon the Wise, Haroun al
Raschid called the Upright, and Owen Glendower; I
summon them to the swordsmeet and weapontake at
the Circle of Guardians in the first sphere of Heaven,
to meet me upon the road of ashes. We ride to war.

"Gerald Samuel Wentworth! You believe I do not
know you eavesdrop where I have forbidden you; you
are mistaken. Call the men of this land to stand ready
for battle, whether it be here or in the dream-lands, I

know not yet. Send the great war-ship called Hairy True Man to the place in the sea I have described. Prepare all your mightiest armaments, including the deadly gasses, diseases, and all-devastating fire at your command. I have here the President's machine, which you have called the football, which can order all these things to readiness. . . . Ah.

"Tell your nation that the Vice President is now in command, that the President has been slain.

"Spirit! You may return to Acheron and take what is in your hand with you. It is still screaming, so I suppose it is still alive.

"By the four angels who are bound in the water of the great river Euphrates, who shall be loosed upon the Earth at the sixth call of the Horn to slay a third part of all mankind, by their names, Nimrod, Ephialtes, Briareus, Anteus, and by the fear you have for them, I charge and compel, conjure and command, that you swiftly and safely depart, taking no more with you than I have said, doing as I have bid, harming none, leaving nothing behind, averting all curses from us, without earthquake, fire, or tempest to herald your departure. Go!"

V

Van Dam dropped his cigarette again. In a hushed whisper, he asked Wentworth, "What do we do?"

"Start Protocol Omega. Call NORAD and SAC and put all systems on general alert. Go to DefCon Two . . ."

"We don't have the authority for that!"

"The Vice President can use the red button. He has the authority."

"What about us?"

"We've got to get out of D.C. It'll be a target."

"Is there any place on Earth that will be safe?"

"Not if Acheron arises; not if nukes start dropping.

The only place to go is Everness. If things go against us, we can get away, into another dimension or something; things go for us, we'll be in the best position to exploit the events. I think I can get Azrael to tell us to take Galen's cloak and the magic bow and arrows to Everness. He's already said how he doesn't trust those magic talismans being here, in the waking world."

"No one has been able to draw that bow, sir. Azrael can't even touch it."

"Doesn't matter. More things happened at the Battle of Everness than Azrael knows about. Shut off those TVs and let's go. Hal has to explain to the vice president who really runs the country."

When the door opened, a triangular swath of light momentarily fell across the room, the conference table, the plush chairs. The silhouettes of two men passed in front of the light of the doorway. The door closed. They were gone.

The room seemed empty.

In the far corner of the room, where the shadows were blackest, stood a tall, black silhouette, invisible and silent. As he raised his head, the shadow of his hat brim revealed first the scarf that hid his mouth, then the slant of his cheekbones, his nose; then, finally, his eyes, which glittered like polished stones; eyes filled with an emotion terrible to behold.

There was the slightest rustle of black cape as the figure turned. No further noise betrayed his further movements.

Now, the room was truly empty.

7

The Heart of the Storm

I

The bus stopped in front of the general store where Main Street crossed Port Street. A big man in a black Inverness coat got off, and the wind tugged at his hair and beard.

The street was deserted. A few stray papers blew across it. The windows of the general store, the bank, and the grocery were boarded up. On the diner's door was a hand-printed sign: CLOSED ON ACCOUNT OF DORIS.

The bus swayed in the wind as it pulled away. Trees by the roadside bowed and swept their branches through the air, and telephone poles shook.

The man looked up. The sky directly overhead was blue. The little town was on a rise; down Port Street he could see the promontory and the sea.

Purple clouds and black clouds, like battlements and towers, loomed over the sea all along the horizon.

Great swirling arms and convoluted knots reached up across the sky.

"This is not looking very good, I am thinking," said the man in a deep Russian voice, stroking his beard. "Franklin! You did not warn me when I dreamed about you on the bus! Call the Princes, you said. Did not say would bring storm with them. Hah! But I must let no anger, no frustration touch me now. . . ." On his finger glittered a massive ring of white gold.

By the time he had walked to the edge of town, the towers and battlements of clouds had grown and outlying squadrons and flotillas of storm-clouds were streaming across the sky overhead, their movement visible to the eye.

There was a lighthouse on a high promontory overlooking the sea. Raven put up his coat collar and bent into the wind, walking forward in heavy strides. Now he put his hand before his face and squinted, and the wind screamed in his ears.

In the distance, between the sea and sky, a ripple of lightning danced. A few moments later, thunder rolled across the landscape.

II

Tim Kearns opened the door to the light, gentle knocking. A little girl stood there, squinting in the wind, holding a big brown dog in her arms.

"Are you the lighthouse keeper?" she asked brightly.

"Get in here. Aren't you Lilly Rushcock's little girl?"

"My name's *Megan*! This is Ralph. She can say her own name." The dog barked and wagged her tail.

"Yeah, that's great. Look, do your parents know where you are?"

"Ralph ran away. The nice man found her for me."

She added in a confidential tone of great seriousness: "We have a deal."

"Yeah, great. Do you know your phone number? Let me see if I can get your parents. Hey! Don't touch that stuff."

"What is it?"

"Radar. Satellite telemetry. That sort of stuff. Those are my schoolbooks and don't touch them either."

"Are you the lighthouse keeper?"

"Naval Meteorology Research Post. It's not a lighthouse anymore."

"Oh. Uh . . . Okay."

"Who are you talking to, Megan, honey?"

"The man. He found my dog. He looked at the ground. He says everyone has to get out of town or hide in a cellar."

"Are you worried about the storm, Megan? We're only at a severe storm warning right now. Hurricane Doris is moving away from us, see? I hope. The satellites say it's going away. But you still shouldn't be out."

"Raven says it's coming. Raven says he's *sorry*."

Tim Kearns had just come across the word "horripilation" in his studies, referring to the sensation of gooseflesh when one's nape hairs prickled from fear or cold. It had never actually happened to him before.

Without another word, Tim Kerns picked up the green phone hanging next to his instrument rack pressed redial. "Sheriff Brody? Remember I told you we were only going to get the edges of Hurricane Doris? I was wrong. The storm path turned, and it's coming this way. We need to get everyone in the bunker after all. Oh. Megan Rushcock wandered into my post here. Can you send a cruiser around to pick her up? Her parents must be frantic. And . . . what do you mean? I don't care what the regional bureau says; they're wrong. They're looking at the same information I am, and I'm telling you the storm has turned. Yes, it's official. I'm issuing a storm emergency warning. I don't care if I'm not allowed to; I'm issuing it anyway. That's right. You want to call the radio station and tell them or do you want me to? Okay. Remember Megan Rush-cock's here. Fine. Bye." He hung up the phone, muttering, "Idiot!"

The light in the window grew visibly darker.

"Megan. Where is this Raven you were talking to?"

She pointed out the window. "He went over there."

"Where?"

"Up the big hill."

"Can you see him right now?"

"Sure. Can't you?"

"I guess not, honey." But Tim Kearns kept his eye on the hill she had pointed out.

It was less than an hour later, and the policeman had just come in to get Megan. Tim Kearns was still staring at the hill. The sky had turned all black, and fat drops of rain and hail were flying down from rumbling clouds. The wind was making a continuous roar.

The officer shouted over the wind, "You got to come too, sir. Sheriff said everybody!"

Tim was actually staring right at the exact spot where the lightningbolt struck the hilltop. The officer flinched, and Megan screamed.

Blinking in the purple afterimage, Tim could see, for the briefest moment, high on the hill above, ghost-like, wind-whipped, the huge, bearded man in a black cloak wrestling the lightning bolt to the ground, like a man strangling a snake of blue fire with his hands.

"Come on, sir!" said the police officer.

Kearns shouted back, "Get the little girl out into the car. I've got to lock up. Only take a sec!"

The policeman stepped out. The man who called himself Tim Kearns removed a circuit card from a compartment in his wallet, opened the electronic panel next to the phone, and plugged the card into the circuit board. Then he plugged the phone jack into the same panel.

"Calling Burbank! Calling Burbank! Tell Pendrake that Raven is here; he's got the ring and is attempting to allay Hurricane Doris. I can't stay in this position; must retreat to storm bunker. Will contact you when possible. Out."

III

Raven sat upon the hill beneath a blasted oak tree, his face calm, his hands folded in his lap. Downhill, the sea was before him, black waves rearing and plunging. To his left, was forest; to his right, the little town.

His face was very calm. His eyes were half closed. He was breathing slowly and deeply. Up from his palms came a trickle of vapor, as if he had just grappled with some force of immense heat. But his palms were unscarred, unblistered.

Lightning passed across the town to his right, and all the lights went dark.

Despite the rain and driving hail, Raven's garments were not wet.

A whine of bagpipes sounded from his left. The trees in the forest bowed like wheat in a planted field bowing in the wind. A dozen trees, two dozen, were uprooted and whirled through the air. A wall of devastation, like a continuous explosion, ripped through the forest, approaching.

When Raven put his palm on the root of the oak next to him, the tree stopped trembling.

Splinters from the whirlwind ripping through the forest, propelled by hundred-mile-an-hour winds, fell to the left and to the right of him, but did not touch him.

Raven, eyes half closed, did not look up. He wore the smile a man might wear who was listening to distant, soft music.

He touched two fingers to the ground. For three paces to each side of him, the grass ceased to bow to the wind. The grass there bowed once to Raven, then stood straight, and the hail and rain did not disturb them.

Raven drew a breath, closed his eyes, laid his palm flat upon the ground. The effect around him grew till it was four paces wide, six, then ten.

A noise louder than any other noise on Earth exploded from overhead, deafening. In the light from a lightning flash, the silhouette of a creature in Roman armor could be seen, hanging between two gnarled storm-clouds, shield raised.

"Murderer!" called a voice louder than a thunderbolt.

The corner of Raven's mouth twitched. The circle became four paces wide, then three, shrinking. Stinging hail splattered his garments.

A creature in a kilt and cloak, breathing out a tornado from his bagpipes, came striding across the crest of the hill; and where he stepped, thunders boomed. Behind was a path where everything had been flattened. He took the flute from his mouth to call out, "Your pretty wife is gone away! Your worthless life must end this day!"

The tree behind Raven began to shake again; his coat was yanked up, streaming, and his own hair pelted his face.

Lightning struck the tree. Standing tall amidst the flaming branches was a creature in black, wearing lace, his whole body crawling with sparks and darts of electricity. He shook his javelin. "Impotent now, I think you must be! Will you stay wed, when you cannot bed, nor do a bridegroom's one duty? The ring was meant for a monk to wear, shy and pale, a porridge eater in a shirt of hair."

Raven smiled, and spoke in a quiet voice, and the storm grew quiet to hear him. "Love has deep roots, Fulmenos. Love last long after tempest of infatuation blows by, you know? Love is both for fair weather and for foul. You like to think I must give up much to command you, eh? You are not so great, I am thinking. I give up nothing."

Lighting spurted from the creature's eyes and mouth as it shouted. Bolts fell to each side of Raven, but he did not flinch, and so they did not touch him.

"You think to tame your passions thus? It cannot be! Men cannot be men unless they let their souls run free! Join us! The strife of life is meant for life, not for cautious thinking-through! Forget the future! Do not reflect, but do! Shake these cobwebs from your strength! Let whatever impulse blows you now, now whirl you aloft! How else to fly? Reason is deceit! Your senses cheat! Logic is a lie! Morality is meant to chain the soft!"

Raven raised his hand, and a great unearthly hush came out from him. The rain diminished suddenly, as if the eye of the storm were overhead. "You say logic lies, eh? And so therefore I must be illogical? But that is argument you make. With logic, no? So you are lying, yes?"

He stood up. The tree behind him stopped trembling. The rain diminished to a drizzle.

"I am not a child," said Raven. "I do not listen to children-fears. I do not act like child, first crying, then laughing, then crying again, changing as the wind changes. I am not a spoiled baby to do whatever I like without thinking. Now then, Tempestos! Attonitus! Come here and be quiet."

Attonitus raised his shield and sword. "Murderer! You cannot control us, who cannot control yourself!"

Tempestos stepped forward reluctantly, but he squeezed on his bag with his elbow, producing a droning hiss, and the wind behind him began to rush through the trees, building. He said softly, "Aye, and what of your wife, mortal man? You bring Galen back to life; she dies. Does this not make fear blow through you?"

"No," said Raven. "There was a storm in me, fear

and anger, and I blew down Galen's life. Now it has rained in me, and I have wept. Weeping done. Now I must have calm weather again. I can quiet myself; I can quiet the storm. Storm-Princes! Whirlwind, Thunderbolt, Lightning! Hail and welcome. Come and obey!"

The three figures gathered before him where he stood, and, kneeling, each one, in turn, kissed the white gold ring.

The clouds parted and a single beam of sunlight came streaming through the gentle rain to light on Raven where he stood, unmoving, beneath the blasted oak tree.

IV

"First," said Raven, "I have parachute from army surplus store at last bus stop. Stole it, yes, but left some money librarian gave, so maybe is alright. I am thinking, Wendy flies, eh? So why not Raven?"

Tempestos picked up his pipes but said, "You think to unleash us, and then bottle us once more? If so, where do you wish to go? I can bear you where e'er winds will blow. Go ahead and try it. Icarus tried before."

"We fly to Everness and maybe to the Moon," said Raven.

"We cannot carry you to Luna's sphere, wise master, for no winds blow from here to there."

Raven said, "Be calm. I solve that problem later.

"Now then, second order: You, there, Thunder! Go make it rain on fires in Southwest. Put them out. Wherever Surtvitnir is, it rains. And no more snow for Bergelmir, eh? He can make it cold, but if there is no moisture, then it is not snowing."

"And if they are together, great Master? For even I, I cannot make it at once both wet and dry!"

"Be quiet there!" said Raven, shaking his finger.

"Don't get yourself worked up, eh? If they are to-gether, make wet mist. Cold will turn mist to frost and nothing burns, you know?"

Raven turned to the last figure.

"For you, I have an idea. Do you think you can make a rainbow all across the sky here? A nice pretty one, lots of colors? I think the people in the town de-serve it."

"Your will, in all, for me, is law," he said, standing. Somehow, his robe had changed from black to a gray-edged and fluffy white. His lace was now of many col-ors. But when he smiled, flickers of electricity ran across his teeth, and his inhuman eyes were like two sparks.

The rain stopped.

8

The
Black Ship
Sails

I

Raven approached Everness by sea so that the wind of his passage would not blow down houses and forests as he passed.

There were three black ships, a clipper and two galleons, moored to the cliffs below the ruins of the sea-wall. It was daylight, and no kelpie were in view. The giants, last he had seen on the news, were still in the midwest and west. Of the three dark supernatural beings whom Apollo had driven away, there was no sign.

But the grounds were crawling with gunmen in black uniforms and blue helmets. There were a few men in purple robes, and a group of seal-sailors camped out on the lawn. The south wing was under repair; and scaffolding surrounded damaged sections.

Raven dropped toward the ground, gray clouds streaming out to the right and left, and gale-force winds announced his coming.

His first realization that normal men could see him came when he heard the crack of a rifle shot, and saw a bullet hole appear in the canopy of his parachute.

Before he could restrain his momentary anger, lightning had destroyed the gunman who had shot at him and forked bolts played among the screaming crowd.

He landed amid the corpses. The grass was smoldering. He struggled with the buckles of his parachute, unfastened them. His ankles hurt.

"Calmly, now!" he told himself. "Thunder! Everyone in the house and grounds! Drive them unconscious! Have fog and cloud gather around me to make it hard to see. Ah, wait . . . Are there reenforcements coming from the ships? Whirlwind! Blow them far out to sea."

Raven strode through the gathering fog toward the house. He only had to electrocute three more men. Less than ten minutes later, all the enemies in the house and grounds lay on their stomachs in the side yard, with their hands clasped over their necks, surrendered, except for those who were carrying the thunderstruck out into the yard.

Raven created a wall of lightning to circle and to guard them. Then he donned his parachute again and let himself be blown off the cliff. He overtook three ships. The one that struck her colors he spared; the other two he sank, and pods of seals swam away through the flotsam.

Raven landed on the poop deck of the remaining ship, and, after some negotiation, accepted the cutlass of the ship's captain in token of surrender.

"I am thinking, you know," he murmured to himself, "I could be getting to like this magic ring very much, yes?"

And he ordered the captain to set sail for the dark side of the Moon.

II

Raven realized he was in strange waters when constellations rose he did not recognize.

He came up from the captain's cabin, stepping over the bodies unconscious on the stair, onto the deck.

The horizon of night was vast, and everywhere was wide, wild sea, with tall waves, like hills of water, gleaming in the starlight, restlessly passing back and forth across the rippling deep. The smell of salt had diminished, as they were far from shore.

In the gloom, Raven could see how the deck of the ship was littered with rubbish, and coils of unslung rope lay in heaps across the planks and rusted bits of brightwork.

Nothing on the ship showed a bit of polish or repair, except the flaying racks, which Raven had thrown overboard last night.

As he came amidships, some sailor in the rigging dropped a bag of filth and offal, which missed his head by inches, splattering across the deck and dotting his clothes with drops of fecal matter. "Sorry, Milord!" called a cheerful voice.

Raven saw two deckhands, seal-faced men in sailor suits with knotted neckerchiefs, clinging to the ropes high above.

They both pointed at each other. "He did it!" they cried in unison.

Raven sighed. The selkie had made the unfortunate discovery somehow that Raven's control over the weather depended on his ability to keep his temper. He might not survive if the Storm-Princes turned on him.

He called, "Where is navigator, eh?"

The two deckhands pointed in opposite directions, one fore, the other, aft. Then they looked at each other and shrugged.

"Maybe he's gone overboard, Milord!" offered one. Thunder rolled through the air, and an angry gust rocked the boat. Raven took a deep, slow breath. The wind grew calm.

Another voice, a baritone, called, "Up here, so please you, Milord."

Raven climbed to the poop deck, which was lit with many lanterns. A large selkie with a human face and a peg leg stood at the wheel. By the deckhouse compass stood two selkie with seal-faces, one was dressed in a long, blue coat with polished silver buttons; the other wore the captain's bright red coat and plumed bicorn hat, but the long wig of white ringlets he wore was tilted askew.

The one in the long, blue coat said, "I be the navigator, Milord."

"Ah? When is last time we spoke?" asked Raven.

The navigator's nose twitched. He stroked his fine whiskers with a furry hand, looking at Raven sidelong. "Yesterday at eight bells 'twas, as I recall, Milord. Milord had asked me why we be sailing in a circle, it was, before I knew sure Milord knew something of sea lore, as it were."

Then he leaned closer and showed his sharp, white teeth, "But Milord shouldn't bother to ask. You know there be no way to get a body's first true skin off except to kill him; and I don't take kindly to the implication that there's a man jack aboard this tub who could best me in any brawl-play, square or foul!"

Raven let that comment pass without reply. Instead, he asked, "What stars are these to our bow? These, they are not northern constellations, nor southern. The Great Bear, he is sunk, but is no Southern Cross rising, eh?"

"We be in the Third Hemisphere, Milord, having passed over the terminator when ye were below. They have two more seasons here, which ye hardly ever get on man's Earth. The constellation just rising there we call Eurydice, the Lost Lady, and beside it, Peirithous, the Forsaken One. So called, on account of neither of them ever rises quite far enough get out of these here skies, if you catch the reference, ha har! The bright star between them is the planet we call Psychompompos; not many mariners of Earth have seen that wandering star, Milord, not and lived to tell the tale."

"Then we are in dreaming-ocean, yes?"

"That be a matter of opinion and dispute, Milord. I would not say yes or no, if you take my meaning. But they be strange waters to be sure. Strange waters."

At that point, someone threw a wet rag at the back of Raven's head. It had been soaked in some sort of filth which stuck to his hair. Hoots of barking laughter sounded from behind. Raven brushed off the rag without turning.

"Captain," said Raven to the selkie in the red coat and wig, "Three more deckhands I am finding lying thunderstruck outside my door when I get up just now. You understand you must send no more assassins, eh? My spirit protects the door. I have told everyone to leave door alone when it is closed."

The captain looked nervous, blinking his big black eyes and twitching his whiskers.

The navigator spoke up. "Begging your pardon, Milord, but once the lads found out how you were defending yourself like that whilst ye were sleeping, well, naturally, it became sort of a game with them to see how close they could get, and wrestle and push each other into your door, so as to get the thunderbolt to knock them senseless what lost the game, so to speak. Hope the noise weren't keeping ye awake?"

Raven said to the captain, "And you said you would show me charts and maps of Moon, once daylight come. Dawn come soon. Where are charts?"

"Been meaning to talk to ye about that, Milord, privatelike, if ye see?" said the captain nervously, scratching at his dangling wig.

The captain drew Raven over to one side, near the railing, and he hissed, "I ain't the captain!"

Raven groaned. "Must we go through this again?"

"No! For true! This time I really ain't! The captain, he made me change garments with him last watch! He's skulking among the men, ye know?"

"Tell him change back. He must obey you now, eh?"

"Nar! And I ain't sure who he is anyhow!"

"What? You are saying *what* to me? He is in your face now, eh? Don't know what your own face was looking like?"

"He's planning some awful mischief, I tell ye that for true and certain, Milord! Don't know what might be, but it's awful mischief a-brewing!"

The pink light of dawn appeared off the bow with surprising suddenness, and the clouds all along the horizon were tinted with rose and tawny colors.

Raven stroked his beard, wondering at the captain's words. He was puzzled as to why the Selkie did not simply jump overboard, turn to seals, and swim away.

At first he had thought that it was their avarice that held them. He had gathered all their trunks and chests and rolls of leather together in the captain's cabin and locked them in the captain's trunk. He assumed they would not be willing to leave without their wardrobes.

Perhaps this was a trap. But, if so, what else should he be doing?

"Well," said Raven, "thank you for warning. One more question. Just curious, you know? Why some of you have human faces, others do not?"

"Ah, well, Milord, wearing those hoods and masks all the time can get pretty sweaty and stuffy, if you take my meaning. Mosttimes, only the officers are allowed to show their faces; but you have to be careful your seam don't come undone, or your sleeves and gloves fall off, and then what can ye do, save some flopping on your face?"

"Eh? How do you zip up disguises without fingers?"

"Ar! Ye are simple, ain't ye! Our girls put the witch-mark tabs right where we can get at 'em with our teeth, see?" And he pulled at the lace of his throat to display a triangle of three white discolorations on his neck, like bruises the size and shape of fingerprints.

"And where are charts showing secrets paths to Moon? In captain's gear? In his pockets, eh?" Raven stepped forward.

The Sun came up over the horizon like an enormous ball of gold, and a hot wind struck over the ship from the East. The Sun seemed many times the size of Earth's Sun, and the sunrise was swifter than sunrise in the tropics.

In the sudden light, Raven could see the captain shrinking back in fear, his muzzle wrinkled in a snarl. The captain turned and fled but stumbled on the gangway to the midships, raising mocking laughter from the crew.

Raven turned and squinted up at the blue-white sky. Enormous gusts of wind began to toss the ship. Clouds turned dark and darker, and the air began to feel tense and close. The bow dipped into a high wave, sending spray along the deck. A violent crosswind then heeled the ship far to the starboard. The masts creaked alarmingly, and some selkie screamed in fear, while others hooted and laughed.

The navigator grabbed the taffrail, shouting, "Luff the mizzen shrouds, ye lubbers! Get them canvass furled before we lose the mast! Hop to!"

Seal-men on deck scurried to obey the orders.

Raven raised his hand and the wind fell to a gentle breeze. He put his hand on the shoulder of the selkie who had shouted out orders during an emergency, the one who happened to look like the navigator at the moment.

"Captain!" he said to the navigator, "last night I could not examine charts to find path to Moon since was no light. Is now light. I have waited. Which is way?"

The navigator snarled. "Ar! Garn! That was a regular Mannannan trick, that was."

"The charts!"

"Ha har! There be no charts! No map shows the searoute to the Moon, and the seas between the stars be vaster than any sea of Earth! We cannot go to the forbidden sphere save what they calls us, and they call not for us too often, I tell ye sure! We come and go at their pleasure, not ours, for the Moon faces halfway toward earthly things, and half toward outer darks, and those what dwell there bow to strange gods, and have deals with them. Horrible deals. We hates them as much as they hates us!"

"This, I find hard to believe."

"That's as ye like, ye hulk. We have to bribe and bootlick the Eech-Uisge of Uhnuman to get ships. Do ye think we selkie could ever get ourselves together long enough to build a ship, with no bickering, no knife-work, and no tricky play? Har har! We're lucky if we can pull together long enough to hold a tea party. 'Twill be different once the Seal-King gets the Moly Wand; and all the crimes but his alone, his and his close pals, will come to light! Then, 'tis the very world we'll be having for our own!"

The name he had used: Eech-Uisge. It sent a thrill of horror down Raven's spine, as if he remembered it from some dream. Images from dim memory came into his mind, clear and strong.

"I can summon up the Moon, if you will sail me there," Raven whispered. "Their cities and ports will lay undefended to your cannon."

"Are you such a magician then?"

Raven pointed his finger at the navigator's whiskered nose. "You want see lightning bolt very up close to inspect, yes?"

"I see yer point, there! There! There! Put that finger away! But 'tis a right foolish idea to dream of us at-

tacking them. I won't hear of it . . . ," whispered the
navigator with thoughtful curiosity.

"So I attack them, me. You? You can pick through
rubble and loot survivors as you wish. Or not, as you
wish. I don't care. Who will know it is you if you are
not caught? No trustworthy evidence, you are innocent, no? But I must sail to Moon! Must reach Uhnuman before the Eech-Uisge realize what Galen
Waylock is!"

The navigator squinted his big brown eyes and
cocked his head sideways. "And what is this Waylock
lad to ye?"

Raven spoke in an eager voice. "You know Galen's
soul is linked with my wife's? The girl Mannannan
saw at Everness? That woman, she is such fool! She
carried off the most powerful . . . Uh. I mean, of
course, I love her very much, and must find her right
away, before anyone else gets the . . . I mean, before
she comes to harm. Since I love her so much, you
know. Galen must know where stupid girl is! He must
be able to find his soul. Is instinct."

The navigator whispered, "You call up the Moon,
you got a deal, mate. We sail you straight to the docks
of Uhnuman."

"No tricks! I keep my eye on you at all times!"

"Har. Not to worry. I swear by the beard of Oberon,
you'll not find me pulling any tricks, at all, Ar. Har."

III

Raven climbed up to the bow of the ship and stood
with one leg on the bowsprit, which was carven in the
shape of a bat-winged king.

Raven chanted: "Sulva! Where fell sprites abide!
Heave up your icy horns to me, your sterile plains,
your lifeless sea, that I may journey to your hidden,
farther side! I know the cause of your inconsistency,

and why your light ebbs and fails; I know a planetary angel where sin prevails. Last to fall, lowest sphere of all, put shame aside; unhide yourself to me!"

The Moon began to come over the brink of the world, enormous; mountains, valleys, and oceans, gray, stark white, and gray-black in the sunlight. Only half the lunar globe came over the rim; and the whole pock-marked, silent, blasted lunar landscape filled a third of the sky. The lunar ocean directly ahead seemed to be mingling its waters with the waves on the horizon. Streams of pale water and black water began to mingle in the waves below, amid the floating corpses of schools of poisoned fish.

The Moon grew larger still, but began to set. Yet as she set, her globe widened and flattened, occupying half the horizon, then more than half. Then mountains on the edge of the Moon's globe now were on the horizon ahead, and had swollen in Raven's vision to such size that his eye could see no curve to the horizon.

Blue sky faded into black, and a harsh and terrible hot Sun glared down amidst a nocturnal sky, and bright, unwinking stars gleamed down onto a lifeless, sunlit sea.

The waves here were vast, like tidal waves, their slopes more peaked, their motions strange and swift, alien to the eye.

"Is this Moon?" asked Raven in surprise, and shock, and awe.

"Look behind, Milord," said the navigator softly.

Raven turned. Off the starboard stern, a silver-and-blue crescent, lovely with swirled cloud and green land, and crowned with sparkling arctic zones, hung above a glittering path of Earth-light scattered on the waves. Between horns of the crescent of the great blue globe, the cities of mankind glowed with many lights.

IV

The ship was burning.

The iron monolith guarding the harbor shot out another beam of molten iron, which splashed across sails and planks. The cannons on the starboard fired, those that still had living gun crews, and a white cloud reached up skyward. Cannonballs rang against the rusted iron plates of the windowless tower.

The bay was surrounded on two sides by basalt dikes and walls; before rose the great stepped pyramid, blind and windowless, from which the flocks of wyverns and bronze-winged harpies rose, shrieking, to harass the ship with vile droppings and vomitous gushes of smoking acid.

The stepped pyramid loomed over the lifeless waters. On the crowns of pikes that bristled from its each battlement, writhing bodies dripped blood in streams down the pyramid, stinking red and brown waterfalls dropping into the bay.

The landing party had successfully piled kegs of powder against the base of the portside tower, and Raven had ignited it with a lightning bolt; that tower had tilted drunkenly on its shattered base. The globes of poisonous glue which that tower had been firing fell short, and a green chlorinous mass now stretched along the tower's base and side, a dripping web of steaming venom.

Raven's winds threw back the harpies and shrieking wyverns, but stream after stream of liquid metal spewed from the iron tower to starboard, propelled by some unearthly machine. Whenever Raven's thunder rolled, the aim was spoiled; and the molten stream discharged at random, whenever the ship fired her cannon, the streams found her again, as if the unearthly gunners manning that machine aimed by hearing alone.

Many of the selkie were jumping into the water to

escape the fire. The navigator, standing next to Raven, shouted, "Call them cowards back, my Captain! The Eech-Uisge release the eels from underwater gates!"

The deck heeled suddenly to starboard, and Raven grabbed at the rail. A selkie next to Raven, a marine with a musket, raised his spyglass. "The sea be frightened, Captain!" he called, putting the instrument to his eye. "The Eech-Uisge must be unleashing a new monster on us! Aha—!"

And the marine turned to stone. The statue, look of horror frozen forever into his features, cracked through the railing next to Raven and fell into the sea.

The navigator hissed. "Don't look up! It be the Basilisk! Time to retreat, Captain, no matter what Raven says!"

Raven was angry. He had been watching to see when the navigator would change his skin and slip away, but the Selkie had been too clever for him. Raven had not seen when the substitution had taken place. And it would be no use to ask the selkie, who now looked like the navigator, where the real captain was; he evidently thought Raven was.

Raven leaned out over the rail. Sure enough, the stern window leading to the captain's cabin had been shattered. He guessed the trunk holding the selkie-coats had been taken. But which of the scores of selkie in the water or with the landing party was his man?

A few moments later, Raven was folding his parachute on the gray and ashy shoreline. Far behind him, the black ship of the selkie was burning to the waterline, and the screams of selkie on the surface, mauled by eels, hung in the calm air.

Around him lay the craters, dust, and broken rock of the arid shores of the Moon. He had calmed the air to save the footprints in the sand.

Behind him, lightning played continuously over the iron ziggurat and towers, and the stench of the hundreds of unseen monsters electrocuted and cooked within those windowless, metal walls, rose up to the black, lunar sky. Raven knew Galen was not in this strange fortress-city. Now that the futile attack had served Raven's purpose, he saw no reason to allow the blind monsters to continue. This city was not Uhnuman, nor had Raven ever actually thought it was. For one thing, it was not on a plateau.

There: one set of webbed seal-feet was deeper in imprint than the others, but the size of the stride did not indicate a tall man. It was a short man with a burden, perhaps the weight of the missing sea chest.

The prints had other prints over them at places. They had been laid down first. Apparently the selkie— captain or navigator or whomever he was—had abandoned ship almost immediately when the battle was joined.

Raven rushed after him, silent, swift, his black coat blending with harsh shadows and outcroppings of volcanic obsidian that twisted across the broken landscape. Raven moved quickly from rock to rock, crater to crater.

For there was no time to lose. There was only one destination the selkie could be seeking; and Raven had to reach it first.

Raven followed the selkie toward Galen.

9
The City
of
Torment

The tracks went over hard stone and were almost lost, but Raven saw where one drop of blood rested on the sharp edge of an obsidian outcropping. Closer, he saw a sandy depression beyond the outcropping.

Lying on the sand was the sea chest. The selkie had cut his foot, tired of the burden, and opened it to get a new skin to wear.

There were leather coats of white and black and red, from every clime, every race of man, strewn along the sand. Evidently this wealth of selkie-coats had been too much to carry.

The selkie had no one to share these coats with, since he was convinced the Raven was hunting for the Moly Wand, he could not trust any of his fellows. The lure of absolute power over all of his kin drew him onward. Raven smiled at how well his plan was working.

Then Raven saw the pelts and animal skins and

feathered coats lying abandoned on the sand as well. And the only tracks leading away from the place were hoofprints.

Raven frowned. It was an unexpected problem. He climbed to the top of the next rise and surveyed the rugged peaks, chasms, and cracks of the tortured landscape. He thought the selkie had actually made a poor choice; little of this ground was suitable for horses, and it should get more broken and hilly as they headed toward the mountains, where the plateau probably was. His eye picked out the likely path the selkie was following.

And then he ran.

Not long after, in the hills, he found the hoofprints again. They led into a canyon. Here, Raven found a pit the selkie had dug and filled up again. In the pit were folded a number of animal skins. No doubt the position of this hole was carefully marked on some treasure map the selkie carried. The selkie had taken his time, no doubt confident that he wasn't being followed.

Human footprints surrounded the site; here was the stone the selkie had used as a crude shovel. At one point the shovel had been abandoned, and the wide paw marks of a badger continued the digging. Raven found to his pleasure that this desert was not entirely void of life; here was a nest of poisonous insects, which the claw prints of an anteater circled. The selkie had stopped for a meal.

Wolf tracks led away from the site. They were recent. He was not far ahead. Evidently the wolf had not been able to carry as many spare coats as the horse.

II

In the mountains, Raven almost lost the trail where the selkie turned into a goat. Then, at one place where the black peaks were cut with an enormous chasm, Raven came across what he had feared: the prints of a winged creature, a bat.

The ground was soft here, and Raven could see the bat had made four trips, each time carrying a coat that dragged along the ground while the bat struggled to become airborne. At his guess, a seal-coat, a wolf-coat, a goat. And . . . what? A man? The selkie's original skin? Something else?

The goat was for climbing; and the blind bat, perhaps, to approach a city guarded by basilisks. The wolf was a good choice for finding a man among a city of stinking monsters; his scent would stand out. What was the other coat too precious to spare?

The chasm was too wide for anything on feet to cross.

Raven opened his parachute and summoned a whirlwind. Atop the next peak, he saw the plateau.

The huge tableland had been thrust by some titanic volcanic convulsion in times far past high above all the surrounding peaks, and it loomed like a thunderhead. Even from here, Raven could see the black metal dome midmost in the plateau, ringed with windowless towers like broken teeth and with spidery, jagged minarets. Aqueducts on crooked metallic legs ran out from the dome toward the surrounding bunkers and towers.

Raven found, by chance, the place where the bat had become a wolf again.

He crept closer to the city, a mile away, then half a mile. He could smell the stench of blood, like the effluvia of many slaughterhouses. Faintly, in the distance, he heard a sound like the moaning and wailing of the wind. It was the sound of many voices, bellowing, shrieking, wailing, begging, moaning, sobbing. It was like the noise of a crowd in a stadium, a thousand voices, a thousand different pitches and tones of agony.

The noise went on and on. At each moment a hundred voices fell silent or shouted themselves hoarse, and a hundred new voices, shrill and deep, broke from soft weeping into loud screams.

Then he came across a point where the wolf tracks showed the faintest double imprint. The selkie had been stepping backward in his own footsteps here. Which meant the selkie had heard the winds Raven had summoned to carry himself across the chasm to the plateau. The game knew now he was being hunted.

Raven crawled on his stomach across a fractured jut of gray rock. In the distance was a pillar of iron, one of many dotting the plain around the city. Atop the pillar was looped fold on fold of sinuous length, which had its head raised, its cobra-hood spread, its rooster's comb red and erect.

Raven could see the pattern on the back of the snakelike hood; the monster had its swaying, feathered head turned away just at that moment. As the monster started to turn, Raven closed his eyes and scuttled quickly and silently back down the slope.

He did not know quite what a basilisk looked like; but he had seen what had happened to the marine selkie back aboard the ship, and he thanked God and Saint Katherine he had not seen the creature.

At that moment, the screams from the city died off. Choked sighs and horrid gagging noises echoed out across the blasted landscape for a moment. Then, oppressive silence fell.

Raven felt as if an immense listening watchfulness, brooding and intent, had spread out from the black dome.

He opened his eyes. He was in a gully between two black ridges. Framed between them, past the edge of the gully, rose the black, windowless dome in the distance, and Raven could see the corpses hanging from impaling poles atop every minaret.

A slight rustle of motion disturbed a pebble nearby.

He turned, sprang to his feet.

The thing came suddenly over the rise to the right, cutlass in one hand and flintlock pistol in the other. He looked like a satyr with a wolf's head. Raven realized that the selkie was wearing the gloves of the man-skin, the hood of the wolfskin, only the pantaloons of the goat; his jacket was some other black fabric. His goat's hoof found swift purchase on the steep rock of the slope, and he came much faster than any man could run, and his wolf's nostrils dilated as he scented Raven, and ran down the slope toward him.

Raven raised his hand, fighting to summon up the calm that would summon his powers. The wolf head snarled. The creature raised his flintlock and fired, running forward at full speed down the steep slope. There was a flash in the pan and a stench of gunpowder, but the weapon failed to fire.

Sparks crawled around Raven's fingertips, but he lost his nerve and was jolted by an electric shock, thrown from his feet.

Two vast bat wings spread out from the selkie's back and he launched himself into the air on wings of membrane.

It was the strange wonder of the sight that saved Raven. He was so startled by the appearance, by the selkie being able to use the coat from the bat-skin in this size, that he forgot his fear.

It was as the monster fell down on him, slashing with cutlass and snapping with wolf teeth, that Raven thought of Galen and, face calm, slapped his hands together.

At his hand clap came a noise louder than any noise on Earth, and the selkie diving down on him was unconscious as he plunged into Raven. The two of them rolled in the dirt.

III

The selkie regained his senses, blinking through the dizziness clouding his vision. He saw Raven, standing with his back to the charred remnant of a snaky body, pointing behind himself, eyes closed.

One lightning bolt after another snapped between his finger and the dead strand of smoking meat. The air smelled of ozone.

" 'Tis tight dead, shipmate!" shouted the selkie. "Ye can leave be, now! But the whole force of Uhnuman heard that racket ye made to blow me down. They be a-coming, for sure. Now give me back me coat! I feel a right fool, a seal in a desert!" And he flapped his flippers against the sand and rock chips.

Raven opened his eyes. He had the several selkiecoats tied at his belt. He looked up at the selkie. "So! This Oberon fellow, he has no beard after all, eh?"

"Ye think of that fine phrase to say while ye were skulking after me? Sounded a mite rehearsed."

"You are very big for seal. Look more like whale. Fine color, too! You are albino, white as snow. Make fine coat for many ladies, or perhaps one big fat lady."

"The fat ones will be here, aye, too soon for my liking! Great, stinking, fat, blind things they be, with nasty beasties serving them. You killed one basilisk; good for ye. Six thousand more be coming! Give me my coat!"

Raven took the goat-skin and threw it up into the air. He pointed; a lance of blue-white flame destroyed the coat.

The selkie cried out in horror and pain. "Oh no! No! No!" Raven took out another coat; this one white, man-skin.

The selkie said, "Not that one, Master, I beg ye! Take any other coat of mine, take everything, but not that one! My life is in it! Me whole life!"

Raven paused, his arm drawn back, ready to throw the coat up. "Explain."

"That is the face and form of the Keeper of the King's Falcon, a high officer at court! I came upon it by merest accident, and shan't never find another like it, not in a million years! The beautiful people live at court, handsome, fine, and rich! Ye don't understand! As soon as I found out more about the man, I was going to go back and issue a bill of divorce! A bill of divorce, don't ye see?"

"Tell me."

"My wife ran off with another man and left some trollop she hired behind to take her place. Gave up her best coat, too, to do it! I been searching for my wife for years! For years! Watching all the women at court, and any man who seemed too effete and dainty, if ye catch me drift. But I found her! The Countess of Noatun be she, I'm sure! But I can't have her back unless I can divorce her from the Count, and only a member of the Inner Court can write a bill like that! Pity, Master! Pity! It's all my dreams ye be holding in yer hand!"

"Pity? Don't you have to kill a man, flay him, in order to become a selkie in the first place?"

"Please . . ."

"Is there a single member of your race who is not a murderer?"

"Arrrgh! 'Tis true. But even murderers have dreams! I'm begging ye, sir . . . and I'll help ye find your wife if ye'll let me have a chance at finding mine. Spare that coat!"

Raven hefted the coat in his hand.

"Garn! Me Lord, ye ain't got too long to calculate about it! The Eech-Uisge be coming across the plain! Them and all their rout of monsters! At a hundred paces they can hear a mosquito what clears its tiny throat to spit!"

"Tell me how to trust you, liar of lying race? You see how weak a thing a selkie is. Once a man knows you, once he knows truth, he will not hand you his trust. You must ask me to hand you the very weapon, my trust, you use to hurt me."

"Keep the coat. Give it back when we're done."

"Very well. Here is wolf-skin. You can find scent?" Raven threw the wolf-coat toward him. The selkie reached down, picked up a tuck of the fur in his teeth, and shrugged his head to throw the coat across his shoulder. He twisted and shrank, and a wolf stood there.

The wolf spoke in a breathy, growling voice, "Galen Amadeus Waylock of the High House of Everness? Find his scent? Ye don't know who ye speak of or ye would not ask!

" 'Twas he who slew the seven-headed troll of the House of Capricorn, found the hidden heart of the Land Beyond the Northern Wind, and drove the nightmares out of Tir-na-Nog'th with a drop of water from the Well at the World's End. 'Twas he who healed the Hermit Prince, and found the drowned lands of Lemuria, not to mention taught the Bird of Fire how to sing again when she had lost her song. Nar! He is a Great Dreamer, that one is, and they've carved a palace for him atop the forbidden mountain of Kadath in the Cold Waste, when his time comes.

"Think I can't find one such as he? A living man, with the Blood of Everness in his veins, Wizard's blood and fairy-blood and blood of English kings! Can't smell that, here among the meepers and mewlers the Eech-Uisge use to fuel their nightmares? Ha! Be like looking for a prince among swineherds. A bonfire next to candles! He can call the unicorn down from behind the shoulder of Orion, that one can; and if they're smart, they won't let him kiss his shadow!"

At that moment, a hoard of cockatrices and naga-snakes came slithering over the crest of the rise, and a flock of grotesque birds like ostriches with plumes of sharpened bronze and faces of hags.

Raven calmly turned, calmly closed his eyes, and

calmly clapped his hands. A dozen bolts of white-hot lightning spurted from between his fingers and a cannonade of noise too loud for senses to tolerate shook the heavens.

IV

For Raven, there followed a nightmarish period of groping through the battlefield, blindfolded, climbing over and around the fallen and thunderstruck monstrosities and fell beasts of Uhnuman. His hands touched slimy serpent scales, knife-sharp harpy plumage, and the bloated, leprous flesh of some disgusting creature that seemed composed of diseased wads of flab.

In one hand Raven held the pelt of the selkie-wolf, who led him; at the selkie's request, Raven had put the cap of the bat-skin over his head so that the selkie was now a chimera with the body of a wolf and the head of a bat. Every now and again, Raven's sharp ears felt a painful throb, and he guessed the selkie was using his echolocation.

Legion after legion they passed. Then came a long time of walking through a plain of dusty rock. The stink of rotten blood grew stronger and stronger until Raven's nose grew almost numb.

Then the surface underfoot turned to riveted metal planks. The wolf said, "Look now. I think 'tis clear."

Raven was afraid. He remembered the look of fear carven forever on the face of a statue now sunk in the sea.

The wolf said, "In the pockets of my courtier's coat, you might find a small mirror."

Raven's fingers found a round, smooth glass in the cloth folded at his belt. Now he looked.

The street in which they stood was lined on both sides by gibbets from which corpses dangled. The buildings to either side were windowless, squat, iron blocks. Their massive doors and portals were closed shut, so that the whole street was as if it were a metal canyon. There were no decorations nor signs in this ugly city of blank metal, except for hand-high railings along the sides of the streets, cut with angular bas-reliefs, some sort of crude cuneiform, worn smooth by centuries of finger-touch.

The wolf trotted down the street, sniffing, his eyes shut, his bat ears quivering. "This way!"

There were barred gates hanging open at each cross-roads, with lines of heads on spikes above, mummified by the lunar air. The next street was lined on both sides with starvation-cages, and the one beyond that was lined with impaling screws.

They turned again, passed a gate hung with severed hands. In the near distance was the central dome. The archstone of the main gates had the head of a medusa hanging from it, with hair of snakes and eyes of viper-hate.

Even the shadow of the medusa in the mirror was almost too much for Raven; there was a stinging pain in his eyes, and he felt faint. He had to bow and clutch his stomach, struggling not to retch. Raven wondered what it would be like to see the thing with naked eye and was not surprised that creatures turned to stone.

When he recovered, they crossed over a moat filled with blood into the shadow of the central dome.

Suddenly, the gates opened with a hiss of pent air. Raven saw they were thicker than bank-vault doors. Within was a passageway wider than a street, leading back into darkness. A sound, as of many people softly sobbing or moaning, issued forth. Then gates behind them, one at each crossroad, swung silently shut, making each street a series of cages.

From overhead, aqueducts carrying poisonous and vile liquids began opening their floodgates, and sending rains of venom into the locked streets. Before the

first sprinkles of stinking poison ever reached the
street they were in, Raven's whirlwinds had shattered
and overthrown the legs of aqueducts, and the vast
structures collapsed all across the city, crushing buildings and towers.

Out from the main gates of the dome came a swarm
of cock-headed snakes, their each glance petrifying
and deadly.

Waddling behind them were the rulers of this horrible city of pain. The Eech-Uisge were fat, nude things
of obscene obesity, their empty eyesockets filled with
pus or scars. In their fat hands, they held long rods of
iron with which they felt their way, and with these rods
they herded the cockatrices before them.

The bloated, pale men formed a line from one side of
the street to the other, holding hands and linking arms.

Raven raised his hand but paused. If he destroyed
this troop, those within would merely close the gates.

He threw pebbles among the basilisks, so that they
all hissed, not just those that had seen him. The Eech-
Uisge swung their great heads from side to side, waiting for some clear signal from the serpent-monsters.

Raven put the bat-skin around the shoulders of the
wolf and gestured for the selkie to don it. The bat fluttered as Raven put in his pocket. Taking an iron rod
from a nearby gibbet, Raven used it to thrust away the
snakes he saw in his mirror.

Then he moved with all the stealth he possessed,
guided by the little mirror held before his face, stepping between snakes, till he was right before the advancing line of Eech-Uisge.

He snapped his fingers between two of them. They
both raised heavy lanterns and worked a lever. Raven
silently moved aside. Beams of molten metal spurted
from the machines; two of the Eech-Uisge were
splashed with white-hot iron and fell, gasping, screaming, burning.

Raven stepped over the burning corpses and to one

side, ducking below or hopping above the iron rods the neighboring Eech-Uisge swept through the area. It took a moment of confusion for the Eech-Uisge to reform their line.

One of the Eech-Uisge uttered a hiss. All the cockatrices fell silent.

Raven, within arm's length of the monsters, stood still, silent, motionless.

Their blind heads turned from side to side, their ugly nostrils wrinkling.

A shattered segment of a destroyed aqueduct chose that moment to lean away from its supports and clatter to the ground.

The line began to march in step in that direction, driving the basilisks before them, leaving Raven behind.

The gates before him were open; but it required all of Raven's skill to move in between the pair of ungainly mole-eyed gargoyles crouched on pedestals to either side of the gate. Their huge, misshapen ears were cocked, and they flailed the air between them with their canes at any slightest noise.

Within, all was dark. This place had no lamps, no windows. Raven heard heavy footsteps on the metal floor. Where he heard movement, he crept carefully around.

Guiding himself by touch, he went deeper into the structure, down a flight of stairs.

At one point he heard low sobs. At another, a strong odor told him there was a living being nearby, something that moved in utter silence. Raven stood motionless till the odor faded.

Now he drew the bat from his pocket. He felt it ripple under his hands and grow into a wolf. The wolf nose nuzzled him, urging him toward a certain direction. He followed.

Once he heard a steady dripping. Another time he heard a voice begging to be let out, then a solid clangor as if a heavy weight had been dropped into place.

There was a point where the echoes of distant screaming told him he walked through a vast space. Then, a movement of air told him he walked on an unrailed bridge. He heard the throbbing murmur of some unknown machinery, the groaning of wheels, the rattle of chains. The wolf led him into a narrow place where he was forced to go on hands and knees, shuddering from the touch of wet things growing on the walls.

The wolf started. Raven felt with his hands, found an opening in the floor, stairs steep as a ladder leading downward. He heard a gargled cough from below. The noise, distorted and horrid as it was, nonetheless sounded human.

The sensation that he was being watched overtook him. Raven stood there on the stairs, shuddering for a moment in the darkness. It took him a long moment to regain his calm. He twisted his fingers tightly in the mane of the wolf, who led him warily down the stairs.

The wolf stopped and would go no farther. Raven wondered whether that meant the selkie had found Galen's cell or scented an enemy ahead. He had no choice but to look. Raven touched the heavy gold ring he wore, concentrated his thought, grew calm, and when he raised his hand, he held a dazzling ball of Saint Elmo's Fire, dripping sparks and shivering between his fingers.

The light twinkled on gold and crystal and on the bulks of pallid flesh that loomed to each side.

The carpeting was rich and luxurious, and carven ornaments of gold and spun glass lined the walls, hung with panels of polished wood or drapes of finest silk.

One of the obese monstrosities turned toward him and a sticky, sucking sound came with its horrible, slow movement. When it opened its drooling mouth, Raven winced at the stench that came from the white throat, the black stumps of teeth. The thing's eye sockets were gaping wounds, dripping strands of corruption across its flabby cheeks.

"Intruder, we can smell you, hear your breath. Why do you disturb our delicate meditations? Now you must join us; we intend to dine . . ."

An arm hung with layers and rolls of fat raised and pointed. Highlights glinted off the crystal and silver with which the banquet table was appointed, the tall candlesticks, fragile glass vases, and hanging thuribles of perfume. The light also glinted from the chains and shackles coiled atop the centerpiece, which was a box of sharpened steel slats shaped like a coffin.

Arms stronger than any human arms caught Raven suddenly from behind, pinning his own. Beneath the gelatinous folds of fat sagging from those arms were muscles harder than steel bars. Raven's strength was like an infant's compared to this inhuman might.

Raven's fist, pinned against his side, still tightened on the wolf's mane, who pulled and snapped, but could not escape Raven's grip.

The wolf twisted his head around and touched his teeth to his shoulder; and Raven found himself holding nothing but a long wolf-pelt. A bat, wings flopping energetically, fluttered up the stairs and was gone.

The fat arms clutching Raven lifted his feet from the ground with easy strength. The creatures, giggling and drooling, waddled toward the feast-table, holding Raven.

The floor trembled almost imperceptibly, and a thundering murmur rolled down from far, far overhead. There was rain and wild wind suddenly above, and rolling thunder, but Raven was below, behind vast and airtight doors, where weather could not reach. And he was afraid.

Raven heard the voice of Tempestos, the Storm Prince, in his imagination, calling, "Brothers, heed! Once fear and anger shake his soul, the Raven's spell is gone away, him we slay, and take the ring withal!"

One of the blind creatures picked up a length of chain with pudgy fingers; another began to heat a rack of jagged knives and iron forks over black coals from which a terrible heat radiated, but no light.

A deep, bass voice rumbled, "Our guest must suffer pain on pain 'til he be cured. Ready the eye-spoons and castration scissors! Sharpen the amputation scalpels, and ready needles to sew his wounds and orifices tightly shut! We will feast on arms and legs and other outward parts, and pare away his shrieking flesh till only purity remains, a living mass without distraction or sensation. A life of contemplation is best."

Raven got his feet against the table's edge and, straining with his whole strength, kept his captor for a moment from hauling him toward the iron box. The monster was infinitely stronger than he, but pushed at a weak angle, not seeing what was in the way.

A pockmarked lumpish body, bloated and babyish with fat, pushed its eyeless face toward Raven, and two strands of filth dangled from its nostrils. "Join our holy order, mortal man! We are the eremites of Uhnuman, the handsome Eech-Uisge! Our strength is Herculean, and our beauty and grace exceeds that of Adonis!"

Raven kicked at the thing, but his boot only sent wobbling ripples through the mounds of pale flesh. "You brag of beauty!" Raven shouted, "You are stinking pile of goo!"

Thunder rolled angrily somewhere far above; but beneath the miles of iron and rock, all was calm as a tomb.

His captor now lifted him overhead so that his leg lost purchase with the table.

A glottal voice from the darkness answered. "We tolerate your difference; can you not return the courtesy? We make no judgments, for we cannot be deceived by outward appearances. Try to be a little more understanding."

His captor slammed him into the iron framework; a dozen sharpened slats and nails made shallow wounds all along his arms and legs, buttocks and back.

He was held down by the hands of his captor. A dozen heads pushed up close, slavering and grunting, and began to lick his wounds with long, black tongues, their noses and fat cheeks pressed into his garments and scratched flesh.

Raven spoke in a loud, calm voice. "Is this courtesy? Is this inner beauty?" His face was motionless, with a look of intense, quiet effort. As he spoke, the patter of rain on the dome so far above grew still, and the rolling thunder quieted.

A voice said, "But we are starving!"

Another said, "Selfish brute! You must give and we must have!"

Another: "All must share their fellow man's suffering. In times of desperation, when we are pale and weak with starvation, who would not steal from those who have to feed those who lack? Who would not eat another man to save himself? You have done the same, Galen tells us you ate him to feed your wife!"

Raven spoke in a voice of steady strength. "That was evil deed. I will undo it. You will not stop me, Moon-creature!"

A flabby hand pushed through the press to jab at Raven with a fork. The wielder said in self-righteous tones, "How will you stop us, you judgmental weakling? We have the strength of many men within us, for we consume the parts the selkie cast aside. They wish only for outward skins and shapes; we take inner selfishness and self away."

A final voice called out, "Eat his tongue first! You know how weak we grow when we know our own true . . . I mean, when lies and propaganda erode our resolve!"

By that time, a dozen groping hands were holding

the chains, ready to throw them across Raven; a dozen monstrous faces were nuzzling and licking him; the others, as far as he could tell in the gloom, were pressing forward, whining and complaining, fat folds pressed against their comrades, and, like baby piglets squeezing in to reach a teat, fought for a position to reach Raven's flesh.

Raven could only move his fingers; he put the hand which still held the ball of lightning, palm down, on the iron bars around him.

Every monster in the room was either touching the metal bars or chains or touching someone who was. The fat limbs jerked and spasmed, and the huge monsters sagged aside, too round to fall. Some moaned; others gargled phlegm; others were silent.

It now was utterly dark.

"Galen! Was that your moan I heard?"

A moan answered him, then the slithering scraping of a chain, three short scrapes, three long, three short—an SOS.

Raven felt his way toward the source of the sound. His fingers found flesh, shackles and needles holding some mutilated body crucified to a wheel. He tried to find Galen's neck and shuddered when his fingers discovered that the creatures had removed Galen's tongue and teeth and lower jaw. There was some sort of tube and plunger leading from a cage to Galen's throat so that whatever insect or animal had been in the cage could be forced living into his stomach.

Raven's hands shook, overcome by squeamishness.

He did not want to discover whatever other horrors had been perpetrated on Galen's body. He put the wolf-skin around Galen's neck, shut the clasps.

Whatever chains or clamps that had been meant to restrain human limbs had no hold on the slimmer, smaller body of the wolf, which fell to the ground and landed on its feet, barking happily.

Raven bent immediately and fitted the courtier's

robe so prized by the selkie around the dog's throat. Beneath his hands a naked man stood up.

"Thank you, sir, whoever you are."

"My name is Raven, son of Raven."

The voice sounded young, and shook. "Darn! I was hoping you were someone from the waking world. But, I guess with a name like that, you're from faerie-land, aren't you?"

IO

The Arrows
of the Sun

I

Raven replied, "I am a man. Am not a magic being. I come to save you."

"Oh, god! Oh, god! Not another trick, I think. The Agoshkoi aren't that subtle. Can you get your light back? It's really hard to change light levels."

Raven made a lightning bolt appear in his hand.

Galen stared at him; at his black beard and wild hair, the long Inverness cape he wore, magic ring on one finger, mirror in that hand, a crackling length of jagged lightning in the other, face of strange serenity.

Galen laughed and said, "No, not a magic being at all! How silly of me to think so! Hahahahah!"

He grabbed the mirror out of Raven's hand and stared at it. "Jeez! I'm an old man!"

In the glass, the reflection showed a silver-haired man with a heavy brow and wide cheekbones, jutting jaw emphasized by the beard he wore, streaked with black and silver.

Fear twisted his face. Galen held up his hands, thumbs and pinkies touching, like a Boy Scout's salute. "This is the body of Dylan of Njord! How do you come by it! Speak." He gestured with both hands at Raven.

Raven found his limbs locked in a strange paralysis. "I came because of Wendy."

"W—Wendy . . ." The sudden look of inexpressible hope that lit Galen's features was a joy to see.

"I am her husband."

Galen suddenly threw his arms about Raven and hugged him. Raven's paralysis had passed. To his infinite embarrassment, he found a silver-haired man weeping in his arms, crying like a baby, and he patted him on the back with one hand, saying, "There, there!" The other hand he held back above his head, so the man he had rescued wouldn't be electrocuted.

Galen sobbed. "She—she was the only one—the only one who knew I was here . . . The only thing I thought . . . if she could tell Grampa . . . but I was fooling myself, some crazy lady in a hospital. People always forget their dreams, you know? Then when they cut my tongue, I thought I could only thank her by a touch of my hand . . . but then my hands were . . . my eyes, they dripped stuff in them, and they told me . . . I thought she would barf if she saw me, you know, just barf . . . and I couldn't even, couldn't even . . ."

"Pull yourself together!" said Raven. "Stop acting like child!"

"Heh—heh—that's what started all this, you know. I wanted so much to prove to Grampa . . . How I was . . . How I could be trusted . . ."

"Your grandfather in much worse place than this! He is in Acheron, Apollo god said! You must make yourself a man to save him! Stop crying! Listen,

Wendy also in danger, maybe. Your father, Peter, was taken under the arrest when I was."

"Dad? Arrested for what?"

"He killed two giants."

A look of wonder and joy overcame Galen. He threw his arms up in the air and spun around, whooping. "So Dad's finally joined the party! Gramps will love it! Killed a giant? Two? That's great! I bet he sure believes in magic now! How'd he do it?"

"He took the Rod of Mollner when Wendy got the Moly Wand."

A sudden noise from overhead interrupted them. There came a roar like a great rushing of waters, and blood mixed with floating bits of bone and organs began to pour into the room through spouts in the walls.

Raven and Galen jumped upon the table, watching the blood rise around them. Parts of the mass began to pulsate, and floating organs began to intertwine, growing complex.

"This most gross thing I ever have been seeing . . . ," said Raven, clutching his nostrils. A flicker of lightning across the blood broke apart some of the organic masses. Others collected rapidly.

The blood level rose. The fat, twitching bodies of the Eech-Uisge began to float, stirring as if the loathsome touch revived them.

A cluster of eyeballs gathered together and glared up at Raven and Galen with insane hatred. Bones grew, forming jagged antlers and claws, and muscle tissues began to web the bones together.

"Sorry, Galen," said Raven. "I try to rescue, but this, I don't know what to do. We be inside huge mouth full of teeth in a few seconds, I am thinking. Wait! You know magic stuff. Anything we can do?"

Galen said, "The Agoshkoi are a type of kelpie. The only thing that stops them is the Bow of Belphanes. But I don't know where . . ."

"Maybe I can blast hole in ceiling. . . ."

Lightning sputtered along the metal roof futilely. The lightning began to fail as fear and anger grew in Raven's chest. Blood was lapping at their boots.

One of the Eech-Uisge bobbed upright, lapping at the blood, and giggled.

Raven, with a look of self-anger, surprise, and sudden memory illuminating his face, took a crumpled dollar bill out of his pocket, fumbling with the hand that wasn't full of lightning. "In here! How stupid of me not to remember, eh? Is here! In country of gold! Look on back! Great Seal! Arrows in eagle's claw!"

Galen reached for the bill, a sudden light in his eyes. At that same moment, a tentacle grabbed Raven by the leg. He sent a jolt of failing lightning into it. It jerked and released him.

In the darkness, an Eech-Uisge tittered.

Galen spoke. "As was foretold, the day is come; let the Horn blow doom and open the City of Gold. I vow by the light in my soul to use this weapon only for such deeds as sunlight will be proud to shine upon, full, faithfully, and well, as befits right reason and the light of truth; nor shall I cast them aside or surrender them to any enemy till battle's end. With pride but without vainglory I take; yield them to me, Spirit."

Golden sunlight came into the room, and the rays formed themselves into a solid length of wood in Galen's hands. Other rays fell at his feet, golden arrows quivering in the wood of the tabletop.

The blood drew away from him.

One of the Eech-Uisge screamed and fled, clawing at the walls and floor for some escape, splashing waves of red muck around him as he wallowed. Most backed up, wondering at the heat they felt.

One screamed, "Foolish child! Only those free of vainglory can draw that bow! Pull with all your strength! It will not flex an inch!"

Galen said, "You will be the first to feel its might, foul spirit." He did not even try to put his leg to the bow to bend and string it. Instead, he put the longbow's heel on the tabletop on which he stood, and he bowed, saying, "Good greetings to you. I ask you humbly for your aid in this good cause, most merciful of all weapons. I bow my head, but I do not grovel, nor is my spirit broken. Can you not do the same?"

The wooden length bowed to him. Galen slipped the bowstring around the bow. Then Galen straightened, saying, "I stand again, back straight and proud, but not so stiff that I snap aside all restraint put on me. Can you not do the same?"

The bow flexed, and the bowstring hummed with tension. Particles of light streamed from the bow, golden, luxurious, warm.

The Eech-Uisge floated backward through the muck, failing their ungainly limbs, hissing and whispering.

Raven, looking wildly around him at the limbs and teeth and horns growing up out of the swampy mass surrounding them, said, "Can that hurt the blood-gook?"

Galen lifted an arrow and fitted it to the string. He drew the bow in a strange fashion, holding it overhead as if saluting an unseen sun, standing with legs braced, then drawing the string down to his ear. There was something vaguely Oriental in the gesture.

Galen said in a happy, calm voice, "Don't worry about their soup. They tried to get me to dissolve into it a dozen times. They think all their servants get stronger if they grind them all together into one common pool. But all they get is a pool of blood. It's actually just one huge wound."

"But arrows can hurt it?"

Galen directed the Bow of Belphanes downward. "No. These arrows never hurt anyone."

He fired an arrow into the blood, and the bloody mass pulled itself instantly through vents and grates up out of the room.

In the distance Raven could hear faint cheers and cries of hope.

"We are still stronger than a score of men!" cried the Eech-Uisge, who had dared Galen to draw the bow.

Galen shot him. The man blinked, and his eyes appeared in his head.

In a sarcastic voice, Galen said, "Look at yourself! You're fat, and you're filthy."

The man stared at his leprosy-streaked hands, at the pale lumps of fat dangling from his arms, his eyes wide, his bloated face a soft mask of horror and surprise. And then his legs failed, as if his muscles could no longer support his enormous mass.

"It's all lies!" cried another. "It's not true if we don't admit it!" He was the one Galen shot next, and the Eech-Uisge knelt, unable to bear his own weight, weeping with his new eyes.

In a moment, all the other bloated men lay aghast upon the floor. One cried out, "But why didn't they tell us! How were we to know?"

"What is that cheering?" asked Raven.

Galen said, "All the blood and strength they stole has been returned to its true owners when I healed it. Hah! And speaking of blood, I've been waiting for this! Glad I have my mouth back!"

He put the bow behind and above him, so that the golden light cast his shadow before and below him. Galen knelt and kissed his shadow. Then he said, "My blood has been spilled upon the ground and cries out for vengeance."

The shadow stood up, swelling with darkness. "Speak your blood-curse. The ground below, and those who dwell there, heed. All who drank of your blood are in your shadow now, and you have power over them."

Raven, who had been quite unnerved by this whole procedure, said, "Quick! Speak your curse, blast the city, and let's go!"

"With all due respect, Mr. Raven, I was impatient once. Now I'd like to think this out before I do anything. First, let's get all the prisoners out of the dome and heal them."

Raven fell silent, humbled. For he remembered the fortress he had electrocuted in a single indiscriminate wash of lightning. He had not checked for prisoners, noncombatants, innocent bystanders.

"What about snakes?" Asked Raven.

"Snakes?"

"Turn-you-to-stone snakes!"

"Ah. Wait. I think I have a spell behind the bathroom mirror in the west wing . . . Let me remember. Yeah, I open it and there is a garden beyond, not medicine, and three women sewing . . ."

"What are you doing?"

"My memory is organized like my house. It's real handy because you can't take pencil and paper with you when you dream. Here. Watch." And Galen held up the mirror, saying, "Maiden, Mother, Crone! All things revere you once they're grown!"

And the tiny mirror swelled like a moon growing till it was larger than a shield and twice as bright.

"Here," Galen handed the mirror to Raven. "The Basilisks and stuff have the same problem these guys do; they can't stand to see themselves."

Less than an hour later, Galen stood on a hill outside the ruins of the city of Uhnuman; and the beautiful, naked people, handsome men and fair women, who danced in the sand and rock below the hill, sang praise of Galen and thanked him that they had been healed of all the scars and horror of the tortures they had endured. They danced among statues of cock-headed snakes, whose stone heads were all gap-mouthed, as if hissing and crowing at a terrible reflection.

Galen had taken a thread from Raven's cloak and uttered, "Spin, thread, weave all on your own! And I believe you'll be the best garb I'll own! Arachne,

Penelope, Urth!" And put on the splendid white chlamys that gushed from his fingers.

Raven said over the sound of singing, "Shouldn't we go back to Earth now?"

Galen said, "Only takes a moment. Don't want to be stupid again. Like, what are these guys going to eat? What about the other Agoshkoi cities on this planet?"

He held up his hand. The freed slaves fell silent. "Your nightmares are over!" cried Galen.

They cheered.

"Help me now to cure this world! Pray with me to the Sun, which is the source of all life, and to the Almighty Hand that fashioned the stars, the source of life beyond life!"

Everyone knelt, except for Galen, who was drawing his bow and pointing it at the Earth between his feet; and except for Raven, who thought this was silly, and fought to maintain his all-important calm.

Galen, his brow furrowed in terrible concentration, shot the arrow into the soil. Immediately it took root and sprouted leaves.

"Now what?" said Raven.

"Now I utter my blood-curse," said Galen. By this time, the arrow had grown into a sapling taller than a man.

Galen raised his bow and looked at the stars shining in the black sky near the blazing Sun.

A black shadow rose up beside him.

The shadow said, "What is your curse?"

By this time, the tree was full grown, and they stood within a small grove of saplings.

Galen said, "I curse them with forgiveness. Let them eat of the tree of knowledge of good and evil, and let that knowledge never pass from them, no matter what blindness they try to wish upon themselves. Let each passing year deepen and widen their understanding, until they are creatures of great sympathy and wisdom, and so that each thing they see will remind them of their crimes and stir their consciences. And I call upon the Archangel Raphael to come to this sphere to minister to them and govern them until three generations have passed, whereupon the Archangel may dwell here or return to the empyrean of the thrones, as he wishes. Look! I deliver the angel to this sphere with the stroke of this bow!"

And he fired an arrow into the air. It rose into the air, and rose and rose, till it was lost to sight.

The shadow whispered, "You have chosen your curse wisely, mortal man. For had you chosen in wrath and haste, you would have destroyed the wife of him who stands next to you for she has drunk your blood no less than these here . . ."

By this time, the grove had grown, and they stood on a grassy knoll in a forest. Green vines were already beginning to bury the cracked dome of the torture-city.

From the region of the sky into which Galen's arrow had disappeared, Raven now saw a falling star descending.

"Is just meteor, right?" said Raven. "Didn't actually shoot star down out of sky?"

"Raphael's coming," said Galen. "Now, one last thing before I summon a dream-colt to carry us home. Don't look. This is going to be pretty ugly, but I'm not going to wear Dylan's face any longer than I have to!"

He shot an arrow straight directly overhead. It paused at the apogee of its flight, turned, fell. By this time Galen had pulled open the hood and cloak of the selkie-coat he wore, so that his disfigured face and mangled chest were exposed to the daylight. The arrow struck him in the chest and turned to a beam of warmth. He shed his old skin and stood beneath sky, naked and whole, newly reborn.

The sky overhead was beginning to turn blue.

Galen drew on his white chlamys, and four fair

maidens came out from between the trees, bearing silver arms. One buckled on his spurs, telling him to let courage spur him onward; one drew a coat of silver scale across his shoulders, telling him to let moderate desires guard his heart; one placed a peaked helmet on his head, telling him to let prudent thoughts ward his head; the last one knelt and buckled a swordbelt around his waist. This belt had no scabbard, but a quiver of arrows hung from it. She told him to use his weapon justly, not in anger or pride.

The girls all kissed him, one after another, and walked away through the green wood, swaying with graceful steps, their faces grave.

Raven was staring in gap-mouthed confusion, "What! Who was this? Who in the world these women were, eh?"

Galen smiled. "Some parts of this job I really like. See that light behind the mountains there?"

"Sunrise?"

"No. Sun's overhead. That's the guy I called: Raphael. I want to get out of here before he comes. Talking to Seraphim is kind of scary. Stand back so I can draw a line on the ground for my pretend wall."

Galen said a poem, and a shape of winged beauty lightly lit down from the heavens, her silvery hoofs not bending the newborn grass.

Galen petted the winged fawn's nose, and little curls of mist and light seemed to caress his fingers.

Raven looked at the light behind the mountains (which was approaching with the music of trumpet, drum, and cymbal) up at the new blue sky, around him at the newly born forest, and then at the vision eating a newly plucked apple from Galen's hand. Raven stood with his mouth hanging open in awe.

Galen looked over his shoulder at Raven and laughed. "Don't look so surprised! This is only a dream, after all . . ."

Raven frowned, for he did not recall falling asleep.

II

At that moment, a scrap of darkness fluttered down from overhead in the shape of a bat. The bat clung, upside-down, from a nearby tree branch, and spoke in a high, thin voice: "The deed be done! I call upon ye, Raven, to yield to me the cloak as promised!"

Galen said, "I know your voice, Dylan! You've got a lot of nerve! How come I shouldn't kill you right now, huhn?" and he lifted the bow, but he could not draw it.

Raven said, "Evil creature! You run out on me, eh?"

But the dream-colt spoke in a voice like rippling music, saying, "Raven, son of Raven, you must keep your promised word. Here, in this realm, gold we do not esteem, for it grows like autumnal leaves on trees, nor wine, which flows from generous springs. But a word, once given, may not be taken back; for our great enemy here is called Forgetfulness, and our only weapon against him, is to remember our promises."

Raven stooped and picked up the man-skin coat, which he threw to the roots of the tree from which the bat dangled. "Here! Is yours. Take it."

The bat dropped down into the mass of leather, and a silver-haired, bearded man stood up. "Don't ye be so high and mighty with me, boyo!" said Dylan. "Who's to blame for anything we selkie do to humankind? The first of us was but a seal, ye know. 'Twas human fingers clasped the first coat around our necks; we had no hands to do the deed, back then!"

Galen, with studied casualness, picked up the wolf-skin he had shed as well, and tossed it to the selkie's feet, saying nonchalantly, "Oh, I guess this is yours as well. Take it."

Dylan picked it up.

Galen pointed at Dylan with three fingers, saying, "A gift of fairy-land, freely taken!"

Dylan stiffened. "Aye? What be all this ye say?"

Galen shouted, "I claim the gift you had from me,

the wolf-skin pelt! I claim the hand that took the gift, and the whole body that hand is part of, and the soul that moves that body! Your soul is mine, now, Dylan of Njord, I know, I know, I know your name!"

"Ar! There be no such spell as that!" snarled Dylan uncertainly.

"I am of the blood of Azrael de Gray. I call now upon ancestral spirits, bound by him, and beholden to my house, to carry out my . . ."

"Wait! Wait!" screamed Dylan in panic.

"Is there something you can give us in equal value to your soul, lying spirit?" asked Galen with great dignity.

Dylan's eyes darted from side to side, frightened. But his voice was controlled, as he said tensely, "What would ye have me tell? Is the fate of the Raven's little wife worth a soul to ye?"

"Speak!" shouted Raven.

"Azrael's leading ninety hordes of Svartalfar and evil Peri against the land of Neverdale, where she was last. But Mannannan has betrayed him, and speeds ahead, to save the pretty lassy for his own self!"

"I release you from my curse!" shouted Galen, who had already mounted the dream-colt, who reared and flailed her magnificent wide plumes. "Raven, get up here! Take my hand! Mnemosyne, can you get us there first?"

The dream-colt said, "Faster than thought and hope am I, destined to carry heroes to final combat and war on the bloody plains of Vigrid and Armageddon. But as fast as swiftest fear would have me fly? Even I must strain. It will be a near chase."

With Raven atop her, she had left the ground behind her, and the Moon had dwindled to a sphere before she had finished her sentence.

Later, Raven sat in front of Galen on the dream-colt, clutching her mane uncomfortably, as stars flowed by to either side, and rearing constellations bowed and parted before their wild flight. Raven, who knew how to ride a horse, was unnerved nonetheless by this dizzying sweep of mystic speed, as they dropped through planetary spheres and epicycles, luminous clouds, and passed strange cometary messengers.

To cover his nervousness, he said, "Good thinking, getting Dylan Selkie to talk that way, eh? You seem to know much spells and dreaming things."

Galen was wreathed in smiles, but tried to speak humbly when he said, "Oh, not really. That was just a trick. He was right, and there wasn't any such spell as that. Some of these fairy-types are really suckers for a good reputation, you know?"

But he sounded so pleased.

II

*Crime
Does Not Pay!*

It was dark, past midnight, as they drove, and Washington D.C. had been left far behind. Before the car, two men disguised in the heavy coats and helmets of motorcycle police sped on, blue lights flashing.

The highway was deserted. Except for government vehicles, no traffic was permitted on the roads past curfew, not while the state of national emergency existed.

Within the gray sedan, two men sat in the rearmost seat: Wentworth and Van Dam. In the front was a driver, and next to him, a beefy Treasury agent with a submachine gun in his lap and the earplug of a radio in his ear. All of these men, and the two motorcyclists in uniform outside, were members of the inner circle. None of them had friends or relatives in Los Angeles, or not any that they particularly cared to warn.

There had been checkpoints at all the major roads leading out of D.C., making each street a series of cages with many gates to pass through, albeit the gates were lines of yellow sawhorses guarded by troops in heavy combat gear.

But the last checkpoint had been left behind, and blank and barren highway stretched ahead, the tarmac a dark ribbon beneath the bleak glare of infrequent streetlamps.

Van Dam's hand rested on the white metal box between them, and his fingers drummed a nervous tattoo. Every now and then, he said, "Are you sure about this?" to Wentworth, who sat stony faced, staring out at empty overpasses and empty crossroads they passed.

At the fortieth or fiftieth repetition of the question, Wentworth snapped, "Garn! Shut yer trap, ye great fool!" in a strange, archaic accent. Then, in his normal tone of voice, Wentworth said, "Sorry, Van Dam. But we really have no choice. We didn't think the riots would escalate this far! How could we know that shopkeepers and small businesses would arm themselves like this, and start fighting back? Or the truck drivers? The FCC has to find and shut down those pirate radio stations! We can't let people know that state militia have opened fire on federal military units! We should have burned those judges and their stupid injunction!"

Wentworth was clutching the briefcase on his lap. Inside was a folded white leather selkie-coat. The golden bow and quiver of arrows had been missing from the vault in the Pentagon. No one had reported the mysterious loss to Azrael de Gray, who was also missing.

"I thought the Vice President looked good on TV. People will come around . . ." Van Dam's fingers tightened on the box.

Wentworth said, "The places where our people aren't being shot at by local citizens are New York and D.C., and parts of California. Urban centers. Thank God for gun control! Only the drug dealers have guns there, and they know where their next welfare check is coming from. But the flyover states, how dare they fight back? Handguns! Har har! Handguns are toys now-a-days! We'll show them what real firepower means!"

As Wentworth said this, Van Dam jerked a hand away from the box he was touching, as if the box had stung him. Van Dam stared down at the box wide-eyed, his breathing ragged.

"Are you sure about this?" he asked yet again.

"It will break their spirit! They'll have to give in . . . !"

"But we're not even supposed to have this thing! Only the Vice President and the President can carry the white box!"

Wentworth said, "We both know the access codes. We can reprogram the missile to its new target and remote-fire it from here, thanks to the computer interlink. The silo personnel have already been told to stand by and assist the launch. NORAD is at DefCon One. The other countries are scared witless and won't dare interfere. No one wants to get involved in the first nuclear civil war in history."

Van Dam said, "Will . . . will the missile silo crew obey the order?"

Wentworth laughed a strange laugh. "There's one that will, and aye, for me shipmates . . . ahem. We have our men, loyal crews, standing by in at least one location. They have been told to maintain communication blackout. No recall order, no change of command codes will reach them. Only the signal from this box."

Van Dam shivered. "Last night I dreamed a hideous beast was loose in the streets. Its fangs were dripping red. And where it went, people turned into mobs, and armed themselves, and burned down their houses . . ."

The T-man in the front seat turned around and rapped on the glass. Wentworth opened the partition between the seats.

The T-man said, "Just lost contact with checkpoint 235-12. Might just be radio problems. Wouldn't have mentioned it, except we lost contact with checkpoint 235-11 a few minutes ago."

Van Dam said, "Could be a coincidence. . . ."

Wentworth said, "Eleven, then Twelve went out? Could be someone coming up behind us. . . ."

The T-man shook his head doubtfully, saying, "Maybe so, sir, but they'd have to be coming up awfully fast. Ten, fifteen minutes? Checkpoints twenty miles apart? He'd have to be traveling at a hundred miles an hour. And satellite watch would have seen the headlights on the road."

Wentworth and Van Dam both turned and looked out the rear window.

A long, lonely ribbon of highway stretched away behind them, dark, speeding backward in the gloom. There was nothing in sight.

Wentworth said, "Have one of the escort drop back to see if there is anyone following us."

Van Dam said, "That might not be wise, sir. Shouldn't we call for reinforcements?"

Wentworth said, "Reinforcements! We're not even supposed to be heading this direction! Azrael doesn't want us in Everness! Why do you think we didn't take Air Force One?"

The T-man radioed one of the men on the police motorcycles. Van Dam watched with a strange sense of desolation as the motorcycle on the left fell behind, turned, and sped away down the highway, traveling in the wrong lane. The blue flickering lights faded in the distance and were gone.

A slow minute crawled by.

The T-man held his hand to his ear. He said, "I'm not getting an answer on the radio, sir. We lost him." And he lifted his submachine gun and worked the action.

Wentworth leaned forward. "Step on it! Get us out of here!"

Van Dam was staring out the rear window. "But there's nothing back there. It's just empty road. . . ."

The man dressed as a motorcycle cop ahead of them had drawn a shotgun out of a long, leather holster strapped to the bike. He hunched down behind the handlebars, and, steering with one hand, he cast glances back over his shoulders, to the left and right, and the motorcycle weaved slightly.

"Driver! Top speed!" shouted Wentworth.

The engine roared. Acceleration pressed them back into their seats. They came even with the motorcycle and began to overtake it.

The T-man snatched the earplug out of his ear looked at it in horror.

"What's wrong?" snapped Wentworth.

"Uh—we're being jammed, sir! He—a voice came over our channel—and he said—he called me by name . . ."

"What was it? What!" Wentworth leaned forward, shouting.

"He said we had to surrender. . . ."

Wentworth's face went blank, and he sank back in the seat. Van Dam shouted, "Look! *It's him!*"

Out from the darkness behind them came a black, armored limousine, running without lights. Smoothly accelerating, powerful, swift, the streamlined dark machine surged forward, growing in their view. The body was wide, low to the ground, heavy, and the pavement streamed backward under its tires in a smooth, silent, effortless rush of speed. Its headlamps were folded shut, and the only light came from the single orange line across the blunt prow of the dark vehicle, gleaming just above the streaming pavement. The window-panes were metal panels cut by thin, black slits.

"How can he see?"

"He's running on infrared," said Van Dam. Then, half aloud to himself, "Heh, looks like a 1966 Chrystler Im-

perial. Good car. Modified it to a high-speed fighting vehicle."

"Faster!" shouted Wentworth to the driver.

"We're maxed out now, sir!" the driver, hunched over the wheel, called out above the laboring whine of the engines. The needle of the speedometer hovered at 150 mph, and the chassis quivered and shook.

The black car came smoothly forward.

"He's using nitrous oxide," said the T-man.

The driver said, "He's using more than that. No car in the world that heavy can be that fast. What the hell has he got under that hood? A rocket?"

The motorcyclist twisted backward in his saddle, right arm straight, aiming. A flash of flame spat from the bore of his shotgun. Pellets dashed harmlessly against the armored plates of the black machine.

The headlamps of the black machine unfolded; there was a brief, dazzling, silent explosion of magnesium light. The motorcyclist put his elbow up before his faceplate, momentarily blinded.

In that blind moment, the black machine accelerated with a deep-throated hum of mighty engines. The prow of the machine brushed against the rear wheel of the motorcycle. The front wheel bent sideways, and the motorcycle spun away, a twisted tangle, and the rolling body of the gunman slid across the tarmac, over the railing, and out of sight.

The headlamps folded. The armored machine was behind the sedan.

"This guy doesn't fool around," growled the T-man, rolling down his window. He leaned out. A hammering, thunderous roar erupted from his submachine gun. Sparks flickered across the hull of the black vehicle, and ricochets whined.

"What the hell's that stuff made of?" whispered Wentworth in awe. Then: "Shoot the tires!"

"I've shot the tires!" snapped the T-man, his hair

tossed by the streaming wind. He slapped his second magazine into place. "They're solid rubber."

The black machine swung away to the left of the sedan, spoiling the T-man's aim. The T-man unbuckled his safety belt, and climbed up out of the window, his rump on the car door, his arms across the roof of the car.

Another volley of gunfire rang out. The two cars swerved back and forth across the highway as the armored limosine tried to maneuver out of the line of fire, and the sedan, tires squealing, swerved to block it from passing.

The T-man reached down through the window, one hand groping. "Hand me up another clip!"

Van Dam could see through his window the T-man balanced over the top the sedan. He saw the little red dot of an aiming laser appear on the T-man's forehead, right between the eyes. The T-man was unaware of it. "Give me another clip!"

There was a slight whisper of noise; the T-man's head exploded in a mass of blood. His corpse went flying out the window, legs thrashing, into the night, yanked out by hundred-mile-an-hour winds.

Van Dam looked back.

He saw a black figure leaning out from the right rear passenger's compartment of the armored limousine, one hand holding a long, narrow weapon. No features could be glimpsed of the mysterious figure. His cloak and hood and gas mask, his sleeve, the weapon he held, and the vehicle were all the same dull hue of nonreflective black, so that all the shadows blended into one inky mass. Up from his shoulder, the tail of his cape streamed back from the window, slithering and flapping.

A red laser light shined from the weapon.

Van Dam turned his head. He saw the tiny red spot reflected off the rear window next to him. He turned his head farther. The driver was staring in horror at the tiny red dot gleaming on his hand where it clutched the wheel.

There was a whispering hiss. The rear window exploded into powder. The driver's hand opened up into jags of bleeding bone and torn flesh.

The air bag in front of Van Dam inflated just as the sedan began to roll.

Groggy, half conscious, Van Dam saw a tall figure step from the rear of the armored limosine, pause to don a wide-brimmed black hat, and move toward him, silent as a shadow.

His vision went black. Vaguely, he felt strong hands pull him from the wreckage. He felt the touch of a stethoscope on his neck and chest, then fingers touching his wrist, feeling for a pulse. The cool bite of a needle touched his arm. Then his hands were twisted behind his back and cold handcuffs circled his wrists with a ratcheting click.

Whatever he had been injected with brought him back awake. Van Dam blinked the haze out of his eyes. The only light came from the one unbroken headlamp of the sedan, pointing toward the ground. The driver lay, one hand bandaged, moving on the pavement next to him, also chained.

A man dressed from head to toe in black, hidden in a voluminous black cape, face shadowed by a wide-brimmed black hat, was hunched over the white box Van Dam had been carrying. The magnetic lock had been opened, and tiny, luminescent readouts and status lights glistened like fireflies. The casing itself had been dismantled, and the interior computer circuits were exposed.

The black figure held some kind of instrument, and wires ran from it to the opened inner workings of the white box. The mysterious fire-opal he wore on one black-gloved hand glittered and flashed hypnotically as he typed on the keyboard, first of the instrument he carried, then on the keypad of the white box.

Wentworth's voice rang out from the gloom beyond the sedan's headlamp. "Pendrake! You'll never get away with this! You should have joined us when you had the chance!"

A strong, calm voice, chilling and pitiless, issued softly from the shadows beneath the black hat. "There is an order to the universe, gentlemen. Azrael's curse can delay, but not deflect, the terrible consequences of his acts: the retribution for his wrong seeks him. For men, justice is dealt out by the hand of the law. For darker things the law cannot see or reach, there is a darker vengeance.

"I have a secret place where those I wish to examine are taken. There, under hypnosis, they testify in my court with exact precision. From that court there is no appeal. But I do not take suspects there who are still within the reach of human laws, nor may I supersede that law's authority, while that law still is free to act. But be warned! For in that secret place I keep accurate files of those destined to be brought before me; and your file is thick indeed, the record of your crimes long and black.

"Van Dam!" came the pitiless voice. "I know you are awake. Heed the warning I gave your master. It may not be too late to repent, and, if you cooperate now in the undoing of some part of your crimes, I may be lenient when your time comes. Tell me the access codes."

Wentworth shouted, "He'll never talk!"

Without hesitating, in a loud and clear voice, Van Dam recited the string of numbers.

"Very good!" said the voice. He raised a glove toward the face hidden beneath the hat brim, and spoke into his fist: "Burbank! Reconfigure your instruments to this channel! Redirect the warhead to the longitude and latitude my wife has given you."

A black-gloved hand reached out from the cloak to pick up the briefcase Wentworth had been guarding.

"And this I impound as evidence; to return to Galen Waylock what was stolen from him. I have sent for an ambulance from the nearest hospital; they should arrive after they are done with the first motorcyclist. You will not see me again, Van Dam. This does not imply I shall not see you. Be warned!"

With a whispering rustle of cape, the mysterious figure, the briefcase, and the white box were gone.

12

*The
Salvation
of Lemuel*

I

He had passed beyond agony into blackest despair. He had forgotten his own name. The music that poured from the walls spun his soul in a terrible rapture, a music driving his thoughts, compelling beyond all compelling beauties, horrid beyond all nightmares, and the dark majesty of the choir quenched his spirit.

It was the music of angelic hosts, but fallen angels; they gave life to songs composed of genius, but genius turned to themes of fear.

He hung suspended in the middle of a flooded cell, pinned by four chains that racked his four limbs. The black and freezing water long ago had choked him, but when his lungs had ceased, he had failed to die. When his heart grew cold and still within his chest, again, he failed to die.

At times, the music swelled, and he forgot how much he longed for death, for the haunting lovely anguish of the songs would not allow him to recall what death was or to imagine escape from agony.

And when the choir fell away to allow a lone soprano's high, clear voice to soar in paeans praising pain, then he recalled the grave, and how he longed for it; and he could not tell if it were deeper torment to remember, or deeper torment to forget.

At other times, ringing melodies wove through the choir of fear, to allow him to recollect the beauty of a snowy night in starlight, or the cold glint of the Moon above the desert, the lonely notes of nightingales lost in frozen forests, or the smile of a dreaming maiden, her face pure and pale, lying quiet in a velvet coffin, withered lilies on her breast.

These images would recollect to him that once he had possessed the gift of sight before he had been plunged in blindness so profound that all images of light within his memory went dark.

And this was torment worse, for as the music swelled again, harmonies ringing with evil glory would grow to drown the memories in themes of black despair. For the gentle counterpoints were there only to increase his pain, to remind him of his loss, and to confirm that loss to be eternal.

Once or twice a golden voice, deep, haunting, pure, and kingly, rose above the choir of darkness, weaving music into beauty beyond all words. And that voice would recall his one best-loved memory.

This one memory he had, cherished above all others, he loved as a drenched man in a freezing wasteland might love the single failing spark hesitating on the tinder of his hoped-for fire that might save him. He sought to save this one dim memory, as a freezing man might gently blow upon his spark, still hoping for fire, long after his hands and feet had gone numb and black with frostbite.

The faint, happy memory was of a face and form more magnificent, more filled with glory, that the human eyes could tolerate. It was a kingly face, noble, wise, serene, and pure, and starlight was in his eyes. It was like the face of an angel, gray-eyed and dark haired, with a single diamond of purest fire on his brow. This countenance was without weakness or fear, a face of haunting aspect, like one bright star seen above an ice-crowned mountain, remote from all the dirtiness and pathetic frailty of man.

When the memory of that perfect face came clearer, he would cherish it secretly in his heart, hoping his captors could not reach this inmost, hidden treasure of his mind. Outwardly, he tried to hide his one last happiness by filling the surface of his mind with thoughts of terror and hopelessness, so as not to give himself away by any show of joy. For he feared the immortals that had him could see his thoughts, and he rejoiced when he deceived them.

The image of that face was like a beacon, recalling hope. For if such a perfect creature as this could possibly exist, then not all the universe was an abattoir of meaningless suffering.

But when the dark choir rose in praise and greeting of that golden voice then, only then, did he recall he had been deceived. Then he wept like a baby, remembering as well that he had been deceived this way many times before. He resolved not to forget, not to be so lightly taken in again; yet he recalled he, many times, had made such vain resolutions before.

For the face was the face of Morningstar, the Emperor of Night, and Acheron's Lord, of course; the glory of that face had been what blinded him, a sight more fair than men had faculties to see.

Worst, and worst of all, was that he could not recall his crimes. The thought that he was innocent was pain to him, but he comforted himself with the hope that so brave and great and gracious a prince as Morningstar could not have condemned him without just cause. The fear that this hope would, too, prove vain, was also painful to him.

The terror and fear and love he had for Morningstar was his only comfort in the midst of woe. Gladly he would have sacrificed his innocence, to make himself deserve his punishments, if only it would keep that noble, mighty being from any stain or slander.

II

His salvation, when it came, came with the swiftness of a tropic sunrise. In one moment the immortal choir's song was choked away, made raucous and ridiculous, a cacophony, by a single clear and piercing song that utterly overwhelmed it. The choir's voice turned to calls of anger, and then blew a trumpet-blast of war; and that blast was answered by the singing of a harp-string, or perhaps it was a bow.

He forgot his love of Morningstar as quickly as a man forgets a bad dream on waking.

Warmth came into him again, and he felt growth within him waking to life, like flowers opening their heads in a summer field. Not without pain, his heart began to beat again, and his lungs began again to fight the stinking filth and waters beneath which he was chained.

That was when he remembered the look of sunlight on the hair of his wife, many years ago when they first were wed, and little Peter running in the grass in spring, playing in the sunshine, he recalled the look of daylight through the windows as he opened them, craning his neck to see a falcon overhead in swift, fierce flight. He recalled the triumph of a sunrise after cloudy nights, and the lusty call of roosters crowing for the dawn.

The structure in which he was penned shook to its

foundations, and he saw one part of the ceiling of his prison glowing red, surrounded by streams of bubbling steam. He remembered the look of light; his blindness had passed.

A voice of perfect calmness called out: "Lemuel! I am come!"

Only then did he recall his name, and choking, spitting water, he tried to call back. But he made only the feeblest noise, and fear embraced his heart, for he thought his rescuer could never hear him, and that he would be overlooked.

But even the smallest cry for help had been enough. A hand of gold and white, with fingers taller than five birch trees, tore away the ceiling of the prison cell.

A face larger than a sunrise looked within, crowned with laurel leaves and rays of living light. "My son!" called out the voice with joy, and a look of anger from those eyes shattered the chains into molten drops.

Warm hands folded around Lemuel and lifted him from the pit where he had been. Here, there was air to breathe, as if the darkness and pressure of these deep waters had no power to come near the prince of light.

Lemuel saw he stood upon a wide and desolate plain of blackest metal, which everywhere showed monuments like gravestones. And he realized that he stood upon an endless prison place, within pits on pits below, and doors welded shut, buried beneath the monuments, meant never to be opened evermore.

In the wide gloom around the plain, rising out of sight into the blackness, cold and pressure of the waters overhead, loomed seven towers of adamantine metal, black as starlessness, rising bastion upon bastion, endlessly upward in proud, unconquerable strength. And Lemuel's heart quailed to realize how far within the power of the enemy he was, and how remote from Heaven.

For in the darkness all about them, and endlessly above, rank on rank and legion on legion, swam clouds of demon-kind, their beautiful and perfect faces terrible with wrath, their wide pinions, plumed with raven feathers, beating slowly in the watery gloom. On their heads were crowns of darkness; their breastplates gleamed with seven precious stones; their spears were tipped with hell-fire.

The prince of light hugged Lemuel close by his side, beneath the warmth and comfort of his wide eagle-wings. "Cling close to me, my son, for both my hands must be free to pluck the bowstring. Let no fearful thought darken your mind, but be lighthearted, and turn your thoughts on high to Heaven, for we both must mingle our full strength to overcome what might oppose our ascent from this deep chasm."

The gates of the greatest tower now slammed wide with brazen clangor. Within were seven maidens, more lovely than any women of the Earth, save that their faces were deathly pale and their eyes were the eyes of vipers. When they paced with downcast eyes, modest lovely they seemed; but when a man might look them straight in the eye, they were horrors.

The maidens came forward, holding torches that shed not light, but gloom; and where the shadows of those torches passed, the water glittered with black ice.

Behind them—heralded by trumpets, drums, and cymbals—came a chariot drawn by writhing dragons; and the dragons belched mists of venom into the water. Upon the chariot-car, armored with gold and darkest adamantium, adorned with black opals, came one who bore a star of perfect light upon his brow. In one gauntlet the mighty Presence held a scepter whose head was a spike-studded orb of adamantium.

"Gaze not at this one, my son," said the prince of light, and lowered his great wings so that eagle-plumes were all around Lemuel like a warm and scented blanket. "Nor will your eyes sustain the full measure of my power as I put it forth this day."

Another voice spoke then, as perfect and as beautiful, or even more so, than the first, but bitterly cold, majestic, terrible, and inhuman. "Archangel Uriel! Why are you come to my dark empire, and by what law dare you to stray from that high empyrean circle to which divinity constrains you? Is high Helion stoopt now lowly thus that he is turned sneak-thief, and would hale away the small beasts I have penned within, my promised prey?"

"I am also called Apollo, the Destroyer, as your coming grief will testify, great Morningstar, should you dare to trouble Heaven's messenger!"

"My eye pierces you, Apollo, and I see the monkey's son who clings with trembling paw to your broad back. Return what is mine to me; you demean your high estate, and mine as well, to let the loathsome touch of such a creature befoul your back. Or, if me you defy, say by what law you dare oppose me in my place of power, far from the pathways of the Sun?"

"I do defy, and ever will, the reign of darkness which follows you, sad Morningstar. Nor need I answer law for law to you, traitor to our order; for while you are greater than am I, I yet am a highest messenger of Celebradon and in service to a power whom only folly dares oppose."

"Smynthian! Well named are you, mouse-hearted mouse-god! To boast of servitude, glorying in unglory, upright in knee-service! With stealthy foot you trespass on my majesty, and that, when well you know my main strength has gone forth from this place, led by the Wizard's will against the Court of Oberon. Yet that strength that fortune leaves suffices, for fortune is my slave. Now I raise my truncheon high, and signal for the onslaught. The seraphim of darkness shall rejoice this day the overthrow of proud Hyperion!"

And at that, Morningstar uttered another word, which Lemuel's ear would not allow him hear; and that word was darkness, which streamed from Morningstar's mouth like the ink of an octopus, and quenched Apollo's light.

Apollo's crown flickered and failed, and all was black as oblivion itself.

"Do not despair, my child, but rise with me," he softly said. Dark, but still warm, Apollo rose, and Lemuel clutched to his back, strummed by the feathers of the eagle-wings as they flailed against the black and freezing waters.

And now the thrones, dominations, cherubim, and potentates of Acheron drove in at Apollo, their spear-points glimmering like evil stars, and a paean-song of blackest victory rose through the gloom.

Apollo's laughter and light song cut through their harmonies in clear, pure tones; and at the singing of his bowstring, the darkness shattered and fled. Apollo's arrows each became a hundred arrows as they flew, a thousand, and ignited into golden rays, and Apollo sang, "Who thinks the stars can smother the approach of day? Even the morning star, at dawn, turns pale and dies away!"

The angels of darkness fled, scattering before the reborn light, at first rosy, then bright and golden, that showered bounteously from Apollo's crown.

Below the dark grew blacker, and writhing smoke rose up between the towers of Acheron, which no arrows and no ray could pierce. Morningstar was coming, and the hiss of the dragons of his chariot shivered through the darkness as he came. Like frightened children flocking behind their mother, the Archangels of Acheron dove into the gloom and hid below their master, hiding behind his growing cape, their weapons glinting like embers. The cape was swollen like a thundercloud to cover the cowering host.

Morningstar stretched his great wings wide, stirring black currents of cold waters from the deep, raising columns of silt and gloom before him as he rose up.

Swift as death he came, the star of his crown gleaming like a beacon of deep hate, and a great majestic music followed him.

He sang in a voice greater, deeper, and more pure than Apollo's. "Petty victory if dawn must conquer night each day; for bloody dusk awaits to rape that briefest life away; we wait, we wait, once more to rise; for Morningstar is Evenstar as well, brightest lord of darkest hell; and Evenstar shall always drive the dying sunlight from the skies!"

Something dark, cold, sharp, and black slashed heavily through the eagle-pinions in motion around Lemuel. It was the head of Morningstar's scepter, a cut, black gem of perfect diamond. Lemuel's hand was but inches from where it struck, and that near passage numbed his fingers merely with the brush of wind from the cursed weapon. He did not look directly at it and so was not blinded.

Then there came a moment of emerald light, and then a crash of noise and freedom. Lemuel clung to the god's back as the vast, winged figure flung himself skyward out of the ocean, and a circle of glittering foam and spray rushed up from them and fell away.

Then they were in the blue heavens, drinking the brisk Spring sea winds, squinting in the glitter and gleam of sunlight dancing on the sea, marveling at clouds, and laughing, laughing with great joy. Lemuel hugged the god with his full strength, feeling pins and needles of life returning into his numb hand.

"Alive again!" shouted Lemuel. "Alive again, and free! I feel so young!"

Apollo slung his bow and tossed the old man up into the air so that he shrieked, and the young god caught him again, laughing with golden tones.

"Again! Again!" gasped Lemuel.

"You are too fresh to fly, my fledgling; though the Judge who waits at the gates of my world weaves wings you one day there shall wear. For each good deed, he fits another feather to the frame; for each ill, he sadly plucks, and lets fall fluttering away. The blessed and damned alike are cast from the same cliff on judgment day, and only some shall soar. Be of good cheer; for he tells me your wings already are longer than a condor's, with plumage thick and rich!"

Lemuel said, his eyes shining, "Come with me to earth, Father, and help set right what's gone wrong there!"

"No. Morningstar smote me as I fled; a single drop of my ichor is falling toward my grandmother Earth; where it lands, there will be deadliest and all-destroying fire. He whom you call Azrael prays to have that drop on the city of angels in the West; the Pendragon seeks to turn it to another course. If my smallest touch can work such harm, how then if my whole foot should step on Earth? I will not repeat poor Phaethon's well-meant mistake, or make a next Sahara."

"That blood was shed for my sake," said Lemuel, "Tell me how to make restitution, and I will do it."

"You say so, even if you do not know the price?"

"I say so. It doesn't matter to me what it is; I can't have people suffer for my sake."

"Well said." Apollo smiled. "I hear the rustle now of another plume being threaded to your wings. So be it! The quest I put on you is to save the girl who holds your grandson's life within herself. Because you asked, am I allowed to tell you what to do."

"And what must I do?"

"Think clearly. Logic is a weapon fairies cannot wield."

And at that word, the god, his pinions streaming, reached down his hand to place Lemuel atop a grassy mountain overlooking the sea in a place where the laurel bushes and sunflowers had all turned and spread their petals toward the god as he approached.

Lemuel's foot touched the grass, and he found nothing in his arms but a beam of sunlight.

He spread his arms, looking upward. "Thank you," he said.

III

And then he woke up. A figure was bent over him.

"Galen . . . ?"

"No, Dad. Sorry to disappoint you. It's me, Peter."

IV

He was in a hospital room. The bed was pushed away from the wall so that sunlight falling through the window shone across the white sheets. Peter sat in a wheelchair next to the bed, two canes across his lap. In one callused hand Peter held a supernatural weapon shaped like an iron hammer. Steam was coming from the hammerhead. In the other hand he held the small, brown corpse of a mouse. Peter's face was grizzled with beard-stubble, his eyes lined and darkened with fatigue.

The hammer vibrated. "What is it, boy?" whispered Peter, talking to the weapon. Without bothering to get up, Peter tossed the weapon in an overhead arc through the window, saying, "Snipers on the roof opposite! Get their guns only! Trash the engines of any moving vehicles, then come on back. Through the window this time! No more holes in the walls."

There was a whistling noise outside, shouts, explosions. Peter rubbed his chin and sighed. "Great little toy, that Mollner. If I tell it to hit the nearest target, it'll wag its tail when they move nearer. Smart weapon. Fucking smart weapon. Heh. Oh, by the way, we're trapped."

"What year is it?" asked Lemuel. "Galen's trapped. I saw him in Nastrond. When I went to Vindyamar to consult with the Three Queens, I was snared by the selkie. I shouldn't have gone to sleep without someone watching me, but you weren't . . . there wasn't anyone around once Galen got in trouble. The Archangel Uriel saved me from Acheron. He said we had to save the girl who holds Galen's soul within herself, and that logic, which is a weapon fairies cannot use, will allow us to save her."

"That would be Wendy Ravenson. So Uriel saved you, huhn? I guess everything I did was just extra. So you're welcome anyway." Lemuel reached up and felt the crown of laurel leaves around his head; and he saw the laurel leaves, sunflowers, and birchleaves tied in garlands arranged along the foot of his bedspread.

Lemuel started to get up, "I'm glad that, after all these years, you have returned to your appointed duties as Guardian of Everness. But men only get thanked for doing what is above and beyond what the minimum . . ."

Peter thrust himself one-handed out of the wheelchair, grabbed Lemuel's shoulder, and they both fell to one side of the bed and to the floor.

"Son! What the . . ."

A smoke canister smashed into the window, emitting fumes, and sailed through the air above the bed, clattering off the far wall. A rifle shot also cracked through the air. At that noise, Lemuel started violently, uttering an involuntary shriek of panic. He had, after all, never heard a gun go off near him before.

Peter carefully put the mouse corpse in his shirt pocket, said, "Shut up. Heads down. Mollner, back to my hand. Fast!"

A whistling roar tore the air. The smoking hammer, wet with machine oil and gasoline, slapped into Peter's upraised hand. "Kill the fucker who just took a potshot at us," he said. "But golf that gas shell out of the window first."

And he threw it.

Lemuel, in a heap on the floor, took a moment to regain his breath. He rubbed one hand across his bald head, amazed at how frightened he was. He said, "The Rod is meant for giants! You mustn't use the powers to kill other men!"

"Watch me."

The hammer, dripping blood, sailed lightly back in through the window and landed in Peter's palm.

A voice, electronically amplified, roared in from outside: "Peter Waylock! You're only making it worse! You know you can't get away! We have armored reinforcements coming . . ."

Peter said, "Knock that bullhorn out of his hands, don't hit him, come back. Use the window. Wait. Use the door, go down the corridor, don't hit anybody along the way. They must be watching the window to see when I throw. You got all that, boy? Good boy. Go!" And he threw the hammer.

The door was smashed to flinders. The hammer turned the corner and rocketed down the corridor.

"So you believe in magic now, I take it?"

"Gloat if you want, Dad. But makes you look like a dumb-ass."

"And the mouse?"

Peter lightly touched his shirt pocket. "Saved my fucking life. Couldn't help the little guy; couldn't get the doctors here to do shit for it. All I could do was Morpheus-zap it so it was asleep when it went, not in pain."

The electronic voice fell silent with a snarled shriek. Peter shouted in a loud voice: "Hey! You out there! We still got sick people in here! You gas this place, lot of sick people going to kick off!"

The hammer shot back in through the window and landed in Peter's hand.

There was no reply, but there was motion, voices murmuring in fear. "They're up to something . . ." snarled Peter.

Lemuel whispered, "Where is the Key?"

Peter grunted, "Wendy's got it. Don't know where she is. She flew off. Galen got killed by a guy named Raven. Nice guy. Wendy's husband. I'm going to hate to have to kill him."

"You talk about killing a lot, son."

"He murdered Galen, or helped someone murder him, and let all this shit, all these nightmare-things, into the world."

"Still, to speak so lightly of killing, my son. That's not good."

"What the hell do you know about good, Dad? You had this magic stuff all these years, and you never used it. I'm not even going to ask you about my legs again. If I had just had this hammer when I was in the field, do you know how many of my people would still be alive?"

"I won't open an old argument, son, but you know I could do nothing about your paralysis. The day after we argued, the day after you left for the last time, I had a dream that night that Oberon himself said we could not use the magic except for our high cause . . ."

"Shut up about your fucking high cause! There's riots in the street right now. Chicago is in flames! So's LA. They got tanks on the highways blowing up trucks 'cause some truckers shot at some roadblocks! Don't you get it? This ain't America anymore! We're some bumfucked Third World banana republic. We're about to have a civil war."

Lemuel went pale, and he whispered to himself aloud: " 'The falcon cannot hear the falconer; things fall apart; the centre cannot hold; mere anarchy is loosed upon the world, the blood-dimmed tide is loosed . . . ' "

"That a spell?"

"I wish it were. Yeats. He had second sight."

"Can you Morpheus the guys out there shooting at us? I don't know their names."

"Easily. I could do it with a magnet out of the phone there. But I won't. We are supposed to be maintaining the barrier between worlds, not weakening it."

"Listen, Dad. Have you ever thought that maybe your orders were out of date?"

"What?"

"Your HQ gave you a certain post to guard, right? King Arthur or someone, right? Have you ever guarded a real post in real life? No? Well, I have. When the wire is cut, and your lines are breached, and the enemy is already in the camp, you don't fucking stay at the gatehouse. You get your piece and start blowing the bad guys away."

"But these are men outside. They have been deceived by the Enemy."

"Listen. You think the troopers I fought in Southeast Asia and South America weren't deceived by the enemy? Kids too young to shave, farm-boys drafted from some stone-age village in the middle of the jungle, probably after their family's one cow was collectivized by the Reds. Brainwashed, told lies, and handed a gun. You think the young Jap boys they welded into their cockpits to go nosedive into a Yankee warship for the glory of the emperor weren't deceived, or the Arab kids the Mullahs wrap up in belts of dynamite to go blow up some Jewish old folk's home for the glory of Allah aren't deceived? I fucking know they're deceived. And I'm trying to be nice to these guys, nicer than it's smart to be. But the rule is: someone shoots at you; you shoot back."

Lemuel flinched again when he heard a loud noise outside. His heart was hammering. But he saw the calm, hard look on his son's face, and his heart expanded with an unexpected pride. Here, on the bloody battlefield, was his son's place.

"I'm sorry, Son. Sorry for a lot of things. Who is guarding the house?"

"Yeah. I'm sorry too, Dad. For a lot of things. Azrael de Gray's men have the house."

"If he gets the Silver Key as well, the world is doomed. How far from the house are we?"

"Texas. You got some magic way of getting from Texas to Maine real fast?"

"No. But you do. Smite the hammer on the ground and call out these names three times: Tanngrisner and Tanngjost."

"Who they hell are they?"

Another rifle shot rang out. Peter threw the hammer and it came back blood caked.

Lemuel was saying, ". . . like the dream-colts but from the world of Vanir. They will serve whoever holds the Rod of Mollner."

"Great. Snooze these guys before the reinforcements arrive. If we still had free press in this country, they wouldn't be taking shots at us. These aren't cops. Soon as they decide the sick people here are expendable, they'll gas us."

Lemuel said, "What happened to the press?"

Peter said, "For the duration of the emergency. They passed a law. I think your goblins hypnotized Congress, or replaced them with look-alikes or something."

Lemuel said in a voice of quiet horror, "Selkie murder and flay the men they impersonate. If the selkie replaced them, those men are dead."

"Then there is a lot of dead guys in the government these days, in the press, and anywhere else anybody starts asking questions. I bet half these officers out here are seals, and I don't mean Special Forces. If you don't want me to hammer 'em, find us a way to get the hell outta here."

Lemuel crawled along the floor, pulled on the phone cord, and the phone dropped into his hand. "North Star's blood! On thee I call, let all below your unblinking eye now understand; they are in your power; you are in my hand . . ."

Meanwhile, Peter struck the floor and called the names.

He didn't expect the roof of the corridor to collapse.

Out of the wreckage, shouldering their way through the doorfame, came two goats. Their eyes were made of flame, and they chewed on sparks of lightning-bolts, and fire spurted from their hooves when they stepped, breaking floorboards underfoot. Straps of a harness made of bone and woven hair crisscrossed their shoulders.

"Shit!" shouted Peter, when one of the beasts put its horns below the bed and flung the whole huge weight across the room with a toss of its neck. Lemuel, scrambling to his feet, dodged out of the way, and the toppling bed missed him.

The other goat put its head through the concrete blocks of the wall, and was knocking bricks out with sweeps of its horns, as if trying to bring the wall down.

Peter raised the hammer. "Mollner! Smash them!" But both goats dropped to their knees when he said that and bowed their fiery heads.

It was silent outside now, except for an occasional snore.

Lemuel said, "They won't let anyone on their backs. But they will pull a chariot. I don't know where to find a . . ."

"Use the wheelchair. You can sit in my lap."

Lemuel helped drag Peter over. The goats snorted sparks and lowered their horns when they saw someone touching Peter, but Peter waved them back by threatening them with the hammer.

Lemuel said softly, "Think you can handle them?"

"No worse than any raw recruits. Here! Tanngjost! Come here or I'll whap your fucking face off! Good boy. Hey, you like to be scratched behind the ear?" He ran his nails through the hair of the demonic creature, who snorted happily, drooling sparks on the broken floor. "Now, let me hook your harness here up to . . . uh, the chair arms I guess. Dad? You know how to drive a chariot?"

"Yes. That's the guide strap. No, the other one. Don't use the arms; tie the yoke straps under here. Look. I'll stand on the back of the wheelchair and hang on. Keep one hand free to hold the hammer."

"This ain't going to work."

Lemuel put his feet on the little metal crossbar at the base of the wheelchair and tied himself in place with his belt. Then he put a gentle hand on his son's broad shoulder. "We had best pray it does work, my son. The glad fact that I am here among the living is a bad omen. Very bad. It means Acheron is rising. We have less than a day left. Once the City of Hideous Night raises its towers into the air of Earth, the Morningstar will rise to the zenith, the Sun will fail, and only those whom it amuses the Emperor of Darkness to preserve as pets will be spared."

"Giddyup. Take off, boys. Hey! Tanngrisner! You want me to stick this hammer up your ass?"

The goats ran forward, struck down the wall with their horns, and leapt into the air. Peter felt the wheelchair begin to fall, and he put the Hammer underneath his seat. The same force that propelled the hammer and allowed it to change course in midair now gently held up the wheelchair.

A five-story drop opened up beneath them. Lemuel, face green, watched the bricks and rubble toppling slowly into the alleyway underfoot.

Then they were above the level of the buildings, in some small, widespread suburbia Lemuel had never seen before. Beyond was desert. The streets surrounding the hospital were crowded with sleeping soldiers and armored vehicles, and a pair of sharpshooters lay in pools of blood on a rooftop falling away below.

Fog obscured the view; then they were above the clouds. "Where to?" shouted Peter, back over the roar of the wind.

"Everness! All forces of light and dark must be gathering there! Whoever has the Key must go there to use it; and maybe we can get there in time to save this Wendy. And . . . Well. Thank you for saving me, Son."

"No sweat, Dad. Let's go." But Peter was beaming.

Now Peter shouted at the goats: "Faster, boys! You wimps! A lame moose could crawl faster than this! Come on! Hyah! Giddup! Show me something to make your mamas proud!"

The two demon creatures roared in wrath, belching fire and smoke, put down their shaggy heads, and ran across the tops of the clouds. The screaming pressure of the wind grew and grew.

It grew suddenly, strangely silent when they passed the speed of sound.

13

In the Court
of the
Faerie King

I

Once, within a midnight grove, a pavilion as lightly built and silvery-fair as falling water stood, and, to either side, climbed trellises of white and dusky roses, and their dew-touched petals breathing perfumes. Behind this fair pavilion stood rank on rank of sober and silent trees, ancient as the world, heavily cloaked in green, heavily shadowed, and before the pavilion, a small, clear pool had captured the image of the Moon within its marble circle.

Reclining on a couch within the pavilion was a dark-haired beauty raimented in a tight-bodiced, puff-shouldered gown of mingled emerald and forest greens hugging her with lightest silks. Little silver chains circled her neck and hips; and on her finger was a girasol like a spot of blood.

On the grass floor of the pavilion, near where her white fingers gently drooped, burned a miniature lantern like a star. Her face was without blemish, her features finely chiseled, small of chin, high of cheek, and her darling nose was tip-tilted like the petal of a flower.

So young and fair was she, that to look at her white hands, delicate shoulders, round bosom, slim waist, and well-shaped legs, one would have thought her a maiden of less than seventeen summers; if she had raised her lidded, dreaming gaze, and if one had the misfortune to be caught within the gaze of her clear, gray eyes, one would have thought her older than a thousand winter times. And if one saw the faint shadow of a smile that which curved her perfect rose-red lips, one would have been curious, and, if one were not of heroic character, curiosity would have grown to fear. For the smiles of immortals always should give pause to mortals, to whom death is not a stranger.

It was clear she was dreaming of her lover, for her smile was sweet, and her one hand drifted lightly across the scented fabric of her gown, wistfully, and ever and anon her lips would part.

The smile sharpened, and the dreaminess turned to coldness in her eye when a voice came from the forest.

"Ill met by moonlight, proud Titania!"

She swayed to her feet as lightly as a flower, but with the silken suppleness of a bent épée returning to true. She reached out with her hand to where streaks of moonlight rayed through the trellis-work; she broke off a section of moonbeam in her hand to be her scepter. The blossoms of pale roses behind her fluttered in the air, like white butterflies, and circled her head, to poise atop her coiffure, a delicate crown.

The tall trees now bowed and moved aside with a whispering rustle of roots. Within the newborn corridor of trunks stood a king crowned in the plumages of black swans, two wings of midnight rising to either side from his floating hair of storm-cloud hue. His face was youthful and beardless, but pale as polished horn. Beneath the straight strokes of his eyebrows, his left eye was a deep, unfathomable pool of archaic wisdom. His right eye, if eye he had, was hidden behind a patch, and perhaps he kept it in another world, or to see things others could not view.

He had a philosopher's brow and a long, straight nose; serious lines embraced a wide, thin-lipped mouth, pursed in a kingly gravity; and yet a foxy cleverness curved at the corners of the mouth, promising dimples; as if this soul held a vast and wild mirth, a trickster's mania, held, for now, in check.

A gorget of silver links protected his shoulders and throat. A web of black tissue floated from his shoulder-boards. His breastplate and kilt and greaves were of vertical strips of silver and jet, alternately polished as mirrors and dark as night, so that, in the striping of the Moon-shadows through the trees, no right judgment could be made of him; so that he may have been man-sized and standing close at hand, or yet he may have been gigantic, and standing far off, or both at once.

Behind him came his train of courtiers and paladins, which, unlike her own, were visible.

"What, jealous Oberon! Fairies, skip hence; I have forsworn his bed and company." Her voice rang cold with pride, soft, but clear. She turned. A murmuring rustle in the grass, a chime of silver voices in the air, made as if to follow in her wake.

Oberon raised a regal hand: "Tarry, rash wanton! Am I not thy lord?"

She looked across her shoulder, her face made more beautiful with amusement and hauteur. "Then I must be thy lady. But I know my daughter thou hast stolen out of my keeping, and swept on secret wing to thy close-faced citadel of high Mommur, there to prison her with toys and idle figments."

"Stolen to her safety, ill-spoken Queen. For your Neverdale is now the rout of monsters; and dragons sent by Morningstar gulf those happy meadows with

Vulcan's spews, while lordly elfs of darkness stride the ruins, ensigns proud on high, and kick through embers with sullen boot to seek thy bastard get, and what she bears. Now both she and it be safely clasped within Mommur's orichalcum doors. Nor does she weep, but plays at simple small delights; she hath forgotten earthly things, herself . . . and thee."

She said, "Oh, webbed in thy own weft, thou spider! Hopest thou to swallow down the plum of victory she carries lightly in her palm? And within thine own court as well, ever in thy shadow, ever in thy one-eyed sight? What torment dost thou pike thyself upon, to scent the savor of that plum, yet ne'er to taste!"

Oberon held up the scepter he carried; it was the horn of a unicorn.

"Behold the Silver Key of Everness, once more clasped in destined gauntlet."

"Vaunt not, Oberon, for it avails thee not. Freely given, 'twould yield thee sovereignty o'er all men's world as thou hast now of fairyland; stolen, 'tis but trinket dross."

Now he laughed in light self-mockery, and a moment of firefly-light came and went in his one eye. "Freely given, and by her hand, it was, and a dozen times it was, yestere'en and yestere'en before that, and so a dozen eventides: once as a jest, once at my pretty asking, once more staked in a game of chess, and again, this she gave to see me whistle a pond-frog to hop high, and again, to see me charm a wren to build a nest within the tangles of mine hair, while I stood stock-still from moon's noon to moonset, and thus, while she ever tickled me. I could love her, were she not the egg of thy unlawful love."

He tucked the unicorn horn in his belt, and crossed his arms across his chest, while the wind played with his filmy cape, which rose like fogs about him. Now he said, "Fairy-knights and courtiers of my great house,

depart! What secret things to pass 'twixt lord and wife
are too fine for your ears!"

But she said, "Nuada Silverhand, and thou, Taliesin,
I charge thee stay; and Hermod, who braved the si-
lences of hell; Donohue and Diancecht, fly not hence;
nor stir thy foot, Tam Lin; for here is matter for a song!
Wise Gwydion, your wisdom will grow greater if you
tarry; and I promise you, sweet Puck, favorite of my
lord, you will know his mind the better if you quell
your winged shoe, and lean on thy caduceus, to hear
great Oberon admit his fault, and crawl to his wronged
queen for favor!"

"What? Hence, my court! I bid thee fly!" he said.

"I fly as well, fairy-land's foul king, if they not stay.
What boots a triumph without ovation and the bay-leaf
crown?" said Titania, and a night breeze began to
pulse and blow at her, and she grew weightless as a
thistledown.

Oberon raised his hand; the gentle wind stilled. And
he said, "I cry defeat, good madam, if thou wilt restore
thy foot to grass. But wronged? What word is that
which spoils thy fair lip? Tell me which hand of mine
wronged thee by slap or scratch and I'll hold it to cold
iron!"

She descended, but her foot did not bend the tips of
the grass where she placed one slipper-toe.

"Not by thy hand, O King, but by thy cruelty, who
would cage mankind in paradise."

"And is this wrong so wrong when measured out by
hands as treason-red as thine? Who had made a cuck-
old of the king, adultery and treason at once? Who has
sent her lover to slay the sacred beast that guarded
once our realm, now shrunken, weakened, blackened
in memory, and made a mock for children? Once wide
empires of the daylit world trembled at my frown;
now only out-of-fashion poets know me; and even
they, in children's tale, would shrink my lords and

gentlemen of this fair court to thumb-sized imps, and deck them out with lepidoptera wings! Ah, grief! Not to be endured!"

Now he took on a frown, and his voice darkened to a deeper note. "And where now is my brightest knight, peerless in war and deep in wisdom, once the glory and the terror of a thousand lands? In what dark pits is Morningstar sunk low, and whose fair hands have pushed him hence? Were I to credit woman's cunning equal to a man's, would I idly toy with notions that all that has occurred is at thy weaving."

"You forget yourself, sir. I am older than art thou, and annual kings once died at Nemi to placate me."

"Madam? Shall I call down the constellations?" and he raised his hand on high.

She laughed a silver laugh. "Shatter not thy heaven's dome to show thou art its architect and master. Ere we were wed, thou wast the king of sky as I was queen of earth, I well recall, and cherish still the lights and gifts sent down to woo me. Yet I recall as well the recent causes of mine royal ire; nor will my majesty be put aside for thee. Come! This gathered company awaits the word of thy defeat! Ask thou me for quarter?"

"Quarter?" Now he pursed his lips, and his single eye, mysterious and gray, looked challengingly upon the queen. "Admit I will that the Silver Key of Everness must be given by its holder unto me, yea, full freely. And now I know as well that thy daughter's right wits must be restored to her before such gift be gift. What is given in giddiness remains ungiven still."

"She is half our blood, and the sly tricks and sleights of mutable law which render mortal kind such fools and play for our cruel delight cannot bespot her."

"But here is matter for a wager, if the fairy-queen has gall for it. Titania would loose the bounds of sovereignty, which once immortals held to check men's folly, and delighteth she to see the golden age forsaken, drown'd in mist of passing aeons. But how now? Are mortals indeed so worthy to rule earth? Rule, aye, and poison? When rulership is folly, even fools would abdicate. So wager I. Is Titania willing to put her light speech to heavy test?"

"Speak thy terms, king of dreams."

"Just this. Restore thy daughter's right full wits, and I will show her a vision of what the earth would be were the scepter of ivory mine once more. You shall not be there, nor any serf of thine speak any word of yours to her. If I ask, and she refuse, very well, instantly, and with no harm nor loss, no geas, nor lien, I shall place her to any boundary of my realm she choose, free as air, to go or stay, so please her. But if I ask and she grant than I am king of earth and sky once more, father both of gods and men; the same true king whom once you wed; and thy pale excuse, that you wed earth's king and not earth's king in exile shall be shown all false; and you shall come to my bed again and be thou mine, and foreswear quite this Anton Pendrake whose ring you wear. Have you so much trust in these foolish mortals that you will put their freedom, and your own, into the balance scales against the simple judgment of a girl?"

"Upon such simple judgments do all free republics stand or fall. I take thy terms, but on this condition strict: utter truth must thou speak to her, and must ask her within this hour, and at her first refusal, thou art lost, and with no second asking."

Oberon laughed. "Within the month."

"To-day. It will not avail thee to rule earth if earth is not more than an ash-heap in the shadow of black Acheron."

"'Tis done, 'tis done. I'll ask to-day, for 'tis all one."

"Then take this courtier of mine, an humble meadow mouse, who has saved your wayward servant Peter Waylock, and was sent back to sleep here before grim Death ate his earthly flesh. He carries her name, and can restore her. Muris! Rise! I name thee now Paridae! The lightest brush of my wand gives you the shape always you have craved, and cloaks you in feathered wings. Mouse no more, but Titmouse now, go to, and sing my daughter's memory to life. But, as at my word, nor further speak to her, for Oberon must plead and fail his case ere she escapes his gilded cage."

" 'Tis done, then, madam; and when next we meet, see thou wear thy bridal-dress again for I carry you to bridal-bed."

"What are your dreams? Small things stood next to glories wrought by heroes as my Pendrake is!"

II

Oberon was not pleased to hear the name of Pendrake.

"He shall not be king, madam, for his blood runs untrue."

"Untrue, sayst thou? The child of Mordred and Gwenhwyfach was Melehan, who wed Lisanor and bore Loholt, father of Amhar, father of Borre, father of Woden, called the Terrible, from whom all the Northmen of the Conquest times and after claim their patrimony: and from Uther's line, his grandfather was Constantine, whose Latin house is rooted in the seed of wandering Aeneas, who comes of ill-starred Priam; and by that reckoning, all Europe and all Asia falls within his scepter's sway, and every land over which the Roman Eagles flew, or the twinned crosses of British sovereigns, supported by fair unicorn and savage lion, or purer lilies of France, and what was claimed of old by Spanish kings or fierce Germanic tribes, or of the Hapsburg emperors, or else the Labarum of Byzantine fame. Is there an inch of Earth where never fell the conquering footstep of some child of Troy, or Rome, or Camelot? Was not Arthur Priam come again, and imperator of Rome?"

"What was Arthur," Oberon replied, with dry, ironic scorn, "but a single king whose dynasty ended with himself, betrayed by barren wife unfaithful, and at his highest power, ruled but a little bit of Welsh and Northumbrian Land? Through what twisted and forgotten genealogies can you trace the golden thread of deposed monarchs long crownless and unnamed, and put the wreath of bold Aeneas on the brow of some common man, and claim, Here is the Lord of Troy and Troynovant, and all the Earth besides?"

"First by birth, and next by merit of his deeds: for though the world has long forgotten who is eldest of the eldest line, the fairy-queen has not: nor has Fame dispraised all the Drakes and Gordons of his line, or all the gray-eyed men (which is the mark and legacy of his blood) whose strange adventures, though swallowed up in Mists of Everness, yet still the Queen of Otherworld, and all her courtiers, recall and praise: Carter, Caine, and Kinnison, their escutcheons bright, still grace the silver walls of Sessremnir, my hall, and deeds there figured are not forgotten, though unremarked on Earth: and all these heroes of the latter days share common ancestors with the Pendrake name. And he is greatest of his great house; nor am I ungrateful for the deed my Anton did in Inquanok, which earned of him thy enmity."

"What boots it?" said the dark monarch. "Great deeds or none done by his hand, yet they shall never grasp the scepter. There is nowhere in human lands where kings are kings, save where toiling multitudes suffer under iron rods of tyrants in Arabic sands or sad Affrick shores; crowned heads who bow to parliaments, I reckon not."

"And yet in dreams when men say Here is King, tis Arthur's name who first comes to praising lips, not Barbarosa, thy ward. Who of the sleeping kings has greatest fame, sayst thou? Brian Boru, or Heimdall's sons, or your forgotten emperor, or the lord who held the sword I yielded him from the lake-waters of Avalon, and, at my behest, drove with the Cross of Christ all Fir-bolg of the faerie-mounds and pagan imps away from British towns and hearts? Ah, how your piskies shrieked and fled when churchbells rang!"

"And thine as well. You wound yourself to wound me: is your womanish hate so fierce?"

"I need not the praise of all the world, and do not covet lands when moon-light does not shine: the praise of my mortal lover is enough, and he be my true lord, true of heart."

"No lordship, his. The Pendragon heir will not be crowned."

She laughed a silvery laugh. "That, I yield thee. For coronets he holds in scorn. Proud and wild America will not endure the scepter that the sleepy sons of Europe seek: and when they dream of justice, it is of Robin Hood, and Gaberlunzie they speak, for Americans deem Justice flies into the wilderness, when the town by savage tyranny is ruled, and lives in the hearts of simple men, when she is missing from the halls and courts of high estate."

"Then he knows his humble place, nor should his common hands, mired with the reek of earthly toil, have dared to touch the lily whiteness of my Queen. The day the Horn of Everness is mine again, that same day your Pendrake dies! My wrath will not be gentle with baseborn mortals who make thee harlot."

"Fie on thee, thou two-mouthed hypocrite, who says and unsays his sworn word as swift as mortals breathe but in and out! Bring forth Io and Europa and Leto and Maia, Thetis and Metis and Mnemosyne, Callisto and Gunnlod and Erda, and every buxom English milkmaid you have dragged by the hair into your rough bed, or surprised by night in tangled green wood, and let them vow your constancy! How often Hymenaeus has been abused by you, or Vor who watches marriage vows! I am done with thee, father of bastards; and my hero will defy thee, surely as his daughter will. Your time is done, your tide is ebbed; and even as the changeful moon eclipses her fair face from silver-litten nights, so too I turn my face from thee, who could have been my Lord, had thou been true. Begone! To frown at thee were too much favor!"

His one eye narrowed, and a fire seemed to be in it, but he smiled a small smile and spoke in a mild, lilting whisper: "Exiled of my rightful realm, I know well why I earn thy scorn; but soon the worlds are mine again, nor will my fealty be foresworn, by every mortal who forgets his dreams with morn. 'Tis realmlessness, not faithlessness, thy queenly heart doth shun; when my estate is once more great, thy love and adoration shall triflingly be won."

With this, she flourished high the silver beam that served her as a scepter, crying out, "Arch-seducer, yet so little of womenish-kind you know! No crown regained will win mine heart, nor any dignity sword or scepter can bestow. Now, my faerie folk, away! We will chide thee if we longer stay!"

The wind picked her lightly up, and she whirled away, dancing like an Autumn leaf; and all about her in the air, the gleams of dew from the grass, and the colors of moonlight followed her in wide, wild circles, so that some part of the beauty of the night and the hues and glamour of the night-world seemed to fade and fail as she was gone.

Robin Goodfellow picked up his wand, about which two serpents coiled, saying, "Good, my Lord, vex not thy brow with frowns. Mortal men be fools withal. If they will sell their freedom for a piece of gold on earth, or half of one, how much quicker will they shed all manliness to sup the golden apples of the sun?"

"My faerie court, dance and wassail! 'Tis mine command!" called Oberon, gesturing hugely with his scepter, "Rejoice! The golden vales of paradise un-

lock, once Clavargent rests again in hand, men shall be
free of pain and strife, and we shall walk once more in
waking life; dream-treasures shall unheap a generous
horde, and our empire and empress both restored! The
sea of dreams shall o'erflood and rule again the daylit
land!"

But his one eye still lingered where his queenly wife,
her train, and all her beauty had departed in the moonlight.

III

A princess sat on a bench of carven ivory beneath a
linden tree, dressed in a gown of green and gold which
fell in long, smooth folds of cloth to the mingled grass
and forget-me-nots of the King's walled garden. There
was a silver-basined fountain not far away, where a
path bordered by hedges of red roses crossed a path
boundaried by white lilies. Here and there within the
garden were little statues of antic gnomes on pedestals
of white marble; and she laughed whenever she saw
one twitch or blink when honeybees or little wrens lit
on them.

There were many things to laugh at nowadays, little
delights each twilight and each dusk. (It did not occur
to her to wonder why it never was quite full daylight
here in this lovely land, never noon-time.) The court
went hawking and hunting, dressed as falcons or as
whippet-hounds; and danced each night on hillsides,
or deep forests, by fountains or by brooks; and once
upon the sea-strands the court had held its gay celebrations, and mermaid music welled up from the waves.

At times she played chess with the King, and she had
made friends with the White Queen's Knight, a little
homunculus in armor with a helmet like a horse's head.

But her greatest joy was Tom. Tom had once been

small, but, drinking from a magic spring at midnight deep in a hidden grot, had grown to human size, a tall, fine blond-haired lad, square-jawed and fresh of face. And now he flirted and paid her court with laughter and solemn grace, half-serious and deadly serious at once.

She had put him off again, wondering if she should wed him as he asked. Each time she toyed with the idea of agreeing to the match, some hidden memory would trouble her, some formless doubt, and she would ask again of the King why her mother could not come to visit her here in Mommur.

The King gave the answer he always gave and, to put her off, gave her, in trade for her horn of unicorn, a key to his secret, walled garden behind the palace. It was ever calm here, and only the music, which sprang, spontaneous, from the air, composed of drifting, lilting cords, attended her. It was lit at night with floating lights, and, by twilight, by the silver rainbow that issued from the castle's silver-shingled roof. This was the King's processional way, a road of moonlight leading at once to all parts of his kingdom, guarded by Hiemdall, a quiet, watchful spirit, with hair and beard of white, and eyes so bright no one but she could look directly in them without flinching.

The greatest treasure of the hidden garden was the fountain; for it was a wellspring of knowledge.

She had been playing with the mirror at the bottom of the pond, making it show her what she would look like garbed differently, or with different hair. Then, her fancy running free, she asked to see what she would look like if she were dusky-skinned, or Nubian, or from Cathay; or what she would look like ten years hence, or ten years past; or what she would look like as a red-lipped succubus from Hell. That image was alluring and frightening. Then she asked what she would look like as an angel from high heaven; and the solemn, beautiful face, crowned with living light, had looked back at her with such wisdom and such solemn pity, that she had shrunk back, certain she had done something not quite right, and frightened for the first time she could remember since . . .

Since when . . . ?

The King came gliding along the pathway, passing between tall, slim, cherry blossom trees, and the scarlet and indigo colors of the dusk striping the clouds above him with subtle hues, and the first fireflies flickering in clouds around him, giggling and whispering. The King's one eye burned like a distant star.

The King was dressed in twilight and moonlight, and wore dark fog for his cloak, and he was crowned with the wings of a black swan. In one hand a little gray bird was chirruping merrily.

"A gift for you, Princess. A sad and heavy gift, but one that will make you glad."

The titmouse flew from his hand and landed near her. She reached out a shy hand to pet it. "That's silly! How can it be both?"

"This little bird has your soul in him."

And when she was done with weeping, and had dried her tears, the King came again, and sent away the maidens and jester-monkeys sent to comfort her. Now he pointed at the silver pool. "Tell me what you wish to see."

Wendy looked up. "Where's Raven?"

"Behold." And the image in the pool showed Raven in a prison cell. His cheeks were drawn and pale; his gaze was haggard and haunted. In grim silence he fought with an ugly man who threatened him; not saying a word, Raven broke the man's fingers one at a time.

"My valley," she said.

"Behold." The Weeping Willows had been uprooted, piled into a bonfire, about which gibbering apelike things with heads like swine were leaping and cavorting. Rushing Brook was befouled with filth. Green Meadow was all trampled into bloody muck. Grinning seal-man sailors stood near a derrick, plucking feathers from dead birds. Armored wormlike things with crocodile heads writhed and slid along the ground, snarling, and belching burning sulfur.

On the toppled ruins of the doorless tower, stood Azrael de Gray, dressed in robes of midnight blue and black, gazing out across the devastation. A conical cap begirt with constellations was on his head, and a floating scarf of palest blue drifted down across his back. Near him, plumes waving in the fiery breeze, stood two angels crowned in smoke and hell-flame, creatures of perfect handsomeness.

One was speaking, ". . . the legions still upon yon scarp encounter ever greater numbers of the enemy, and battle waxeth furious. More from Acheron must we summon, wizard."

The other angel spoke, a voice too beautiful and heartless for human voice: "It is our own forces we engage, O wizard. We are caught within the meshes of an enchantment."

Azrael de Gray held up his hand. "We are being overheard. I feel the pressure of a fairy's gaze. Oberon! You shall not acquire the Silver Key! I call upon the four ruling cities of man, Jerusalem the holiest, Enoch the eldest, Agartha the hidden, and Rome the world's crown, to witness my curse . . ."

The King uttered a soft word, and the pool went dark.

He said, "Now I wish to show you, not what you would, but what I would. Here is your world. This is Edoubi Kenzai of Ethiopia. She is starving. The baby she holds, for once, has stopped crying, and she is glad; she does not yet realize she holds a corpse. The babe is dead of malnutrition. This is Dmitri Varechenko. He has been imprisoned in a work camp in Siberia because he survived a battle. He was falsely accused of cowardice and treason. His official sentence expired long ago; but the records have been lost. He suffers because of a clerk's mistake. Here is Alfred Anderson.

He is dying of a cancer. This is Linda Severn. She was to be married this week; see how happily she displays her white dress in the looking glass? Her fiancé is a clerk in a bank who has just been murdered during a failed robbery. This pile of skulls is in a field in Cambodia, victims of conquest. Here are the faces of some of those widowed to make that monument. Here is Sigmund Idverrtsen. He is lost in the snow and shall perish. This is Alison Guicciardio. She is an inmate at an insane asylum. This is Alison's sister Beatrice, who suffers nightmares created by her causeless guilt. This man is Hamir Cohen. He has murdered twelve people in a temple at prayer. This is Elizabeth Rienholt, who is lonely, this man, Henry Vandermer, would be perfect for her, and, if they wed, would cherish her with perfect tenderness and great love. They will never meet. Here is Raschid Washington, dying of a drug overdose, his pants dirtied by his own filth. Here is . . ."

Wendy said, "This is really sad! Gross, too. Why are you showing me these things?"

He turned to her. The eye of Oberon was deep, mysterious, and looking into it was not like looking at any human eye, but like looking into the infinite night sky. "I wish to show you the depth and fullness of human suffering. Know that for each one I have shown you here, a million others share horrors equal, if not in sudden flashes of red blood, then in long, gray days of blind misery."

"You just want the unicorn horn, I bet. I must have given it to you a million times when I didn't know what it was. I guess those times don't count. Do you like being sneaky?"

"You know now my whole purpose in compassing your rescue, and the hidden reason for your happy exile in my palace of delight. The Silver Key of Everness, once mine, I wish to wield again. All these harms can be made hale, and starvation; pestilence, war, and murder can be banished. Even loneliness can be alleviated."

"If I give you the unicorn horn, right?"

Oberon raised his hand and pointed. At the far end of the garden, a space of the wall that was deeply shadowed and hidden by overarching pines, now grew light. Between the pines Wendy now saw a barred gate of gold.

Sunlight streamed through the bars. Wendy saw the green hills and blue pools, wide trees, and lush, bright flowers. The scent brought a freshness and forgotten memory to her, so that to breathe it was to smile.

At one of the nearer ponds, a stately lion lay couchant, with lambs and rabbits nibbling the grass between his paws.

"Oh my!" she said, "How long have we been away . . . ?"

"All your race recalls, perhaps in dreams, this golden age."

"It's the Garden of Eden! Oh, how lovely!"

"Come, child. Let us walk closer." And they strode across the twilight lawns of the King's walled garden to the gate. Wendy put her hands on the bars, closed her eyes, drawing deep breaths. Then she opened them again, looking at the wide champaigns, the stately arbors, and, midmost in the garden, two tall trees atop a high, green hill.

She giggled. "How come paradises always look so much like earth?"

"Ask, rather, why earth so closely resembles paradise. The Demiurge created the daylit world to have all of heaven's glories in her; many of your wild places, untouched by man, have not yet forgotten fairest heaven."

"Can we go in? Oh, please, can we? I won't mess anything up or eat any apples or anything. Please? Pretty please."

Oberon put his head down near her ear, whispering, "The Silver Key can unlock that gate. One wave of the Unicorn Horn, and this dream can step full formed into the waking world. The bounty of the earth can cure all hunger with her abundance."

Wendy tilted her head aside. "I guess that would be nice . . ." She wore her favorite expression, one eyebrow cocked high, her mouth pursed in a skeptical moue.

Oberon raised his hand. In the garden beyond the gates, all the flowering trees put forth fruit, the grasses grain, with the suddenness of dream. "See, the Earth puts forth her full abundance without stint. There can be no hunger here. Nor shall any war or murder go unavenged, not while my well of wisdom, Hlidskjalf, shows me all human secrets. Look at that herb which grows on yon leafy bank; it is called panacea, and it cures all bodily ills, plagues, cancers. Look at that tree round which the mighty and wise serpent curls. Here are the apples of Hesperides, which restore the aged to youth."

He turned to her, drawing himself erect. "Even as we speak, men die. Those deaths we can prevent, once the unicorn horn is mine. Ask what questions you may have for me. I will lay my heart bare."

"Why doesn't Azrael want you to have the Key?"

"He is an evil man, proud and selfish."

"Can people build houses in paradise? My daddy is an architect, and sometimes the zoning people won't let him built the way he wants to."

"Human art shall glorify nature rather than demean, and masons shall labor only in moderation. Beautiful houses only shall be allowed, for ugliness is pain: quaint cottages of wood, noble castles of stone; but not so far as will do forest or mountain harm."

"How about factories? Can we build factories in Eden? Daddy was really proud of one factory he designed in California."

"Industriousness and honest work bring joy, and on

those we smile. But smoke and poison belched out from drab work-houses? We will not allow a man's momentary love for gold to commit eternal desecration on the earth. There will be no need for all this hurly-burly and commerce if all men are fed and sheltered at the hand of the fairy-king. My coffers cannot run dry."

"And what would inventors do in paradise? My daddy is an also an inventor. He made a special lightweight armor alloy, and it's also really really heat resistant, so it can be used for super–high-speed engine parts . . ."

"Earth, wind, and wave will be made all obedient to my will, and elves shall do all things nature must be persuaded to do, whether to swim, or fly, or carry, raise and lower tides, or calm the giddy thunderstorm. What need, in paradise, to build hulking machines to compel the earth to do what otherwise she would do freely?"

"My daddy is also a lawyer . . ."

Oberon smiled thinly. "Human wisdom shall not be called upon to render justice. The judgment of immortals need not entertain lies and rhetoric."

"What about the Second Amendment? My daddy owns a lot of guns. He wins contests."

"What need for arms? The King's officers shall wield the lightning bolt to smite transgression."

"Great. If we don't like your administration, can we vote you out? Or are we stuck for good? My daddy ran for public office once, but he didn't win."

"Patience will teach those who do not understand my ways. The child cannot wrest the rod from his father's hand."

"Okay. I have one more question. Can you make your paradise so that people like you showed me in the pool can come here to get healed, or to rest, but people like my daddy don't have to come if they don't want? A paradise where people can leave if they don't like it?"

Oberon stepped back so that he was no longer in the

light shed from the locked gates of paradise. His face was a shadow, and Wendy could not see his features.

The voice of Oberon came from his silhouette. "Titania's curse compels me speak. Listen: Bread must be baked before it can be eaten. That is the law of your world. So, too, in this world, dreams must be dreamt before they can be enjoyed. It is the great of the world I must have in my kingdom, not the weak; it is their sacrifice that will sustain the poor and helpless."

"Hmph. I think I see what kind of sacrifice you're talking about. It's my daddy's life, isn't it? You're going to take away everything that makes his life worth living. You just want to kill people like him, don't you? People who make their own dreams come true without any help from you! I'll bet you're jealous!"

Oberon grew to twice his normal size, and there was a murmur of thunder in the echoes of his voice. "It is but one life balanced against so many others!"

"Would you give up your own life?"

"Certainly not! Don't be absurd. But among men it is the great who must be sacrificed to the weak. The Pendragon must shed his blood to feed the earth, that the earth might feed all mankind! It is your modern conceit that kings must no more pay the ancient price that renders your earth so sterile and barren. You recoil?"

"You're talking about human sacrifice! Yeach! Are you crazy?"

"There are worse things. Recall the horror of the faces in the pool! Their suffering is real! Are you utterly without pity? You would not spend one life to save a million?"

"It's not yours to spend! You're just another Koschei the Deathless, except bigger! Now tell me who this Pendragon fellow is. And don't tell me he'll be someone I don't know!"

"You know him."

The sky overhead turned black. Oberon looked up in a posture of surprise. The constellations were fighting. Even as they watched, Orion with his bow shot Scorpio, and the stars all turned to meteoric streaks of falling light.

The earth and sky began to shake, and comets appeared, as planetary spheres jarred against each other.

Volcanoes erupted on the horizon. Against their lurid light, rank on rank, and cloud on cloud of dark angels shined, rising above the storm-winds. To their rear rose leviathans and chimerae, basilisks of more than titan size, brazen scolopendra, medusa shaking snaky locks, and krakens rising like swollen moons, reaching out with many arms like fire.

In the vanguard was a giant with a hundred arms, and on the crest of his huge helmet was a howdah, large as a citadel of iron. On the balconies of that citadel, was a figure too small in the distance to be seen. By some intuition, Wendy knew it was Azrael de Gray.

Oberon stamped his foot; the earthquakes fell silent. "Mother Earth! Raise this my city of Mommur a thousand leagues above the plain; allow my three mighty, all-encircling walls, of copper, of tin, and of orichalcum, to likewise grow."

Suddenly the pure aether was around them, and the constellations equal with the level of the outer wall, or underfoot.

Oberon said aloud: "Eli! Send old age in a fusillade of years among the attacking crew, to render instantly any not of immortal blood withered hulks. My faerie court, attend to me!"

There came a rustle in the air, and princely knights garbed in green and silver knelt now at their sovereign's feet.

"Where is Hiemdall? Why did his all-seeing eye not spy the foe from afar?"

One dressed in winged helm, winged shoes, and holding a wand spiraled by two snakes answered: "Slain, my lord, by treason, and his sword, Hofud, was still sheathed. One came upon him in disguise. I suspect Tom Lanthorn, who has fled."

"Where is Vidar the Silent?"

A one-handed man carrying a sword so sharp that it was painful to look upon it spoke. "From the south came a mighty wolf, whose lower jaws scraped the earth while his upper scraped the sky. Vidar said no word, but went to wrestle with the beast."

"Who else is absent from my call?"

A huge man dressed in a lion's skin and carrying a club of oak now spoke: "Lord Freyr is dead, burnt by the giant Surtvitnir. The weapon destined to destroy him is in the hands of Galen Waylock's father, a mortal whose name I cannot recall. Also, Cu Chulainn in wrath leapt from the walls to grapple with the giant Enceladus."

Oberon turned to Wendy and said, "Yield me the Silver Key, and I will destroy thine enemies, and mine, and drive Acheron down into the bottom of the sea. In Celebradon, guarded by silent angels, sleepers wait for this final battle. Will you not wake them now?"

Wendy said, "No." And she reached over and took the unicorn horn from his hand.

"Mad girl! Will you choose destruction and war above peace and paradise?"

Wendy smiled and laughed. "We'll win our own war, thank you, and build our own Paradise as well, without giving up all our freedom to you, Oberon!"

"Very well," said the elf-king softly. "Yet I will allow you still to yield the Key to me once Acheron's forces enter your homeland. You will have no choice then but to wake the sleepers. Robin! Bear this girl away to any boundary of my wide empire she desires, safely and without mishap."

A dark-skinned knight with an Oriental bow spoke up, "Why is the Key in her hands? Where is Galen Waylock?"

With a rustle, a tall, green-skinned knight dressed

all in green, with hollyhocks in the crest of his helm and bearing a great ax, stepped forward out of empty air. He answered the dark-skinned knight. "Galen Waylock is at the east gate, Arjuna. He bears the Bow of Belphanes. Raven the Titan's son is there as well. He wears the Ring of Niflungar."

Oberon said, "What news, Sir Bertolak?"

"Galen Waylock craves audience, good sire. But not with you; with the young princess here. He says he wishes to plead for her to extend forgiveness to his friend and savior, Raven, son of Raven, whom he excuses from any blame."

Oberon asked, "Why has the enemy not fallen on him?"

"Lightning, thunder, and whirlwind protect them from the foe; and even fallen angels remember to fear the lightning that once blasted them from paradise down to hell."

The ground shook. Arms of flame came over the outer walls, and eerie music. Oberon said, "My court is not for lover's trysts! War rears his head. Let loose the wild hunt! We will show the foe how the rose of Mommur has thorns! Lady? Are you not yet gone? Puck, if she will not choose a place to go, then throw her from the walls!"

"I want to go to Everness," said Wendy. For she was not quite sure whether she wanted to see Raven again or not.

Puck said softly in her ear: "Then, milady, wake! The dream is done; the day is nigh to break!"

And when she had vanished, Puck smiled and muttered, "Or is it that the storm is nigh to break?"

Oberon said, "Go, herald, and tell the wizard called Azrael that the Key of Everness is no more within these walls."

And when, a few moment later, the skies grew clear, and the flames and roars and pure songs of the enemy had faded into silence, the knights of the faerie-court gave forth a cheer, and called for music; and a spring of wine came up from the grass at their feet in celebration, and blossoms from nearby bushes grew into chalices.

Only Oberon looked grim. He was staring at the locked gates of gold between the pines, and he watched while the light grew dim, and the gates were hidden in deep shadow once again, invisible and lost.

IV

"My lord," said Puck, "Will you not take cheer with us?"

Oberon said heavily, "Let us gather our noble and august dead into the Cauldron of Rebirth that they may join us in our revelry on tomorrow's dawn. And where is Tom Lanthorn? I want him brought to me."

But Tom was gone from the court of the faerie-king.

14

The Storm Gathers

I

Squad leader Gilbert Eckhart was miserable. He liked the uniform he had been issued, all black leather and bright polish, and he liked the feel and look of his weapon in his hand, a heavy, solid, and deadly M-16 with a slung M-101 grenade launcher beneath.

He also liked being a member of one of Wentworth's special fighting units. Eckhart hated his country and wanted to see it changed: and he was young and did not care how the change was made. Orders allowed them to take prisoners and hold them without charge, without warrant, without cause, for as long as they liked: and anyone deemed to be a danger was subject to summary execution. No complications, no mess, and, above all, no lawyers. What could be better? The elite squad was meant to act swiftly, with drastic and certain results.

But here he was on a lonely road in upstate Maine,

one of the hundreds of Wentworth's units in the area, guarding some mansion some miles away. Swift? Drastic? He was sitting on his ass doing a whole lot of nothing.

Somewhere there were riots going on. Somewhere there were units of state volunteers in open rebellion against the federal government. Somewhere there was action happening. Somewhere.

Not here.

The morning sunlight streaming through the leaves of early springtime did not lighten his mood. He sat on the hood of the Abrams M1-A1 tank that stood in the middle of this narrow country road, watching some of his men sleeping on the blockade of sandbags, and others arguing over a card game. He knew he should whip them into shape, call them back into order. But somehow, he didn't have the heart.

It was his friend, Sergeant Furlough. Furlough had been acting strangely. At first Eckhart thought it was a joke; that Furlough was playing some sort of mind game with him, trying to weird him out.

Thinking that, Eckhart slid off the tank hull, landing upright on the road. He walked over to where Furlough was crouching on the pavement, staring off down the road, and sniffing.

"Hey, Furlough, what's up? What'ch going to do with your bonus money when it comes? I was going to go in town and find a fine woman and a keg, hey?"

Furlow cocked his head sideways. "Ar! Aye, now, would ye be? But afore ye count yer gold, there's something strange on the winds, ar! Har! Ho, hoy, me bucko! Something powerful bad dangerous I reckon!"

At that point the radioman spoke up, shouting down from the back of the transport truck. "Squad leader, sir! Post Six just gave me a strange report!"

Eckhart walked over, looking over his shoulder at his friend Furlough only once. Then he said, "What's up?"

The radioman's name was Petroff. He was all spit

and polish, upright of posture, and did everything by the book. He thought Elkhart ran a sloppy unit, and he did not bother to hide the sneer in his voice as he spoke: "Sir, Post Six just reported something broke through their perimeter. Sounded like they said it was an old goat in a wheelchair. Something like that."

"Huhn. That's funny."

"Sir? Shouldn't we go to general quarters?"

"Uh. Yeah. I guess so."

Eckhart started giving out orders; the men listlessly moved to obey; the tank raised its cannon and pointed down the road.

"This is stupid," whispered Eckhart to himself. "Nothing can get through Posts Seven and Eight. They've got APCs and LAW rockets . . ."

The radioman jumped up. "Sir! Post Seven has been hit! Post Twenty-two is under attack!"

Eckhart said, "But—Twenty-two is on the road north of here. They're coming in two different directions!" And he worked the action on his piece, a sudden, heady joy in his heart. Action at last!

"Get ready, people!" he shouted. "Rebels coming!"

One of the men laughed. "Shit! Ain't nothing coming through Murphy's squad. They APC shoot them so full of lead, they be shitting pencils!" Some of the men chuckled, but they all kept their eyes on the road south.

"Petroff, what's hitting Post Twenty-two?"

"They said it was a black, armored limousine before they went off the air."

A chill feeling touched Eckhart's spine. "Wh— why would they be off the air?"

"Post Twenty-three is calling for reinforcements— no—static now . . . I think we're being jammed."

"Get on it! Raise somebody! Anybody!"

"Wait— It's Tolland's unit, at sea with the Coast Guard cutter. There's some sort of paratrooper just sank two of our gunboats . . ."

"Paratroopers?" Eckhart's voice broke into a high-pitched note.

"Keep calm, sir," said Petroff, with an open sneer of contempt on his features. "No, just one paratrooper. He has some sort of particle beam weapon like a lightning bolt. They just reported that he's . . . wait . . . now they're off the air, too . . ."

In the distance, down the road, a huge tree erupted into splinters and fell across the road, blocking the way. Oddly enough, there was no flash of flame nor any smoke, almost as if no explosives had been used.

"They're coming!" shouted one man.

Eckhart saw Furlough turn and slink away into the woods.

There was a whistling in the air. The line of sandbags exploded, and hundreds of pounds of sand were flung skyward.

That was enough for Eckhart. "Petroff, you're in charge!" he shouted.

He turned deserter and ran into the woods. Looking over his shoulder, he saw Petroff hesitantly raising his rifle, as if debating whether or not to shoot Eckhart in the back as he fled.

At that same moment, the tank fired, and the front of the tank crumpled and fell in on itself, with a noise like the end of the world tearing the air. Scraps of heavy tank armor flew through the air as an iron hammer pulled itself backward out of the wreckage and flew away. Petroff was hit by the shrapnel and fell.

Everyone fired. The air shook with the continuous hammering fire of machine-gun bullets.

Eckhart looked back again when everything fell silent. He wondered if his hearing had gone or if . . .

Since he was running away, and since he was looking back, and, since the leaves and shrubs nearby had been cut away by the gunfire, Eckhart may have been the only person alive who saw the sight of two monster goats, running at impossible speeds, breathing fire and pulling a wheelchair, who rammed their horns into the hulk of the tank, broke it in two, and threw it from the road.

They didn't even slow down.

And because Eckhart had dropped his rifle a few steps to the left, he was not near it when some whistling instrument of destruction ripped aside the trees, smashing the rifle into flinders in the bottom of a smoking crater. He blinked for a moment at the white-hot, smoking weapon. It was a sledgehammer with a short haft.

The falling tree (cut in half when the hammer pulled itself out of the crater and flew away) missed Eckhart by several feet. He did not look back thereafter, but put down his head, and ran.

II

Peter shouted over the thrumming of fiery goat hooves on the road, "Dad! How come your Morpheus spell didn't work?"

Lemuel, clinging breathlessly to the rear of the wheelchair bumping and flying down the road, gasped out, "Don't . . . know . . ." The goats skidded to a stop before the main gates of Everness. The platoon of astonished men raised their weapons, and the war-machines behind them began to elevate their heavy guns and rotate the turrets of their miniguns toward the goat-drawn wheelchair.

"Mollner! Kick all the bullets and shells out of the air before they reach us!" shouted Peter, throwing.

"Somnus! Hypnos! Morpheus! Slumber!" whispered Lemuel, holding up the magnet in his hand.

A moment later, Lemuel dismounted from the back of the wheelchair to stare in fascination at the fragments of the heavy tank shells lying, flattened, in craters to either side of the wheelchair. Then he started pulling sleeping men aside to make room for the wheelchair to pass through. Tanngjost put down its horns and was shoving the armored personnel carrier off the road; Tanngrisner, still excited by the noise of the deflected gunfire, was kicking holes in the side of the Bradley Tank.

Lemuel straightened up. "There's still so much I don't know. Perhaps those squads infested with selkie have been warded by Azrael; perhaps he has raised the Yellow Sign and put on the Pallid Mask. It could be the stars. Mars is in opposition to Venus, now, and Mercury is in retrograde in the house of Aquarius, a water sign. This may be making my magic weaker; but these are very bad times for Azrael."

"I don't know what all that means . . ."

"Perhaps if you had studied your lessons . . . ," began Lemuel.

Peter cut him off. "I don't think you know what it means either. You're all dealing with book learning, here. You never did a lick of magic in the waking world before." And then he smiled. "I guess we're just going to have to make allowances for each other, huh, Dad?"

Lemuel's expression softened. Then he smiled too. "Forgive me. I suppose we shall. After all these years, I finally know why you were meant to go into the military. We are a warrior race; our blood has a love of honor, of faithfulness, which must come to the fore."

Peter looked skeptical. "Whatever. Let's take the grounds slowly. According to their radio here," he hefted the walkie-talkie he had taken from a sleeping man, "they sent most of their units north to stop some big black car. We don't know what they left behind to guard the . . ."

Out from between the trees lining the main drive, it came, huge, black, monstrous, walking forward on padded paws, its horrible cat's eyes slitted into thin crescents in the sun. The odor from it's rank fur smelled of napalm and blood.

Peter raised his hammer. Lemuel said, "Wait . . . I don't know if Mollner can stop it . . ."

The beast reared up on its hind legs, like a grizzly rearing up, and stood looking down at them. The two goats snorted flame and pawed the ground nervously. Lemuel whispered prayers beneath his breath, eyes downcast. Peter looked the creature in the face without flinching.

The beast raised one mighty paw. It beckoned.

"Welcome, henchman of Ares. Come! Increase my kingdom. Soon the Horn shall come to light; when the final note is sounded, then my kingdom shall encompass all the worlds, and yea, hell and heaven also! I will not oppose thy path . . ."

Falling again to all fours, the monster turned and lumbered off, pausing only once, briefly, to smile back over its shoulder at Peter. It expanded, becoming rarified, swelling to fill the whole landscape, faded into smoke, and was invisible.

"I got a bad feeling about that . . . ," said Peter.

"We must acquire the Sword!" whispered Lemuel.

"Let's get going!" grunted Peter.

When they came upon the main house, everyone was asleep, except for a group on the front steps, in the distance.

"What do you think that is?" asked Peter, pointing to the side-yard. A circular barrier of snapping electric bolts surrounded a large group of sleeping men. Next to the barrier were two large trucks with generators and dynamos filling their truckbeds. Heavy cables ran from the trucks to the edge of the electric wall; technicians in bulky radiation suits were slumped over their instruments. There was a burnt-out shell of some sort of circuit-breaker board smoking nearby.

Lemuel said, "The scientists here were trying to impede the Storm-Princes' power. They were succeeding. Note how the electricity is dying down."

"What about those guys up there?"

They came closer to the main doors.

A cluster of pale-faced lepers stood three ranks deep on the steps, blocking the doorway. Here were sickly men; frail, thin women; and wide-eyed children standing, sad, silent, and motionless. Each face was gaunt and slack with despair; what tears they had once shed were long since gone. They stared at Peter and Lemuel with the apathy of concentration camp prisoners.

Each bony hand, even the hand of each child, was holding some pathetic weapon: a knife, a tire iron, a chain.

In front of the steps were huddles of corpses, skulls, and ribcages strewn amidst rotting garments and stinking flesh. The one or two crows that had picked at the diseased flesh there had fallen over dead.

Peter reined in the goats well away, and he held a scarf over his nose and mouth, his eyes watering in the gangrenous stench that came from the living, the putrid odor from the dead.

One old man covered with sores and boils, near the front, said softly, "Wait! If you approach, we must attack you . . ." His voice trailed off feebly.

Peter asked, "Who the hell are you?"

One old woman raised a ruined, pockmarked face, and peered out with bleary eyes from between the ratted tangles of her gray hair. "Lemuel Waylock. It's me. Freda Teeldrum. Don't make us fight. Let us alone . . ."

Lemuel whispered in horror, "Mrs. Teeldrum . . . ?"

Her dry, thin voice whispered, "Let us alone so we can die. . . ."

"Where's Mr. Teeldrum?"

One of the figures pointed with a gray and skeletal hand at the ring of disease-eaten corpses surrounding the stairs. "That's what happens if we don't do what they say. We can't let you in."

One little boy's voice from the back wailed thinly, "Mama! I want to sit down. I'm so tired . . ."

A hard, harsh voice answered, "You stay on your feet! I'm not going to lose you and Cathy, too!"

Lemuel said, "Mr. Milliard! Reverend Shipley! Joseph? Ellen?"

There was a stir among the crowd of invalids. One tired voice said, "You best be going away, Lem. We might like you as a partner for bridge, but we sure ain't going to die for you. You step up here, we got to try to stop you."

A woman's voice from near the back hissed, "Let's get them anyway! It's all his weird antics and eccentric ways brought this plague on us! It's this house!"

Lemuel backed up, face pale, unable to speak against that accusation.

Peter raised the hammer. Lemuel said, "Wait. These people are innocent."

"Those bastards there aren't." Because around the corners of the house, to the right and left, came two lines of armored knights. The horses were lame and sickly, ghastly to behold, creatures of rotting flesh and peeling skin. The knights were handsome, with sober, pious faces. And their swords and lances dripped blood and corruption.

The knight banneret who led them, a plumed cavalier carrying the sign of a leprous face on his shield, now smiled with false warmth, and said unctuously, "Beloved friends . . ."

Peter whirled the hammer and threw it with an angry convulsion of his powerful arm.

The Kelpie-knight did not even bother to raise his shield, but swatted the hammer aside with his palm as if it were an annoying insect. The mighty hammer fell to the grass with a dull noise. One of the other knights shook his head sorrowfully. "Poor, ignorant man! Does he think diseases can be vanquished with bludgeons? You do not kill a fever by stabbing the patient!"

The knight banneret said; "Beloved friends, the

citadel of the chiefs of our high order on the dark side of the moon has been ruthlessly destroyed by one of this house. While we forgive you, it is not right that you should have while we do without. Therefore we intend that you should share your house with us. Is this not simple fairness? In return, we will share the blessings of our diseases with you. Poxes! Plagues! Instruct them in our wisdom!"

Peter gestured; the hammer jumped back into his hand; he threw again; a smiling knight lightly brushed the hammer aside with a small movement of his shield, ignoring it.

With a flourish, and a murmur of polite excuses, the knights lowered their dripping lances, spurred their grotesque horses, and charged.

Lemuel jumped on the back of the wheelchair. Peter screamed at the goats, who spun and raced down the road.

Clouds of dust erupted from the tires of the shuddering wheelchair. Racing horses were to either side of them, half-hidden in the smoke billowing from the flying hoofs of the goat-monsters. The horses, ears flattened, necks tense with veins, yellow teeth bared, galloped at supernatural speeds equal to the goats'. The knights, with condescending smiles on their faces, jabbed with vile spears and lashed out with stinking swords.

One horse leapt ahead, a hurricane of speed, rearing up before them, its rider standing in the saddle, glorious in his armor and crested helm, black blade held high.

The goats trampled him; he smiled as he fell, thankful words on his lips. Tanngjost began to stumble and vomit black blood.

"Through there!" shouted Lemuel, pointing at a line of trees crossing the southwest lawn.

Peter cut Tanngjost out of the traces with a sweep of his hammer. The monster goat, dying, turned and fell upon the pursuing knights, spitting blood and fire, kicking with hoofs like meteors. Two ranks of knights were crushed and burnt before the row behind swept over the falling Tanngjost, whose hair had fallen out, and flesh grown pale, leprous, and corroded.

They passed through the trees, the Kelpie-knights only strides behind them. When the knights encountered the line of the trees, however, they smashed into an invisible wall; some were flattened and others thrown.

There was a single moment while the trees turned sickly, rotted, and fell, and the cavalry passed though the unseen barrier. During that moment the wheelchair had flown to the front gate. The front gate was held against them by a vaster cavalry than they had seen before, including charioteers of obscenely fat blind men, whose cars were drawn by pairs of the rotting, horrible Kelpie-steeds.

They turned again, now pursued on both sides. Lemuel shouted and pointed, "The cabin!" They flew beyond the shrubs that hid the smaller, modern house. There was no time to open the front door; Peter shattered it with a throw from his hammer.

Tanngrisner stumbled, his flesh crawling with sores and boils, his fur peeling off in clumps. The goat-monster fell sideways, and momentum carried Peter and Lemuel, and the wheelchair, over the goat-monster's shoulder in through the door. They fell and slid across the carpet, yanked out of the wheelchair when the reins around Tanngrisner went taut. The great beast had bent the doorposts, but was too bulky to pass through the frame.

The Kelpie-knights reined in, coming instantly from their impossible velocities to a dead stop. The corroded Kelpie-steeds stamped impatiently, and pulled on their bits.

One knight leaned from the saddle, doffing his helm. He said politely, "May we come in?"

Peter pulled himself, hand over hand, out of the toppled bookshelves of his son's tapes and recorded music, which he had crashed into. "Dad! What do we do now?"

Lemuel had risen weakly to his feet, and was staring in horror at a tiny cut on the back of his hand. It was the tiniest of cuts; but his wrist was becoming inflamed and swollen, and blisters were visibly growing and crawling down his forearm.

III

At that same moment, there came a great commotion and noise from the east of the little cabin. Two gigantic hands coated with ice plunged in through the east wall, ripped it out of its foundations, and opened that side to the sky.

Bergelmir the ice giant, face hidden behind its featureless mask of ice, raised the wall on high. But it was not attacking those within the cabin; it was facing the other direction, toward the southern forest.

Through the drenching downpour of rain, which was, somehow, on that side of the cabin, Peter could see the forest on fire, and, wading through the burning trees, the flame giant Surtvitnir came, breathing out conflagrations.

At the edge of the trees, walking calmly, dry, untouched by wind, was Raven, son of Raven. There was also a squad of Kelpie trying to close with him, and armed men; but they were being whirled away by the tremendous winds that flattened the nearby trees. The only creatures large enough to stand were the two giants.

Bergelmir threw the wall at Raven. Lightning danced off the ice-giant with no noticeable effect. The tons of brick and masonry fell; a hurricanic wind threw Raven to one side. During that moment, Surtvitnir, his fiery body also unharmed by the lightning, stepped out from the forest fire and stooped toward Raven, raising his burning bludgeon on high.

Peter curved his shot so that the hammer passed through Bergelmir before it sheared off Surtvitnir's head, and then, coming again back to his hand, the hammer passed through both their falling bodies. One turned to ash and was blown away; the other collapsed into powdery light snow.

The hurricane stopped at a nod from Raven. Peter waited till Raven had come close enough before he spoke. "You killed my son! It's payback time!" And he drew back the hammer.

Lemuel said, ". . . Beware . . . the wall broken . . . ward broken . . ."

The Kelpie-knights dismounted and came in through the door, stepping over the fallen goat.

"You will thank us for this, in time," said one, raising his sword and coming toward Peter. Another stooped over Lemuel, who had fainted.

Raven said loudly, "Peter, wait!"

Peter glanced at the knight closing with him. He only had one short moment to avenge his son. He threw the hammer.

Galen stepped out from the woods behind Raven and raised his shining bow. He shot.

Suddenly, Lemuel's daze passed. A sharp warmth stabbed into him. He opened his eyes to stare in awe at the arrow which, touching his freshly healed arm, was transforming into a beam of sunlight. The Kelpie-knight bent over Lemuel, who had just been missed by the shaft, was staring at the arrow, his face slack with guilty fear. In the light from the shaft, the knight looked pale and unhealthy.

The other Kelpie-knights had frozen in shock and shame. One stared toward Galen and shouted, "It's not my fault!"

That one doubled over the shaft that pierced his

midriff, and transformed immediately into a disease-ridden hulk. Two others fell, their wholesome appearance vanquished by the radiant shafts. One sobbed, "We were wrong! It's not them! It's us! It was always us!"

Lemuel stood, his heart expanding with pride and happiness to see the heroic figure of his grandson bending the great bow. "Good boy, Galen!" he cried.

At that, Galen, smiling happily, walked forward. He shot, took a step, shot, took a step. Some kelpie ran away; some ran at Galen, brandishing weapons. Galen took an arrow from his quiver and pushed it into his chest over his heart. It became a beam of light, and the kelpie-weapons did not bite on him.

He fired shafts among the horses, who, immediately becoming handsome, whole, and strong, would no longer tolerate the stinking burdens of their diseased riders, but bucked, threw, and trampled them.

Whether the knights ran or stayed, the result was the same. In a moment, twoscore knights lay helpless on the ground, too disease-ridden and leprous to move.

Galen spoke in a loud voice: "Those who wish to rise, rise up! For you are healed! Those who will not accept my healing, pass away, back into the shadows from whence you came!"

One, their leader, the leper-knight who had killed Lancelot, whispered defiance through his disintegrating mouth, coughing bile. "No! We couldn't help it! It's all your fault!" And he passed into a miserable death, excreting his own entrails.

The others slowly rose, their limbs weak but whole, and knelt toward Galen. One said, "We were wrong. We wish to resume the burden of humanity again."

Galen handed them a handful of arrows. "Go! Heal those you have deluded into believing themselves sick. For the next year and a day you are bound to do them any service they might require of you." The knights, now human beings, bowed and departed.

He turned. Lemuel was watching him with shining eyes. Lemuel put out his arms.

They embraced.

Lemuel said, "I've always been so proud of you, Galen. You didn't have to prove anything to me."

Galen felt the bow vibrate in his hand, stiffening, and he let whatever vanity was growing in his mind to relax and go away. Instead of boasting, he said, "This all is my fault. I should have been more careful. I'll be careful from now on."

Lemuel looked him deep in his eyes, saying, "Your faults are forgiven; you have saved us both. Grandson, you are a true Guardian of the Everness."

Peter, sitting nearby, said, "Yeah, he's right, Son. I'm sorry too, about, well, shit, about a lot of things. A lot of things I said about you wasting your life and stuff, okay? That was a real smooth military operation you just pulled off. And, yeah, I guess I believe in magic nowadays, too."

Galen straightened up in shock.

"Where's Raven?" cried Galen.

IV

Peter said, "You know, I'm sure glad I can call that hammer back to my hand before it hits its target . . ."

"Me, I am also very glad," nodded Raven, pulling Peter's wheelchair upright and bringing it over.

There was a rumble of hoofs outside as the riderless horses of the kelpie, now strong and healthy looking, ran with flowing manes and tails, past the broken cabin wall toward the sea.

Peter asked, "So what the hell do we do now?"

And they turned and looked at Lemuel.

Lemuel ran his hand across his bald head, trying to hide his embarrassment. It was clear everyone here regarded him as some sort of wise man.

He resolved to do his best to live up to that expectation. "Galen, shoot those goats; they may not be quite dead, not if their bones are intact. We can use them to uproot any other enemy forces in the area. I think we won't be getting any other major opposition until sunset; the three outer gods are very weak when the Sun is in the sky. Unfortunately, their governing planets are very strong; all three are above the horizon now. Worse still, Acheron is rising; we would not be seeing the kelpie abroad in broad daylight except that Morningstar himself is very near the earth."

Raven said, "Does each evil race have a talisman to drive it back?"

Lemuel nodded, "Except Morningstar himself."

Galen said, "What can we do?"

Lemuel said, "Find the Horn. Blow it. Wake the sleepers. Call an end to this world, and the beginning of the next."

V

It was Raven who spoke next. "We have not so much time, I fear. Azrael de Gray and Acheron-things, they were all around Mommur, city of Oberon. We saw them fly up like great black cloud. They leave. Galen, he catch kelpie, forced to tell us black legions coming here, Everness. They following Wendy, who we are thinking has the Moly Wand, and has Silver Key. We got here more fast on dream-colt, you see? And dream-colt say horrible thing. Galen, he . . ." Raven's voice trailed off and he looked at Galen sadly.

Galen spoke with dignity. "Father, Grandfather, Look behind me. I don't cast a shadow. I'm a ghost. Unless we can get me my life back, at dawn tomorrow, Apollo has to kill me. They're giving me this one day, today, as a grace period."

Peter whispered, "Holy shit. Got to be some way out of that."

Lemuel hid his reaction. He only said, "Let's sit down. I'd like everyone to tell me what they know. Let's coordinate our information."

15

The
Pendragon's
Daughter

I

Wendy woke up. She was lying in a large, four-poster bed. She heard sea-mews calling; overhead, reflections formed moving webs of light which danced across the polished wood of the ceiling.

She sat up. Wendy was in a large chamber overlooking the sea, decorated in four styles; Arabian, Oriental, Viking, Norman. To her left, the window was guarded by Mameluke armor; to the right, by Viking armor; behind her, the bay windows overlooking the sea were watched by a rack of Samurai armor with a scowling faceplate; to one side of the door, before her was a Norman helm, kilt, and chain mail.

The door was open. A long corridor decorated with ship models, with paintings of ships, Neptunes and nautiloids, mermaids and sunken cities stretched away before her. The carpet was navy blue, and the wainscoting was a wood polished till it gleamed like gold.

The pedestals and carven archways ranked down the corridor's length gave it the sobriety and sublimity of a museum.

At the far end, she could see the shoulder and trident of the god guarding the corridor and a glimpse of the white marble floor of the central circular corridor.

"This is Everness," she whispered. "I never saw it by daylight before! Gosh, it's beautiful! But I thought it was all blown up and burnt!"

A tall, blond man with a lace cravat and dressed in a long-tailed coat and carrying a covered tray came in from the map room, a room Wendy recalled had been collapsed when the figure of Atlas holding the ceiling had attacked a group of selkie. A wonderful smell came from the tray: bacon, hot chocolate, and buttered toast.

"Hello, Tom," she said, sitting up. The folds of silk covers, gathered in her lap as she sat, spreading to either side of her along the bed.

"Top of the morning to ye, me darling. The Wizard Azrael, he's been making to fix up what harms were done here right quick as he may. But he be afar gone now, off in Oberon's fairy-land a-chasing you. Eat your breakfast up quick! For we must be away from here before Azrael gets home."

She fluffed the pillows behind her, smoothed the sheet, and set the little legs of the tray to either side of her. She saw she was wearing the green-and-gold princess dress with the puffy sleeves she had had on in Oberon's court.

Tom removed the tray cover with a flourish, displaying the china and crystal. There was parsley on the omelet and a rosebud in a slim, glass vase.

Wendy picked up a slice of buttered toast from a cute little rack designed just to hold toast. She nibbled on a corner. "Thank you very much! Breakfast in bed!" Now she looked up at him. He had sat on the side of the bed next to her and was staring into her eyes.

She smiled, showing her dimples, and said softly, "And who are you really?"

"Your love, before ye recalled that murderer ye married," he said, his voice low and husky. "Yer husband, if ye will wed me." And he leaned down and kissed her.

II

She kissed him back, but without any warmth, and when he put his arm around her shoulder to kiss again, she turned her cheek. "That's not really an answer, Tom," she said softly. She touched him gently on the cheek and smoothed the hair above his ear.

" 'Tis the truest answer me poor old heart can give, sweet missy," he said, in low tones. "I fear me I shall not live unless I can know the answer to whether ye will have me. Have all our days together in King Oberon's fair court meant nothing, then? The hunts, the jousts, the fetes, and festive days? Why come back here to this tired world of old sorrows, when ye could live forever and a day in the Land of Youth? 'Tis joy, not sunlight, which lights that land for all eyes to see! Ah! Aye, come with me, sweet lass, my darling belle, and I shall make ye a queen of a fine and handsome folk!"

"Mm. Sounds nice. But I only have one question, you handsome hunk."

"Aye, me lass . . . ?"

"Where's my Moly Wand? Where's the Silver Key?"

Tom straightened up and stepped backward. He licked his lips and raised both eyebrows. "Er . . . that's two questions, actually, there, girl."

Wendy put the tray aside and swung her feet out onto the floor. "You've got a cute face. I like it."

"Er . . . Thank ye, sweetheart . . ."

"Who did you have to kill to get it?"

"Ah . . ."

She stood, lips pursed, looking up at him, and put her little fists on her hips. "Hmph! As if I wouldn't figure it out! Men! They think they can get away with anything, don't they! Well?"

"Well, what?"

"You took the wand away from my hand while I was waking up and still asleep! You're Mannannan, aren't you? The Seal-King?"

Tom bowed his head, and put one hand to his throat. His face and body wrinkled and fell away, and he swelled up to his true size.

He seemed to be a burly, huge man, robed in white ermine.

His bushy beard was white and streaked with dots of black, as was his long hair, which fell to his shoulders. His face was round, and his neck-muscles were so thick his head seemed almost to flow smoothly into his wide shoulders. He was one of those rare men who was of wide girth without seeming obese. Beneath his huge stomach and chest were layers of hard muscle.

On his head was a crown of gold, caked with age, but still bright, and little fingers of coral had grown from every point of the crown. A smell of sea brine came from his hair.

"Aye, lass," he rumbled in a deep voice. "That I am, indeed."

III

With a flutter of feathers, a wren landed on the rail of the repaired balcony behind her. Then a robin, a thrush, and two pigeons landed there, chirping and cooing.

Wendy turned her head to look at them. A lark and a linnet landed on the sill of the southern windows. The forest to the south showed as an angry line of smoke and flame; to the south, the sky was coiled in knots of thunderheads, gray with driving rain. Everywhere else the sky was blue.

Wendy turned back. "Okay, Mannannan! Enough is enough! Give me back my wand and the Silver Key! Right now! And I don't want to hear any excuses!"

Cardinals and seagulls landed all along the balcony. Mannannan folded his large arms across his massive chest.

"Yer wand I shall give back, me dearest, if yer hand ye give to me. False man I am, perhaps, most false, albeit my love be true as truth! Were it not me what tossed to yer hand that wand in the first place, and let ye render all me own men to mere helplessness?"

"And you who dropped Lemuel out the window!"

Several more birds landed on the windowsills. Birdsong filed the room. The entire balcony was filled with flocks. An owl was next to a lark; a pigeonhawk next to a pigeon.

He stepped forward, "Lassie—ye will not take yer old husband back. I think ye must hate him well for what he done to poor young Sir Galen Waylock."

She tossed back her hair and looked at him with a spark of anger in her eye. "I wouldn't bring that up if I were you! Galen told me everything your people did to him in Nastrond! You're really a goof if you think I'd give up someone like Raven for someone like you! Now give me my Wand!"

A cold, stern voice came from the door. "Enough."

Azrael de Gray came in through the door. He wore a hooded robe woven with constellations; his belt was a living snake biting its own tail. In the shadow of the hood, his eyes gleamed, dark, hypnotic. Angular lines framed his mouth, and had gathered beneath his eyes. In his hand he held the unicorn horn capped with a silver point.

Behind him came two angels with faces too handsome and perfect to gaze upon. They had wings of vultures; circling their long hair were coronas of darkness. They wore ebon breastplates inset with seven stones; on their surcoats was the heraldry of a pentacle reversed, red on a black field. One carried a torch upside-down, and the bleak flames burned downward rather than up; the other held a censor from which poison smoked.

Where the fallen angels cast their gazes, frost gathered. Mannannan fell to his knees. "A few moments more! She would have agreed! Once wed, everything of hers would be mine, and ye could have had yer blasted Key! And the Wand! The Wand would have been mine!"

Wendy sniffed. "Don't flatter yourself. If I left Raven because he acted like you, what makes you think I'd take you? You act more like you than he does!"

She turned to Azrael. The look in his eyes frightened her, but she tried to keep her voice brave. Her fingers only shook slightly when she put out her hand. "Give me back the Silver Key. It won't obey you and you can't use it unless I give it to you. And I won't! You can bet . . . Um. I mean: I'll never give it to you!"

Azrael said, "All time has run; there is no more. This day shall see the ruination or salvation of the world. I shall trifle no more with any of you; the pressure of overhanging doom bids me cast all scruple now away. Yield me the Silver Key, fairy-girl, or I deliver you to torment."

"Never." She floated up off the floor a few inches, then a foot or two, light as thistledown, and her hair and skirts spread and swirled around her.

Azrael's face grew dark with wrath, but he held his expression immobile as a statue's. "Archangels of Darkness! Balphagor and Belial, I charge you by your master's name to seize that girl who floats there like a little bird, wrap her in chains of adamantium, and bear her to the nightmare-pits of Acheron till such time as she relents and speaks the words to render me possession of the Key!"

The angels of darkness took a step forward, growing in size to fill the chamber. As they did so, a music of drums and trumpets roared in the air, a chord of ringing majesty and horror.

The dark angels raised their hands.

There came a music of a woman's voice singing in a language unknown, clear notes of quiet strength and joy. The dark music fell silent in a winding tumble of misplucked chords.

The dark angels covered their faces with their wings for a moment, and stepped back. With a rustle they folded their wings once more on their shoulders. The singing voice blended into silence.

Azrael said, "What is the meaning of these signs? Speak, Balphagor, I charge you by Nimrod!"

The dark angel with the torch said, "She is protected by a rune cast by Oberon; she is circled with the charms sung by Titania."

"Interesting. He cannot have the Key itself, yet still Oberon will keep me from it. Belial! Name the time of this rune, by Iormungandr's fang, I ask."

"Till the world's last day, this strong charm shall hold. The King and Queen of Dreams rarely knit their power together, and might beyond might springs forth when they do. Creatures of our order may not approach till Acheron's power extinguishes the sun, doomsday's dawn."

Azrael said, "The humble must serve where the great fall short. Mannannan! Send your folk against her!"

The Seal-King rose from his knees. "I'll not. 'Tis my own true love ye ask me harry."

Azrael's lips curved in an expression that could not properly be called a smile. "Your true love is yourself, seal-man. Do you recall what promises you made on the burning deck of the sinking ship where last you shed your humanity? Do you remember what you said to the voices in the waves? The flames of that ship still hunger for you; I know their names. I shall burn you with fire if you call not your folk." He gestured toward the windows, and all the casements flew open.

Mannannan did not hesitate for long, but sadly beckoned to the birds. "But don't hurt her too muchly!"

Flock upon flock flew in through the window. Wendy looked at the birds closely for the first time, and screamed in outrage and horror. "How could you! You killed Mr. Owl! And Wren and Skylark and Gray Gull!"

Then the birds were all around her, pecking and clawing.

Wendy threw her hands before her face, and flew away down the corridor, her elf-gown flapping like a green leaf in a wild wind. The birds flew after her.

Azrael turned and strode down the corridor after, his robes billowing around him. "Wind, path, and guide her way; wind her will to wind my way. . . ."

IV

Raven, a lightning-bolt buzzing in one hand, crouched in a corridor decorated with tall Egyptian sarcophagi. Ahead of him were two archways opening to the left and right, and, through them, he could see small bits of a hallway hung with red drapery, with swords displayed on the wall between each set of drapes. Both corridors on either side were decorated symmetrically.

His nostrils twitched. He smelled the scent of blood, freshly spilled, and the lingering acrid odor of gunpowder. His sharp eyes saw the bullet hole scarring the wainscoting near the ceiling. There had been a fight here, and recently, too. But why had he heard no gunshot?

Raven turned and called softly over his shoulder, "Fight here, but I am seeing no sign of who shoots who."

Lemuel and Galen were standing at the doorway down the hall behind him. Galen, with an arrow nocked, was looking from side to side nervously. Peter was "eyes behind," and he sat in his wheelchair in the main hallway beyond the door, one goat in the traces, one goat free to act as combination heavy cavalry and secret weapon should the need arise.

Lemuel hissed, "What does the needle say?"

Raven took out the needle from where he had stuck it in his coat's shoulder. He held it by the thread that Lemuel had carefully tied to the balanced center of the needle.

The needle swung back and forth lazily, then turned and pointed to the left. "Left!"

Not long before, Lemuel had dropped the needle through the center of Raven's wedding band fifty times, each time praying to Saint Anthony and the pagan god Hymenaeus. When it was done, Lemuel claimed it was "magnetized." Raven had his doubts, but he didn't have any better ideas. The needle had led them toward the east wing of the house, until a few moments ago, when it turned, and began leading them toward the central tower. Peter was in the main corridor leading from the south wing to the central rotunda, which, from the noise, they guessed to be held by enemy forces; Raven was trying to find an unguarded path through side-passages toward the main corridor of the east wing. There was no way in sight yet; this corridor seemed to dead end in an alcove holding a sarcophagus.

Galen whispered, "She's moving again. That's a bad sign, I think. Is that a bad sign, Grandpa?"

Peter, from the main hall, said softly, "Everything's a fucking bad sign when you're in enemy territory! We haven't seen one fucking bad guy, except for the noise behind the door to the main tower. Why the hell would they all be gathered there? They're up to something.

Raven! Get a move on up there! I got a feeling we ain't got much time!"

Lemuel said, "The secret latch to the doorway to the left is behind the Egyptian coffin at the end of the hall here."

Raven crept forward. "What? What are you meaning? Is no door here. Archway is open! I . . ."

He saw a movement in the archway as he started to look around the corner. He yelped, threw his lightning bolt.

Lemuel was saying, "No! It's a . . ."

The red-hung corridor to the left seemed to fracture and shatter as the mirror filling that archway cracked.

". . . it's a mirror, Raven . . . ," finished Lemuel.

Only the archway on the right was real, opening up into the corridor lined with weapons and red hangings. The archway to the left had been a mirror held in a sliding frame.

Raven stood blinking at his cracked reflection, which had startled him. Peter called softly, "Easy there, pal. That could have been your wife, you know . . ."

Part of the mirror had fallen away in a large triangular shard. Raven could see the corridor beyond was actually small and dark, paved with large, gray stones, each stone inscribed with letters from the Greek alphabet.

Upright, like pillars, lining the walls were tall sarcophagi. The carven, gold-painted faces of pharaohs looked down with regal, cold disdain.

In the shadow of these ancient coffins, on a stone inscribed with an "omega," lay a dead body in a purple robe, facedown in a puddle of fresh blood.

Raven put his hand though the hole, found the catch and slid the broken mirror aside with a tinkle of glass. "Someone here before us. Enemy of Azrael's, I am thinking."

Peter rolled in through the door, calling his goat-monster after him. With a curt gesture, he signaled Galen to shut the door.

Behind them, Galen softly swung the door leaf shut. Raven was looking at the line of tall coffins nervously, as if he expected some dark shape be hidden in one of them.

Lemuel walked past Raven, stepped gingerly over the corpse, and came to the end of the short passageway paved with letters. Here, flanked by engravings of pyramids, was a door to the large, main east hall.

Lemuel stepped up to a painting of the pyramids and swung it open on hinges, showing a tiny peephole. Peter and Galen stared at the peephole in open surprise.

"No wonder you found out about that time with me and Sue Butterworth . . ." whispered Peter, grimacing.

There came a noise of many running boots outside the door.

Then, shouts. "Radio says she's coming this way! Remember, no shooting, except you guys with blanks! Azrael says herd her toward the middle tower!"

"Captain, let me do something! Give me a weapon! These guys wiped out my squad!"

"Shut up, Eckhardt! Oh, shit, here! Take my sidearm . . ."

Another voice: "Here she comes!"

There was a noise like a rushing wind, and, "There she goes!" Someone said softly, "Damn, she's fast. How does she do that? Wires?"

Raven was at the door, teeth clenched, eyes wide, but Peter warned him to stay calm with a motion of his hand. Then Peter noticed everyone was staring at the door. He touched Galen's shoulder and pointed down the corridor they were in. Galen obediently kept his eyes looking down toward the Egyptian hall.

Beyond the door, meanwhile, came the rushing flutter, chirping and screeching, as if a vast flock of birds, hundreds of birds, were flying by outside. Some of the soldiers called out in fear. One voice said, "Looks like a fucking Hitchcock movie in this place!"

Another: "I'm getting damn sick and tired of all these supernatural manifestations of otherworldy power!"

"Yeah, no shit."

"Hey! Here she comes again! Like a rocket!"

The sound of the birds swelled to agitation.

Wendy screamed.

At that moment Raven kicked open the door, a lightning-bolt in either hand, and a sound louder than any sound on earth echoed from his shout. Drops of sweat flew from his black hair and black beard, and his face was ruddy with anger.

Galen was behind Raven, turning left and shooting with his shining bow while Raven blasted the length of the corridor to the right. Sunlight glanced from the arrowhead, and the bowstring sang a high, pure note.

Peter, bellowing, drove his wheelchair, drawn by Tanngjost, into the gap between them, shouting to Tanngrisner to follow. The fiery hoofs of the goat-monsters dented and blackened the floorboards. With one huge motion of his broad shoulder, his muscular arm, Peter threw the hammer.

Behind them down the corridor, Lemuel raised his magnet and called on Morpheus.

Wendy was high above, near the cathedral-like ceiling of this huge, main corridor. To one side of the corridor were the tall, peaked doors, almost gateways, leading to the central tower; to the other side was a balcony, like a bridge linking two second-story cross-corridors. Beyond, the main hall stretched away and became the pillars and stonework of the east wing.

The air was filled with birds of all kinds, shrieking and screaming, swooping and diving at Wendy. She was trying to keep her hands before her face; her arms and shoulders were dotted with scars and drops and streaks of blood where they had pecked her.

Everywhere were fleeing men, men falling asleep, men dying. In that first second, Raven electrocuted a dozen; Peter smashed and bludgeoned two dozen; Tanngrisner trampled two score and burned five others with his breath. Galen accidentally shot one man who was wounded, who straightened up, unhurt, and ran away.

A clatter of hooves came from overhead. Onto the transverse balcony rode Azrael de Gray, in a chariot of ebony drawn by two monstrous Kelpi-steeds like rotted skeletons. He held up his hand. "As the Guardian of Everness, on Everness land, in my hour of duress, I invoke my swift command! I exclude the magic of the intruders from the wards of Everness! Morpheus! Somnus! Rob their limbs of motion!"

Galen said, "I am the true Guardian of Everness, not you! I call on the world to witness this is true!"

Lemuel held up his magnet. "Hyperion! Cast all sleep away! Slumber cannot bide the coming of the day!"

During this exchange, Peter and Raven slew another two dozen men, with lightning and iron hammer, nor did any fatigue touch them.

Raven began to summon a wind to blow the birds away from Wendy; but either fear hindered his concentration, or else the doors and windows kept the winds outside. Raven shouted for Peter to use his hammer.

Surrounded by steam and gun smoke, the hammer glowing redhot in his hand, Peter ran his monster-drawn wheelchair over the line of men opposing him. When they broke and fled, he used the moment to shout, "Mollner! Get the birds!"

The hammer did not move.

Galen shouted over the din of battle: "Selkie! They are selkie-lords! High selkie!"

"Get the selkie!" The hammer flew up, hindering some of the birds in flight; but it could not strike them.

Mannannan the Seal-King came out on the balcony bridge across from Azrael. He had put down his hood, and now seemed a man of great girth, dressed in ermine, but with the head of a gray seal.

The Seal-King laughed. "Ye cannot fight lies with violence, ye great fool! Yer loud hammer can do us no hurt!"

Peter, without a word, threw the hammer through the balcony floor beneath Mannannan's feet. The balcony floor in that spot became flying splinters. Mannannan fell in a shouting flutter of ermine into the confusion of battle and was lost to sight.

Galen shot into the thick of the flock of birds. The shaft hit Wendy. Immediately the spots of blood dotting her arm vanished. Wendy smiled.

The birds drove in with greater fury now, meaning not just to harass, but to slay, and cut her arms and face with their talons. Raven looked up, sick with horror, while his bloody wife screamed in mid-air; his calm concentration slipped; the lighting bolt he held shocked him; he fell, dazed.

Galen loosed another shaft at Wendy; it turned to sunlight as it touched her and cured her of all wounds inflicted by the selkie. Galen shouted over the din of battle to his grandfather, "Why can Dad call the hammer back to his hand?"

Lemuel brightened, for he understood the point of Galen's question. Cupping his hands around his mouth, Lemuel now shouted up to Wendy, "These weapons are spiritual weapons! Honesty cannot be taken from you unless you throw it away yourself!"

Wendy, flying among the rafters, now put out her hand. As if it had come from nowhere, as if it had appeared from out of a dream, the Moly Wand flew lightly through the air and landed in her palm.

Mannannan, the Seal-King, stood up suddenly from where he had been hiding among a group of fallen bodies. He shouted, "Roost! Come to land, ye fools! Can ye not see 'tis your death she holds in her hand! Obey me! Land! Can ye not see this gold crown upon me head!" He was in tears; his voice shook with anger and frustration: "'Tis I, 'tis I, the Seal-King himself who tells you! Land! Land! Can't ye believe yer eyes for once!"

Only a few of the birds fluttered to the hall floor and landed. They were safe when they turned into seals.

The rest fell. Twisting, barking, screeching, their flippers flailing helplessly for purchase against the air, the enormous streamlined bodies crashed to the floor with sickening noise. Bones were broken, floorboards were broken, and the floor was soaked and splattered with life-blood.

One gray seal, larger than the rest, lay on his belly, his great dark eyes weeping, and the gold crown fell from his streamlined white head and rolled among the corpses.

The battle fell silent during this horrible scene as everyone paused to stare at the carnage. Because of this silence, they all heard Azrael de Gray's indrawn, ragged gasp of breath.

Lemuel and Galen looked. But Azrael was not staring down at the ruination of the selkie, but upward at the rafters. There was still a single bird roosting on the rafters, a bird of prey. This bird spread wing and floated across the air to land on the railing near Azrael. It was a Pigeonhawk.

The Pigeonhawk cocked his fierce eye up at Azrael, and spoke out loud in a voice like a man's. "How shall you redeem your lost name, Wizard? It is not their blood, but your tears, I need to wash the stain away!"

Azrael stumbled backward out of the chariot-car, falling to the carpet of the balcony, his face distorted with grief, and guilt, black anger, wrath, and rage.

"No! No!" he screamed. "All has been for the coming King! I had no choice! No choice! We are torn between the tyranny of heaven and Acheron's oppression! What time have we for courtliness and law when those two loom to our pendant destruction? If the blood of guiltless babes must spill to preserve the kingdom, why, then! So must it be!" And he staggered to his feet, eyes blazing, maddened.

The Pigeonhawk hopped a little ways away from him along the railing, and spoke in a voice of cold disdain, a voice which, strangely, was like of mirror of Azrael's own. "For the King? Is this how you choose to prepare your house for his coming? Your pride has made you so blind, Wizard, that if the King were here, you would not see him; and when you saw him, you knew him not. You cannot earn his praise by doing deeds he holds in deep contempt; nor use injustices to work justice."

Azrael sneered. "You are the puppet-dream of the faerie's false and faithless queen. Why should I heed her glozing lies?"

"Hear your doom! Before the sun sets this day, if you take not up your name again, you will have no name forevermore, but be known only as a slave of Acheron." And the Pigeonhawk spread his pinions, fell from the balcony, swept under it, and winged his way down the hall, through the open casement of a stained-glass window, and away.

The soldiers, meanwhile, had watched this drama, dumbstruck; nor had anyone with Peter's party acted. Now Lemuel shouted up to Azrael. "Surrender the Silver Key to us, Founder; for you know it belongs to Oberon, and he gave it to us in trust!"

Azrael's face grew cold with pride, and he climbed once more to stand in the car of his chariot. "If I am doomed not to have the power of the Key, then let the Darkness take it rather than bend knee to Oberon! Iotun, Kelpie, and Selkie have you overcome of mine? beware! I have powers greater!"

Azrael held his hands overhead, thumbs touching, pinkies extended. He called out, "Morningstar! I call thy servants by your secret names to serve me! Phosphoros, Flammifer, Earendel, Nergal, Sammael! Come, Balphagor, Principality of Deepest Hell . . ."

Galen shouted, "Stop him!"

Peter leaned over, picked up a fallen machine gun, and emptied the clip into Azrael as he was speaking.

The bullets had no effect.

". . . Lord of Peor, Lord of Opening, I summon and conjure thee by thy secret name . . ."

Lemuel held up his hands, palms together. "Uriel, Regent of the Sun, Lord of the Third Circle of Heaven, cherub, one of those seven who face the Supreme unblinking, I call and charge thee by thy vow uttered at the death of Phaeton . . ."

Peter threw his Hammer at Azrael. One of the Kelpie-steeds, rearing, took the blow in its chest, and the hammer glanced aside without harm.

". . . secret names Nisroc, Baal-Peor, Rutrem! Come!" Azrael drew apart his thumbs and flung a gesture at the floor.

Where he pointed a pentagram of brimstone flamed into existence, and an angel of darkness appeared, dressed in a dark breastplate, crowned in blackest glory. Some of the confused soldiers, staring upward, were looking the angel in the eyes when he appeared, and now these soldiers clawed at their eyes in panic, screaming horribly.

"Balphagor! At my command, draw up Mount Pelion by its roots and drop it on the city of . . ."

Lemuel reached to a secret panel in the wall, opened it, and pulled the big double throw switch inside.

Electric lights hidden in the ceiling above the rafters came on, startling in brightness. Lemuel cried out, "I revoke all magic from these wards!"

Azrael stood in an undrawn chariot, as the Kelpiesteeds were gone. Wendy floated near the ceiling. The surviving seals, lying along the floor, had vanished. The angel of darkness was nowhere to be seen.

Azrael laughed. "Excellent! Take them, men!"

Tanngjost and Tanngrisner had vanished. Peter was

alone in his wheelchair in the middle of a ring of armed men. He called for his hammer. Nothing happened.

Raven, rising to his feet, held up his ring. Nothing happened, except that a group of four men grabbed his arms and another man tackled him about the waist.

Lemuel cried out, "Where's Galen?" And then he put up his hands as a soldier waved a gun in his face.

Azrael called out to Wendy, holding up the unicorn horn.

"Yield me possession of the Silver Key or I will kill!"

Wendy said back, "Who? Killing me won't make me give in! You won't kill your own family, will you?"

"Your husband, then!" Azrael gestured. Raven was forced to his knees. A gunman put a barrel to his temple.

Wendy laughed. "I don't care. He deserves it. He killed Galen."

Raven sighed and tried to tilt his head to look up. He wanted the last thing he would see on earth to be the sight of his wife.

The gunman snarled at him. "Keep your head down!"

Raven wondered what the little red dot of light floating between the man's eyes was.

V

A place in the wall, a little below where Lemuel's peephole looked out, now splintered with a cough of noise. Raven's sharp eyes caught the sight of the bullet hole cracking the wooden wainscoting. Because the weapon was almost silent, four of five soldiers had dropped before their comrades knew what was happening.

Then came shouts and screams, as soldiers turned each direction, looking for the source of the unseen force slaying them. The doors that Raven, Galen, and

Peter had charged through now swung wide open. A billowing cloud of black smoke swelled up in the doorway and began expanding into the hallway.

Several soldiers fired into the black cloud.

The men holding Raven's arms were dead, neat bullet holes drilled with surgical precision into their heads and hearts. The explosion of blood from their ragged exit wounds had drenched everything around. Raven lay still, surrounded by corpses, hoping to be overlooked.

From his position, Raven could see the thin beam of an aiming laser swinging through the edges of the black cloud, where the rare smoke caught the beam. From the angle of the beam, he guessed whoever was firing was still behind the door, shooting through the crack at the hinge. Meanwhile all the soldiers were directing their fire directly down the hall, now hidden by smoke, paved with Greek letters, where the sarcophagi stood.

A captain shouted and called for a charge. He and his squad of four men ran into the smoke, shooting.

A moment later their guns fell silent.

When a figure appeared at the edge of the smoke, shrouded in black, the other squads outside the cloud all fired again and again into the form.

The body waved its arms, shouting, and fell over in a wild spray of blood. As it fell, the edge of the cape covering him fell free and was pulled back into the cloud. It had been, not the man in black, but the captain of the gunmen. The captain's body feebly twitched and then rolled face downward in a spreading pool of blood.

The men in the main hall, backing away from the spreading smoke, fingered their guns nervously.

"Its nerve gas?" called a panicky voice.

"We just shot Phillips! Who is in charge?"

Azrael, down the hall and far above, was leaning on

the rail, one eyebrow raised. He made a gesture with
his fingers, then glanced upward in irritation.

With a dull rush of noise, a small black cylinder
shot out from the cloud, and rolled and bounced, erupting with black smoke as it came. There was now a
cloud in the middle of the great hall, and as it swelled,
the spreading smoke from the door began to mingle
with it.

Then a second cylinder shot out, this one farther
down the hall, and began making another spreading
pillar of opaque black smoke.

A panicking soldier shot into one of these new
clouds; the men on the other side shot back. Azrael's
shouts and commands could not be heard over the
thunder of gunfire.

A black figure appeared at the edge of the cloud
advancing out from the Egyptian hallway. The soldiers hesitated, fearing to shoot one of their own in
the confusion.

For the briefest moment, Raven saw the figure step
out from one black cloud bank and pass into another.

It seemed to be a tall man, hidden in a vast black
cape, face unseen beneath a wide-brimmed black hat,
a weapon in either hand: in his left, a machine-gun pistol with a laser aiming device parallel to an elongated
silencer; in his right, the large tube of a grenade
launcher. In the shadow of the hat brim, came a metallic glint; perhaps he was wearing some sort of goggles.

The dark figure raised his gun and shot three times;
each time he fired, another man died. One man threw
down his weapon and was spared; the final man was
struck in the chest with a gas canister shot from the
grenade launcher, throwing him headlong backward
across the floor.

Then the figure was somewhere inside the second
gas cloud. Raven saw a grapnel and wire shoot up out
of the top of the gas cloud, catch on a rafter; but the

wire did not stiffen, as it would have had it been under tension.

"Look out!" cried a voice from near or inside the gas cloud. "He's trying to climb up! Aim high!" Raven recognized the voice as that of the man who had saved him from prison.

A group of men ran in near the gas cloud and sprayed bullets into and through the tops of the cloud. Men on the far side of the cloud were shot, and fired back.

Meanwhile, a dark-clad figure belly crawled from one gas cloud to the next. He now had pistols in both hands, and seemed to be as expert a shot with his left hand as with his right.

There came a rapid staccato of clicks as the wildly firing men ran out of ammo. One man shouted, "Hold up! Squad Three, hold your fire! Squad Two, change clips . . ."

The black-cloaked figure stepped from the gas cloud, raised his weapon, aimed, calmly shot the soldier giving orders, and faded back into the gas cloud.

A corporal stared in horror at the fallen body; even though he was now the ranking man here, he uttered no orders.

When two other men started giving orders, they were shot. A group of men, shouting, charged into the gas cloud. The shouting turned to coughs and screams and trailed into horrible silence.

The squads ignored the orders concerning firing and reloading; the panicked soldiers clenched their triggers with white knuckles, and were surprised, after a moment of wild firing, to find their weapons empty.

Silence fell. The soldiers looked at each other for a stupefied moment, and then started scrambling to get clips.

Peter had gotten his hands on a machine gun when the men guarding him had died. He sat in his wheelchair somewhat down the hall, a look of contempt on his face.

"Boy, you guys' training sure sucks."

And he sent a short, controlled burst of gun fire into the bodies of the four men nearest him before they could turn around.

The figure in black stepped out from the gas cloud, with wisps of black vapor billowing from his cloak and hat. With an unhurried motion of his arm, he raised his weapon and aimed at Azrael. Azrael looked with calm disdain at the red dot focused on his chest, his cold eyes showing no fear at all.

"Throw down your weapons!" the black-cloaked figure's calm voice echoed through the hall. "Or your leader dies!"

There was a metallic clatter as machine guns, pistols, and rifles were dropped to the floor.

Azrael de Gray leaned on the railing. "Who are you, sir? How dare you to interfere with these affairs?"

The man, with his left hand, pulled off and threw aside his hat, gas mask, infrared goggles, and opened the cheek flaps of the Kevlar head armor he wore. He was a stern-eyed man of arresting handsomeness, straight of nose, with firm, deep lines to his cheeks and chin, and a mouth that was one sharp line of determination and pride. His hair was silver.

Raven recognized him as the man who had saved him from prison; but also, strangely, Raven began to recall other times. At the wedding reception, at Wendy's house, visiting on Wendy's birthday . . .

Inside his mind, Raven saw a whole section of his life, buried, forgotten, come to light again.

"You! You cannot be here. . . ." whispered Azrael in horror.

"The time has come for you to pay for your crimes, Sorcerer! You thought to destroy me when I would not join your evil organization, and to make the world forget me. But I have not forgotten you; nor did I need the world to encompass your downfall."

"I am not fallen yet . . ." hissed Azrael.

"I hereby place you under citizen's arrest, according to the laws and principles of this nation."

Lemuel picked himself up off the floor where he had been lying during the firefight. He stared back and forth in confusion. Peter met his gaze from across the room, a question in his eye. Lemuel shook his head and shrugged.

Wendy floated down from up above. Her voice was shrill with excitement and pride. "Daddy! Oh, Daddy!" Then: "It's my Daddy! I *knew* he would come! Isn't he neat . . . ?"

16

A Dying
of the
Light

I

Raven stood. He noticed that the figure in black, arm still straight, still holding Azrael in the aim of his weapon, was nevertheless swaying on his feet. Spots of blood were appearing on the floor beneath the black hem of the cloak, splattering to the floorboards between the black boots.

One of the soldiers said uncertainly, "If we all rush him at once . . ."

Wendy's father turned his head to stare that soldier in the eye. When that man fell silent, he returned his unwavering gaze to Azrael. "You have been defeated, wizard!"

Azrael said coldly, "I will give you the shadow, Anton Pendrake, and take the substance; for I have the pith of victory like wine in my mouth; and you have the rind."

Lemuel put his hand on Raven's elbow, and whispered, "You did not tell me your wife's maiden name!"

"Pendrake," said Raven. "Gwendolyn Moth Pendrake. So what is this? How does this matter?"

Lemuel said, "There has always been an heir to the power of Logres, a power to bring justice to mankind. The head of Bran was brought to America when the English kings became tyrants; that's why America has never been invaded successfully. We lost all touch with the bloodline long ago! Mordred's heirs did not all share his wickedness, but even those heirs have forgotten who they are! This is a miracle!"

"What is miracle? What is all this things?" whispered Raven, rolling his eyes.

Wendy landed behind Anton Pendrake and wound her arms around his chest, pressing her cheek against his back, smiling.

Anton Pendrake did not turn his head, but kept his narrow gaze along his black-clad arm toward Azrael. "Careful, Gwendolyn! Don't spoil Daddy's aim."

"I won't, Daddy. Is Mommy coming, too?"

"Sweetheart, you know your mother can't come out when the sun is up. Now, dear, can you call the Silver Key to your hand the same way you did the magic wand?"

Azrael's face blushed dark when Wendy's mother was mentioned, and the hiss of detestation that escaped his lips was audible to those below. Now he spoke. "Your daughter's claim to Clavargent is without effect and force! Her possession is not lawful; founder of this house am I, and the Silver Key is mine, supreme against all other claims, except the present Guardian!"

Peter said, "That would be my dad over there, pal . . . Or maybe it's me. The Key is ours. Cough it up."

Azrael spoke in a cold voice. "The present Guardian is absent; the claims of yourself and your father to the guardianship of this great house have lapsed! Now,

Pendrake, do you see? Death comes to claim Galen Waylock's ghost; even now it comes. Without him, you have no power over me. Nor have you Belphanes' Bow to heal your wounds. He cannot be in this house until the lights here are quenched and this house is reunited to its counterpart in the world of dreams. Now I raise my hand. At my signal all my men will assault you in one rush. Perhaps you can kill one or two. You cannot kill all."

Peter said to Anton; "Shoot him. Shoot him now."

Azrael raised his hand. He stood on the high balcony bridge, an upright figure in robes of woven stars and constellations. "If I perish, my hand must fall."

Anton Pendrake spoke. "Is that what you really want, sorcerer? Picture the future where both of us are dead and Acheron rules the world. You lose. Morningstar wins. Is that what you want?" Pendrake's arm never wavered; the red dot of the aiming laser was steady on Azrael's chest above his heart, but more drops of Pendrake's blood pattered to the floor at his feet.

Raven whispered to Lemuel, "Explain this! Where does Azrael know Wendy's father from?"

Lemuel said, "I don't think Azrael knows who Pendrake really is. I doubt if Pendrake knows. I heard the voice cry out to me in a dream, and saw the three queens in their barge, rowing the coffin far out to sea . . ."

"Well? Who is he, then?"

"Don't you see? The word 'drake' is another word for 'dragon'."

Raven looked at Wendy across the hall, snuggling against her father for comfort and protection, not against her husband. The impulse to go to her was stifled by two things: the nervous, unarmed soldiers still outnumbered them considerably, and their weapons lay scattered on the floor, close to hand. Raven had seen beasts of prey at bay hesitating between the desire to flee and the desire to kill; any sudden motion might wake the soldiers to the realization that even starting the battle unarmed, they could overcome everyone here.

The second scruple he had was this: Raven said to Lemuel, "We must get Galen out of dream-world. He is alone there, with evil angel Balphagor."

Lemuel was sweating. "I dare not flip the switch. Azrael is nearly all-powerful in the dream-world . . ."

Azrael, meanwhile, was saying to Pendrake, "Foolish once not to have joined me when I sent my dreams far-ranging to all those men of greatness and great worth throughout this land. Now foolish twice to spend your life to buy my death! How dare you defy me, mortal man! Even now if you join me, even now, I will forget your presumption and grant you a place of power and preeminence among the lords of the world who will serve the new king when he comes to claim his kingdom!"

"You're joking. Free men never accept tyrants, Azrael. Certainly we won't accept Morningstar as this new king of yours. Instead, you should surrender and pay for your crimes."

"Thrice fool and fool again! Did you actually think I wish to give this green world to Morningstar, the Lord of Fear and Darkness? Once the Key is mine, I will enslave the powers of hell and heaven both! It is the gods who now will pay for their long list of crimes against mankind; rapes, plagues, temptations, curses, tempests! The ghosts of all innocent firstborn children of Egypt slain by Moses' magic; the world of all those who died in the Great Deluge; the sons of Atlantis; all these and more cry out for vengeance!"

Peter said, "Enough talk! Dad, get ready to throw the switch after I blow away Azzy-boy here. Raven, zap all these guys when the magic turns back on. Any of them who don't surrender, crisp them on deep-fat fry."

All the soldiers stiffened, and turned their eyes up toward Azrael. One or two soldiers had stealthily drawn bayonet knives or were beginning slowly to bend down toward their fallen weapons.

Azrael said, "Men! Recall what spells I have put on you! Recall as well the promise made atop the pyramid of skulls we raised inside the solar obelisk you call Washington Monument! We can only seem to die! Whether I stand or fall, fight on! For I shall assist you, even if you do not see me anymore among you!"

"Wait, Mr. Waylock," said Pendrake. With his left hand, Pendrake drew a small black oblong out from beneath his cloak and, without turning his head, tossed it across the room to Raven. "Mr. Varovitch. Can your control over electricity allow you to duplicate the specific amperage generated by that machine in a field throughout the room? That device emits on the frequency combination that can stimulate the convulsive centers of the nervous system."

"Don't know! Will try!" said Raven. Wendy turned her head to look at him when he spoke. It was the first time their eyes had met.

Raven could not read her expression. He said, "Wendy My love, my darling! I am not knowing if you were lying to Azrael when you said you no care if I live or die. And I do not ask you for forgiveness . . ."

"I should certainly hope not!" she snapped.

Peter raised his rifle toward Azrael. "Are we all going to wait while the two lovebirds make up, or are we going to start shooting?"

Raven said to Wendy, ". . . but if I live through this battle, I will tell you the story of how I lost my name when I lost my love. And maybe you will tell me the story of how I get it back again, eh? I know you love happy endings."

She shouted through her tears, "You're so silly sometimes! Of course I still love you!"

Peter said, "Well, ain't that special?" And he fired a burst of rounds into Azrael.

Azrael de Gray, his chest a bloody mess, his skull

opened and face caved in, his right arm torn from its socket by the power of the shells ripping through him, was thrown back against the far railing of the balcony, and then slumped forward, falling in a shower of red spray to the carpet of the balcony.

The arm turned over and over as it fell from the balcony to the floor of the great hall. It struck with a dull, wet thud.

The mass of soldiers shouted, and attacked in a huge rush.

A vast sweep of black smoke billowed up out from underneath the hem of Pendrake's black cloak, and he was lost to sight. There came six whispering hisses of his weapon; the six men closest to reloading their guns were dead.

A soldier shouted, "Hold that switch! Without magic, we got 'em!"

A thrown knife stabbed into Lemuel's arm before he could pull the switch. He was shocked by the pain. Blindly, he groped for the switch with his other hand, but a soldier tackled him and knocked him from his feet.

The three men jumping Peter were bullet-riddled corpses before their bloody bodies struck him and knocked him from his wheelchair. Next, a booted foot came down on Peter's gun hand. Peter reached up with his other hand and did something horrible to that man's groin. The man was writhing on the ground, and Peter raised his gun. Two more men died before he ran out of ammo. The man who stooped over him with a knife had a surprised look in his eyes when Peter broke his wrist, took the knife, and left it in his throat. Another soldier stood back, trying hurriedly to jam a new clip into his gun. Peter opened his belt buckle into a knife and flung it into the man's forehead. The man's eyes crossed as blood streamed down his nose and cheeks, almost as if he were looking at the knife quivering in his skull. He fell backward.

Peter had no more weapons at hand. Three more men jumped on him. Several soldiers were shouting, "Hold that switch! Hold that switch!"

The men near Raven apparently had no knives, for they merely tackled him in a mass. To his surprise, these men seemed to have no more strength than children; he broke limbs and snapped spines with ease, crushing skulls with his fingers; then he waded through the packed crowd of soldiers, ignoring those hanging off his arms, pulling along those clinging to his legs, and he came toward the switch one step at a time.

The man clinging to his back made a swift motion. Raven felt a cold sensation across his neck, felt the blood pour out of his neck wound, and spread like a red bib across his shirtfront. He saw his vision dim. The strength left his arms and legs; he fell to his knees, reached over his back, and threw the man who had cut his throat into the wall with enough force to break his ribs and snap his spine.

Then he fell to his face, and he was dying one heartbeat at a time.

More voices took up the cry, "Hold the switch! Hold the switch!"

When a squad of soldiers took out clips, reloaded, and shot into the spreading gas cloud, they did not see Wendy, her arms still tightly wrapped around Pendrake, shoot up out of the top of the cloud, trailing black mists. Pendrake dropped a grenade or three behind him as he left.

Pendrake, swooping upward, held by his straining daughter, pointed his arm toward the switch. There was a dull cough, and a grapnel and wire shot out from his black sleeve, and caught a hook around the switch.

Two soldiers pushed frantically on the switch, keeping it in place, and one slashed at the black metal wire of the grapnel with his knife. The whining motorized reel was only drawing Pendrake down through the air toward the soldiers.

"Hold the switch! Hold the switch!" Nearly all the soldiers were shouting it now; it had become their battle cry.

Meanwhile, another soldier, his elbow around Lemuel's throat, hauled Lemuel up before him, putting his back to the switch. Pendrake did not have a clear shot. When he raised his weapon, the soldier with the knife yanked on the wire. Pendrake and Wendy swung widely through the air like a drunken kite.

Wendy screamed, "Raven's dying! We need Galen's bow!"

Pendrake slapped a quick-release catch and the motorized reel fell away out of its housing. Father and daughter, free of the line, bobbed suddenly up among the rafters.

The soldiers cheered when Pendrake dropped his pistol. "The switch is ours! We held the switch! We've won!" Pendrake unscrewed one of the lightbulbs from the ceiling, reached into the socket with a thin metal implement he drew from his belt.

The bulbs flickered as the circuit was shorted, and they all went dark.

The man astride Peter, trying to strangle him, heard his whisper. "Mollner. Waste them." That was the last thing that man heard.

Raven stood up, huge, massive, blood still spurting from his throat, his face unnaturally calm, throwing the electrocuted and smoking corpses from his arms and shoulders. Sparks flickering in the blood that fell from his body. Lightning streamed from his eyes and mouth, and a ring of lightning flashed out from his body as he spread his arms.

With a great, ragged, roaring gasp, he called out Wendy's name. The stained-glass windows down the hall shattered, and the hall shook, when the echoes of her name reverberated down from the sky above, louder than any noise of earth.

The stunned and thunderstruck soldiers were falling like limp dolls.

And Raven fell as well.

II

When his daughter fainted from the thunderclap, Pendrake managed to get an arm around her waist, and grab a passing roofbeam as he fell. There he dangled in air, half-fainting from his wounds, blinking at the bright sunlight that came unexpectedly from underfoot, until a pleasant warmth stole through his body and returned his strength.

He looked down. The head of the gigantic, supernatural being whose wings filled the hall from side to side, was slightly below the level of the balcony, so that the balcony was cast in deep shadow from the rays of brilliant light spreading from the archangel's crown. There was some motion on the balcony; he dimly saw the skeletal Kelpie-steeds backing away, kicking at and pushing the chariot awkwardly behind them. He was not sure what the other black shape, crisscrossed by a pale framework, might be; this shape was hunched down on the balcony near the chariot.

Galen, standing near the foot of the great being, bent his bow and shot a shaft of sunlight into Raven's fallen form. Raven said, "But Balphagor was . . ."

Galen smiled and nodded upward, saying, "Driven back to Acheron by Apollo. I finished Grandpa's invocation!"

Pendrake's command cut through their talk: "Gwendolyn next! We may have trouble up here!"

Galen turned and raised his bow.

In the sunlight shed from the burning shaft sinking

into his daughter's back, Pendrake could see the balcony. A thin, tall, humanoid shape, cloaked in billowing darkness and armored in knitted human bones, was bent over Azrael's corpse. The torn ruination of Azrael's bullet-ridden flesh had fallen open at the throat like a coat, and became no more than a torn white coat in fact. Beneath that coat was another body, whole and unhurt, which looked exactly like the first; and into this body the long razor fingernails of Koschei the Deathless were pushing a little ball of glowing light which flickered and shimmered like a burning butterfly.

The little light was sinking into the chest.

Pendrake said, "Wake up, Gwen! Daddy needs a free hand to shoot the bad guys! Wake up!"

Galen shouted, "Just drop her! I'll heal her if she breaks her legs!"

Raven said, "Apollo! The god can reach her with his hand!" Pendrake let go of his daughter and reached under his cloak. Wendy, yawning and stretching, bobbed slowly through the air like a thistledown. Pendrake's hand encountered three empty holsters, and his forth gun was holstered near the armpit of his free hand, so that when he drew the gun, it was awkwardly backward in his fingertips.

Koschei stood, drifted backward in a billowing flutter. Azrael de Gray regained his feet from a prone position when an invisible, silent thrust of pressure set him slowly upright, with neither his knees nor waist bending at all.

Pendrake flipped his wrist, caught the pistol grip, aimed, fired. No bullet touched Azrael.

Azrael looked at Apollo, and raised his hands, wrists crossed, ring fingers curled. Azrael's robes began to billow and float around him, and the constellations came out from the fabric, burning with eerie starlight, and made a circle in the air around Azrael.

Galen shot a sunlit shaft into Lemuel, waking him. "Grandpa! Wake up! Big trouble!"

"Wake your father. . . ." said Lemuel, rising to his knees.

Peter had one arm around the neck of each goat-monster, who nuzzled him and drooled sparks, and, his legs dragging on the ground, they were stepping toward his wheelchair. "I'm awake!"

Azrael said to Apollo, "As Guardian of Everness, I revoke your permission to be upon these my lands. Go."

Galen shouted up toward the balcony. "He's not the Guardian! Grandpa is!"

Lemuel said softly, "Not I. When Mannannan cast me out of the window, fair or unfair, that ended my guardianship. Your father passed it to you. You are the true Guardian of Everness, Grandson."

Galen drew a deep breath. He said, "Helion! Hyperion! I bid you to stay! I charge you and compel you in the name of the Unicorn, whose Key is in our keeping, and in the name of the head of dragons, from whom our charter comes!"

Raven reached over and threw the switch; but the lightbulbs had all shattered when the windows had, broken by the noise of the thunderclap.

Koschei's icy, hideous voice floated from the balcony. "Great Lord Hyperion, seraph of the Third Circle of Heaven and universal chieftain of the armies of the daylight, have I your leave to address you?"

Azrael said sharply, "Apply to me for such permission! Speak!"

Koschei said nothing. Light danced along the walls when the titanic figure nodded his head crowned with glorious beams. Koschei spoke, "Great Lord Hyperion, Galen Amadeus Waylock, who is called by another name in higher realms, has perished. What you see before you is no more than a ghost. He cannot be the Guardian."

Pendrake, still hanging from the ceiling, said, "Your honor, I object! The same thing could be said of Azrael, who was shot to death just now! You cannot call Galen's claim void unless you also, by the same logic, call Azrael's claim void. Galen's claim would therefore pass to his nearest living heir, who is Peter Waylock!"

Pendrake kicked his legs and flung himself from one rafter to the next. Then he dropped down and landed lightly on the balcony on the far side of the bridge away from Azrael.

Peter spoke up, "Hey! If I'm the Guardian here, my orders are to arrest Azrael, neutralize his magic, and obey Galen. Am I in command? I'm ordering you to ignore Azrael's orders, Mr. Sun-God. So don't leave!"

Azrael stepped onto the back of the Kelpie-drawn chariot. He held up his left hand, first two fingers crossed. "I call upon the final rune to witness! Hyperion, Helion, Apollo, Uriel, I charge you to answer and to speak! Is not Galen Waylock truly past the day when the Book of Judgments records his death? Have I not the authority as Guardian of Everness to banish you?"

The voice of Hyperion filled all the hall, and his breath was like a warm summer wind when he spoke: "Galen is past the day and hour of his death; the Hours who serve me have decreed it . . ."

Azrael shouted, "When a god speaks your name, the ward is broken and permission is granted! Thanatos! Ares! Moira! Step forth! Into the daylit world you now may come!"

The tall doors to the central tower swung open. There, where three great archways opened beneath three great images of the waxing moon, the full moon, and the waning moon, the three outer gods hovered, and in some way that stung and confused the eye, they seemed farther away than the walls behind them, larger than the world they stood upon.

She in the middle was a tower of darkness, and a woman-featured mask of iron hung below her hood like a blood-red moon beneath a black cloud bank. In her hand was a flail of chains.

To her right hand was one who showed an ivory skull, now clearly seen, now fringed in the shadows of a hood, like a January moon seen full through weeping thunderheads. In one gauntlet hovered a reaping hook; in the other, a lantern imprisoning many little lights that fluttered like butterflies: the lights of many souls.

To her left, standing upright, was a figure drenched with blood and stinking of smoke. The face beneath the hood was that of a saber-toothed tiger, whose fangs gleamed like crescents. There were chains around the apelike shoulders and the bearlike waist, but the links were loose, with unshackled chain ends floating in the air in all directions. A vast claw held a terrible red sword.

Azrael said, "The pawns are swept away! Here is my knight, my tower, my queen! You have no defenses to oppose them! Pendrake! Order your daughter to yield the Key to me, or I unleash these things upon the world!"

Fate spoke: WE NEED NOT YOUR PERMISSION LONGER, SLAVE OF ACHERON. THE TIME COMES NIGH FOR DARKNESS TO COVER ALL.

Hyperion spoke. "Both claims are invalid, nor does Peter Waylock take. The guardianship reverts to the heir of the original grantor. I await for him to speak."

Everyone looked back and forth dumbly. Lemuel opened his mouth, looked up at Pendrake, and blinked, as if he had come to a conclusion of which he was unsure.

Azrael said, "I call upon Chronos to sever the time of waiting! By the Final Sign I command a judgment!"

Hyperion's glance flung Azrael reeling to his knees, and the ring of constellations around the warlock broke and faded. Hyperion's words rolled like thunder. "You have no power here, for you have been arrested by an authority, which, in this land, is paramount. Your claim to the guardianship is exhausted. Your name is not your own. The Key is not yours."

Hyperion pointed his finger at the unicorn horn where it had fallen from Azrael's limp hand, and, turning, Hyperion raised a great shining hand toward Wendy. The unicorn horn slid through the air and hung before her.

Hyperion's words rang and echoed in her ears: "Take and guard till the rightful owner shall declare himself."

Lemuel shouted upward. "Anton Pendrake! It's you! You are the one! Order the Sun-God to stop the three seraphim of darkness!"

Pendrake leaned from the balcony and pointed toward the central tower. "Apollo, I hereby deputize you! Arrest those creatures!"

The Sun-God stepped toward the great doors, and his wings fanned out from his golden shoulders to cover all the billowing darkness radiating from the three towering beings. Two themes of world-shaking music rang out, one made of notes of rising triumph, gladness, and majestic light; the other, a swelling pulse of dark drums and crashing horror.

The floor shook when the Sun-God stepped in to fill the door, and the light was blinding; his wings filled all the space of the huge doorway, so that only the tiniest crack of streaming darkness leaked through where his outer feathers failed to overlap.

"Checkmate, Azrael!" shouted Pendrake, pointing down the balcony. "Call off your attack and surrender, or my daughter will use her wand to turn you back into a bullet-ridden corpse!"

Azrael, on his knees in the car of the chariot, was clutching the railings of the car as if they were the bars of a cell. "No, oh no. It cannot be. The Pendragon is here. His name not hidden, I saw no hidden sign because it was open and clear! Hah! The mocking laughter of the goddess rises again in my ears! The King is come. The King is truly come again, and I have made him my enemy! Hah! The wide hat! The disguising cape! To think I did not recognize the garb of Odin! So she would dress him in mockery of older husbands than myself!"

Azrael climbed unsteadily to his feet, and turned his face down the length of the balcony. "Majesty, I sought only the establishment of the foundations of your throne! America would have been yours, and this nation's might is more than great enough to conquer all the lands and peoples of this world, though why the rulers here have not done so long ago, I cannot guess."

Pendrake was walking forward. The house shuddered again, and rays of darkness escaped the edges of Apollo's wide-flung wings. The theme of darkness swelled; the music of daylight bent it into glad harmonies; and the rays of darkness narrowed and failed. But Apollo cried out in pain and the stitched scar on his back pulled open, and a little drop of glowing white blood began trailing down the length of his back.

Lemuel pointed and shouted, but his words were lost in a crashing crescendo of mingled music.

Pendrake, walking closer down the balcony, shouted to Azrael, "Call off your attack!"

Azrael said, "I have summoned what I cannot put down. My authority has been broken. But the Dark Gods can be driven back still, if you yield me the Silver Key! We have but moments!"

The voice of Death rang through the hall, making all hearing, only for a moment, numb: "Reagent of Light, you cannot keep Death from the Dead. However you protect the others, Galen Amadeus Waylock, the Parzifal of this time, must come with me now."

The words of Hyperion healed the hearing of those within the ambit of his golden voice: "Till sunset I suspend your power, Lord of Silence."

The shining one began to beat his mighty wings. A great wind, and gushes and streamers of light, began to emanate from him in all directions. Flashes of darkness pulsed from the door with each wing-beat, scarring the door frame and walls to either side with ice.

Peter put his palm up before his face, squinting. Galen, behind him, his hands on the wheelchair, was trying to shout something in his ear. Lemuel was backing away down the corridor, stepping over dead and sleeping bodies, a look, not of terror, but of exultation on his face.

Wendy floated down and hugged Raven. He put his arms around her. It was utterly calm where he was, and there was no wind.

She said, "Thank you for saving Galen."

Raven patted her shoulder.

Wendy brushed a tear out of her eye. "I think I know how you get your true love back, but I'm afraid the story has a sad ending."

"What? What are you saying?" A coldness and fear touched Raven; the winds began to tug at him.

"I've got to go. In Galen's place. To give back the life you stole for me. It's my time . . ."

She pulled out of his arms and began walking toward the great door. A look of grief so great that it was like terror now drove Raven's calm expression away; and then winds, escaping his control, roared and flung him to the ground before he could put out a hand to stop her.

The winds pushed at her as well, tossing her hair and skirts, but she was walking with her feet above the ground. Streamers of light erupting from the struggling Sun-God splattered and rebounded from the floorboards to her left and right as she walked forward, a very small figure indeed.

Peter's goat-monsters pulled his bucking wheelchair across the floor despite the gales of winds, with Galen clinging to the back. They rolled up next to Raven, and Peter shouted, "What the hell does she think she's up to? What? I can't hear you . . ."

The winds began to grow to hurricane force.

"Enough!" said Raven in a loud, calm voice. He took a deep breath. The winds were gone.

In the unexpected silence, they all heard Pendrake shouting at the top of his lungs, ". . . shut up about this king business already and do something!"

Azrael said, "Majesty, I can do nothing. Not Azrael. Perhaps if . . ."

Lemuel called across to Wendy. "Wendy. Stop being such a silly girl and come right back here! All we need to do is have Koschei give Galen's life back to him, and then have Galen cure you of your illness with his bow!"

Wendy turned, her eyes large and round. "Will that work?" But her tone of voice said, *Does this mean I do not have to die . . . ?*

There was a look of fear and of relief on her face, a look of trembling courage about to fail, a look that only those who walk willingly to their own deaths, and are then reprieved, might wear.

"Hurry up now, darling, we haven't got all day." Lemuel forced a cheerful note into his voice.

Wendy ran back across the floorboards toward them and a tear flew from her cheek.

At that moment, the light from the windows turned gray and then dark. Through the windows they could all see a sudden nighttime cover the land and sea.

Pendrake looked up. "It's an eclipse!"

Lemuel said, "The Moon's in the wrong position."

Azrael de Gray said, "It is a body larger than the Moon, and the shadow of his wings are larger than the Moon's shadow."

The voice of War trembled through the great hall. "Defeated Hyperion, begone! Galen's time and thine are run! For now it is night!"

The Sun-God was flushed with rosy color as he bowed his massive head. His light grew purple, faded, and he was gone. The three gods of darkness stepped into the great hall. The voice of Fate pronounced: BE-GONE, URIEL. THE SUN SHALL NEVER MORE COME AGAIN: ACHERON IS RISEN.

Through the archway behind the three dark gods were windows, and through them, in the deep twilight above the seawall and the waves, low in the East, the morning star pulsed and twinkled with a growing brightness.

17

That Strong, Unmerciful Tyrant

I

High on the balcony, eyes rolling, looking each way at the landscape of unnatural night that extended out from the broken windows, Azrael de Gray lashed at the skeletal rumps of his steeds with the reins in his hand, crying out, "Treason! Treason! I have betrayed all! King, house, kin, and all! I have betrayed my name! Fly, horrors, fly! Fly with wings of fear to where my soul flies off!"

The Kelpie-steeds leapt into the air, passed out through the broken windows with the speed of nightmare.

Galen raised his bow to shoot the steeds and prevent Azrael's escape, but at that moment, the figure of Death advanced into the great hall like a storm front advancing, or the line of a nightfall seen far-off at sea; and a glance from the empty eye sockets of bone struck Galen to the floor, where he lay, unable to move.

Peter raised a gun that he had reloaded and shot at the unearthly huge figure. It had no more affect than as if he had shot at a mountainside, or at a constellation.

Lemuel, throwing himself to his knees, drew out on the golden arrow from Galen's quiver and jabbed Galen with it. The arrow did not glow in Lemuel's hands; the arrowhead drew a spot of blood.

Raven knelt down on the other side.

Galen's lips drew back. Through his teeth, a little flutter of light glimmered. Galen's mouth was filled with a gleaming pearl of lovely light, which began to come up out of his mouth.

Raven could not touch the ball with his hands; his fingers passed through it. Ignoring the light, he put his lips to Galen's, pinched Galen's nose, and breathed. The light bobbled and floated back a little ways into Galen.

Raven found no pulse. He interlaced his fingers, leaned forward, and began to pump Galen's chest above his heart.

"Don't touch him!" Raven said to Lemuel. Raven took out the little box Pendrake had given him, and shocked Galen with the electrode. Galen's body thrashed.

Raven saw a pulse in Galen's neck. Raven put his lips to Galen's once more, and breathed. When he drew his head back, the little light gleamed momentarily in Galen's throat and returned back down into Galen.

Raven asked Lemuel, "What is this light? I was thinking Galen's life was in Wendy."

Lemuel shook his head. "I don't know. A temporary life lent to him by Hyperion? A symbol?"

The three dark gods took another step into the hall. The corpses of the dead men in the hall were being wrapped in the loose chain ends radiating from the figure of War. The chains, like tentacles, pulled the dead men up into the mouth of the Beast, who chewed and consumed them, blood drooling from the terrible fangs.

The figure of Death raised his great sickle, and leaned forward. The shadow of the sickle fell in the large semicircle on the ground around Galen. Then, as the cold, black hand drew the sickle slowly back, the creeping shadow slid across the floorboards, closing in on Galen.

The figure of Fate put her glove on Death's mountainous shoulder. NOT HIM. Fate's flail pointed at Wendy. IT SHALL BE THAT ONE.

Wendy straightened up, a far-off look in her eye. Whatever reprieve she thought Lemuel's hope had given her was gone. In a small and solemn voice, Wendy said, "She's right. This all started because I lived past my time." Then, almost angrily; "Koschei! Come here! I want you to take my life and give it to Galen!"

A wash of darkness slid down from the balcony like a waterfall of mist, and crawled across the floorboards, a carpet of dark fog. As it came near Wendy, the pool collected together, rearing up, shrinking and thickening into the tall, starved, angular form of Koschei. The darkness he wore as a cloak rippled, and bones and skeletal plates rose up into view like stones emerging from sinking stream-beds, and formed his grotesque armor.

His pale, thin hand held up his pale, thin scabbard. The hilts of his blade were wound around with complex knots. "Undo this knot, fairy-girl, and I shall perform."

Raven stepped between where Wendy stood and where Koschei loomed and swayed like a leafless tree. Raven spread his arms, putting Wendy behind his back. "No! Should be me! Take my life instead, Spirit! Is my fault and I must pay!"

Wendy put her hands up onto her husband's shoulders and whispered into his back, "It's past the time to be afraid, Raven. I may be going into a dark place. But it's okay. Really. Because I know that dark place is not a pit. It's just a tunnel. And the tunnel leads to a brighter place on the other side."

The shadow of the sickle of Death still formed a half circle on the floor around Galen. The three outer gods stood like towers, impassive, patient, motionless, looking down gravely at the small beings gathered at their feet.

Koschei offered his sword hilt now toward Raven. In the gaunt and famished gray face, Koschei's eyesockets gleamed like two points of marsh gas, glinting in the shadow of his crown of dead men's severed hands. "Unbind my power, then, son of the Titan; the choice of Alcestis lies before you," came the eerie, echoing voice, "But be comforted: They say the torments in the wood of suicides in the gardens of Dis are lighter for those who take their lives to save another's."

Raven slowly reached out his hand, but he felt a rapid wind blowing in from the broken windows down the hall, and he heard an unsteady rumble of thunder. He drew a deep breath to calm himself. Raven muttered to himself, "Why so afraid? Why should I try to make same mistake again . . . ?"

Meanwhile, Wendy was trying to push in front of him, "No, Raven! I'm just not going to let you do this, that's all! Koschei! I'm ready!"

Lemuel snapped, "Stop it, you two! Anubis! I know your secret name!" He stepped forward, tracing a star shape in the air with his left pinky. Koschei was flung backward across the hall, and he landed in a clatter of bones, his darkness sweeping the floorboards about him.

Lemuel said angrily to Wendy and Raven, "This is very foolish and very dangerous! You don't talk like that to Archons from the spirit-world! Apollo said there was a logical way to solve this, and I'm not going to hear any more talk about anyone dying!"

But Koschei had gathered himself upright again, his

shoulders and head floating upward as the pool of darkness spread at his feet shrank. "Too late, old guardian." The voice of Koschei was like a violin. "You think to match yourself against me? It is only the young who delude themselves to deem that Death can be overcome. You and I, however, old, old man, we know the same fear. You see the grave in your bedsheets each night you lie down, not knowing if you will rise again. You hear the footfall of the psychopomp when the murmur of your heart skips; in your cough, you hear the crow's cry."

Koschei hissed, and his eyes glinted pallid fire as he saw Lemuel blench and stiffen. Koschei's sinister voice purred: "Your knowledge of the night-world is as great as mine, old man; why have you not called upon the Horrid Powers to shed mortality? Be as me, and escape the jail of life; those who cannot live therefore cannot die."

Lemuel took a breath, and calmly said, "I read in my books that you were a shadow, Koschei, a shadow who says the Sun cannot exist because he never sees it. Those shadows who embrace eternal death cannot see sunshine of eternal life. There is always something blocking his way."

Koschei said, "Wise words! Your wisdom is too late, this time. The deed is done. Observe." And he held up his naked blade in his hand.

Raven shouted, "But I didn't untie it this time!"

Koschei's voice hummed with echoes. "A word is sufficient." He pointed the sword at Wendy, made a slashing motion, pointed at Galen. Raven stepped before Wendy, blocking the way.

Behind him, Raven heard Wendy gasp. He turned to catch her as her body fell limp in his arms. A pearl of light flew out from her mouth and darted into Galen. As the light touched him, Galen's eyes flickered open.

The voice of War roared in the hall. "Victory! Take

them both. She is dead of her disease, he is a disembodied spirit."

Raven was looking into his wife's face when he saw her go pale, sallow, hollow cheeked and baggy eyed; as if an instant had recaptured all the hours and days of pain and waiting in the terminal ward at the hospital.

Lemuel was staring in horror at Galen. The little light which dove into his body immediately bobbed out from his mouth again, as if there was nothing inside his flesh to hold it. Galen convulsively came to his knees, snatching at the light with his hands. It slid through his fingers and began to drift away. Galen crawled forward with frantic awkwardness, clawing toward the gently bobbing light.

Koschei said, "The first of mortal race, by his crime, condemns all children of his blood, mixed or pure, into the authority of Death; your life, for that original sin, is forfeit! Do you deny this?"

Raven shouted, "She is not awake and cannot answer you!"

Pendrake, speaking down from the balcony, said in a voice of ice, "I deny it. A child cannot be justly punished for the crime committed by another person, even if that other person is her father. Nor can anyone be justly punished without a trial, without any defense, and without a statement of charges; and to be alive, to be human, these things are not a crime. Galen, shoot her with your bow."

It was with a very brave look on his face that the kneeling Galen, ignoring the living light which floated ever farther from him, put out his hand to have the bow and arrows jump up from the floor into his grasp. He drew the bowstring to his jaw and loosed a shaft. There was sunlight.

When Galen's shaft entered her, Wendy face grew full and healthy again. Her eyes opened slowly. She said, "It's not true."

"What? What is this?" said Raven softly.

Wendy said, "There is no death. A light told me. It's not true."

Pendrake drew a folded leather coat from a deep pocket in his cloak and tossed it, spinning and flapping through the air, down toward Galen. "This is your property, Galen. I should have given it to you earlier, but it took me till just now to figure out what it was. Gwendolyn! If he has any trouble putting that on, see if you can use your wand in reverse to help him."

Wendy kissed her husband, walked over to Galen, knelt, and put the Selkie-coat around his throat. When the clasp was shut, Galen looked no different, except that the light from his bow now cast his shadow on the floorboards. The little bobbing pearl of beautiful light circled around him, closer and closer, and landed on his chest, sank in, and vanished.

"Thank you," said Galen softly, "for saving me . . ."

"You're welcome! Thanks for saving me!"

"And . . . umm . . ." Galen suddenly put his hands on her shoulders and thrust his face into hers for an awkward kiss. "Sorry . . . I mean, I really wanted to do that . . ."

Wendy smiled brightly, rising to her feet. "It's okay. A lot of people have been doing that lately. And never apologize for kissing. It sounds bad."

Galen stood up, still with one hand holding Wendy's, then he saw Raven watching with half-hidden amusement, and he dropped his hand nervously away.

Lemuel made a gesture with his fingers, and this flung Koschei across the great hall. "Begone!" Lemuel said. "Your plans have failed!"

Crouching like a great, ragged spider on splayed limbs, his enveloping darkness billowing like a smoky fire, his head cocked sideways at a strange angle, Koschei opened his mouth wide. His voice issued from that mouth, even though no tongue nor lips moved at all. "The dead are dead, healed or no! Her time has passed; her life returned to Galen! If she has no life in her, then she is dead! Do you deny this?"

Lemuel, facing Koschei, turned his head back, putting out a warning hand, "No one speak! Don't answer him!"

The voice of Fate spoke. TAKE HER.

Death stooped, and it was like a mountainside stooping over. The great black hand of Death, coated with icicles of blood and rottenness, emitting a terrible frost, reached down.

Galen, Raven, and Peter, all attacked the hand, with bow, bolt, bullets, and hammer. It was as if they attacked five pillars of solid iron; the hand did not bother to brush them aside.

Raven had his arms still wrapped around the gigantic thumb joint when the hand closed around his screaming wife and rose back into the air. The stink of the hand, and the terrible penetrating cold, dazed him. The floorboards fell away underfoot, dizzyingly, as if he were being hauling upward by a crane. He tried to pull himself closer to his wife, hammering at the huge plate of the thumbnail.

Wendy had one arm free; the other was pinned to her side. There were tears in her eyes from the pain of the cold and of the grip. In that hand she held the unicorn horn. She brought its silver-tipped point down into the iron flesh; the horn stabbed into the hand of Death like a dagger. Wendy said, "Begone! Back to the dreamrealm with you! Go away! Oh, and leave me here! And my husband!"

Then Raven was falling through midair, his wife's small hands plucking at his broad shoulder. Death had vanished.

But Wendy was not strong enough to hold him. Raven shouted as he fell, "Galen! Get your bow!"

Then a giant goat-monster was in the air next to him, hot smoke breathing from its nostrils. The huge, square yellow teeth of the monster grabbed him unceremoniously by the coattails, and he was momentarily strangled by his own coat.

He heard Wendy's voice call out, "You, too! Fate and War, I banish you!"

YOUR AUTHORITY EXTENDS ONLY SO FAR AS THE PRECINCTS OF THIS HOUSE, AND ONLY UNTIL MORNINGSTAR PLACES HIS BOOT UPON THE EARTH. WE ARE CONTENT TO WAIT.

They vanished like nightmares.

II

Raven was next to Peter. Peter was petting the goat-monster, trying to get Raven's coattails out of its teeth, going, "Good boy! Always teach your pets how to fetch! Okay! Let go, boy! We don't want to have to ask Mr. Hammer to make you let go, do we, you dumb, stinking goat?! That's a good boy!"

Pendrake did a flip over the balcony railing, hung by his hands for a moment, and dropped lightly to the floorboards. He walked up at about the same time Wendy floated down to Raven.

"Let's make a plan," said Pendrake.

Lemuel was staring up at the broken windows. "They're out there."

It was true. As if the funnels of tornadoes were to stand, looming between earth and sky, the three dark gods stood surrounding the house. War was to the West, with treetops around his ankles and floating chain ends writhing like blind arms. Death was to the north, one foot to either side of the range of hills in the distance. To the south was Fate, one foot on the land and one foot on the surface of the sea. All around them the twilight landscape was silent.

III

Pendrake said, "There's nothing to the east."

Lemuel said, "I suspect there is no need. The city of Acheron must be in that direction, rising from the bottom of the sea."

Peter said, "Look! How long do we have? What have we got by way of bigger firepower? Aren't there more magic ordinance hidden around this joint?"

Lemuel said, "Minutes only, I suspect. The Sun hid his face the moment the tallest tower of Acheron, the one called Despair, cleared the waves. The city is vast indeed, and it may take hours to rise up entirely; we may have until the planet Venus reaches the zenith. On the other hand, we may have minutes only."

Pendrake said, "Venus doesn't go to the zenith."

Lemuel nodded, "Not heretofore. It shall hereafter, and if the prophecy is true, it will not sink again, but rise to become the new polestar."

Raven said, "One question, eh? This Morningstar, you know, to get to Earth and put his foot on it. He has to walk through this house? Up from ocean, out front door?"

Lemuel said, "More or less. With the Silver Key you can make another spot with the same properties as this house."

"Blow up house. Burn it."

Lemuel shook his head. "After three days of dream deprivation, people begin to hallucinate; soon they die. We need the dream-world to survive, mankind does, the same way we need bread."

Raven said, "Burn it, then remake it."

Peter said, "What about reinforcements? The Fairy-Queen? The lios-alfar? Glinda, the Good Witch of the North?"

Lemuel said softly, "The time has come to wake the sleepers. In citadels of light they sleep, high above the Autumn Stars for these great ages of the world, prepared at last for this last day. We must blow the Last Horn Call. And perhaps Raven was right after all. We must burn and remake, if not this house, then perhaps the world."

Silence held the group for a moment.

Lemuel said quietly, "You know, I have always hoped to be alive at these times. All the previous Guardians, I'm sure, wished for it, for their long watch against the darkness to draw to an end, to lay down the burden of the guardianship. In dreams they let me see from afar, as if from a mountainside, the shining fields and gardens that the Lords of Light will grant us as a new world to replace this lost old world. I have often wondered what it would be like to lie in those fields of clover, watching clouds roll by, in a long, golden dream, once more like it was when the world was young . . ."

"Maybe I can get my legs back then. Go dancing. Climb a mountain," muttered Peter.

Pendrake said, "It will not happen."

Like a man stirred from a dream, Lemuel said, "I beg your pardon?"

Peter said to Pendrake, "Look, pal, I didn't believe all this shit till just a few days ago myself. But this is it. Curtain call, you know? We ain't got what it takes to fight the big guys, these gods of darkness. Time to cut our losses and retreat to this new world."

Wendy said, "Are you people crazy, or what? You can't just go blowing trumpets and ending worlds like that! Let's beat them up ourselves!"

Lemuel raised his hand, "I realize that you are not of this family, miss, and do not know the prophecies told in secret to the Guardians concerning the end of time, but we all know . . ."

"No." They turned at the sudden voice. It was Galen.

Galen said, "No, we don't. I don't. Sorry, Grandpa, but they're right. We have to find another way. We can't blow the Final Horn Call."

Lemuel smiled and said to Peter, "Perhaps we should have named him Roland."

Peter said, "Look, son, maybe you don't understand the situation. This family, we're guards on post. It's a long war, so we got to wait a few hundred years before we're called into action. But our orders are, when the enemy is sighted, tell headquarters, blow the damn horn, and call the goddamn cavalry. Then we haul our asses out of here and go enjoy some R and R in paradise."

Galen said angrily, "You? I don't need you to be telling me what this family is supposed to stand for! You're the one who walked away, not me! And if all soldiers can do is obey orders without asking questions, then maybe I don't want to be a soldier anymore!"

Lemuel looked a little surprised, but said quietly to Peter, "Son, he might be right. I seem to recall you said a very similar thing to me just a very little while ago."

Raven said, "Look. Am not sure we is having so much time for family squabbling now, eh? Is there plan we can make for fighting Acheron?"

Peter said, "Hey, pal! We didn't butt in when you were having your family squabble!"

Pendrake said, "Gentlemen, please. Let's have a little order in our discussion. Destroying the Earth by calling this celestial cavalry should be out of the question until we exhaust all other possible remedies. It will be much more difficult to overthrow Oberon's government if we are all trapped in his paradise; but a Pyrrhic victory might still be better than no victory, so we cannot rule out blowing the Last Horn Call entirely. Agreed? Next item: finding more magic talismans to fight these three gods of darkness. Lemuel? Where and what are they?"

"The Sword of the Just, called Calipurn, and the Chalice of Hope Renewed are hidden in the Country of Gold. The Country of Gold is a special hidden section of the dream-realm, recently created by the Freemason

Illuminati, so that the American Guardians could hide the talismans where no other dream-creatures could reach. The theory was that the Old World beings do not understand the American Dream. And, yes, they erected the symbols around our money. For better or worse, that is what the root of our dreams are."

Pendrake asked, "How does that work? I would think dreams are amorphous?"

Lemuel said, "Certain symbols and ideas are permanent; certain dreams do not die. A nation or a people can have a spirit, can have a dream, that endures while the nation endures. The American Dream is in the Country of Gold. This country is an artifact, a made thing, created by men who knew my arts, in much the same way Oberon and Titania have made landscapes and castles among the dreaming. These weapons we seek are older and deeper dreams, more permanent still: the dream of justice is as old as mankind."

"Good. Wendy's got the Key; we can get those two," said Pendrake.

Lemuel said, "There is a price for those. No one can lift that Sword except someone worthy to rule the Earth; no one can hold the Chalice except his heart is pure and sinless. While you might be able to hold that Sword without it destroying you; I can tell you that I am certainly not worthy to touch such a Chalice."

Pendrake looked surprised. "I was going to have someone else get the Sword. I'm not a politician. But how sinless does a man have to be to be considered sinless? Have you ever committed murder? Theft? Adultery?"

Lemuel said, "Of course not. But out of all King Arthur's knights . . ."

Peter said, "They committed murders. They were soldiers. Soldiers kill people."

Wendy said, "He's right, you know! Also, I don't think knights were Christians until after King Arthur converted them. So they must have had a lot of fornication, because pagans are more fun people than Christians. And I think you are perfect for getting the Chalice, Lemuel!"

Galen said, "Grandfather, it must be you. Who of us has been steady and unwavering enough to hold onto our hope without spilling a drop?"

Pendrake said, "That's decided."

Lemuel said, "Wendy, find a five-dollar bill; touch the Silver Key to the reverse."

Pendrake said, "The Chalice is in the Lincoln Memorial?"

Lemuel said, "It's actually in the Reflecting Pool before the monument. The president who freed the slaves and reunited the Union was given custody of the talisman of Hope."

"And the Sword?" asked Pendrake, "Let me guess. Washington?"

Lemuel said, "Wendy, touch the one-dollar bill. There is a pyramid without a crown, the edifice for a nation that bows to no earthly monarch. The hidden capstone hides the Sword."

Pendrake said, "Let's discuss the next point before we do anything rash. What do these talismans do?"

Galen said, "The Sword of Justice conquers the Beast called Hate. I don't know about the Chalice . . ."

"Hope of Life Renewed washes away our fear of Death," said Lemuel.

"You never told me that, grandfather . . ." said Galen.

Lemuel said, "I was going to wait till you were older. The temptation to misuse that cup is very great. Koschei the Deathless used to be human, you know. He used to be one of our order, a mage in the court of the Byzantine emperor."

Pendrake said, "Does anything repel the Fate goddess?"

Lemuel said, "Not to my knowledge."

Galen said, "Nothing except the Titan himself. That's what Azrael told me. The Titan."

Raven straightened up, a strange look in his eye. "Koschei called me son of Titan. Prometheus. My father saw on the mountainside. Titan of Fire. Gave to mankind. Fire. What is word in English? Enlightenment."

Pendrake said, "Okay, we launch an expedition into the dream-lands and get the two missing talismans, find and free Prometheus. Can we do it from here? I had to go through a graveyard in Louisiana, back in my day."

Galen said, "This house has special properties. When did you go to the dream-world?"

"It's where I met my wife. I'll tell the story some other time. Next, we have to discover where Acheron is specifically rising. I need to know the exact position. Do we have any magic method of finding out?"

Lemuel said, "The planetarium upstairs can tell us where any awakened magic in the world is centered. We can find Azrael's chariot wherever it goes on Earth. But why do we want to know from what part of the sea Acheron will appear?"

Pendrake smiled. "Maybe these supernatural beings are pretty tough. Let's see how the magic of modern science stands up to them. I have the presidential emergency launch device in my car, and can code in new targets. The bad guys foolishly disabled their own ability to override the launch signal. I can hit any spot on the planet. Let's nuke Acheron."

18

The Name
of the
Raven

I

Lemuel objected. "Such weapons are too dangerous to be used."

Pendrake said coolly, "Really? More dangerous than Morningstar?"

Peter said, "Give it up, Dad. I've served with men whose lives were saved by dropping the A-bomb on Japan. Men who would have died storming the home islands. You can't tell me you'd rather have the powers of Acheron overrunning the Earth than use a bomb. It's just a bomb, just a tool."

Lemuel said, "So is an electric chair a tool; so is a thumbscrew or a torture rack. It is an act of despair to say one has no choice but to use such means! Some third option will always present itself, if fate is gracious."

Pendrake said, "And it is an act of injustice to condemn a world to hell, merely because the means to achieve victory are distasteful to you."

Galen said, "Grandpa, fate is not on our side, this time. She works for the enemy." He pointed out the windows at the iron-faced hag, a column of darkness that stretched from the leafless treetops of a dark earth to the black clouds in a starless heaven. "Besides, my bow might be able to cure any radiation poisoning in the area."

Lemuel said, "What do you two say?"

Wendy shrugged. "You have to understand my daddy. He is a very serious person. He does serious things to people."

Raven blinked. "Why are we talking? In Russia, we prayed you would blow up Moscow, prayed every day, and free us. Except, well, not allowed to pray. You know they burned the churches, killed the priests. Killed the farmers. Killed everyone. Millions die in famine that Stalin orders. My father tells me the stories. So many fewer people would have died, you Americans had blown up Moscow. But you never did. So, blow up Acheron; this seems like not such a bad idea, not to me. You have better idea, eh?"

Lemuel did not have a better idea.

II

Raven went up to the planetarium with Galen. Pendrake and Lemuel were with Wendy in the main tower, summoning their weapons from the dream-world. Peter, who had difficulty getting upstairs anyway, stayed in the main hall guarding the prisoners. When they had left him, Peter had been sitting near the enormous gray Seal-King, puffing on a cigarette, and then holding the butt up to the Seal-King's whiskered muzzle. The seal would take a puff or two, and then Peter would take a puff. The seal had seemed melancholy, lying on his belly among so many corpses of his folk; but the tobacco seemed to give him a small cheer.

The door to the north tower was inscribed with zodiacal signs. To the right, hung a portrait of winged Eros embracing Psyche beneath a starry sky; a plaque beneath read, "Oh, be a fine girl, kiss me." To the left, was a woodcut of a farmwife in a country kitchen, ladling jam out of a jar onto a slice of bread, with an eager little boy below tugging at her skirts, looking upward.

There was seven stairs of seven colors leading upward. The colored marble floor of the planetarium was inscribed with a polar projection map made perhaps two centuries ago, Latin inscriptions curled among the wind-roses; and the interiors of some of the oddly shaped continents were blank, or were drawn with mythic animals.

Seven great armatures rose like brass arches across the height of the dome above, and an intricate clockwork of cycles and epicycles held seven mirrors in the positions of the Sun, the Moon, and the planets between Saturn and Mercury.

Galen put on a white robe he found in a closet, took out a crystal orb from a locked cedar chest. This orb he put atop the tripod that stood atop the North Pole. Beneath the tripod he placed a golden lamp he took from the same chest. He said an invocation and lit a candle.

Galen extinguished his lantern, so that the golden lamp was the only light in the room. Smoke from the lamp made an intricate pattern of smudges across the lower hemisphere of the crystal ball. Rays of light from the upper hemisphere of the ball touched the prisms and mirrors that formed the major stars and the planets on the dome above. Thin, colored rays of red and cerise, blue and blue-green reached down from the dome's heaven. Dots of tinted light rested on the world map. In places where the rays, shining down at different angles from the different planetary mirrors, over-lapped, at these spots the light was white.

Galen consulted an almanac, said another set of in-vocations, and turned the handles of the clockwork to shift the planets into proper positions. Then, with a measuring rod, he paced off the longitude and latitude to where the colored rays formed one or two white dots.

Galen frowned down at the notebook where he had written his results, puzzled. Raven, who thought he had guessed how this magic worked, pointed up at the silver mirror representing Venus, and said, "Venus out of orbit right now, eh?"

Galen smiled in surprise.

They went out on the balcony, measured the height of Venus with an astrolabe, and then Galen carefully raised the mirror to a new calculated position on the dome with a pole.

Galen pointed at the silvery spot trembling in the mountains of Peru. "I think that smaller light there is Azrael. And see this spot up here on the coast of Maine? That's us."

"And this large one, eh?"

"The stronghold of the enemy. Acheron."

Raven squatted down and looked at where the very bright white fleck of light now hovered on the floor. "Marianas Trench," he said. "Middle of Pacific. Deep-est sea trench in world."

Neither of them had noticed Pendrake at the door until he spoke. "Get the coordinates. The aircraft car-rier USS *Harry S. Truman* is in those waters; now we know why Azrael's people ordered it there. They would have used a carrier group out of San Diego, had they not lost control of the Pacific Fleet to mutiny. The mid-Pacific! Good fortune for us; if Acheron had chosen to surface in the Aral Sea, or nearer to the Asiatic coast, our actions would start the first atomic world war."

Raven turned, and his eyes grew wide when he saw the sword Pendrake carried, hand on hilt, naked blade against his shoulder. All the haft twinkled with diamond sparks, myriads of topaz-lights, and jacinth-work with subtlest jewelry. The blade itself was polished to a mirror shine, so that a man would see his own face in it, were the blade close enough to strike him; and the letters etched into the blade spelled out: TAKE ME UP.

Pendrake said, "What about Prometheus?"

Raven pointed glumly to the carven map of western Russia underfoot. No glints of light were there. "We see nothing," said Raven.

Galen said, "The gate to the dream-world must still be shut, there."

Raven said, "Where is Wendy, eh?"

Pendrake said, "Lemuel wanted to talk to her alone. He came back from the dream-world with the Chalice, but it was covered by a white cloth, and he doesn't want to show it to anyone. I asked him what happened when he got the cup, but he seemed really shaken up, and wouldn't talk about it. 'Shaken up' isn't quite the right word. Amazed; reverent. He only made a comment that time in the dream-world is not the way it is here, and that years can pass in a moment of dreaming."

"And you? What did you see?" asked Galen.

Pendrake said, "I was standing at twilight on a marshy moor, with no path nor track to be seen, and up in front of me, there rose a topless pyramid of thirteen blocks. And the twilight was not coming from the sun, for there was no sun in that land, but from the eye of God, which hung above the pyramid . . ."

At that moment, there came a sound of drums crashing and trumpets braying, high up from outside, from the Eastern sky. The noise resolved itself into a tritonal chord, and the source of the eerie music passed from west to east in the heavens, diminished in the distance, and was gone.

Raven was clutching his ears, looking upward at the dome's ceiling, eyes staring and mouth a-gape. Galen started to draw his bow and then lowered it with shaking hands. The arrow fell from his string and lay gleaming on the marble.

Pendrake frowned thoughtfully. "Mr. Waylock? Galen . . . ?"

Galen whispered, "They were the seven Amshaspands of Acheron; Taurvi, Zairicha, Khurdad, Murdad, and two others. They are released from the tower called 'Injustice' to herald the coming of the empire of darkness; the drums they beat are made from the hides of apostate martyrs. It means that the tops of three of the towers, those of the central keep, must be above water at this point, though the gates should still be under. We have a lot less time than Grandpa thought."

Pendrake said, "Let's move it."

Raven said, "How are we finding Prometheus?"

Pendrake said, "Your father is still alive?"

Raven blinked. "Sure. Lives in New York City. He . . ."

"Call him. He knows where the Titan is."

Galen said, "No phones in this old place. And my cabin out there is trashed."

Pendrake, without speaking, took a matte black cellular phone out from a cloak pocket, unfolded it with a flick of his wrist, tossed it to Raven.

Raven wondered why a strange sense of nervousness began to crawl over him as he started to dial.

III

Wendy followed Lemuel into a small room paneled in carven woodcuts. He carried no lantern; the pulse of rosy light breathing out from underneath the large, white veil that draped the chalice cast a fog of light about his feet as he walked, and shadows played along the ceiling.

Wendy watched as Lemuel carefully slid shut the

panel behind him. She said, "Okay! I'm ready. What do I have to do?"

Lemuel bent his stiff knees with a grunt, and motioned for Wendy to kneel. Wendy whispered, "Is this going to be religious?"

Lemuel smiled sadly. "It might be easier if it were. I was hoping we would not fall so far if we fainted. But perhaps that is why people knelt when they saw holy things to begin with."

He put the Chalice carefully down on the floor between them, and the veil stirred and its edges rippled weightlessly, as if the pressure of the light were living in it.

"Now, Wendy, you are a very nice girl, and this should be no problem for you . . . not . . . not like I had . . . don't be nervous . . ."

Wendy could not think of anything he could have said that would have made her more nervous. A tremble went up her spine.

Lemuel closed his eyes for a long moment, as if he were praying. Then he opened them slowly and looked deeply into Wendy's eyes, and he said, "Wendy, please keep in mind that everything we do and say in this life, and even everything we think, is being watched and judged. Judged to see if we will abide by that law which is written into every man's heart from the day he is born. This law has two parts. Men have thoughts and reason, to tell them about the world we know, and any rational man knows he must treat others as he himself wishes to be treated. That is the Golden Rule and it is the law of this world."

He continued, "Men also have feelings and intuitions to tell them that, even if this world we know does not enforce this law, some other world, some next world, a world we don't know, ought to enforce it. We don't know what happens after death. Where we don't know, we can only hope, or despair. We either hope, without evidence, that there is a life after death; or we fear, equally without evidence, that there is not."

Then he said, "Remember what you say is being judged. And tell me whether you have hope in life after death."

Wendy laughed.

She said, "Well, of course! Don't be silly!"

Lemuel licked his lips. He said, "Yes . . . ? And why?"

Wendy rolled her eyes, as if he had asked her the most obvious thing in the world. "If there is nothing after this life, then nobody's story, not a single person's, would have a happy ending, right? And every story with a happy ending would just be a lie. And then there wouldn't be any point in going on with the story, would there? There wouldn't be any point in anything."

Now she smiled like sunshine: "But we all know what happy endings are. We've always known, everybody. Happiness is real. It's the only thing that really is, isn't it?"

Lemuel looked slightly puzzled, and perhaps fearful, as if this were not the answer he'd expected; but his fear turned unexpectedly to joy when he saw the veil stirring and lifting.

Silently, with no hand to touch it, the white cloth floated up, dancing, away from the Chalice, made buoyant by the streams and pulses of light that now inundated the room.

Lemuel's eyes began to water from the brightness of it; but he dared not look away. Wendy, her face transfixed with joy beyond all smiling, looked down at the Chalice.

It was a simple cup with a broad bowl, deep and generous, standing on a square stem, and it was made all of smooth ivory, so that the light that beat through the sides and smoky stem dyed all things rosy red. But the light itself within was diamond and prismatic, for it was a pool of pearls and flock of burning butterflies.

Wendy had seen such a light before; in Galen's hand or being pushed by Raven's breathe back into Galen's body. It was the light of living souls, a multitude of abundant lights. She wondered what great spirit, or what man, had put so much, a living force equal to so many lives, into this cup of hope, that others might one day drink of it.

Where that light fell, the wooden carving on the wall immediately burst into the buds and flowers of each type of tree from which those planks had come. Her cotton skirt put forth bolls and cotton flowers. She giggled when she saw her patent leather shoes grow hair.

Then, her face all solemn, and her eyes all shining with delight, without waiting to be asked, Wendy put down her head and drank her fill.

Strangely, the more she drank, the more the cup seemed to hold, until it overflowed the brim.

When she and Lemuel left the little closet, there was a sapling growing up in the spot where the cup had spilled, and the little closet was filled with leaves and springtime air.

Because Wendy went skipping and floating up ahead of him, laughing for joy and kicking away her shoes, Lemuel was left behind; and he was alone when he heard the monstrous drum beats thunder from the east, and the shriek of strange trumpets pass by overhead, traveling west.

His face was pale with fear, which the rosy light from the Chalice could not blush red again. Lemuel tucked the cup, swathed in its long white veil, beneath his arm as he ran upstairs.

IV

Var sat nodding in his threadbare but comfortable armchair in his small apartment, petting the cat that purred in his lap. He knew he had trouble staying awake nowadays, but, on this day of all days, he had set the two alarm clocks that stood clicking on the mantle-piece, ticking loudly in the quiet little room.

He had not shaved or cut his hair in many, many days, and now his hair lay like a blanket of snow across his shoulders, and the cat was batting at the long curls of the white beard.

The chair faced the window, outside of which there was a little park, the only spot of greenery to be found in acres of surrounding concrete, glass, and steel. Sometimes children played there. Var found it more interesting than television, which stood neglected in the corner where he had pushed it the last time it had broken.

The stove had also broken long ago. Atop the stove stood the electric hotplate and saucepan upon which he warmed the cans of soup he ate for his meals. At times, he got the impulse to walk down to the corner shop to drink a cup of coffee or eat a plate of scrambled eggs made by his friend Hezikiah; sometimes he was actually in his burly coat and pacing slowly down the sidewalk before he recalled that the corner shop had closed four years ago, and that Hezikiah had died five years ago.

Above the window was thumbtacked his calendar, which, page after page, he had waited through, crossing off the days until this one, the day circled in gold and overwritten and surrounded with small pictures and cartoons. Those pictures, during long, boring months and weeks, he had drawn to remind him of everything he had been told about this day.

Here were tiny drawings of black towers rising from the sea, drawn in the margins above the name of the month: there were pictures of flying goats drawing a chariot; a great ship; a heroic figure crucified upon a cliff, the chains that bound him parting; here was a girl with a key, floating in the air; and there was a wizard with the key now in his hands; and the sun going dark at noon.

When he was in the hospital this most recent time, and he saw the other old people dying around him, he knew the cause. They had nothing for which to live. They did not have the pictures. They did not have the awaited day, the day circled in gold.

Var, however, refused to die that time, and his stubbornness pulled him back.

Below the window was the radiator, upon which he had placed a board, draped in a red cloth; here was a picture, drawn in charcoal, now framed under glass, of his long-dead wife. Every day he replaced the flowers in the vases to either side. Almost every day. Sometimes he forgot.

He had been napping when the Sun went dark at noon; one moment, he was nodding in the sunlight; and the next, he jerked his head upright, seeing it was night. He knew, somewhere above the stinks and smokes of this city, the constellations would be all wrong; Autumn Stars shining in the spring.

Var sat with one hand on the telephone, counting down the seconds on his pocket watch. He remembered, about twenty years ago, losing the long speech he had written down in preparation for this day, and how frantically he had, over the next year or two, tried to remember and recreate the wording of that speech. Now he had only the notes he had jotted down four years ago, when he noticed the light of his memory beginning to dim.

He picked up the phone a second before it rang.

"My Son," he said in his native language. "I was told you would call. This I was told when you were less than one year old, when I stood in the mountains, surrounded by snow, surrounded by enemies. Your real father was chained up on the mountainside before me. His love had killed your mother.

"Wait. I am explaining. You listen. She knew a baby born of such a father might be too big for her hips to bear. But she had seen him three times climbing the frozen mountains by herself. Very courageous woman, your mother. Afraid of nothing. I remember how the midwife, her hands all bloody, was all tears. Not your mother. Her eyes were clear, even while she was dying. And she said you must live, even if she were to die, because you would save the world and your children would heal it.

"Listen, Prometheus is chained on the cliffs 1,028 meters northeast-east from the highest point of Mount Kazbek in the Caucasus. But you will find it more swiftly if you take the road to it, which I took from it when I flew away. My daughter-in-law has a silver key, does she not? Prometheus said it would be in her hand. There is a doctor with a bow and arrows with you, is there not? A man who can heal all wounds? Yes. Listen; these are the instructions. I have waited thirty years to say them, so you must listen.

"The doctor must make your wife sleep; he must make her dream that she is standing beneath a high mountain. In the sky above is a raven fighting with a vulture. She must unlock the sky with her key, and the road will come down to her from the door which opens in the sky. There will be a creature guarding the beginning of that road. To that guard, she must say, Piotr Ivanovitch Vanko has lived without his name for thirty years; you must take me to the place where he had hidden it; and she must say these magic names; listen carefully; she must say, 'I order you in the names of the saviors of mankind: by Prometheus, savior of fire; by Ducaleon, savior of flood, his son; by the blind poet Homer, who taught men to sing; by the wise fool Socrates, who taught men to question.'

"The middle of the road is guarded by the mists of forgetfulness; only one of the men from the tower of four moons, the tower of forever, can pass through. The terminus of the road is guarded by the king of vultures. Only a dream can banish a nightmare.

"Are you writing this down, Raven? Write it down.

"You are wondering the name you were born under, no? What do you mean, you don't want to hear this thing? I tell you even so. You are called Vasil Piotrovitch Vanko, and you will be the father of a race of kings.

"There is no more time. Listen and do not speak! There is a warrior with you, a man with a cart pulled by flying goats? When your wife goes to free Prometheus, you must not wait, but go at once to the great ship which is in the ocean where the black towers rise. There, you must unleash the power of the sun. The Lord of the Black Tower must come himself to face you; and when that happens, you must be ready to blow the horn . . . What? What is that terrible noise? Raven? My Son?"

Var blinked sadly at the phone. Then he slowly replaced it in the cradle. He petted his cat, saying, "And I have been waiting all these years to tell you, that, even if another man is your father, you have always been my own true son, and I have always been very proud of you. That what you did on that lifeboat you had to do, and I never blamed you for that. I never blamed your mother for what she had to do. And you may miss me when I am gone, but I am very tired now, and would like to rest."

A few years ago, he had saved up enough money to move to a place outside of the city, away from the seacoast. But when the time came to move, it did not seem worth the effort, and the savings money had been lost in trickles of little expenses.

At the bottom margin of the calendar, in one corner, was a drawing of the great sea-wave crashing over the Empire State Building. Slightly above it, was a doodle of a man stepping onto a long road leading up to the clouds, with a winged angel pointing the way.

Funny. He had never drawn what was at the end of the road. As soon as the cat moved off his lap, Var decided, he would go get his pencil, and draw in a little picture of his wife.

V

Raven was falling, flung from his feet as the marble world cracked underfoot, and the dome of the sky overhead was hurled up and away into space. Wheels and broken gears, torn from the receding dome, showered through the air, and streamers of brick and rock and dust. Raven, on his back, saw the dome turning end over end high above before it disintegrated into shards of masonry.

His fear made lighting and thunder race through heaven. In a lightning flash he saw the enormous black hands of Death, which had ripped away the dome, descending, and the five bloodstained nails gleamed like five icebergs; and the palm, as it came, was like a storm cloud, blotting out the stars as it grew larger, closer. The little telephone spun away out of his grip before his father had finished speaking; it dropped from his hand and was lost in the darkness.

In the gloom, Galen seemed maimed; but three shafts of sunlight streamed from his bow, and at this the light, he straightened, whole and unhurt. One beam of light touched Raven; the other glanced across the billowing dark cape of Pendrake in the air.

Pendrake had jumped upward off the balcony to escape the eruption of brick as the dome was shattered, and he hung for a moment in midair, falling, weightless. Behind him, larger than an October moon, the beast-face of War came toward him, half-obscured by swathes and clouds of cloaking darkness.

Pendrake twisted in midair and raised the sword to strike, and a flash of light, curled and mazed in the intricate hilt, gleamed forth and shivered along the mirror-blade.

The Beast, roaring, was flung backward across the whole length of the sky, twisting in midair like a cat, paws out as if to land on its feet; but where it landed could not be seen, for it fell beyond the horizon. The words it roared still echoed in the air: "I go now to a hidden place! You shall not overcome me until you discover it!"

Raven was blinded by a white, pure light; he squinted in the glare.

There was Lemuel, standing atop the headless remnant of the broken stairs that once had led to the planetarium. Lemuel's hands were folded in prayer; the Chalice swam and hovered in the air before him, and the light which gushed, living, from that bowl, played against the vast form of Death like searchlights, or as if columns of burning butterflies had been released; and where they touched that form, the huge being was gone like smoke.

Death shrank, spinning through the air like streams of autumn leaves blown by a gale. The streams of darkness passed around Lemuel's shoulders and gathered behind him, forming the cloaked figure again, albeit smaller, man-sized.

The Chalice beat with illumination, red from the body of the Chalice, white and silvery from the mouth of the bowl, till all the air was light, and a white rainbow of perfect light haloed the cup in radiance. Where that light was, there was no place for Death to be; and Death became Lemuel's shadow, clinging to his feet.

But Lemuel did not look behind him, and paid no heed to the shadow at his heels. Raven scrambled to his feet. Rock and debris covered the tilted marble floor between himself and where the staircase hung out over nothing. "Behind you!" Raven shouted, "Is behind you! Death is behind you!"

Lemuel, his eyes still downcast, lifted up a cloth and covered over the floating Chalice. "No," he said.

"Is there! Is right there!" Raven pointed.

Lemuel shook his head. "No more for me than for any other man. While we live, we must cast shadows. Don't worry, Mr. Varovitch."

"But—"

"It's all right. Don't worry."

Galen walked across the broken slabs, shining bow in hand, his eyes turned away to where the figure of Fate still loomed, taller than a whirlwind, the uppermost clouds of the twilight sky wreathing her shoulders. Her iron mask rode above the clouds.

Galen spoke, not taking his eyes from the goddess of darkness: "Grandfather, I think I saw Pendrake fall. But why hasn't Fate attacked? We don't have a charm against her . . ."

"I'm up here," came Pendrake's voice from overhead. He was clinging to the back of Peter's wheelchair, which flew down and landed; and the two goat-monsters kicked irritably at the marble floor, cracking chips and tossing fragments of the walls hundreds of feet away into the air.

After Peter calmed his steeds, he said, "Mannannan told me an attack was coming . . ."

Raven asked, "What? What is this? Told how?"

"How the hell do I know how this magic stuff works? A human voice came out of his mouth though, and warned me. He said he could feel the power of Acheron increasing; strong enough to break into our wards."

Lemuel said, "Where is he now?"

"I let him go."

Galen said, "Dad! You did what?"

"Watch my lips. I let him go. We ain't got a man to spare for prisoner detail; I had to fly out the window and deflect the hilltop joyboy there was throwing on the house."

Raven said, "Hill?"

Peter said, "Knocked it out to sea with my hammer. None of you saw it? Oh, fuck it. My moment of glory, and no one saw it."

Wendy floated up over the edge of the roof and landed lightly with one toe atop a toppled marble wall-slab. "Hi, there! Is everyone okay?"

"Wendy? How do you have this growing from your dress?Flowers?" asked Raven.

"Aren't they the *cutest* things? Lemuel gave them to me!"

"Look there," said Pendrake, pointing west with the sword. The huge, celestial figure of Fate had darkened and faded, shimmering as if it were sinking below rippling water. She became fog, turned, and vanished over the horizon.

Galen said, "We can't track their movements with the planetarium destroyed."

Pendrake said thoughtfully, "This was a desperation attack; they must have been trying to stop us from acquiring the Sword and Chalice . . ."

Peter said, "Don't think so. They picked up and threw a real goddam hill on us. They wanted to flatten this place. You see what that means? They got another place besides Everness to come through into the waking world."

Lemuel said, "Acheron itself is such a place. As soon as it is fully above the waves, it can open its great gates and allow the Hosts of Evil to oversweep the world."

Galen said, "If you're right, Dad, they would not have tried to smash the house unless they were dead sure Acheron was going to make it all the way to the surface."

Pendrake said, "No. Excuse me, and I admit I don't know about this dream-science of yours, but aren't they already convinced that they must succeed? We don't have anything to oppose whatever motion is bringing this dark tower to the surface. They were trying to destroy something else."

Wendy said, "The trumpet!"

Pendrake asked, "What's that, sweetie?"

Lemuel said, "We have the horn to sound the last horn-call, to waken the knights from Celebradon. It is the one thing Morningstar fears."

Peter said, "Hey I just thought of something. Why did the big fate-wench poof and go vanish when Wendy here popped up? Why were they sticking around the house until just now?"

Raven said, "Quiet, all of you! There is no time for talk. My father told me that Prometheus foresaw all this, in exact detail. There is one thing we can do to overcome the dark. He says Wendy must take Key and fly to Mount Kazbek to release Prometheus; we must go to ship on ocean near Acheron. Must go now." And he told them in a few words what his father had said.

Wendy said, "Wow! You really are from a fairy-tale. I always knew you had it in you!" And she gave her husband a hug.

Galen stepped forward. "I can send us both to sleep with a magic word. Only take a second. With the Silver Key, we can go there in the flesh, and come out again at Prometheus's mountain."

Wendy said, "Shouldn't we get the trumpet and bring it with us? Just in case?"

Lemuel said, "The Horn will be there by the time you meet us there."

Pendrake said, "And the rest of us have to get to the *Harry S. Truman* as soon as possible. Before we leave, let me get the emergency launch device from the car." He stroked his chin for a moment, looking right and left. "Ah . . . Am I the only one here who can't fly?"

VI

The dream-road writhed like smoke and was gone, leaving him bewildered. His name and memory escaped him; he was lost in icy wilderness, alone. A man in black, carrying the Great Sword Calipurn, had sent him here. Where?

He found himself atop a black, snow-streaked crag of rock, with the august crowns of mountains looming over him, cloud-touched abysses and deep chasms dropping away underfoot. They were so high, those peaks, that the crystalline singing of the stars came faintly to his ear, like an echo of far choirs, remote, wondrous. A sense of holy dread beat in his heart.

Perhaps he had been here a long time, mazed in these mountain passes, lost in this bleak and freezing place. Or perhaps (and this seemed more likely to him) this was a dream, and the rocks here were saturated with time, bathed in aeons, so that the ground itself inspired a sense of eternity.

A vast voice rose up from the cliffside underfoot, a cry of desolation and anguish. It was not a human voice, but was as if a mountainside were crying aloud in pain.

The young man restrained his impulse to rush forward to the aid of whatever so cried out. He recalled he had been in such a place as this before, a place of cliffs, a place of punishments.

The young man said to himself, "I recall this much. I am a Great Dreamer. I stand within my place of power. Now, patience! If I am patient, the way will be made clear."

With his bowstaff, he drew, in the snow, a circle inscribed in a square, and, when this reminded him of the signs of the wardens of the four quadrants, their four weapons, their gates, he drew their four seals, and their four galleries. In the gallery of air were seven

paintings of English hunting scenes, each hung below
the zodiacal sign of a wandering star. Beneath the sigil
of Saturn, the Sphinx sat couchant, in the dappled
shadow of a bush. On the back of the Sphinx, the
mother of memory, he had placed a child in armor,
carrying a balance scale and a padlock.

When he opened the padlock, he remembered his
name.

"Weigh—lock," muttered Galen. "Very funny."

The lock had a white key in it. The key-ring was
shaped like a mirror set above a cross, the symbol for
Venus. In the mirror was an image of a high-heeled
shoe with a pair of little raven wings springing from
the heels.

"I don't wear high heels!" exclaimed Wendy in ex-
asperation. She walked forward, hips swaying, high
heels clattering on the stones. "And I certainly
wouldn't wear them mountain climbing!"

"Sorry. I just put them on you 'cause that's how I remember . . . um . . . so you wouldn't get lost, or forgotten," said Galen. "It's my magic . . ."

"Oh, right!" she snorted skeptically. "And these fish-
nets? And this miniskirt?! It's so tasteless! I think I
know what you remember about me. Look at this!
Hmph. Men!"

Wendy had hiked up the skirt and extended her leg,
clad in black nylon, as if to display the tastelessness of
her garb. Galen stared, then tried not to stare, smiled,
tried not to smile, looked apologetic; then tried to look
serious, blinking, his mouth open, but with nothing to
say. "Uhh . . . Well . . . That is . . ."

"And what are we here for again?" She tossed her
head to fling her hair out of her eyes, and looked,
wide-eyed, up at the huge granite peaks towering
vastly up out of the clouds to either side.

"Yeah. I'm about to remember," said Galen, plucking a raven's feather, and brushing it over the circle in
the snow he had drawn. When he touched the Greater

Sign of the Guardian of the Quadrant of the East, it turned into an eagle's feather in his hand.

A piercing, shrill scream echoed from the mountain peaks, the deadly cry of a bird of prey, but deep in its note, as if the eagles uttering that scream were vast, vast beyond all measure of earthly birds.

"Oops," said Galen, his eyes round. "Now I remember . . ."

He bowed to his longbow. The staff bent. He strung it. A golden arrow glittered like fire beneath his fingertips as he drew the fletching to his cheek. Bow drawn, he stood with his legs spread, his head back, scanning the starry black sky.

From around the shoulder of a peak all blue with snow it came, its wings, as large as sails, spread wide to ride the streaming winds. Its claws, like crooked thunderbolts, dangled below the pillars of muscles which were its legs. The streamlined head was naked like a vulture's, and the two bright eyes gleamed with malice, self-righteousness, and bitter hate.

The giant vulture lowered like a storm cloud, and its cold shadow fell across the crags, darkening the landscape. Wingtip to wingtip, it seemed to fill all the sky above the mountain. The eagle screamed, and its voice was the voice of the thunderclap.

Galen saw the bloodstains on its claws and beak, and the streaks and stains along the sleek sides of its head, as if it were wont to thrust that head into some living flesh to tear at it. But the blood was light, golden in hue, not red or brown, as if, perhaps, it were not the blood of mortal man at all, but the ichor of the immortal.

He thought in fear: this eagle is an ancient symbol, torn from the deepest heart of mankind. It is the punishment the world visits on the genius, on the idealist, on those who are martyred when they seek, as Prometheus sought, to better men's fate. The forces of Enlightenment, everyone since Socrates and Galileo onward, have always been crushed by worldly power. Here is mankind's darkest nightmare, enemy of hope and light—the old, cynical fear that virtue's only reward in life is crucifixion.

How can I fight such a fear? How can I, I alone, overcome that evil dream?

With leaden arms, as if he were mired in the mud (for this was one of those dreams where motion was all but impossible), Galen raised the mighty bow. The arrow at his cheek burned like a ray of sunlight.

VII

The same moment as the arrow left the string, Wendy said, "But wait! Won't those arrows just heal it? You know, just make it better . . . ?"

The arrow was away. It sped, blazing like a comet, a small, golden light shooting toward the overwhelming darkness of the eagle's breast.

The eagle was touched by the gold light. It shrieked in triumph, a terrifying noise, as it swelled in size, growing in strength, and it folded its vast wings, like a storm cloud narrowing into a tornado. Like a thunderbolt, it fell.

"Oops," said Galen. The shadow of the swooping monster fell across him; the shadow spread out from him in each direction.

He dropped the longbow, yanking a length of string from his pocket. With a flip of his wrist, he tied a quick loop. "Father Time! I snare your fleeing foot! Patience bridles time!"

The bird froze in midair. The loop jerked and trembled in Galen's fingers as if massive and invisible forces were struggling with the knot.

Galen said to Wendy, "I don't know how long I can hold the slow-time frustration dream, so listen! I'm going to hand you my life and my arrows. Fly away from the skyfather-eagle. Come back, heal my body with the arrows, put my life back inside. Got it?"

"But—but—" stammered Wendy, looking scared.

"There is no time! I was impatient, and I used the wrong symbol; you don't use enlightenment on tyrants, and you don't try to reason with unreasoning force; it only encourages them and makes them stronger . . ." Galen's fingers began to slip on the knot. "You're just going to have to save me again, okay?"

"Okay!" said Wendy. "But don't make a habit of this!"

Galen rolled his eyes back so that only the whites showed. In a strange voice he said, "Thanatos! Tartaros! Hades, and Dis! Unwind the ties of Orpheus! I call on Hercules, who conquered Hell, and ask you, if I am slain, to answer this, my final spell, and find me my soul and memory again. Let Koschei's rune, which I, alone of living men have seen, render me again as I and I alone have been, both living and unliving, both seen and unseen! Sator! Arepo! Tenet! Opera! Rotas!"

Galen threw back his head and made a horrid choking noise. A crystalline orb, a flicker of living flame pulsing and beating within it, began to come out of his mouth, large as an egg. He dropped the string. With one hand he reached up to pull the egg forth, and filmy flickers of light danced along his fingertips. With his other hand, he plucked a golden shaft from his quiver. With both hands he extended his treasures toward Wendy, swaying on his feet, his mouth lax, his face empty, his eyes extinguished. Wendy caught up the crystal flutter of life quickly, even as Galen dropped it; and she grasped the blazing arrow. Her eyes were wide with horror, for his fingers were as cold as the fingers of a corpse.

The bit of string writhed; the knot snapped open. Galen's lifeless body began to fall. Wendy, light as thistledown, whirled away, thrown weightlessly aside by the winds that swept from the monster-wings.

Like the fall of the hammer of a Titan, the storm-eagle struck.

Blood flew everywhere.

Floating high above the mountain peak, looking down, Wendy could see the skyfather-eagle in the cleft between the peaks, ravaging, clawing: a writhing black shape of inexpressible fury. To her tear-blurred eyes, it seemed as if a whirlwind, winged with storm and clawed with lightning, were churning and swirling in that space between the mountains. The noise was terrifying.

When it was all over, and the eagle had sailed away like vanishing thunderheads, Wendy spent a long, horrid, silent time trying to gather the scattered limbs and severed head, the shreds of meat, the wads of blood, which had once been the young man. Into the bloody heap she thrust the arrow.

A soft miracle came, and the corpse lay whole, undefiled, and silent. Galen's face was gray and cold and calm beneath the cold, gray skies.

Wendy stood, a gleaming light fluttering in her folded hands, and, for a time, she looked down at that still form.

She tried to force the light back into Galen's lips, tried to thrust it into his chest, but to no avail.

She knew there was something she ought to do, some clever thing perhaps to do with the Moly Wand or the Silver Key, or maybe some way to call or summon the Chalice of Hope. But her mind was blank; she was sad and weary; she could think of nothing.

She wept.

"Hey, little lady," came a cheerful, rough voice behind her, "What's the matter?"

Wendy turned. "Hello," she said.

The stranger was hugely muscled, his upper arms bulky knots, the breadth of his chest magnificent. On his head he wore the tawny skull of a lion, the fur and ears and teeth still attached, and the lion skin was thrown across his vast shoulders like a loose robe, with the giant claws tied in front. The nails were made of black iron.

In his right fist the muscular man held a club of oak. His hair was black and long, unkept, and his smile was huge and cheerful.

"Come on! Come on!" he called. "No blubbering! It can't be that bad!"

"My friend is dead," Wendy softly said.

He blew out his cheeks in an immense sigh. "Hey! That's not so bad. I mean, its bad, but it's not really so very bad. The worse thing about death is, you see, how it makes you forget. But this here is Galen Amadeus Waylock! (You've sure got important friends, I'd say!) He found the lost horn of the star-steed, and overthrew the Demon Kings of Uhnuman. He's the Guardian, he is! He's got his whole memory arranged sort of like a house, see? And not a sloppy house like mine with goats in the kitchen and wood cords piled every which ways by the door, no, his house is a real shipshape affair. All we have to do is stuff that soul in your pretty little hand back down his throat."

"His soul won't go."

"Yeah, well, sometimes you just got to force it. Here. Let me."

"Oh! Oh, do be careful! What are you doing?! You're not going to smash it into him? Put down that club!"

"Don't worry, little miss! I've done it before! Ask Theseus . . . er. Except don't ask him about Perithous . . . Hup! Ho!" The stranger had balanced the fiery crystal orb atop Galen's breastbone and raised his club to hammer it in. With giant strokes he pounded the chest.

"Don't fret, ma'am!" he shouted. "Some folk have weak spirits, and their spirits give way before their flesh does, you know? But this here is Galen Amadeus

Waylock! His spirit survived the touch of Cerberus. His soul will hold . . ."

The sky was darkened with a sudden shadow. From overhead came a thunderous shrill cry of a bird of prey.

The club strokes drove the air in and out of Galen's chest. Galen gasped and sat up, eyes wild. "It wasn't impatience at all!" he said breathlessly.

"What?" said Wendy, blinking.

"Welcome back to the living," said the gigantic stranger, leaning on his oaken club. "You're getting to be a regular customer. If I hadn't been following my old enemy Cerberus around, I never would have been close enough to give you a helping hand."

"Who?" asked Wendy.

"Koschei," said Galen. "Cerberus is another name for Koschei . . ."

The sky about rang with horrid shrieks.

Wendy looked up.

"Well, well," said the huge man, toying with his club. "What now, young Parzifal? The world is ending, the sun has died, and the hawk flung from the wrist of the father of all tyrants wheels and stoops again. What now?"

Galen stood up slowly, his face calm. "I thought impatience was my sin. It's not, or, at least, not entirely. I got in this mess because I thought my need, and the emergency, would justify everything I said or did. When I went to Tirion, I killed a man. I lied and said I was the Guardian when I wasn't. I tried to go down and make a deal with the Selkie, our enemies, just because Azrael told me to. Why? Why? I wanted to prove I was a man, not a frightened boy. No, I wanted to prove I was a hero. The first thing men do, when they are old enough to be men, is stop trying to prove that they are men. They stop trying to be the hero and to do everything by themselves." He smiled grimly. "And, unless they want to turn into little copies of Azrael de

Gray, they stop letting needs and emergencies justify their actions."

He stooped and picked up the string and began to loop a knot again. "I'll try to catch the sky-eagle in a frustration dream again. We have a hero here, a real hero, who can fight the eagle and keep it away from us. . . . That is, sir," said Galen, suddenly shy, "if you are willing to . . ."

The huge man laughed. "Of course! What fights tyranny? Not enlightenment, no, not healing. Courage! Strength! Heroism! And cleaning up after tyrants is no worse than mucking out the Augean stables, I can tell you!" He whirled his club and saluted with it.

"Wendy," Galen said, "you and I are going to go save Prometheus. The Silver Key can make him real. I'm hoping the chains will stay in the dream-realm when that happens. If not, we might have to resort to messier measures."

"Messier?" asked Wendy, smiling. She was pleased that she would have something to do in this rescue.

"Yeah. I figure if his liver grows back every day, his hands and feet can grow back, especially with the help of my arrows. A chain can't hold you if it's chained to something you're willing to give up and have cut off."

The huge man pointed. "Prometheus is that way. Legend might report that I got him down from this mountain, but we'll know the real story, my Lord Guardian. Strength is wasted when it's used without patience. And if you want to be a hero, my young lord, don't fret about it! I wanted to be one too, when I was young, and I ended up being not just a hero, but a god. You might not have much time left, now that the end of the world is here, but maybe you'll have a chance to make some difference before the end, eh?"

"How soon is the end?" asked Wendy, looking up fearfully.

"Now. The time is come," said the huge man. He

saluted once more with his club and turned and marched away, whistling. In the distance, the sky was darkened by a vast, approaching shadow.

"Let's go," said Galen, and he drew the sign to summon the chariot that had brought them here. "Piotr! Show us the way!" A small black raven hopped out from the shadow of a rock nearby, cocked its head to look at Galen with a yellow eye. It opened its bill and croaked at them.

Wendy looked at the bird. "That's my father-in-law, isn't it? His spirit. Is he dead?"

VIII

In his seat of power, carven of black opals, sat great Morningstar, his pinions fanned up to either side, and in his hand, his mighty scepter, which also was his mace.

All about his throne, within that vast and nighted hall, fallen angels bowed with adorations hymned to his dark majesty. Each fell spirit paid homage according to its kind: evil seraphim bowed their heads; cherubim knelt on one knee, their crowns like black flame; thrones knelt fully; dominations crouched with hands grasping the black diamonds of the floor; virtues, powers, and principalities were prone; and all the waters shook and breathed with perfect song.

Music there was, but no other light than that one cold fire which the Lord of Acheron wore like a gemstone on his brow.

On balconies and pillar-tops and in far places, near enough to hear, but not to see, were princes and emperors of races in bondage to Morningstar, or heroes who had distinguished themselves in his service; svartalfar and svart-vanir, dragons, vampires, scorpion-worms, necromancer-kings, sarim and lilim, abdals and amshaspands, chimerae, hydrae, hecatoncheire, and krakens.

Beyond and behind all the gathered and adoring hosts of living beings, within an arch, rose a great window, figured around the boundaries with runes of secret meanings, through which Morningstar could view at once the whole of his terror-builded kingdom.

Three times great shudders trembled though the length and breadth of Acheron, and three times great music was let blown as the topmost three towers rose from the waves.

Through the window, as if through eyes of vultures high above, Morningstar beheld drowned towers rising in skirts of spray and waterfalls pouring from windows and gates, splashing over corbels and gushing from the teeth of machicolated bastions. The upper courtyards were now pools; and the streets and steps and bridges of the higher citadel were rivers, streams, and aqueducts.

Morningstar raised his scepter; the hosts fell silent. There was no noise in Acheron except the sobbing of the Tormented echoing from the Houses of Woe.

The oceans parted and fell away from the tall, black walls of the inner citadel. The four towers of the outer citadel now rose up, broke the shivering curtain of water overhead, and touched the air. With a hideous roaring and confusion, which tossed his court this way and that, the seawaters rushed from the hall.

Morningstar rose to his feet, and the single light that burned from his brow cast out a beam that turned the rushing waters of the presence hall instantly to silent ice, which lay in frozen waves like hills and mountains all around his throne.

Now he nodded, and, at that nod, the far window opened, as it had not opened in a thousand years or more.

And, without the window, Morningstar beheld a great waste of empty waters, dark beneath a sunless sky, and here and there a drift of toppled iceberg floated, released from Acheron's black walls. The cold of the towers had pierced the sky, and it began to snow.

Morningstar looked up to that vast dark shape, riding in the heavens, which had blotted out the Sun. And now he smiled.

His chest swelled as he breathed in air.

"The time is come," he said.

IX

Prometheus hung in chains on the mountainside, his muscles aching once again with agony, his nude body shivering with pain as his torn flesh, once again, was slowly reknitting itself. He had been watching when the full Moon suddenly went dark, and, by this, he knew night had fallen across the noon on the other side of the world.

Yet the features of his face showed no fear, no pain, no uncertainty, only a remorseless, intent, alertness.

Now he raised his pain-stiffened head, and shook the icicles of sweat which clung to his long, tangled locks of hair. This slight motion caused chips of bloody ice to pull away from the lips of the wound in his side, and sent another shiver of pain like a needle into his body.

His eyes narrowed as he looked in the distance.

And he saw, far off and flying down across the mountain peaks of ice and granite, led here by the shade of a raven, a girl in a flowering dress, a wand of truth in one hand, and the key of dreaming in the other. Behind her was a young magician on a dream-colt, with a bow, and the scars of his battle with the vulture of heaven were closing and healing in the light from the arrow on his bowstring.

And now he smiled. "The time is come," he said.

X

Azrael de Gray Waylock lay on his stomach on the edge of an icy ledge, high on a cliff overlooking a darkened world. He inched forward, his face contorted as if in pain. A few inches in front of his outstretched hand, the smallest distance beyond the reach of his imploring fingers, stood a fierce, small bird of prey, feathered in blue and black, with bright eyes, a pigeonhawk.

He inched forward, crawling on his belly like a worm, and the slippery and rotten ice beneath him creaked ominously. He knew that if he moved forward another inch, or half inch, the ice would give way and he would plunge down the steel-hard slopes of cold rock into the abyss below.

The pigeonhawk looked at him disdainfully, and hopped a few more inches away.

"Do not flee from me," Azrael whispered. "Do not despise me."

He crawled forward. The ice began to crack and snap.

The pigeonhawk hopped a few more inches away, ruffling its wings, preparing to fly.

"Wait!" breathed Azrael de Gray Waylock, "I have pursued you from high heaven, where there is no air, across the face of the Earth, flying at the speed of thought, past blasted desert, frozen glacier, and the wilderness of the salt sea. Now, so close! Why must you ever fly from me? What do you disdain so in me?"

The bird spoke in a voice like unto the voice of a man. "I am no more than your mirror, slave of Acheron. Ask yourself what you disdain so in yourself, and you shall know your answer."

With a crack, the ice beneath him tilted. He began to slip sideways, an inch, six inches, a foot. He clawed at the slithering pebbles beneath his hands and said, "Call me not by that name! Tell me what I must do to regain what once I was, I compel you by . . . by the name of . . ."

"The only name with which I may be compelled is your own, slave of Acheron, and you have forgotten it."

"Shall time come when it will be recalled?"

"The time is come," said the pigeonhawk, flying up.

And Azrael, falling from the ice, called for his kelpie chariot in midair, and, mounting, flew up out from the chasm, to give chase to the bird once more.

They passed in a moment across continent and ocean. In the midst of a great fleet of the warships of mankind, the pigeonhawk flew down to roost upon a mighty flagship, built of cold iron, large as a floating city.

On the deck, surrounded by armed men, he saw the chariot pulled by Tanngrisner and Tannjost. Here also, gleaming with fairy-light, beautiful and swift as song itself, a dream-colt reared and plunged, made nervous by the closing circle of sailors.

The young Titan was here, and Peter, and Lemuel, whom he had betrayed; and here as well stood a proud figure in black, a sword of mythic power shining in his hands; the Pendragon.

Even as he watched, he saw Van Dam order the men to stand at ease. Van Dam saluted the Pendragon and asked for orders.

XI

Oberon, Lord of Heaven, stood alone within the private garden which gloamed with twilight hues, lit only by the reflected silver and gemwork of the Towers of Mommur. Now and again, the scented breeze played about the locked gate to the east and breathed the perfumes of paradise across the lawns and hedges.

Oberon stood, hands clasped behind his back, gazing down into his seeing pool.

All at once he grimaced with wrath, wincing. "Fools! Do not let so dangerous a creature loose!"

And then, upon another image, said to himself,

"Wind the Horn! Do not forget the Horn! Have I not promised the whole might of Celebradon shall follow where that horn-call sounds?"

Now he stood in black abstraction, crown of swan plumes bowed. His one eye glittered gray and clear as a winter dusk. Then he spoke. "Must Oberon's own hand make whole what clumsy mortals mar? The time is come."

And drawing on his cloak of mist and shadows, invisible, he dropped down from heaven toward the earth, and he flew with the same speed with which a man wakes from deepest dream instantly to day.

19

Darkness,
Darkness Covers
All

I

The smell of the sea brought back memories, but he had never served on a ship like this. Raven stood on the deck of the aircraft carrier and was amazed that he could feel no pitch nor roll. The vessel was so enormous that it was perfectly steady even in the roughest seas. The upper deck was larger than a football field; jet aircraft, launched by steam catapult, rushed with a thunderous roar down the immense length of the deck and were flung into space, engines blazing. Even more amazing was the sight of other aircraft, rocketing down from the sky to touch the deck, wheels squealing, only to catch a cable with a tail-hook and jerk to an alarming stop. Massive elevators could lower the fighter jets into vast hangar spaces belowdecks.

Raven saw the faces of the fighter pilots as they climbed down from their cockpits. They would take their fibreglass helmets from their heads, shaking back their sweat-streaked hair, and glance around the decks with looks like panthers. The fighter pilots walked with a jaunty step, and there was an arrogance to their posture, a fighting spirit in their eyes.

For a time, every crewman and pilot was so busy that no one noticed or had time to deal with the intruders, despite the supernatural beasts they had brought, goats and dream-colts.

In the far distance, across the tropic seas, a flotilla of icebergs floated out from the heart of the darkness. Above the tops of the spreading clouds on the horizon, three tall towers rose, like straight shafts of impenetrable night. Even from this distance, Raven could see sparks of light crawling along the towers' bastions and balconies; strange lanterns held by cloaked monstrosities, and explosions and raging fires flung down by the darting swarms of fighter jets.

There were other swarms around the towers; circling and wheeling bat-winged shapes, much too large to be bats. And, goddesslike, each tower was crowned by a supernatural figure of a winged titaness. Twin beams of reddish light streamed forth from their eyes, reaching like searchlights through the clouds, and whichever way the titanesses gazed, fighter jets dropped from the sky or silently vanished.

Great battleships struggled in the wave-swept, ice-crowded sea, and the smoke and thunder of their guns was a shock and an amazement to Raven. With immense concussions, rolling clouds of flame-lit smoke would appear before the main guns of the battleships when they fired, clouds of smoke larger than the ships themselves, and the power of those guns was so great that even those huge ships would sway, driven backward in the sea several feet from the force of the recoil.

Raven borrowed Pendrake's photomultiplying telescopic site, and saw warships continuously shelling the rising towers, and the armies and hordes of creatures gathered on the roofs, upper courtyards, and in the vast windows were slain by the hundreds. Yet even through the clouds of smoke and flame, Raven caught glimpses of vast, slow, graceful silhouettes, undisturbed by shell or shockwave, shrapnel, gas, or flame, moving among the shadows, carrying tall torches, pennants, or lances; and, unless he was deceived by the distance, the confusion, the flame, the gloom, Raven thought these vast shapes were washing and decorating the towers in preparation for some rite or celebration.

A squad of marines came to surround them. Pendrake spoke with them briefly, warning them of the coming nuclear strike. Perhaps because he spoke with such calm authority; or perhaps because he was holding a magic sword and was escorted by obviously supernatural cohorts, the deck officer ordered them brought up to the conning tower.

Raven looked at Peter, then up at the tall, angular shape of the conning tower, with the narrow stairways and gangways leading upward. Peter understood the look, and snorted, and said, "Don't worry about me, friend. I'll be waiting for you by the time you get there." And his goats ran up onto the air, dragging the wheelchair aloft.

When one of the marines ordered Pendrake to put away the sword, Lemuel whispered something in to Pendrake's ear. Pendrake nodded, and surrendered the blade to a marine officer.

They climbed up the narrow stair, through an oval door, then another, and found themselves in a tall space, surrounded on all sides by slanting windows of greenish glass, crowded by ranks and rows of computer boards, radar screens, and readouts. Men with faces of frantic calm were bent over the microphones, and Raven overheard, from more than one speaker, voices requesting help and rescue in urgent monotones, terse descriptions of casualties, or of the unnatural monsters causing them, and, in the far background, sounds of eerie screaming, chanting, or inhuman voices shouting praises to the darkness.

Pendrake seemed to recognize the civilian officer in charge. "I think I can be of some help here, Van Dam," said Pendrake, and he nodded to Raven.

Raven held up his hand. The thunderstorms and screaming winds around the towers rising from the sea died away and fell silent. In the distance, through the windows, Raven saw the clouds shrouding the towers of night thin away; the bat-winged horrors were strafed by passing jets, able to maneuver more freely as the turbulence calmed. A tinny-sounding cheer rang out from some of the microphones, and little whoops of triumph.

Pendrake said, "I have a partial understanding of the oneiric phenomena involved. Observe." And when he held up his hand, rainbows of gold and silver sparkled into existence in his palm, intertwined, became solid, and the mystic sword materialized in his hand.

"I . . . I believe you . . . ," said Van Dam. "Uh. Sir."

"What's the tactical situation?"

"Uh . . . We're facing sea-monsters and, well, dragons. The dragons have no long-range weapons to hinder our forward air group, and we have reinforcement squadrons coming from the SS *Liberty*."

"Raven, see if you can give those guys a tailwind. What else, Van Dam?"

"Well, sir, our ships are shelling the enemy, uh, structure, but are being attacked by sea-serpents and huge, uh, things. Some of our destroyers and missile cruisers have been pulled under by the sea-monsters, but our submarine support can keep the sea-monsters away from our major-class vessels. Right now most of our casualties are from suicides. Pilots and officers go suddenly berserk."

Pendrake gravely listened to several more reports; and Raven was impressed how the radarmen and officers who spoke with him, unlike the gunmen who had attacked them at the house, hid whatever fear they felt behind expressions of stoic professionalism. Raven realized that, unlike the men who had attacked the house, these were true military men, not merely goons in borrowed uniforms.

Pendrake turned to Raven: "They're having trouble with their long-range satellite phototelemetry. See if you can clear up the cloud cover."

To Peter: "These sea-monsters may be similar to the two giant creatures killed at Everness. Find out if your hammer has underwater capability. Also, does it have an outside range? Can you throw it a mile? Twenty miles? If so, you can launch strikes against specific targets on the towers, like a sharpshooter."

To Lemuel: "The rash of suicides sound like demonic possession. Can that Chalice protect us in any way?"

Lemuel said, "Mr. Pendrake, the absence of any selkie or kelpie, or of any of the races of darkness with which I am familiar, troubles me. We should assume that the Emperor of Night knows we have the talismans, and is not putting into the fray those creatures we can banish with the magic at our command."

Pendrake nodded brusquely. He asked Van Dam: "I assume there are no ships of any other navies in the area?"

Van Dam said, "Azrael didn't control their governments. There are only American ships here, except for foreign nuclear submarines that they have tracking our nuclear submarines."

Pendrake said to Van Dam, "I should tell you, Van Dam, that three thermonuclear multiple-warhead missiles have been launched from a silo in Nevada and Oregon, a primary and two backups, which we can abort if the primary is successful. The nuclear strike will hit here within twelve minutes. All our forces must be clear of the blast radius before that time, and be operating under radiation-environment protocols. Vessels not equipped to operate in a high-roentgen scenario must withdraw immediately; those that are radiation-worthy should lay down a suppressing fire to guard their withdrawal. I suggest you maintain your carpet bombing. Use incendiaries where possible. Many of these magical creatures, even if they are not hurt by bullets, are hurt by flames and fire. As soon as Carrier Air Wing Eight arrives from the Roosevelt Carrier Battle Group, have them drop their full payloads."

There was a silence on the bridge for a moment. All the officers within earshot had stopped in the middle of whatever they were doing to turn and look.

One officer muttered, "This is the big one . . ."

Another said to himself, "My God. It's World War Three."

A younger officer, staring out at the flame-crowned towers of darkness thrusting cloudward through icy tidal waves, murmured, "Oh, man! We're going to toast those freak-show fuckers good!"

Van Dam turned to the captain. "Mr. Pendrake is here in an advisory capacity, but I urge you to follow his advice to the letter. The nuclear strike he has warned us of has already been cleared at the highest levels."

The captain said briefly, "Gentlemen! To your stations!"

Raven whispered to Pendrake. "Am very glad Wendy used unicorn horn key to make you visible to awake people again. Look at faces; they remember you. Remember your famous work. Am glad they trust you."

"Trust is earned by deeds," said Pendrake, not turning his head. "Isn't that right, Mr. de Gray?"

Lemuel, Peter, and Raven all turned their heads in surprise, looking back and forth. It was not until he spoke that they saw him, as if a mist had been hiding him from their eyes. There he stood in his now-tattered star-woven robes, his peaked cap missing. His black hair, streaked with white, lay in disarray to his shoulders. His face was pale and drawn, his eyes bright, as if fierce emotion pained him. Near his foot stood a small, fierce bird of prey. Azrael did not take his eyes from the bird as he spoke.

"Pendragon, in vain do these brave men shed life's blood. For what comes against you now is not the armed might of Acheron; these are but playthings, the hunting dogs and falcons of the dark lord. When the final towers invade the realm of air, first shall come forth his heralds and squires; and only then will he let sound the dire call, and let his damned angelic knighthood take the field, armed and ready to oppose the soldiery, not of man, but of Heaven's wide empire."

The captain said sharply, "Sailor: Get back to your duty!" to the one or two bridge officers who were watching this scene.

Pendrake pointed the magic sword at Azrael. "Mr. de Gray, why are you here?"

Now the wizard looked up from the pigeonhawk at his feet, and he looked into Pendrake's stern, alert eyes with eyes that were haunted by a strange emotion.

Slowly, the wizard sank to his knees. "For justice, do I come, my Liege, and to pay you fealty. I am a traitor; I confess this freely and with my own mouth. I give my life to your justice. Strike! My blood has properties which may be useful to your cause."

Pendrake said, "Until we can hold a proper hearing, and until all evidence is presented and weighed, I can make no determination. But we will take this favorably into account and might mitigate what sentence, if any, you receive if you will voluntarily submit yourself to a probation before judgment, binding yourself to accept the verdict of this court, and accepting a period of community service."

"My lord, I vow I shall accept what doom you decree, and shall fully perform your each command. I swear this by my name," said the wizard.

Lemuel squinted and pursed his lips when he heard

that last phrase. But he swallowed whatever he was about to say, and waited.

Pendrake said, "Rise. Advise us."

Azrael stood. "My Liege, the Silver Key could have kept Acheron beneath the waves before the tower called Infidelity arose. Now it is too late. No weapon of man can harm an angel, even fallen. Nothing but the power of the Sun himself can drive them off, and even the Shining One is unequal to the sovereign of angels, the lordly Morningstar. The lesser creatures in the dark Lord's service can be slain however. But if Fate should take the field, her mere command can turn all chances against us. Should she come and decree our defeat, then our defeat is assured, for no man can escape fate."

Raven looked out the high windows of the conning tower. Even as far away as they were from the main action, his sharp eyes could still see, lit by explosions, the vast waves radiating out from where seven black towers rose on the horizon.

Even as he watched, he saw the dark goddess rise from the waves as a walled courtyard and temple before the main gates, surrounded by carven statues of demigods and chimerae, opened its doors and released a flood of ice. There she sat, throned in the midst of the waters, and raised her flail.

II

The battle group was made up of twelve surface ships and submarines, including a fighter squadron and two fighter attack squadrons attached to the Third Air Wing. Fighter attack Squadron 105, "The Gunslingers," had engaged the great dragon Crommcruach high above the sea while there were still only two towers showing above the waves. The dragon-worm rose in flame, his wings a hurricane, but the deadly fire and poison of his breath could not reach but a few hundred yards.

The squadron lost two men when the pilot of one FA-18B Hornet saw the eyes of Crommcruach too clearly through his canopy, the monsters' face lit with the hellfire it vomited from terrible jaws. They all heard his insane shrieks as he dove his craft into the sea. The rest of the fighter attack squadron, flying by instruments or night-vision goggles, were not so affected; they launched their Sidewinder air-to-air missiles from several miles away. Their warheads could not penetrate Crommcruach's age-crusted armored hide; but the vast wings of membrane were tattered at once by flak, and the mighty dragon toppled from the sky.

The children spawned of Crommcruach rose on wings of flame in their thousands when they saw their great patriarch fall in defeat.

The fighter jets engaged them with air-to-air cannon, slaying the younger dragons whose armor had not hardened fully; nor could the monsters accelerate past Mach One, which allowed the jets easily to escape. Radar-directed fire of Sparrow missiles carrying heavy warheads shot down the elder dragons with harder armor.

The path was cleared for the dive bombers, who flew low over the maelstrom-boiling ocean, and unleashed column after column of concentrated explosive across the surface of the sinister black towers. The winged beings atop the towers were not disturbed, but the cataphracts and janissaries of Acheron were slain in droves, helpless where they stood among the bridges and boulevards of the upper citadel. Wire-guided missiles flew in through open window casements and archer slits, and sent shrapnel and jellied gasoline ricocheting along the somber basalt maze of corridors and naves within. The soldiery of the Dark Tower, those who were human or nearly so, stood in their gleaming armor, fraught with ancient magic, drew their rune-crusted swords, and died without ever seeing the foe that slew them. One or two squads from the nearer arches were pulled by the suction of the fire-storms out from windows and flung, bullet-ridden, onto their comrades on the walls below.

However, when the fourth tower, the one called Cowering Dread, rose up, two destroyers and an AEGIS Cruiser from the carrier battle group were swamped in the resulting tidal wave, and the winged being opened the upper gates of her tower, and displayed the Medusa to the fighter bombers.

The SS *Mitscher,* the SS *Donald Cook,* and the SS *San Jacinto* shattered and capsized, sank beneath the flood, and their brave crew perished to a man. High above, those pilots and bombardiers who were relying on visual targeting were turned to stone, and their aircraft plunged into the sea, to the songs and delight of the black naiades who sported in those icy waves. The rest of the attack wing released instrument-guided missiles.

Meanwhile, a kraken had risen from the bottom, larger than an island, and engulfed the frigate USS *Hawes* and the destroyer USS *Oscar Austin,* but took major damage to its beak and to the roof of its mouth from the guided missiles launched point-blank from the decks of those ships. Because of the damage to its beak, it was unable to swallow the cruiser *Yorktown,* but gnawed at and bit off the prow of that ship, until the concentrated fire power of her 20-mm Phalanx guns, three thousand rounds per minute of depleted uranium shells, drove the monster from the surface. There, the attack submarine USS *Virginia* fired twelve tactical nuclear warhead-tipped torpedoes into the great beast's hide as it chased her. One of the torpedoes found the kraken's mighty heart, and the immense hulk of the monster floated to the surface, dead. Unfortunately, the fleet oiler USNS *Kanawha* was not able to maneuver clear, and ran aground on the carcass. The fuel supplies of a dozen heavy ships now spread over carcass and sea-wave, and a stray missile lit the oil slick afire.

The crews of the submarines gave a great cheer when the kraken died, until look-down sonar showed the hundreds of krakens and leviathans rising from the deep, some with towers and armies carried among the crusted plates of their backs.

III

The walls of the outer citadel rose up above the waves, vast sheer slabs of admantium brick, like a range of mountains, rising up, and threw down gigantic wings and sprays of froth. Along the wall were salt-crusted minarets and plates of titanic citadels, never before exposed to air.

Streaming like a hundred waterfalls, dark water gushed from the teeth of the machicolations, and here and there, flopping misshapen limbs, choking, lay blind, pale monsters of the deep, caught unawares. Along the bastions stood the nightmare-legions of a race of giants, water sluicing from their helmets and spears, and, with a roar, they turned and saluted the four vast and hideous towers which loomed at the corners of the square outer walls.

When the tower called Madness, sixth to rise, came shining darkly above the waves, the first of the angels of darkness came from the windows, coming aloft in song, foretelling the coming of Morningstar. No jet was swift enough to outpace the beat of his immortal wings, and whichever way he turned his deadly glance, shrieking men committed suicide with what weapon came first to hand.

When the final tower, called Blindness, rose up, the gates of darkness were opened, and all the stars above were blotted and smothered up with storm-clouds, except for one bright, pale planet in the East, now rising to the zenith.

Taller than the other servants of Morningstar, the

dread goddess Fate sat in the courtyard of the risen palace, outside the great gates of darkness, raising her scepter and pronouncing the defeat of the forces of man.

All the gates and windows of Acheron now opened, and a pale light which cast no shadows poured forth in mighty beams, creating glaciers where it brushed the raging sea. Thrones, Dominions, Seraphim, and Cherubim rose up in their hosts, and sang what music as made men die if they chanced to hear it.

The Angels of Acheron swept through the air, shining beings, whose wings drew cloaks of snow behind them.

In a great circle around their master's throne, uttering hymns, the seraphim of evil passed, destroying all life in the sea where their shadows fell, friend and foe alike; and they were robed in constellations which do not appear in earthly skies, and their triple sets of wings clothed their legs, girdled their waists, and shaded their haloed heads from the sight of the imperial gates of Acheron.

"Glory, glory, glory," they sang, but the imperial gates did not yet open. A great voice spoke from the darkness, saying, "The way has not yet been made ready! Let Earth prepare to greet her master!"

At this, the Archangels of Acheron passed back and forth across the waves, and their wings stirred up tidal waves taller than any mountain. The archangels, like shepherds, led these tidal waves to the great fleet and gathered armament that mankind had placed against them. The waves came against the ships.

All but one of the ships foundered and sank; sailors who were dashed from the decks were eaten by naiades and sea-serpents.

IV

The helmsman turned the prow of the aircraft carrier toward the waters as they began to rise and rise. Raven saw, through the windows of the bridge, a rushing slope of water like a mountain, trembling with streaks of foam, coming toward them, swelling, growing—a wall of water whose top he could not see.

A sound of alarms beat through the bridge. Quickly, without much fuss or wasted motion, the bridge crew abandoned their stations and fled below decks. Raven was carried along in the orderly rush. He found himself thrown into a compartment with a dozen other sailors; hands strapped him into a padded chair that folded out from the bulkhead.

The chamber was long but not wide, and the oval watertight hatches at each end were chocked shut.

Raven turned to ask the sailor next to him a question when a hammer blow shook the room; Raven's breath was knocked out of him by the jar of the straps cutting into his chest and waist.

The lights went out; orange emergency lights came on.

The deck was heeling over at a forty-five-degree angle, then at a ninety-degree angle. Raven was now dangling as if from a wall.

A horrifying sound, a sound Raven had heard once and prayed never to hear again, shrieked through the chamber. It was the sound of metal in agony, the sound of steel beams being twisted and torn. Screams and snaps of metal rang out, like the cries of dying beasts, and the gunshot noise of rivets popping. It was the sound of hull plates being breached.

An earsplitting crash thundered, and the chamber shook.

Then, Raven was suddenly hanging head downward.

The sailor next to him said, "Well. There goes the hangar space. Ocean's in the whole compartment."

Another sailor said, "Listen. Hear those crashes? Aircraft falling up into the upper deck space. We just lost them all."

"Hope the reactor core hasn't been breached . . ."

Raven said, "We're capsized!" He could not keep the fear and astonishment from his voice. He could not even imagine the force necessary to capsize a vessel the size of this one.

The sailor next to him said, "Actually, I think we're under. Hear how quiet it's become?"

Raven heard no thunder rumble at his fear; his power over storm was meaningless below the sea. He was helpless.

The sailor continued, "But don't worry. This old tub is well-designed. Compartmentalized, you know. We should right ourselves and come to surface automatically."

Even as he spoke, with a creaking whine of metal, the floor and ceiling suddenly reversed themselves. Raven heard a roaring all around him, electronic alarms squealing in the near distance.

The sailors began to unstrap themselves. "It's going to be a mess out there!" said one. "Nothing was strapped down!"

"Hear that? Something's triggered the fire-suppressor foam."

Red light spilled in through the unchocked hatch. An officer waved impatiently, barking orders. Raven, struggling to maintain his calm at all cost, found himself carried forward by the surge of sailors rushing to their emergency stations.

A confused moment later he found himself lost in the huge, interior hangar space of the upper deck. Overhead, great wounds were opened to the sky, and ragged metal plates had been wrenched up in jagged rips. The hangar bays were awash with seawater, and the elevator shafts were pools. Aircraft fuel floated in a thin layer across these ponds, and some were burning. Seawater was pouring out from gangways and hatches all across the deck.

Raven climbed an undamaged ladder to the main deck.

Whatever aircraft had once been on deck were gone, except for one wreck, dangling by its tail-hook from a cable, half over the edge. There were fires on deck.

In the near distance, wreckage and flotsam floated on the waves, and mountains of ice gleamed pale against the dark waters. On the horizon, the seven towers of Acheron were darker than the nighted clouds beyond them. Between here and there, angels and archangels of evil stood atop the frozen peaks of the icebergs, wings spread, saluting the towers with their swords and whips. The ocean was seething with a thousand wriggling shapes, serpents and sea-dragons, many-armed krakens, and swimming chimerae with triple heads, and mermaids of haunting beauty. The angels paid no heed to the lifeboats and struggling figures in the water, but Raven heard faint screams as playful mermaids dragged sailors from lifeboats, or sea-imps capsized them.

A triumphal march began to ring through the air, a superhuman and perfect music. Dark figures rose from the waves, bearing torches and drawn swords, forming a double line leading toward the last closed gate of the dark citadel, a gate taller than all others, flanked by the towers called Injustice and Inhumanity.

Raven jerked his head sharply aside and saw Pendrake, Lemuel, and Peter with some other men standing near Azrael on the runway. Raven jogged over. The scene was lit by the ball of rosy light emanating from the fabric covering Lemuel's hovering cup.

Pendrake was saying, "We have a second dive-bomber wave coming in five minutes, and a nuclear strike in ten. Are you telling me we must lose? Must?"

Azrael was saying, "'Tis the working of Fate, my Liege. No arms of man can prevail."

Van Dam was there as well, and he said the coming

bomber wave from the Roosevelt and Washington Carrier Battle Groups was composed of over a dozen squadrons, many more than were presently in the air, and that the reinforcements included antisubmarine-warfare systems that might be able to target and destroy the shoals of kraken.

A naval officer standing near Pendrake said, "Yes, sir; but the boys up in the air now have no place to land. And we're no longer capable of any radiation protocol. And we can't get these fires under control. Everything's going wrong! Systems that never fail are breaking. It's like we are under a curse! Maybe it *is* fate! These fires . . ."

Raven saw water pouring out through great portals beneath the runway, lit by fires burning in the interior of the ship. It looked also to him, like a sign of doom.

Pendrake said, "Your opinion, Mr. Waylock?"

Both answered. Peter said, "I don't hold with this mystical mumbo-jumbo, but this ship isn't a battleship, and doesn't carry capital-class guns. We should start bugging out as quick as we can, and hope we're far enough away when the nuclear shit hits the fan."

Lemuel said, "All the powers placed against us are repelled by certain ancient talismans; all but her power. If there is a talisman against doom, I do not know what it might be. Our magic has failed. We have no weapon against fate."

Another voice spoke, and each word rang out crisp and clear, light, swift and sure, as if the speaker knew no doubt nor hesitation. The voice was very deep, like Raven's voice, and there was a note of impatient joy trembling in the basso profundo notes. It did not sound like a human voice at all.

"There is no fate, for man cannot be bound."

Raven, and the others, turned.

A golden Titan, taller than the wreckage of the conning tower, stood upon the deck, sixty feet high; and his long, black hair curled and tossed about his shoulders,

as if moved by a wind that touched no other object. A
mantle of red cloth was billowing and swinging from
his shoulders, belted, as if in haste, with a rude length
of cord at his waist, leaving his arms and legs free.

He stood balanced on the balls of his feet, legs
spread, as if an active, energetic impulse might suddenly swing him in any direction, to whatever engaged
his interest. With musing smile and glittering eyes he
surveyed the machinery and weaponry intact upon the
deck. His smile was one a teacher might have for the
accomplishments of a prize student, but there was a
deeper joy here too; he smiled as if he savored a long-
awaited victory.

From one manacled wrist there swung some links of
broken chain.

In the other hand, the way a man might hold a house
cat, the titan held Galen Waylock. In the air above his
head, floating like a bird, was Wendy.

Wendy waved energetically. "Hi, guys! Look,
Raven! Look, Daddy! Guess what I found!"

20

The Last Horn Call

Lemuel, his eyes wide with recognition and with awe, seemed like a child again, filled with joy at seeing what no hope had ever promised. There was a glint of hero worship in his eyes as he whispered, " 'To defy power, which seems omnipotent; neither to change, nor falter, nor repent; this, like thy glory, Titan!' 'And thy godlike crime was to be kind, to render with thy precepts, less the sum of human wretchedness, and strengthen man with his own mind.' "

The naval officer next to Van Dam said, "Who the hell is this?"

Lemuel whispered reverently, "Prometheus. He stole divine fire from the gods and gave it to mankind."

Prometheus, in swift, long strides, came across the deck and stooped to place Galen near the others.

The Titan's voice was deep and rich; he spoke quickly, with a curious haunting rhythm to his words, as if the syllables were spoken to an inner music only he could hear.

In a laughing voice, he said, "I see that those who honor me have been very busy here, for look! There are fires, fires everywhere."

He turned and spoke to the masses of oily flame burning in spilled pools across the deck. "Children! I cannot curtail your freedom, nor command; but if it please you to reverence your sire still, who freed you from the Thunderer's proud will, and put you into gentler, more uncertain, mortal hand, show ye then your younger brethren, things of clay, distant courtesy, and embrace them not this day."

The fires burning here and there across the deck flamed suddenly higher, bowed toward them, and then turned all silvery and cold, became wafts of light, and faded like ghosts.

Prometheus smiled and spread his hands. "Radiations escaped from the reactor core! Invisible, but no less dear to me, nor no less deadly; therefore I ask you alike and gently to go. You know you take my love with you, for all the bounties you bestow! Adieu!"

And now he turned and knelt, avalanchelike, as if a mountainside were kneeling; and his mysterious gaze rested on Raven.

"Son of my body are you, who is called, here, Raven; yet I have not earned to call you my son, for no support nor patrimony, rearing, gift, or counsel did I give through all your swift youth. Ask what you will, that I may amend; speak quickly!"

Raven stepped backward, craning back his head. Even when kneeling the colossal figure was too much to take in all at once.

"Can you save us?"

"No," the golden figure answered, "but tools sufficient to allow you to save yourselves are eagerly at hand. Ask your questions."

Raven blinked, backing up. "But I don't have any questions . . ."

"Then you are doomed."

A great, thin screech of inhuman hate echoed across the icy waves from the citadel on the horizon. It was the figure of Fate, shrilling like a banshee, and in one gauntleted hand was a severed head writhing with snakes in place of hair.

The appearance of the Titan had attracted attention; sea-monsters and naiades began swimming purposefully toward the battered shape of the great aircraft carrier. Yet they were still many fathoms away, and the carrier's engines roared into an unsteady life, throbbing and hesitating.

They had begun to outdistance any pursuit, for their engines of metal were swifter than any monster's fin; but then, after less than a minute of power, the engines suddenly fell silent.

Galen said, "This is more than just bad luck . . ."

A sailor a short distance away from Raven on the deck raised a pair of binoculars to his eyes. The man stiffened; Raven called out a warning, but it was too late; the man turned into a marble statue.

Prometheus put up his hand. "Guard your eyes and do not look! Only the one called Raven, the son of Raven, may look; and he must describe what he sees to the rest of us. Only he is blessed by me to be free from fear, which otherwise would petrify you."

Raven took the photomultiplying telescopic sight from Pendrake, and he looked toward Acheron, while the others turned their backs. Raven jerked the instrument away from his face, blinking and hissing as if his eyes had stung him. "Fate has medusa head in hand. Same as I saw on Moon. She wading toward us through water, far ahead of other monsters. But do not look at her to aim guns!"

Van Dam said, "We don't have large guns on this class of vessel. . . ."

Wendy asked Prometheus, "I have a question! How come every enemy of Everness has a thing to stop it but this one? Fate? That doesn't make any sense! She tried to kill me once, did you know that?"

Prometheus put out his hand and Wendy lit on his finger like a little bird lighting on the finger of a man. He nodded his great, handsome head forward, and spoke softly, his black hair weaving and tossing, never still. Raven heard part of the Titan's comment: ". . . guardians of Everness promised tokens to repel all their foes, even as there is a virtue to repel every vice. If there is no talisman to repel Fate, then does one of the other talismans repel her?"

Wendy said back, "I don't know . . ."

Prometheus lifted his finger as if he were tossing a falcon into flight, and he laughed, and asked, "Oh! Come now! What is the true nature of fate? What type of men worship her?"

And at this, Wendy's face lit up, as if she saw the simple answer to a puzzle. Without even bothering to look, she raised the Moly Wand.

Prometheus now gestured, waving his hand and beckoning for the men to look behind them.

Raven's instrument gave the best view, and he passed it from one pair of hands to the next, and the people gathered there eagerly applied their eyes to the lens.

What they saw, lit from behind by the lamps and torches of Acheron, wading through the iceberg-troubled deeps, with black and frozen waters swirling around her legs, was the figure of Fate, collapsing like a wash of turbulent smoke. The medusa head she held dropped from her now-empty gloves and was lost in the sea.

Her mask of iron, which had loomed so huge and grim, now fell. Behind, was a tiny, deformed, hairless, pale, and squealing ratlike face, with twisted jaws and eyes grown mad with spiteful fear and snarling malice. The tiny rat-creature jumped from the toppling mass of empty robes, smaller, after all, than a human being, and fearfully tried to scurry and hide itself under the snow of the ice floes around her.

Wendy shouted happily, "There isn't a fate after all! She's just another selkie!"

The engines of the aircraft carrier, as if by magic, began their action once more, perhaps repaired just at this moment by frantic engineers somewhere belowdecks. Long-range missiles were launched from the two remaining functioning firing stations on deck; red explosions rose up amidst the endless swarms of sea-snakes that had been flowing after the goddess.

The sea was seething with writhing shapes; almost a solid mass of sea-dragons surrounded the waters all about the risen citadel, which had come up to its full height, taller than any mountains of Earth.

The angels and dark elves hovered in a great, motionless chorus of concentric rings all around the mighty citadel; and all at once the lights and lanterns were darkened. There now was but a single ray of pale and ghastly light issuing from the smallest crack that gaped in the main gates of Acheron. These last set of gates, wider and taller than all others, were the only doors yet shut in all the dark facade of Acheron.

The only other light came from burning hulks of vessels scattered among the icebergs on the sea.

Raven said, "Everyone ignoring us, except sea-serpents."

Azrael stood with his head bowed. "It is the vainglory of Morningstar displayed. That light comes from the coronet he wears upon his brow; he will tolerate to have no light other challenge it, while he comes forth to glory."

Galen said, "What are they waiting for?"

Azrael said, "The wandering star Venus must rise to the zenith."

Lemuel said, "That's about twenty minutes. No time to do anything."

Prometheus rumbled, "Lose no hope."

A terrible, soft music began to steal over the gathered hosts of angels, and then pure and perfect voices, terrifying and inhuman, rose in hymn.

> *"Hail to our master!—Prince of Earth and Air!*
> *Who walks the clouds and waters—in his hand*
> *The scepter of the elements, which tear*
> *Themselves to chaos at his high command!*
>
> *"He breatheth—and a tempest shakes the sea;*
> *He speaketh—and the clouds reply in thunder;*
> *He gazeth—from his glance the sunbeams flee*
> *He moveth—earthquakes rend the world asunder.*
>
> *"Beneath his footsteps the volcanoes rise;*
> *His shadow is Pestilence; his path*
> *The comets herald through crackling skies;*
> *And planets turn to ashes at his wrath.*
>
> *"To him War offers daily sacrifice;*
> *To him Death pays his tribute; Fate is his,*
> *With all her infinite of agonies!—*
> *All proud, majestic things, he is!"*

A chill came across the group at the sound of that music, and Raven wondered if the fallen angels were exaggerating their master's might, or were underpraising it. . . .

There was no motion on the deck as that song grew and filled the heavens. All were awed.

Lemuel whispered, a note of surprise entering his monotone: "That's Byron. That poem is from Lord Byron . . ."

Azrael spoke like a sleepwalker, but his words took on strength and scorn as he spoke: "The Demon-Kings make no new things for themselves; all the substance of the dream-worlds, even to their songs and festivals, are taken from mankind."

The deep, energetic voice of Prometheus jarred Raven and the others from the apathy and horror which that mighty and angelic song had cast over them.

Prometheus said, "Do not listen to their music! A greater song, one of my making, shall soon drive it forth. Do not listen! Their songs are false! Aha! Now my chorus comes to outshout their pride . . ."

Peter cocked up his head. "I hear 'em. Jets."

A roaring began to fill the sky, coming from somewhere above the cloud cover. The angelic song swelled louder, but it could not cover the long, high-pitched whistles of the descending bombs, the roar of guided missiles.

The ordnance came down out of the clouds like hailstones, by thousands. Ton after ton of explosive, dropped among the sea of monsters, and air-launched antisubmarine torpedoes fell swiftly into the sea. Balls of light like little pale suns appeared beneath the waves, as tactical nuclear charges tore monsters of measureless bulk and strength into bleeding acres of meat.

All sound was drowned by the continuous earth-shaking roar of explosions, one after another, in huge masses of unthinkably violent concussions.

Red light from the fires which spread from horizon to horizon now lit the scene; it was a scene from an inferno.

The bombing went on and on.

In the firelight of the bombing, they saw that the mortal servants of Acheron were dead. Dragons, chimerae, scolopendra, naiades, leviathans, and sea-worms, all wore reduced to broken and scattered flesh. The sea was red with blood and flame.

The immortals, however, were untouched. The angels of darkness continued their song, albeit unheard, oblivious to the destruction around them. When they were done with hymning, the seven figures atop the seven towers spread their wings and raised their hands.

The clouds parted and the scores and scores of fighter-bomber squadrons were revealed to view.

In a moment, half of the immense air fleet was destroyed, swept from the air into the sea, or consumed with fire; the other half turned and accelerated away. At a nod from a seraphim, three of the lesser angels, out of the hosts of thousands, opened their immortal wings and instantly overtook them; the three angels of darkness passed through the aerial armada, where they pointed, steel wings snapped; when they spoke, blood exploded outward from shattering canopies; when they nodded, planes by the score were instantly consumed with flame; where their shadows passed, pilots grew silent and died without a mark or sign on them.

The action of these three herded the frantic jets toward each other on converging courses, so that their wakes interfered with each other, or closer still, so that they crashed. The sky was torn with a column of flame and rained flaming gasoline.

The seven winged figures waved their wings; the clouds grew together once more, and there was darkness over all.

The pale and hideous beam of light issuing from the half-open gates reached up and touched those clouds. It immediately began to snow, and the fires burned dimly in the sudden, terrible cold.

A dismal wind passed along the breadth of the sea; all the waves grew calm as a millpond. The water was as still and flat as a black mirror. In terrible quiet, they watched the last of the immense air fleet drop to destruction, annihilated by the tiniest effort of the unearthly forces of Acheron.

The gates slowly began to inch open.

Peter muttered, "The goddamn radiation didn't even faze 'em."

Azrael said, "The final gates now open. Morningstar prepares to issue forth to claim his kingdom, and put all Earth beneath his scepter's sway. Observe where, like columns of luminous mist, pacing with bowed haloes, and weeping blood, the four Guardians of the Four Quarters of the Earth are drawn, compelled to come pay homage to their new sovereign! Their steps are slow, and stir up the sea as they linger. Morningstar abides their coming. . . ."

In the far distance, gleaming like comets, great luminous beings, their heads wrapped in the lower clouds, came silently over the sea toward Acheron.

Pendrake ignored the sight and called up to Prometheus, "Sir! I have a question! Is the megaton yield of the nuclear warhead I've launched sufficient to destroy Acheron?"

The Titan's gaze jumped aside, and he pierced Pendrake with his glittering eyes. And now he laughed a carefree laugh, a quick, rising patter of notes. "Why, no! The resistance of the adamantium, combined with the power of the ice and seawater to dispel the heat and radiation, will render the blow ineffective. However, observe. . . ." And the Titan's restless hands pulled up a length of pipe from the wreckage which lay sprawled across the deck, and bent it into a doubly curved shape something like the stitching on a baseball might look if seen without the ball.

Prometheus raised a finger, and stared deeply into Pendrake's eyes, saying in a low voice, "At extremely high temperatures, the behavior of subatomic exchange particles becomes symmetrical for all forces: electromagnetic, nucleonic, gravitic. This was the condition of the universe within the first three seconds of time after cosmogenisis. What you do not know, is that the same condition applies to supersaturated high-gauss magnetic fields. If the electromagnetic pulse of a thermonuclear explosive of ninety megatons is directed along a field of this shape, what would be the result?"

The Titan held perfectly still, almost as if holding his breath, and waited for Pendrake's answer.

Pendrake said, "A toroidal field of symmetrical particles; if what you are saying is correct. . . ."

"Aha! No! Picture not a field but a beam. What is the torsional diffraction of such a beam at that temperature?" The Titan impatiently interrupted.

"It would depend on the behavior of the field at such high temperatures. Surely the field would be unstable."

Prometheus said, "Assume it was kept stable!"

"The beam would curve."

"Aha! How far?"

"That would depend on the aperture of the zone . . ."

"And suppose, oh, suppose, that it were equal to the wavelength involved?"

"It would curve back on itself."

"Would the resulting field interact constructively or destructively? And if it were constructive interaction, would the field strength build again?"

Pendrake looked shocked. "It would continue to build asymptotically."

Now a calm look came over the Titan's handsome face, as if all expression had been wiped clean by some breathless eagerness. He whispered softly: "Approaching zero or approaching infinity?"

Pendrake's face went entirely blank. Wendy, who had her arms around her husband, but her feet hovering above the deck, now leaned out and tugged on her father's arm. "Daddy! I'm bored! What are you two talking about?"

Pendrake said, "Quiet, darling. Daddy's trying to figure out if he's just been told the secret of an infinite power source of superatomic energy. No. It's only nearly infinite. The energy levels would fall off as additional created particles were reabsorbed. Right?"

"Correct, correct! Clever man! The energy level falls off in the inverse of the particular wave form, according to this formula." The Titan scratched a few simple symbols with his forefinger into the steel deck-plates.

Pendrake, stooping to look at the formula, said, "Would this ignite the free carbon in the atmosphere? A carbon chain reaction would destroy the entire atmosphere if it spread."

Prometheus said, "Observe your reaction mass figure. Outside of this field, normal asymmetrical particular interactions obtain. What is your conclusion?"

"The initial sphere of reaction would reproduce a carbon fusion, producing higher elements. Outside that sphere, we are below critical mass and temperature thresholds. It should be safe. It might be safe. Is it safe?"

Prometheus smiled but did not answer the question.

Pendrake asked, "Will it destroy Acheron?"

"The power of Creation can always overcome the servants of Destruction. Only Morningstar himself is great enough to withstand such a primal force."

Lemuel asked, "What is he talking about?"

Pendrake said, "He just told me how to use a hydrogen explosion as an igniter to create a higher-level energy reaction, similar to what took place at the origin of the Universe. Imagine a little Big Bang. The explosion's energy would keep turning back on itself, and create a hotter and hotter explosion. Not only does this have great potential for making cheap, easy-to-make weapons, but you could have cheap, almost free, almost infinite power. All you need is reaction mass to start the first explosion; it drives itself after that."

Prometheus smiled and spread his hands and said, "Such is the hallmark of all well-made creations."

Raven said, "You said is same as at beginning of universe. Would it make a new universe?"

Prometheus smiled, his eyes lit with delight, and he answered in grave, measured tones, saying, "The topology of space is elastic according to the force applied. Sufficiently high-energy explosions would create singularities of any desired dimensions. The laws of nature within the singularity fields would depend on the initial conditions."

Raven said, "Say that again."

Prometheus said, "Yes. Yes, you could make little worlds. Don't you want to? Having children is such a delight! The small sacrifices, which, from time to time, one might have to make for them, are always worth the pain."

The naval officer standing near Van Dam spoke up. "This is too dangerous. It might blow up the atmosphere, you said. Cheaper and easier to build than an atomic bomb, you said. Don't we have enough to worry about already?"

"Ah," said Prometheus, "at last he speaks; and yet, as ever, anonymously. If one needs to feed on fear, one cannot speak aloud, and proud, and clear."

Azrael said, "My lords, it is past time for debate. For look! The Guardians of the Four Quarters of Earth have bowed before the half-open gate, and proffer sheaves of grain, bowls of wine, wreaths of flowers, and gems without price, all to grant the foe the bounties of the Earth. Pendragon, if you can call fire from heaven, call it forth, and smite Acheron. Whether we perish in flame or no, death is lovelier than the iron hells of Acheron."

Pendrake, for some reason, looked at Lemuel. "Any objections?"

Lemuel said, "He's right. He's right. I've been there. He's right."

"No time to waste," said Pendrake. "Let's get busy."

"But we've just lost," said the naval officer next to Van Dam. "Our air fleet was just wiped out. Wiped out! Unless you wake the sleepers, we have no forces that can halt the forces of the enemy. Look at what just happened!"

Azrael said, "All is lost. Name and fame and all. I have failed . . ."

Galen said, "I, I, uh, want to help, Mr. Pendrake. But we can't build your superbomb in the next two minutes . . ."

Pendrake said, "We can build it in one. We have all the elements here. All we have to do is put together what we have learned how to do logically. These fairies and all their magic can't stop that."

Lemuel said, "How?"

They all waited for his answer.

Pendrake said, "Simple. Where did Wendy get that dress she's wearing now?" They all looked at the green dress with cotton flowers growing along the skirts.

"Fairy-land," said Wendy. "It's just something I dreamed up."

"She dreamed it. Then, when she woke up in Everness, it was a real, physical object. What is Everness? A place where (except when Lemuel turned on the lights) whatever happens in the dream-universe is exactly reflected here. Peter's wheelchair can go fast enough to intercept the missile and recover the warhead we need. I can draw the technical plans and schematics for what we will need to make the cosmogenesis ignition system. Galen or Lemuel; one of you can go to sleep. You said you could do it in a moment, with a magic name. Galen, how good is your memory?"

"Perfect," said Galen. "The only thing I ever did my whole life was practice mnemonics."

"Good enough to memorize a technical drawing even if your didn't understand it?"

"The one-thousandth digit of pi is a nine. The one before that is a . . . let's see, 'wheat fields are white in August' . . . an eight. That answer your question?"

"Good. You go to sleep. You have a lucid dream exactly matching my specifications. Wendy touches her horn between my real drawing and the materials and hardware in your lucid dream. Is there any reason why

my technical drawings cannot act like the design on
the back of a dollar bill, in your dream-science?"

Galen said, "It will work."

"Fine. The appliances become real. We connect
them to the warhead. We use Peter's Hammer to accelerate the warhead back into position over Acheron. We
cure ourselves of radiation sickness with your arrows
and your grandfather's Grail."

Raven said, "And me? What I am to do?"

Pendrake pointed to the curved metal shape
Prometheus had bent. "You guide the electrical flows
generated from the electromagnetic pulse of the primary explosion."

"What?"

"If you can throw lightning, then you can spin lightning in a circle. That creates a magnetic field. The reason why fusion power projects have not worked
heretofore is because sufficiently stable magnetic
fields could not be generated to contain the plasma.
But you, Raven, you are going to be our field genera-
tor. And since you are guiding it with your mind, it will
be as perfectly stable as you can imagine."

The naval officer next to Van Dam said sharply,
"This is insane! Recreating the Big Bang? Such a
weapon, such power will destroy mankind! It's like
giving matches to children!"

Prometheus smiled grimly, his red mantle stirring
and billowing around him like agitated wings. "If you
don't give matches to children, how will they learn to
build forges? Your objection is an utterance of craven
fear; or, no! I give you too much credit! It is weak-
minded jealousy of one's betters. The same objection I
heard the time Hercules released me, and I showed
them how to grind gunpowder before I was caught
again. Look! All the lesser slaves of freezing Acheron
were reduced to ash by gunpowder, nitrates, and fire!
Fire! Beautiful fire! Observe the efficiency!"

The naval officer said sharply, "Mr. Pendrake! Don't listen to this anarchist pyromaniac!"

Raven said to his wife, "Wendy. Find out for us who this navy man really is, eh?"

Wendy rolled her eyes. "Oh, come on. It's obviously Oberon." She pointed the Moly Wand at the naval officer.

The naval officer's body rippled like an image seen underwater; they all had the sensation of suddenly waking up, and realizing the naval officer was nine feet tall, that his right eye-socket was an empty pit, that his left eye was a lambent gray pool, trembling with mysterious wisdom, and that he was dressed all in silks of gold, dark blue, and black, and that, for his crown, the two wings of a black swan rose up to either side of his shadowed visage.

In the palm of his hand he carried a light like a star.

Oberon said, "Pendrake, make not your terrible weapon; you will render the Earth entire to smoldering devastation. Put aside all weapons, and rely on the swords I have stored in heaven to defend you. They are not mortal weapons; they cannot fail. Have faith in me. It has been deemed to be thus: this world will fail, and a new world shall rise. Do not question what lies beyond all understanding."

Prometheus, looking down, smiled softly. "Require him to produce his evidence, and proofs of logic."

Wendy said, "Daddy, look out! He wants to kill you!"

Pendrake smiled. "Men like him always want to kill men like me. Don't worry, baby, Daddy knows what's behind his creed. Daddy isn't fooled."

Oberon turned toward Lemuel, saying, "I know your secret name, Bedevere Waylock, last faithful Guardian of Everness. You have stayed at your weary post so long, so very long, when brothers, wife, son, kith and country, and all the world besides, has scoffed and forgotten. How often have you wished for travel; how often have you broken faith with aliened kin, when you would not leave your house, your dutiful bed, not even for celebrations, for marriages, not even for funerals! Long have you waited your reward. Yet you have not waited in vain; for in my kingdom a chair of honor at my feast-table awaits, a crown of glory, raiment of light; youth, and pleasure, bounty, and bliss; and your fathers and brothers shall come forth to be glad with you. No pain of your long-suffering patience shall go without its balm; great faithfulness you have shown me, I shall be faithful to my promises in turn. Rejoice! For the hour of your reward is nigh. Yet one last trial and last temptation you now must overcome. For look! She who holds the horn must realize she cannot wield it to create what so her father wishes; she has not the art; only you, last Guardian of Everness. Deny to them the secret of the key; unleash not this terrible fire in the hand of unruly men; wake instead the sleepers who shall renew the world; and blow the herald note of paradise!"

Galen said, "Hey! What about me? I thought I was a real Guardian at last, now, too!"

Oberon's shadowed head bent toward Galen. "But I see in you, your heart is turned away from me. Do you wish for honors from my hand? Then practice the patience and faithfulness which is your motto; repent; serve righteousness; become the instrument of the destiny of Earth; let wind the final horn-call!"

Prometheus said, "There is no destiny, for I took from the stars the powers to guides men's fates and gave this to men, little tyrant."

"Traitor!" and now Oberon's voice crashed like a thunderclap. "And where was your loyalty to your own kind when I and my two brethren made war against your father! Where was your vowed loyalty to me when you led mankind astray!" Oberon turned to Lemuel. "You admire how he suffered for mankind when he was bound. But he loves not your race, no, not one whit!"

"I was never bound, Lord of Envy," said Prometheus, "only this body I wear. The vultures of destructions tore at it, true, true, but every dawn I had the pleasure of creating it anew."

Raven looked at the joyful, restless, ever-moving figure of the titan of fire; and he thought what a horrid crime it would be to chain so active a being as this; how much worse than imprisoning a man. Men grow weary and sometimes wish for solitude, motionlessness. Not Prometheus . . .

Raven felt a warmth in his heart for the Titan. Fondness? Love? It was too early to say.

Oberon was speaking in bitter, yet majestic tones. "Lemuel! Ask this Titan you so admire why he plans to study your machines that think, and what he dreams to make them into . . ."

Prometheus looked pleased and said, "The machine intelligences that shall supercede mankind will have vastly greater intellect, which they will be able to increase at need and will accomplish in microseconds what requires men years. It will be wonderful! At last the blind weapons of the Thunderer shall be tamed, made into electricity, and turned to some useful . . ."

Pendrake interrupted, saying, "We really do not have the time for this. Honestly. Oberon, you've been overruled. Wendy . . . ?"

She shrugged and said, "But he's right, Daddy. I really don't know what to do to make a dream-gate; all I can do with this Unicorn horn is open and shut them. There isn't time for me to guess and try and guess again, you know?"

Lemuel had a frowning squint on his face. "Miss Wendy, I don't see what all this debate is about. Even Prometheus admits that this superbomb cannot ever hurt Morningstar himself, only his servants. It is hopeless. Human might cannot win against the supernatural. Blow the Horn. Call the sleepers. End the world."

Wendy blinked. "I don't have any horn to blow," she said.

Galen clapped his hands to his head, "Of course! It is not the gates of ivory and horn! It is the gates of an ivory horn! Wendy! You've had it in your hand all this time! It is not a horn like a trumpet-style horn. It is a horn like a unicorn horn."

Wendy held up the unicorn horn, which she drew from her belt. She looked carefully at it, and them pried up the silver cap that covered the tip. Underneath was a mouthpiece. The horn itself was hollow.

Wendy looked at Raven. "What should I do?"

Raven said, "Hand horn to Galen. He is only one who knows both sides of the big picture. He is Guardian of Everness."

"Well said, my son . . . ," murmured the Titan.

Before anyone could say anything, or interfere, the horn was in Galen's hands. He stared at it in shock, "Thanks a lot! Now I've got to decide the damned fate of the world!"

Pendrake said, "One of you—I can't remember who it was—said the horn could be made to make a place like Everness. Galen, if you know how to do such a thing, use them on these plans I've drawn up. I sketched them out in my calendar book while you people were jabbering."

Galen said, "Grandpa never told me the spell . . ."

Pendrake said, "Peter? Do you know it?"

Peter had been watching the corpse-choked ocean, the angels of Acheron. He didn't turn his head. "Course not! Hey, Dad. Help him make his damned bomb. We should have had all this talked out and set before we got here!"

Pendrake said, "Fine. Take off. I'll give you instructions about how to dismantle the warhead once you match course and speed . . ."

Lemuel had put out his hand. "Give me the horn, Grandson."

Galen looked at his grandfather suspiciously. And he saw the wounded look on his grandfather's face as that suspicion hung between them.

Galen said, "You're not going to blow the horn, right? You're going to help Pendrake conjure his bomb?"

Lemuel smiled. "I will do my duty as I see fit, Galen. Give me the horn. I thought you had learned your lesson about how you should listen to your elders' wisdom. If you had listened to me at the beginning, none of this would have happened. Listen to me now. Trust me. Give me the horn."

Galen extended his hand toward Lemuel, the horn glimmering like white bone.

Azrael said, "By Morpheus, stop! Hold your hand!"

Galen's hand tingled, went numb, and jerked the horn up away from Lemuel's grasp. Galen grasped his possessed hand with his other hand, and said a name of power. The tingling stopped.

Azrael stepped between Lemuel and Galen. "Fool! He intends to wind the horn and end the earth! See how the tangles of his hair make the Sephiroth Binah tangled with the rune Tiwaz! It is a sign of treason!"

Oberon intoned. "We have had treasons and treasons enough!" and he raised his hand to the sky.

A lightning bolt, called by Oberon, snapped down from the clouds, a white shaft of electricity, which struck toward Azrael; but Raven, forewarned by Prometheus, stepped in the way, and caught the lightning bolt in his hand.

Galen said, "No! Stop it!"

Lemuel said, "Son, I order you to give me that horn. There is no point now in doing otherwise. If your father had tended to his duties, he might know the charm. He doesn't. He disobeyed the sacred trust of our family. I am very disappointed—very disappointed, mind you—that you also are toying with treason. But it doesn't matter. This world is old, and tired, and its time is up. Give me the horn. We have always loved and trusted each other, even when the rest of the world laughed. Don't leave me all alone now, at the last hour of time. Be a member of this family. Give me the horn. There is no one else to give it to!"

Galen said, "I'm sorry, Grandfather. But I think the world is young and has a long way to go yet. And I'm not so sure anymore if I'd like paradise if it was just given to me. It wouldn't really be mine, then, would it? And you're wrong. There is someone else who knows how to use the horn. The founder who made the first tower of Everness."

And he turned and offered the horn toward Azrael.

"I accept!" shouted Azrael, and his hand snatched the horn. But Galen did not let go. There they stood, both holding the horn, and Galen was staring Azrael in the eye.

For some reason, it was Azrael's gaze that faltered and wavered. He could not meet Galen's eye, but lowered his head. Galen said, "I gave you my cloak off my back once, because I thought you were cold. Well, you were a lot colder than I thought. Take it."

Azrael yanked the horn to his chest, where he caressed it with both hands, staring at it. Then he looked up at Galen, a puzzled, guarded look in his eye. "You—you have given me the ultimate power over the earth and sky. All I can dream, now I can make real. Why?"

Galen said, "You don't want Oberon to win, or Morningstar. So you have to help Pendrake make his bomb."

Azrael said, "And thereafter, the world is mine to do with as I see fit, first, perhaps to revenge myself on the man who has stolen my wife and cuckolded me . . ."

Oberon said, "You are not alone in that, Wizard. For such a purpose I would set aside my enmity with you, till Pendrake has been taught humility . . ."

Azrael snarled and Oberon recoiled, drifting backward like a column of smoke in a slow wind.

Galen said, "See? That's what you don't want to be like."

Azrael said darkly, "Boy, why do you so trust me?"

Galen spoke slowly, thoughtfully. "I don't trust Azrael, not at all. But I trust Merlin. Merlin is the one who founded our family; and maybe he's forgotten why he built his tower, or why he rebelled against heaven. May be he's forgotten who he is. I haven't forgotten. Look at that pigeonhawk you've been following around. A merlin is just another name for a pigeonhawk. I know who you are. I can read the signs. Maybe it's a gift I get from my ancestor."

Galen now turned toward Lemuel. "Grandfather, I do want to be part of this family. But I think the family has been lied to somewhere along the line. I was told we were given the horn. Azrael says he stole it. Excuse me. I mean Merlin. It was not because of treason or failure that Merlin was in a cage in Tirion, it was only because of Oberon's hatred. Oberon was just too weak or too scared to come take the horn once we had it; so he did the next best thing, and told our forefathers that we worked for him."

The wizard put the unicorn horn back into Galen's hand. "It is simple to use. Wound yourself, and let your blood drip into the hollow of the horn. With the blood drops that reach the tip, trace the image and the lines of what you wish; touch both the drawing and the object the drawing represents with the horn; sleep with it beneath your pillow, and dream of the dream you wish to make real. In just this fashion, long ago, Oberon, a man, stole the dream-kingdom from Ouranos, the Demiurge who dreamed this world into being."

Oberon stepped forward, raising his hand. "I will with patient grace abide no longer this poor folly. Enough! Behold, I raise my hand and call on all powers of earth and sky . . ."

Azrael reached out, touched the unicorn horn, said, "Coming, as you did, over the wall of Everness, I have power over thee. Thou art a man; I revoke the law of dreaming!" And pointed at Oberon.

Oberon shrank to mortal stature, becoming solid and whole. His features were now plain to see; a handsome man, but not supernaturally so. He had weight; his knees made noise on the deck when he sank down; he cast a shadow. The glamour of unreality had fled.

He clapped his hand to his empty right eye socket as if that pained him now. His splendid garbs and silks, now folded in absurd lengths across his too-small frame, were wilting and evaporating.

Pendrake said, "Why don't you just sit there till we decide what to do with you?"

Galen said, "Do you give me this horn now, relinquishing your claim to and power over it?"

The wizard had to draw a deep breath before he spoke. "I do. The power is no more mine." And he looked sad for a moment.

A pigeonhawk flew down from nowhere, landed on his shoulder, and immediately, the wizard was garbed in a great cloak of merlin feathers, dappled brown and white, with a hood of slate blue, which sprang, dreamlike, from the plumage of the bird. The black robes inscribed with constellations lay in a heap at Merlin's feet, shed along with his old name.

Peter landed at that moment, the cylindrical warhead carried across the shoulders of the irked goatmonsters pulling his wheelchair.

"Now," said Pendrake, "This should only take five minutes . . ."

It actually only took four and a half. Curving bars of magnetic superconductors appeared around the warhead with the suddenness of a dream. Pendrake opened the casings, attaching drawings of machinery and circuits, which then unfolded and became solid. He made adjustments, altered his drawings. Galen stirred and muttered in his sleep, clutching the horn, waking, hearing instructions, and throwing himself immediately back to sleep with the secret names of Morpheus.

Azrael, or, rather, Merlin Waylock, guided and directed each step of the process. Raven practiced generating perfect magnetic fields. Prometheus made suggestions and looked eager. Van Dam brought up radiation suits and leaded glass goggles from a locker and passed them out. Wendy floated around, trying to help, and got in everyone's way.

Peter lashed his hammer to a heavy cable tied to the framework holding the warhead. "Ready? Come on, let me throw it. Not many men going to be able to say they threw a nuke. Ready? Goddamn it! I'm waiting around here, y'know!"

"Ready," said Pendrake.

Galen passed out arrows. "In case this new radiation doesn't listen to Prometheus."

Raven said, "Am ready." He had a little picture on a piece of notebook paper in his palm, diagramming the internal structure of the cosmogenesis weapon, with concentric circular arrows in blue ink showing where and how he had to rotate the fields.

Wendy hopped up and down with excitement, "Go, Daddy, go! Blast them to smithereens!"

Prometheus said, "Actually, I just thought of a much more effective way of dopplering the field recurvature, if only we had a tetrahedron of neutronium point sources rotating around a common axis. Well . . . perhaps next time . . ."

Lemuel said to Peter, "Throw it, Son. We watchmen have watched long enough. The foe is here; the watch is done. Now is the time to strike . . ."

Peter threw his hammer in the air. The cable snapped taught. The warhead was yanked aloft.

Peter pointed with his finger to a spot overtop Acheron, some twenty miles away. Raven was squinting at the picture in his hand.

"Too late," whispered Azrael Merlin Waylock,

The clouds parted to reveal the wandering star at zenith . . .

A fanfare began to blow from the citadel of Acheron. The gates swung open. The single beam of pale light began to swell and widen.

"In position," said Peter Waylock.

Galen Waylock pointed the unicorn horn; "Laws be one, both waking and asleep; it is done!"

"Say . . . ," said Wendy, looking back and forth, "where'd Oberon go?"

"Now, Raven," said Pendrake, "now!"

Raven put his finger on the wiring diagram of the ignition circuit.

21

Morningstar

I

The imperial gates of Acheron swung open, and the processional which went before great Morningstar marched, singing, out into the waves; and the waters grew still as crystal beneath their angelic footsteps.

Great Morningstar himself, taller than the tallest church steeple, heralded by the pallid light which shone and darted from his brow, stepped over the threshold, and paused, one foot upon the iron steps of Acheron, one foot on the water.

His proud eyes viewed at once the whole of Earth, his promised kingdom, for the eyes of angels do not fail with distance, and are not deceived by the surfaces of things. He saw the whole business of mankind and all their works; and his mind, wiser and swifter than any mortal mind, instantly apprehended all the sins and woes of all humanity. And now his lip curled in disdain.

The seraphim to his left were crowned in black Hell-fire, and wore vestments red as blood; the seraphim to his right wore crowns like the aurorae that appear over arctic snows, and their vestments were pale as corpses. Seven candlesticks of gold went before him, issuing smoke without light, held in the hands of the seven Virtues which were his handmaidens: Inhumanity, Despair, Infidelity, Madness, Blindness, Injustice, and Cowardice. And behind him came the great Archangel Mulciber, Prince of the Abyss, carrying the scroll wherein the doom of all the world was written; and the scroll was sealed with seven seals.

Morningstar halted in his processional, and spoke to Mulciber, saying, "My house has not yet been prepared to receive me, for, behold, the vermin mankind still infests this green Earth. You have not yet opened the Seal of Doom, nor let free the utter destruction contained therein to cleanse this, my world, of that filth which the Thunderer dared to set before me in priority. Even now the fallen creatures conspire to direct a weapon against me; yet still they live. Where, in this, is wisdom?"

Mulciber bowed low, saying, "Glory, glory, glory to you in the highest! Majesty, your own command allowed that those who worship you, and committed crimes in your name, would be permitted to live as slaves, forever condemned to die and deserving of death, yet forever spared. We cannot unleash undiscriminate devastations to rule, with horror, the Earth, till your loyal worshippers have been winnowed out from the body of mankind; to do otherwise would be to put a falsehood into the mouth of Morningstar, our brightest, and that cannot be."

Morningstar raised his head to gaze upon the darkened clouds and darkened sky. "Behold, their weapon ignites. Glory, and empire, hesitate. How shall we sponge away this blot upon our honor? For we have, with conquering footstep, set forth to receive the homage of the Earth, and yet we have trodden on a scorpion."

Mulciber spoke: "What are the weapons of creatures such as they to spirits such as we? No flame of man's making can hinder pure and higher entities; only the sun can drive us back, and we have overcome and banished him. Mere men, I deem, cannot draw down the sun at their command from heaven!"

Morningstar said, "Yet so they have done. Behold."

A white light appeared above their heads, and in the midst of that light, Hyperion, crowned in glory, whipped his chariot of fire down upon Acheron, and raised his bow of light.

Morningstar stepped forth, swelling in an instant to a stature overtopping his own towers, and his wings, like winter storm clouds, spread hugely across the sky. Those Angels of Acheron who fled into his shadow were spared; those who did not were withered like autumn leaves in a fire.

Acheron was destroyed; the flames cast fragments of the broken towers, hugely crumbling, cloaked with smoke, into the steaming sea and up on high into the bright, burning air.

Morningstar strode gigantically up into the sky, slaying the steeds of the sun-chariot with the first sweep of his scepter. Hyperion, his wings of gold fanning out to grip the air, toppled from the wreckage to the chariot, drawing his great sword Adustus as he fell.

The second blow from the scepter of Morningstar broke the sword in fragments, shattered Hyperion's golden breastplate, and struck the Sun-God to the heart.

II

Raven pulled the leaded goggles over his eyes and looked up the moment he triggered the ignition.

A sphere of perfect white light appeared in the air above Acheron, surrounded instantly by a shock wave of electricity and Saint Elmo's Fire, which fled like sparks across the sea as the sphere reddened and expanded. Ripples of blue-white and silvery light flickered across the face of the sphere as it swelled; and the seascape behind the sphere to either side vibrated and twisted, as if the light near the explosion were bent aside, or as if space itself were bending.

The towers of Acheron melted like wax. The sea and the huge rebounding fragments of blasted towers flew up into the expanding explosion as if gravity were suspended in the immediate radius.

A dark fragment, surrounded by smoke and darkness, larger than the rest, pierced through the center of the sphere.

The sphere popped like a soap bubble, and a wash of heat and fire flashed across the seascape from horizon to horizon, and a mighty mushroom cloud, knotted like a turbulent great fist, thundered upward, red light cooling and swallowed in black.

The light became darkness as the fire of the explosion was consumed by the rising, all-consuming clouds.

The sound and shockwave shook the ship.

Raven cried out, "Look!"

III

In the midst of the explosion, stepping forth from the smolder and cloud-mass of which he seemed a part, rose a vast figure of perfect angelic beauty, his dark visage stern and contemptuous beneath the single pale light which burned like a third eye upon his coronet, his black wings like smoke spreading the cloud far out across the heavens. And in those arms was the dead body of a golden angel, withered laurel leaves dropping from his golden head, broken sword and snapped bow dropping from his relaxed fingers.

As the after light of the explosion faded from the sky, Morningstar, with a contemptuous thrust of his arm, dropped the corpse into the sea, where it floated, face downward, sodden wings collapsed crookedly upon the waves like two islands.

Morningstar strode across the surface of the sea, and put one foot upon the deck of the aircraft carrier. Such was his size that his heel and toe covered the forward part of the deck from port to starboard; and the pressure of his step overcame the power of the engines, so that the laboring propellers churned the sea without effect.

The pale light from the supreme angel's brow gathered itself into a beam and glanced down at the deck, as Morningstar looked down. Lemuel yanked the cover off his Chalice and spilled the living light into the air all around him, so that, while Pendrake, Raven, Galen, and the others were sickened, robbed of all strength and beaten prone by that light, they were not instantly slain. They lay on their faces, shivering, limbs cold.

Morningstar raised his great scepter, and the muscles of his upraised arm were like the pillars that hold up the world. The ship was in the shadow of his arm, and of his scepter.

Snow began to drift gently down from the clouds that had gathered in the shadow of his measureless, vast wings.

Only Prometheus was on his feet, and even his size was nothing compared to Morningstar's; he was as a tall pine tree growing the shadow of a vast mountain-glacier. But Prometheus was not even looking upward; he had taken the engine out of the wreckage of a helicopter, and was holding it in one hand, taking it apart with the other, fascinated.

Raven was looking at where his wife's face was pressed into the deck not far from his own. There were tears in her eyes; she was frightened. Through blue and shivering lips, she whispered feebly, "Raven! Do something! I'm scared!"

Raven feebly twitched and put his hands under him. Morningstar's perfect and beautiful voice floated down from heaven. "Prometheus Loki. Bow down to me, trickster, and yield me homage, and, even now, I will spare the filthy race you have created. Bow! Or I send the tidal wave to swallow the cities of mankind, one for each minute you resist." He opened and closed his wings, and great waves gathered on the far horizons and fled away across the sea.

Prometheus looked up, as if puzzled. "Pay honor to you, eldest brother? How have you earned it? What have you invented?"

"The great city of New York has been overwhelmed and inundated. Yield to me. Am I not your elder?"

Raven, warm sparks crawling over his trembling limbs, and leaning heavily upon the lightning bolt he held like a crutch, had found, from somewhere, a superhuman strength to rise again to his feet.

Raven could not meet the gaze of the Emperor of Night, but looked up at his chin, and shouted, "Morningstar! Stop! Or we destroy you now!"

Morningstar eye's narrowed in withering contempt. "Prometheus Loki! Order the things you have made of dirt to bow to me, and I will, perhaps, entertain to restore the Sun whom I have slain."

Prometheus said, "Should you receive bows from my mankind? Well, that's for them to say. They are not mine to give away."

Raven said, "Galen, blow horn. All heaven fall! Fall down and crush this evil angel!"

Morningstar, perhaps irked by the whining noise of the carrier's engines, glanced toward the stern, and his cold glance froze the rear third of the ship into a wide iceberg. "Prometheus Loki, silence your crawling vermin. Do they not know their little place in the vastness of the universe? Dare they attempt deception to a mind superior without measure to their own? For I can see into their very hearts, and I know that he who holds the horn has no will to wind it."

Azrael Merlin, his face darkened with effort, his eyes bright with rage and fear, had struggled up to his knees, his breath laboring. "Great Morningstar, paramount and without peer among the hosts of angelic powers, though fallen; hail and greetings, and glory, glory, glory unto thee, wonder of heaven! Have I your leave to address you, unworthy though I am?" And with unsteady fingers, he picked up the unicorn horn out of Galen's hand and pointed it like a weapon at the mountainous vast figure of Morningstar, who loomed, mace still upraised, across the whole heavens overhead.

The words of the dark archangel, luminous, perfect, filled the night. "Merlin Azrael Waylock, it was your hand and with that horn which first gave me the passions and ambitions of mankind, to which all other angels, save me alone, are ignorant, frozen in their pale duties, unambitious, content. This has pleased me, you may speak; but know first that all you intend to say I see within your heart. Shall you tell me that Acheron behind me is destroyed, and that I cannot return to the dream-world, except through Everness? Shall you tell me that you will have the authority to embody me as you have had to Oberon, should I so put myself beneath your authority and pass back through your Everness gate? Your schemes are nothing to me, wizard, for I foresaw all your treasons when first we met before the cadaver of the unicorn; I knew them even before you had conceived them. My herald, Koschei Anubis Cerebus, the littlest of all my servants, already has raised my colors above Everness, and received the fealty of the lares, genus loci, and guardian angels loyal, once to you, now to me. Prometheus did not give your race wit enough even to remember an enemy you saw within your wards; you fled here and left him there. Fool. Your house is mine; your magic has failed. Now speak. What will you say to me, Merlin Azrael Waylock? Will you, too, threaten to blow the horn? I see in your heart that you would rather die than give victory, and this world, to Oberon. I await. Have you nothing, after all, to say?"

Azrael Merlin slumped forward, beaten down by the contempt of the angel's gaze; and he knelt, leaning heavily upon the deck.

Raven, breathing in strained gasps, said, "Merlin! Apollo, he said magic not save us—only courage."

Azrael Merlin, his strength failing, rolled the horn across the deck with trembling fingers. "Take it! You have endured the horror of Acheron. Your courage is greater than any of ours."

The horn rolled into Lemuel's grasp. He put his other hand on the Chalice, leaning heavily upon it; and when the Chalice began to float upward, beating against the tide of hideous pale light radiating from Morningstar's disdain, Lemuel was raised to his knees.

"Blow!" snarled Azrael Merlin. "Blow your precious paradise to come and blow me back to hell!"

Lemuel raised the horn to his lips.

At the mere touch of his lips, the clouds above parted, and the constellations were gathering together. A shining city, gleaming like a star, with silvered domes and towers of sheer crystal, silent as a ghost, beautiful as a gem, began to descend.

Lemuel drew in his breath.

"Stop," said Morningstar, "I concede. Well done, Prometheus Loki; your tricks have prevailed once more. I shall withdraw if your creature blows not that horn, and wait again in darkness for an aeon. Time is nothing to me; the Guardians of Everness, in generations to come, shall once more forget their charge. Sloth and idleness shall undermine your walls and grant me victory. A century of years or a millennium; it is all one, to me."

Prometheus had just taken apart the ignition system of the helicopter, and was staring in fascination at the distributor cap. Without looking up, he muttered, "Certainly, that's as you wish, eldest brother. But none of this is my work."

Morningstar removed his foot from the carrier and stepped back onto the surface of the sea, which turned to ice in his shadow. And he lowered his great scepter.

Pendrake, leaning on the magic sword, face red with effort, heaved himself slowly upright. "That's not enough, Morningstar! You have not yet heard our demands; we have not yet accepted your surrender!"

Wendy, stilled pinned to the ground by the weight and horror of the dark angelic gaze, said in a worried tone, "Daddy? Daddy! What are you doing?! Why don't you let the nice angel go away now!"

Azrael Merlin had collapsed back to the deck. He hissed, "My Liege! Do not tamper with such powers! Do not tempt such a miracle as this our escape!"

Pendrake barked, "Now, Lemuel! Blow the horn. This is a matter of principle, and it is better that the world be destroyed than that we compromise one inch!"

Galen, face down on the deck, said weakly, "Please, Mr. Pendrake, can't we just live and go home?"

Morningstar turned the pressure of his terrible gaze upon Pendrake, who raised the sword as if to parry a blow. Pendrake staggered but did not fall. Morningstar spoke in a mild and lovely voice: "Who are you, vermin, to make demands of one such as I am?"

Pendrake was able to look him in the eyes unflinchingly. "I am a free man. I bow to no one. And we will blow the horn unless you agree to return control of Everness to the Waylocks; agree to restore the sun which you have extinguished; to recall all tidal waves presently set in motion; to restore Venus to its proper orbit; and undo any other damage in the sky. Or does your angelic intelligence regard my demands as unjust?"

Morningstar gazed down. "I see in your heart that you put aside all temptation to ask for more, demanding only what is just and fair. So be it: I agree. I will, if it please me, wait till you are passed away, little bee, before I raise again my hand to pluck the honeycomb of this world. But you have wished your worse curse alive again: for only if you restore the tyrant Oberon to his power, can he use the Cauldron of Life to coax the soul of the Sun to flame again. I pray he will destroy you, filth, as you deserve. Enough! I am departed."

And Morningstar turned, his great black wings folding over his shoulder like thunderheads, and he strode away into the airs and disappeared, passing over the waves to the East faster than the eyes of men could trace.

IV

They all climbed to their feet, looking around themselves at the devastation and wreckage. The aircraft carrier deck was dented with the footprint of Morningstar, and a light powder of snow lay across all surfaces. The aft of the great ship was locked within the mass of iceberg.

All around on the sea was blood, corpses of monsters, floating hulks of destroyed ships, ice-flows, and a scattered few lifeboats.

Overhead, like a crystal chandelier, hovered the lovely aethereal citadel of Celebradon, silent, hushed, and lovely, and with banners and pennants flying from its battlements. Tinted clouds rose hung in a great ring all around it.

The sky above was nighted and eclipsed. The Sun had not reappeared.

Galen said in a tired voice, "How come I don't feel like cheering . . . ? Haven't we won . . . ?"

Pendrake looked back and forth. "Where did Oberon get to?"

Wendy said, "No one noticed when I said that!"

Raven looked at the snow that ran in streaks across the deck; but the snow had fallen after Oberon had vanished, and he saw no footprints.

He looked up and down across the deck, seeing nothing out of the ordinary. He hesitated, looking again.

Wendy said, "Raven! Can you find him?"

Azrael Merlin said, "Look at how the stars come joyfully from behind the edges of retreating clouds; the shapes in the clouds form images of nestlings, flowers, elongated fingers. Oberon has already returned to Celebradon. But I do not know how." Now Azrael Merlin's nostrils flared, and he turned his head his head to look up at the eastern sky.

Raven pointed the other way across the deck. "Look!"

Galen said, "I don't see anything."

Raven nodded. "Where is dream-colt Lemuel riding to get here, eh? All dream-colts are belonging to Oberon, no?"

Then he turned his head to follow Azrael Merlin's stare.

Wendy looked up, too. "Now what?"

Pendrake looked at a Geiger counter he held, then took off his radiation suit and threw it down. He raised a pair of complex-looking binoculars to his eyes.

Where the clouds had parted, in the far distance, they saw a moving point of light like a falling star. As it dropped closer, speeding toward them between cloud and sea, they saw a gleaming, slim chariot of lacy silver. The traces were a score of silk threads; the chariot was being drawn through the air by a cluster of cats, their furred, graceful bodies leaping through the air in long, curved lunges.

Closer still, they saw a slim and stately young

woman leaned backward against the pull of the reins, skirts and train floating; and her hair was a dark cloud, wind-whipped back from her face. She was slight of build, like a girl in the first bloom of womanhood; but she carried herself with the carriage and dignity of an empress.

And even closer still, they saw the cryptic smile which touched those perfect lips, the smoldering gaze which gleamed mysterious from beneath those wide, dark lashes.

On her hand was a ring burning like a drop of blood, the twin of the mysterious fire opal on the hand of Pendrake.

The flying chariot circled the deck twice, and then came down for a landing. Slim chariot wheels spun blurring across the deck, as the queenly figure reined in her tiny steeds. The cats all landed on their feet, pulled the chariot to a stop with impatient shrugs of their little shoulders, and padded softly to a halt. There they sat and lay, some washing their whiskers, as dignified as pharaohs.

Wendy was hopping up and down with excitement as the chariot was circling. "Mommy! Mommy! It's my mommy! Isn't she pretty! Look, Raven, look! I bet you forgot what she looked like!"

And then when the chariot landed, Wendy, as if carried forward on a breeze, spun across the air and landed in the lady's arms. They hugged each other fiercely, and the lady stroked Wendy's hair and whispered to her. The mother seemed as young or younger than the daughter, if one did not see the ancient wisdom in her eyes.

Then Wendy was on her knees, surrounded by the cats. "Hello, Fluffy! Hello, Smudge! Can I pet you? Whiskers! Have you been a good girl? Look, Raven!" Cats were purring and crawling all over the giggling Wendy. Raven thought he had never seen his wife look so pretty.

Pendrake stepped forward and put his arms around the lady's waist, and lifted her off the chariot car to the deck.

He bent to kiss her, but she turned her cheek and looked at Azrael Merlin. Pendrake took her chin in his fingers and turned it back toward him. "What is this?"

She said, "It may not be polite, Anton. Not in front of my old husband. . . ." Her voice was husky and musical, delightful to the ear.

Pendrake snorted. "Titania! I'm not going to falsify reality for him, or any man. If he doesn't want to see, he can close his eyes."

"No . . . Anton . . . Mm . . . no . . ." She shrugged her shoulder and tried to pull away from his grasp. Her bent her backward over his arm, his fingers tightening in the fragrant masses of her hair, and pulled her tightly to his chest. She could not escape, and, beneath his fierce kiss, whatever murmur of protest she had been speaking softened into a warm moan in her throat, like the purr of a kitten.

Raven, embarrassed, turned his gaze away. He saw the look of deadly hate burning like fire in Azrael Merlin's narrowed gaze.

When they straightened up, Titania had both her arms twined around her husband's arm, leaning her head against his shoulder; and she was smiling a soft, triumphant smile. She never moved far from his side thereafter, but kept herself pressed close to him.

Raven stepped forward, but stood gaping, unable to think of what to say. Lemuel at that moment also stepped forward, bowing low, his hands held out, palms up. Lemuel intoned a phrase in an ancient language, perhaps Egyptian, perhaps Babylonian.

Titania smiled, looked out from under dark lashes, and arched one eyebrow high. (Raven was surprised to recognize Wendy's favorite expression.) She said to Lemuel in English, "You are polite, sir, and recall the old ways other men forget. But a lady doesn't like to be reminded of her age."

Lemuel said in English, "Great Mother Isis, I rely upon your bounteous good nature to mend any fault of mine."

She said, "Pour one drop from the Grail you hold into the sea, and all this blood, these miles of corpses, shall be cleansed away, and the waters made sweet again."

Raven found his voice, and said, "I know you . . . don't I? From at the reception . . ."

She laughed, a sultry, musical laugh deep in her throat. "I should be dismayed you forget me, son-in-law, did I not blame the Mists of Everness. Once, long ago, the Earth was all heat and volcanic passion, and the sky was nothing but cloud, and Heaven had never been seen. The clouds parted for my first husband, so that he could come down to earth to see me. The spirits of earth were amazed when they first saw the stars. Earth and sky now saw each other; and they were married. Lightning, his weapon, now yours, caressed the seas, and brought forth life. The world thereafter was utterly changed, due to the coming of heaven. For you, now, Raven, and for mankind, the Mists of Forgetfulness which cloak the Earth now part; and you will see the wonder, deep, sublime, and ancient, which stands beyond what you thought formed the boundary of the world. The world will be changed again, profoundly."

Azrael Merlin said in a voice that cracked and snapped with hate: "Indeed the world shall change; it shall be ice from pole to pole; and every herb and grass shall die in darkness; for the Sun is fallen and shall not rise again."

Titania turned, looking at him sidelong from the corner of her eyes, and smiled a slow, languid smile. "How so? Oberon already is in Celebradon with the Cauldron of Rebirth. He merely awaits that you revoke the curse you spoke, to resume his power, that he may work the cauldron to reignite the Sun. It is a miracle, I know, but one which will not try him; hasn't he done it every dawn?"

"And if I do not revoke my curse?" Azrael Merlin stood with his arms crossed, his head thrown back, his eyes blazing.

Titania turned to Pendrake, and she said, "I came to tell you, Anton, that you had no time to tarry here; already the servants of evil seek to reap the grain their masters, defeated by you, have sown. Even if the battle among the gods is suspended, the battle among men is not, and may continue for many years before the wounds are bound up and forgiven. You must go immediately to the Capitol Building and stop them before a state of martial law is proclaimed. It is cold there, and you should wear something heavier than that black cape of yours. And are you wearing a flak jacket? You know how I hate it when you go out without a flak jacket."

Raven was shocked when he saw Pendrake, smiling grimly, swat Titania on the bottom. She squealed, her pose of queenly dignity forgotten, and danced away from him, her palms on the bustle of her dress.

Titania laughed like a little girl, shrugging her shoulders and tossing back her hair. "You had best be as quick to smite the evil ones as you are to smite your wife, Anton. Take my chariot and my daughter and go! There is not time to spend even on a kiss!"

Pendrake stepped over, put his arms around her, dipped her, and kissed her till she was breathless. He said in a voice of fierce calm, "I shall conquer them as easily and absolutely as I have conquered you, my dear."

She lay curved gracefully back over his arm, and whispered through parted lips, "Oh, yes."

He put his lips to her ear and whispered something. She stood erect, dignified once more, and with a gentle hand pushed Pendrake back. She said, "You must go. I need to have a word with Merlin Azrael in private. Go! What happens hereafter you may learn in time."

Azrael Merlin said, "What words would I have to spend on thee, Queen of Witches?" But he did not walk away, but stood glowering.

Pendrake stepped up onto the car of the cat-drawn chariot, and took up the silk reins in his hands. "Raven, I may need your help, too. Wendy, come along. Van Dam, you come too; if what I think is happening is happening, I may need your help. Prometheus, I'm afraid you won't fit . . ."

The titan did not look up from the partly disassembled helicopter, but said, "If you curled your rotor blades at the tip, you would avoid the turbulence caused when the outer part of the lifting surface goes supersonic."

"Right," said Pendrake, who turned back. "Titania, I'm assuming you think Peter and his goats can't take us because they are going somewhere else?"

She turned to Lemuel. "The house of Everness has been destroyed by Morningstar as he passed through it to the sea. In less than a week, all mankind shall perish, for, without their dreams, men go slowly mad, hallucinate, and die. You must go at once and make what reparations you might."

Lemuel turned and bowed to Pendrake. "Mr. Pendrake, I need your permission to do this work."

"Certainly, you have it," said Pendrake, hiding whether he felt any puzzlement.

"Then touch me on the shoulder with your sword."

Pendrake snorted as if he thought the idea was mildly absurd, and it was somewhat awkward raising the enchanted blade with two people crowded around him on the chariot car. But, leaning out, he touched Lemuel on the shoulder with the flat of the gleaming blade.

Then, with no more ado, Pendrake snapped the ribbons holding the cats, shouting, "Hey up, Whiskers, Muffin, Snuggles! On Smudge, on Frisky! On Fluffy!"

Several cats turned and regarded Pendrake with looks of infinite dignity and infinite disdain. One yawned, her little pink tongue flicking in the air. Another began to wash her paws.

"I hate cats . . . ," muttered Pendrake, then, louder, "Titania, can you get your pets to move their tails?"

Titania nodded and pointed to the East, and immediately the tiny, furry figures were leaping into the air. The chariot was yanked skyward in one long, dizzying swoop of motion. Pendrake wrestled with the reins, his black cape flapping around him. To his left and right Van Dam and Raven clung to the slim, silver rails with both hands. Wendy was flying in the midst of the cluster of cats, sometimes on her face, sometimes on her back with her fingers twined behind her head.

Pendrake said to Raven over the noise of the wind, "There is a navigational instrument in my weapons harness under my right armpit, could you get it for me? I don't have a free hand. Do you see the coil of fiber-optic of my television periscope? It's a little black box in the holster just under that."

"Everything here is little black box! Is it this?"

"No, that's my radar jammer. Leave that on anyway; it will make sure we don't get shot down. The Loran box is right there under my right arm. Do you see the line of grenades on a bandolier? Okay, moving up the belt, you should see three pockets, one with a filter mask, one with an ultraviolet lamp, and then . . ."

"I have it."

"Can you give me a reading?"

"Yes, is same as we use aboard ship." And he read off their longitude and latitude, and gave the bearing the instrument showed.

"I should hope it is considerably smaller than the Loran you have aboard ship," said Pendrake.

Raven turned his head. The darkened sea had fallen

away in long swooping plunges of swift motion; the aircraft carrier and the ruins of Acheron were gone from sight. "Wish I could hear what Titania saying to Merlin, you know?"

"Ah," said Pendrake "dial the radio-phone clipped to my belt to the channel marked 'memory six.' That should tune us in to the bugging device I left on Azrael."

22

The Sword
of the Just

I

Titania's voice came over the tiny radio. They had missed the beginnings of her conversation with Merlin Azrael.

"Behold the wise magician! So wise. Wise enough to find the heir of Uther when Uther left no heir. Wagging tongues claimed the child was some bastard son of Gorlois or of Ector. How cleverly you stilled those tongues by showing all the land the miracle of the sword in the stone! But why was it none ever guessed that the babe the magician found, and proved to be the rightwise king born of England by a magic trick, was indeed the magician's own son? A miracle indeed!"

Azrael Merlin's voice: "A hidden catch held the sword in place till Arthur's hand was on the hilt. He never guessed that I stood nearby on the platform, with my toe upon the switch. To him it seemed a miracle indeed. Do you question my rightness? I faced terrible foes; all the kingdom was torn; that small lie let Arthur never doubt his rightness to rule!"

"A great and enduring rightness, Emrys. How ran the rest of your little lie? You said he was the son of Uther and Igraine, oh, happy fate! To be thus the heir both of Caer Leon and likewise of King Lot's estate! Blood of mingled houses, he, to whom both houses owed due loyalty."

"Mingled blood indeed, O Lady of the Lake. Your own son you mock; though, by law, you could not deny him the arms which he rowed out upon the lake to take. All men saw those who came on Easter Day to do him homage, the petty kings and barons of great estate. But only you and I saw what ancient ones came forth from the deep greenwood on that moonless night to dance him fairy-rings and anoint him with immortal powers, for they could not deny him what fealty to thy blood, O Vivian, required."

"Were you pleased, then, with your works, O Mage? What matters it if a dead king and a living widow were name-blackened and branded with adultery?"

"You dare, madame, to upbraid me, that I branded others with a name better deserved by you?"

"Your part in that was not small, as I recall, my lover."

"Indeed; but I hold it as a unstained honor. I made a kingdom!"

"And what did you give the king?"

"In that first fairy-ring which danced around him, he saw the mystery and power; and he bad me devise for him a table of like shape, to make all equal who sat there, a table without head or foot, and all the tiresome squabbling of priority and precedent made hush. The dolmens at Stonehenge he likewise commanded I erect, to bind the spirits of heaven, that his Round Table never fail while ancient stones still stood. But there was a secret flaw within the staunchest pillar which I took for my main support, the mighty champion of the Lady of the Lake, Sir Lancelot. Your champion, madame!"

"And what else did you give the king?"

"I do not know your meaning, madame."

"Where was the Moly Wand that was meant to be his scepter? To allow him to see the truth and falsehood in all hearts? The treasons of Lancelot would have been discovered in an instant, had he had it. But, no, I forget. Your lies would have been discovered all as well. How necessary to the kingdom's weal were your practical, dark-minded schemings now?"

"Is this, finally, the reason for your terrible betrayal of me? My long imprisonment?"

"What imprisonment was that? Surely if the Silver Key had been in the King's hand, as we agreed when I told you how to slay my husband's unicorn, and steal the power of the beast Oberon used to betray and slaughter Ouranos (the power I gave you!), the High King, my son, he could have instantly released you, for that is the nature of keys. Was it cold in the roots of the world-tree where I locked you? I thought the kingdom might prevail without your meddling; yet I was wrong; and I was equally as cold as I stood upon the boat looking down at my dying son after Mordred's blow; cold in the sea-wind, terribly cold, without the arrows of Belphanes to warm me, without the Grail to give me hope. He had sent them out to find it, don't you know, but could not uncover where you had hidden it. And so I took my son back home."

"My son as well, who should have stayed on Earth, with me! I could have dream-cursed Mordred, had I been free, or blamed him for some horrid crime, or met him with venom-coated dart shot in secret from afar. Any of these means would have served the King, provided always that he never learned of them. But now, what evil fate oppresses me! I shall never see my son awake until the world's last day! You stole my son and stole my life, Queen of the Other World! And now you ask me to restore the pomp and power of Oberon, another husband you have betrayed!"

"To let the Sun be reborn, and bring the world to life again. No one knows the secret of Oberon's Cauldron but he. Are you still so loyal to the Pendragon? Another holds the Pendragonship today. He is of your blood. He, and all the Waylock line, and all the world alike will die in darkness, if you lift not your curse on Oberon. Think, think, O Wizard, and all your pride in all your dark service to the kingdom; where is your pride now? Where your loyalty? Swept away by jealousy? By hate? How then is this world of today so different from our failures in Albion? How are you different?"

There was a long silence. The signal began to fade.

"And if I say I will lift my curse on Oberon, if the Pendragon will lift his arrest of me, and grant me liberty?"

"You saw him speak to Morningstar. Do you think he will agree? Do you think anything you do will persuade him to allow you to escape the punishments you have earned for your many murders? Why do you turn away? Do you realize, now, at last, that no just kingdom can be built upon injustice?"

"Prometheus! I see you there. Put that down and answer me; you can see the future! Should I demand my freedom, even if it means the world die in frozen gloom? Will the Pendragon capitulate to my demand? What does your wisdom say?"

There was a long pause over the radio. Then the deep, rapid voice of Prometheus came over the channel. "I don't see it matters. With a simple application of the technology I showed them, men can build their own sun now. A sufficient charge of antimatter directed at the planet Jupiter would ignite . . ."

The signal began to fade in washes of static.

Raven said, "Prometheus really my father? Is nothing like me!"

Wendy called back over her shoulder, "I wouldn't say that, you little titan, you!" and she laughed.

Pendrake said, "Is that Merlin fellow related to me? The man's a bloodthirsty maniac. Scary guy. He's nothing like me."

Van Dam, clinging with both hands to the chariot railing at Pendrake's elbow, stared up at the tall figure in wind-whipped black billows, the deadly weapons and amazing equipment neatly holstered in his black harness, the magic sword thrust unsheathed through his belt. Van Dam whispered to himself, "I wouldn't say that . . ."

II

As the cat-drawn chariot flew over Los Angeles, they saw the city still standing; but the electrical power was out, and there were torches and fires in the streets, screams and mob-roars.

Pendrake saw the Beast of War crouched over the city.

It turned and fled at his coming.

Raven held the instrument Pendrake had given him, which stimulated the sleep center of the brain. When they landed the chariot in the midst of the rioters, the electricity that streamed from Raven's hands caused people in the mobs to fall, but only into sleep. In a moment half the people were down.

The other half stared in awe at the black-cloaked figure hovering in the chariot. Pendrake brandished the sword. An instrument electronically amplified his voice to echo across the city: "Return to your homes! Every crime you commit is being watched! You cannot hide because those around you do evil! Looters will be punished! Whatever injustice you imagine you have suffered at the hands of others shall be redressed!"

The mob became a crowd, and thinned, and fled like fog before the sun.

In the air, passing over the Rocky Mountains, Raven said, "Why did they believe you?"

Wendy, surrounded by flying cats, called back, "I think I did that! Something Mommy said, and I thought that maybe the Moly Wand can make a person feel when someone is lying. I let them feel Daddy's words. And they thought they were true! Or maybe I just waved the wand in the air and nothing actually happened . . ."

They landed again in Kansas City, and in Baltimore. Only once did Raven have to call down a thunderstroke to daze the mobs. Where they found federal troops fighting local militia, Van Dam was able to order the federal officers to disarm. Along three major highways they cleared roadblocks and ordered the tanks to stand aside. The truck drivers with their shotguns, who had been besieging the federal troops, cheered as they flew off, shooting into the air to salute them.

As they flew over Washington D.C., they saw troops on every street corner, tanks and armored vehicles blockading the streets; but in other places, wrecked cars had been piled one atop the other, blockading the federal troops in turn; and militia from Virginia and Maryland prevented the federal troops from moving. The capital was paralyzed.

Pendrake, looking down, said, "This city was designed for barricades."

Raven said, "Always heard had bad traffic here, you know?"

Van Dam said, "Why are the Virginians here in arms but not the Districters who live here?"

Pendrake said, "The only people with guns in the District are criminals. Here is the Capitol. Van Dam, I'm going to land between those two machine-gun nests on the Capitol stairs next to that armored personnel carrier. Do you think your badge can get us into the building?"

"Well, sir, I can try. But look at all that television equipment; the Vice President, excuse me, I mean the President, is addressing Congress, like the announcement said over your radio. We might have some trouble."

Raven looked up at the still-nighted sky, the autumn constellations hanging, despite the season, above streams of black clouds. At his frown, lightnings flickered around the outline of those clouds. "Am ready for trouble," said Raven, "but those who try to make this country, free country, like Russia? *Ha!* They are not ready."

The chariot landed.

III

Van Dam's credentials got them past the first set of guards at the outer doors and then past the next set who were guarding the lobby with drawn machine guns. The security officer merely looked at Van Dam's face, grunted, saluted, and waved him on through. But they made Pendrake leave his sword in the lobby, and his weapons. He carefully tied his weapon harness to the sword hilt, wrapping them together with a leather band, before turning it over to the sergeant-at-arms.

Once they were beyond that guard post and out of sight, Pendrake opened his hand, and spirals of gold rainbows formed themselves into his sword again. The harness was still attached, with all his gear, and he took a moment to shrug back into it.

They continued forward, footsteps echoing off the wainscoting and the vaulted ceilings.

Then they were in the long, main marbled corridor leading to the congressional chambers. There were a line of sandbags across the corridor, and fifty-caliber machine guns on tripod mounts peered out across the top of the bags to cover the length of the corridor. A voice from behind the bags shouted for them to halt.

Van Dam stepped forward, raised his badge overhead, and identified himself.

A voice said, "I'm sorry, Colonel Van Dam, but we have orders to shoot anyone who tries to come down this corridor, no matter who it is, till the President has finished his broadcast."

"But this is an emergency!"

A warning shot ricocheted off the marble near his feet.

The group backed up around a corner. They stood in a narrower side corridor, one carpeted in red, lined in dark wood paneling, interrupted by large, oak doors.

Raven said, "Pendrake, think I can knock them all out, even if not outdoors, with thunder."

Pendrake took out his grenade launcher and put on his goggles. "We don't have much time before the announcement. I don't have any spare photomultiplier goggles; you'll all have to hang on to my cape. Raven, on my mark, thunderstrike them, and douse the area with a nonlethal electric charge." He had his launcher in one hand, a long-barreled dart gun in the other. "These men are not criminals, and the neurotoxin I'm using takes three seconds to take effect. Ready?"

Raven stepped out, his face unnaturally calm; and when he snapped his fingers, the echo from the walls shattered the air, breaking windows and chandeliers.

A group of overeager soldiers came over the top of the sandbags, guns ready. Beams of lightning gushed from Raven's eyes; and where he glanced, soldiers toppled, paralyzed with convulsions.

Pendrake leaned around the corner and fired. The sandbags were obscured in black smoke. The soldiers, unable to see, held their fire. Pendrake strode quickly down the corridor, spreading smoke as he went, Van

Dam, Raven, and his daughter behind him, holding on
to his cape hem.

Inside the gas cloud, Raven, despite that he could
not see, made no noise as he walked, and Wendy
floated. Pendrake, who could see everything clearly,
stepped around the groping and blinded soldiers, those
few who had not been rendered unconscious by Raven.

Twice Van Dam bumbled into a soldier; both times
Pendrake casually turned and shot a dart into an exposed arm or neck before the soldier could react. The
lieutenant on duty was shouting to his men to gather in
a line and block the corridor. Pendrake turned on his
pocket tape recorder, taped a sentence or two of the
lieutenant's voice, shot the man with a dart, and then
threw the tape machine down the corridor, where it re-
peated a phrase calling for the men to gather to him.

Raven's fingers stiffened on Pendrake's shoulder.
"Smell grave-dirt."

"I see him, Mr. Varovitch."

Pendrake's goggles gave him a clear view of the
skeletal hand, with elongated fingernails, reaching
around the edge of the corridor up ahead and then the
unnaturally tall, hideously thin shadow which followed it.

Koschei took a position in front of the great doors
leading into the congressional chamber. His famished,
thin face floated near the level of the upper lintel; his
crown of severed fingers was higher still. The dark fog
he wore stretched from one side of the door to the
other, and bones like chicken claws reached down
from his greaves to scratch the marble to either side of
his thin feet.

Koschei loomed horribly in Pendrake's view, and
the rib cages he wore as breastplate opened and closed
like a man drumming his fingernails, sharp ribs folding and unfolding from Koschei's midsection.

One of the soldiers called out, "Get them when they
try for the door!" and then sagged, a moment later, as

Pendrake, without turning his head, casually shot a dart into him.

Koschei said, "You shall not pass, Pendragon! You shall not pass by me." The points of green light that served him for eyes were not deceived by the smoke or by Pendrake's black garments, but they stared with sinister hatred at Pendrake.

When the dart he shot into Koschei had no effect, Pendrake drew his magic sword. "You have to let go of me, Raven, Van Dam. I fenced a bit in college. Let's see how much I recall."

Raven said, "But he has no sword, unless another draws it for him!" And the soldiers who heard Raven's voice, when they tried to grab him, were flung to the ground by the mild electric charge which he was keeping in his coat.

Koschei's laugh sounded like the rattle of a poisonous snake. "There are many, oh, so very many, in the chamber beyond who would draw out Pity to use as a weapon." And in the electronic image in his goggles, Pendrake saw the white bone blade glisten like an icicle as Koschei raised it and saluted him.

A noise came from behind the doors at that moment, applause and cheers. And a voice, "Ladies and Gentlemen, the President of the United States!" More cheers.

Pendrake saluted with his blade, and made an adjustment to his goggles, turning up the gain.

Koschei came forward like a black wave, feinting and disengaging, his thin blade rapid as the stinger of a wasp. His bone-covered arms were so long, his reach so great, that Pendrake was forced to retreat in a quick shuffle of footsteps, parrying rapidly left and right. The stench from Koschei was overpowering. The ringing slither of blade on blade echoed from the walls.

A voice from behind the door was speaking: ". . . as my words go out, both to those loyal Americans who know their place and know how to have faith, keep the peace and obey their lawful magistrates, and to those criminal rebels who do not, they also go out to the powers abroad, to the world . . ."

Pendrake did a rapid jump-lunge, and the point of his blade corkscrewed down the length of Koschei's blade, but rebounded from the bony plates guarding Koschei's wrist.

Koschei, lithe and quick as a striking snake, dropped to one knee as he lunged, his face now low to the floor, and his blade feinted high and came in low, under Pendrake's guard, stabbing at his groin. The fold of Pendrake's swinging cape hem slowed the blow enough for Pendrake to parry in a low line, chop toward Koschei's head, and retreat again.

Koschei pulled his head back, brushing the chandelier with his crown, and aimed several short, rapid strokes at Pendrake's head and shoulders. Pendrake parried, aimed a cut at Koschei's leg, and backed out of range, panting. The sweat in his goggles was beginning to obscure his vision.

Raven, meanwhile, crouched low to the floor, listening for the tap of soldier's boot's on marble, listening for the ring of blade on blade. He heard the voice from the other room, suddenly sounding much louder, saying, ". . . to our allies, with all the reassurance that your trust in me requires, that the explosion of the nuclear warhead over the Pacific waters less than an hour ago was the first act of a terrorist group which has stolen American nuclear material. The criminal act the American government utterly denounces . . ."

Koschei swung his white blade in a quick figure eight, lunged forward. Koschei's abnormally long arms and legs gave him a reach that could keep mortal foes at bay, but Pendrake saw that this also made the monster slightly slower to lunge and recover. Pendrake did not take the feint, parried, and ran past the monster as soon as he saw that Koschei was extended in full lunge, stabbing the other's back as he fled past. Koschei parried, and swung at Pendrake's back, missed.

Pendrake was at the edge of the gas-cloud now, and the smoke had thinned to wisps of dark, hanging fog. He only had a moment to regain his footing before Koschei billowed up out of the smoke-cloud behind him, his thin, white blade whistling and stabbing.

Raven found the edge of the gas-cloud at the same time. He wondered why the gas was dispersing in the enclosed corridor. Raven was right next to a soldier who was raising his rifle and taking aim at the two figures locked in the deadly dance of swordplay.

Raven touched the man's shoulder, and a small electric charge made the man's muscles spasm. The rifle flipped out of the soldier's grip before he could fire. With his other hand, Raven snapped his fingers in the young man's ear, and caught him as he fell.

Other soldiers came out from the smoke, but could not shoot Pendrake for the same reason that Raven could not dash Koschei with a lightning bolt; the combatants were too close to each other.

Raven and the soldiers stood and watched, momentarily fascinated.

Pendrake and Koschei moved quickly back and forth, white blade and gold blade ringing—Pendrake stamping, lunging, and shuffling; Koschei billowing and fluttering like a loose sail in a high wind.

They clashed together in a corps à corps; their sword hilts locked together in a brief contest of strength. Koschei swelled to full height, and bore down; Pendrake, caught in midlunge, was driven to one knee, blade high above his head.

"Fool!" hissed Koschei's terrible, cold voice, "When can your sword of justice overcome my Pity?"

Pendrake let go of his sword. Koschei, overbalanced, toppled forward toward Pendrake's empty hand. But Pendrake had already closed his fingers again, and the swirl of golden light that formed around his fingers brought his blade up from the floor and into his hand just in time to slide in between two rib bones in Koschei's breastplate, through his chest, and protrude two feet out from his back. Koschei was now draped over Pendrake in a crouch.

Koschei smiled, and the lights in his eye sockets burned with sinister mirth. "I do not keep a heart in my body, and I cannot be reached by any touch of Justice."

And he raised his white blade and stabbed it into Pendrake's chest.

The speech in the other room went on, loudly, clearly: ". . . in order to track down Anton Pendrake and his terrorist allies, we hereby order all civil rights suspended for the duration of the emergency. Police may make arrests without warrant and search wherever, in their discretion, they see fit. Because of the dangers of weapons falling into such hands, the privilege to own firearms, which this government generously granted its loyal citizens at the outset of this republic, is hereby revoked. Disloyal speeches and publications must also be shut down until the unrest caused by the fear of these terrorists is abated . . ."

Raven then heard Wendy's voice ringing out, clear and loud overhead, "It's not true! He's just a big liar!"

Raven spun, and saw that the doors Koschei had been guarding were opened, and that the gas-cloud was dissipating into the greater space beyond. Wendy had simply flown overhead, found the doors, opened them, and gone through.

He heard gasps of wonder and surprise, and then scattered laughter.

Pendrake straightened slowly. "This battle was pointless, Koschei." He began to pull the white, thin blade out of his chest. "You tricked me into thinking I had to fight. But I think your weapon can only hurt people who let Pity affect their judgment." And when he pulled the bone blade out of his body, he was not hurt, and his heart did not bleed.

He laughed a sarcastic laugh, and the blade, which blows and strength could not chip, shivered in his fingers and was shattered by that laugh.

Koschei floated backward, gathering himself into a spiderish shadow in one corner of the remote ceiling. "Laugh, for now, mortal man. All works of men will one day pass away. And I shall always be armed; for though you break my blade, there are many, many traitors to your kind, eager, so very eager, to forge that sword for me again. I am banished, but not vanquished. While envy lives, my lifeless evil cannot die." Silently, insubstantially, he evaporated.

Wentworth's voice came from inside the congressional chamber: "Someone shoot that floating girl!"

The soldiers had surrounded Pendrake. "You're under arrest, sir!" said one young man.

Pendrake said in measured tones: "Under arrest I may be, but I am going into that room." He started forward with a firm footstep.

Another soldier said, "Stop!" and jumped in the way, raising his rifle.

Pendrake stared at him coolly. "Soldier, do you recognize me?"

"Uh—no . . ."

The first soldier said, "You should read the papers. He's Anton Pendrake."

A third man said, "He owns the papers . . ."

The first soldier said, "He won the Nobel prize last year for physics, and the year before that . . ."

Pendrake looked at the soldier who was speaking. "Son, do you want to be responsible for having me murdered on your watch?"

"Uh—"

"You can stay around me in a group; you can keep me under arrest; but I am going into that room!"

And when he walked forward, for some reason, no one stopped him.

23

The Wand
of Truth

Raven had been standing near the great doors and, still
half shrouded by the smoke, he was through the doors
before any guard thought to stop him.

Passing through the black cloud, however, he came
face to face with a line of armed men in business suits,
who covered the door with their pistols. Raven stopped
suddenly, staring at the many barrels pointed at him.

Van Dam had somehow gotten through even before
Raven, and was arguing with two of the men, calling
them by name, asking to be let through. These men
wore dark glasses and stony expressions, which hid
any reaction they might have had.

Two or three of the Secret Service men were looking up, but, despite Wentworth's calls, none of them
had raised a pistol toward Wendy. Raven thought that
was a good thing: these men did not look particularly
wicked, and it would be a shame to fry the first one
who began to point a weapon at his wife.

The chambers were full; the congressmen filled the aisles, and the gallery was filled with press and television cameras. Some of the cameras had swung up to cover the girl floating in midair, who swooped slowly from one side of the vast chamber to another, her skirts flapping and dropping cotton-flower petals.

Wendy was calling out, "We dropped the bomb on the bad guys and saved the earth! It was magic! Look at me flying! Magic! Stop laughing! It is not so wires!" Her voice was growing shrill and tearful with anger and frustration.

Some of the congressmen laughed in nervous, high-pitched bursts, guilty laughter. Some congressmen were snarling in fear, guilty fear. Others looked up with a boredom drained of hope.

Wentworth had been sitting near the president but had leaped to his feet, shaking his fist and snarling. He froze in embarrassment when some cameras turned on him.

The congressional chaplain was Kyle Coldgrave, not dressed in his purple robe, but wearing the collar and crucifix of a faith not his own. His thin face was twitching with rage and malice: his squint and hairlip were pronounced. Beneath the gray stubble of his skull, his complexion was sallow. Whatever advantages or preferment Azrael had bestowed upon his henchmen, health and tranquility were not among them.

Coldgrave shouted, "Shoot that girl! She's armed and dangerous!"

There was a group of his acolytes, dressed in their purple robes, but seated in a line of folding chairs nearby—allowed into the proceedings for no reason made clear to any outsiders. They did not understand Coldgrave's orders, but, loyally, they took up the cry as well. "Shoot her! Shoot her! She's armed and dangerous!"

A Secret Service officer near them shouted them down in a bored voice: "She's carrying a broomstick."

"Shoot her!" cried Coldgrave.

"I don't take orders from you, sir."

The man who had been, until recently, the Vice President (and he still had trouble remembering that he was no longer) stood at the podium, confronted by a battery of microphones. The recent troubles had worn on him; his polished demeanor had given way to a harassed, frightened look. He had lived his life by appearing to lead, while following public opinion; by appearing resolute while ignorant; by appearing wise while uttering platitudes. Now that the emergency had come, demanding real leadership, real resolve, real wisdom, the Vice President had no such qualities, and lived in the continual fear that this would be discovered, and in the even deeper fear that it already had been, long ago, and that he wasn't fooling anyone.

It was that fear which made him grip the podium and stare when Pendrake came through the smoking doorway, dressed in black, armed with a sword, and walked toward him up the aisle with a majestic stride. The armed soldiers coming behind him, who had allegedly arrested him, seemed, at first glance, to be following him.

It was the expression of certainty in Pendrake's face, of clear, dispassionate, inflexible judgment, which frightened the vice president.

Wentworth shouted, "It's Anton Pendrake! Shoot him!"

A murmur of awe ran through the chamber: Everyone had just been told that this man had control of a nuclear bomb.

The Vice President cringed and said, "Don't shoot anyone on camera! It will look terrible!"

Wentworth turned and glared at him, "Shut up, you fool!" The Vice President flinched, and looked up in fear at the cameras. "We can edit this out later, can't we?"

A ripple of disgusted laughter ran through the chamber.

Wentworth said, "We're live, you idiot!" He pointed at the cameras. "Shut off the satellite feed! No broadcasts are leaving this room!"

Pendrake said in a loud, clear voice: "The time you have feared has come! Now you will pay for your crimes!"

Wentworth grabbed a Secret Service man next to him and wrestled the gun out of his holster. People screamed.

Raven raised his voice: "Wendy! Now! And the chaplain, too!"

Floating on high, Wendy pointed her Moly Wand at Wentworth, who was brandishing the gun in the air.

Wentworth was pointing the gun at Pendrake, screaming, "You're just a filthy terrorist, Pendrake! You can't prove anything . . . ar! Ar! Ar! Awk! Awk! Awk! Arwwwk!" And Wentworth's face and skin fell open as he slid to his furry belly near the podium, the gun dropping from his flippers. He was a seal.

Raven said, "The chaplain! I saw their flayed corpses at Everness, with Koschei! Azrael had killed them!"

Coldgrave, in a huge flap of his coattails, tried to leap over a line of chairs and run away. When his false skin fell off, he turned into a seal and rolled heavily to the floor, coming to rest almost at the feet of his erstwhile acolytes.

There was a moment of silent horror in the room. The men and women in purple robes stared down at their feet at the inhuman creature they had been following and worshipping.

The seal-creature flapped it flippers and choked out a croaking bark.

A cry of rage broke the silence; a dozen men in purple robes seized their folding chairs and clubbed the creature mercilessly to death, while it rolled and squealed pathetically.

Blood flew. The rich carpet was stained. The horrid deed was done. The men in purple robes straightened suddenly when they saw the cameras pointing at them.

Numbly, they dropped their chairs. Numbly, they began to strip off and discard their purple robes.

It was Van Dam who spoke next. He called on two or three people in the room by name, saying, "Wentworth is a selkie. Look at him! Take a good look! We were being played for suckers! Is this what we owe our loyalty to? Is this seal-thing what was going to lead us to power and glory? The damn thing can't even pick up a gun for itself! Can't do anything unless we help it! And we're not going to help it anymore! You there! Put down those guns!"

Pendrake stepped up to the podium. One of the Secret Service men set to guard the Vice President stepped in his way. "Get back, sir! I can't let you near the President!" He spoke in a calm, strong voice, like the voice of a man who knows his duty. He held a gun in his fist.

"Please!" whined the Vice President. "You can't shoot anyone on television! Wait till later!"

Pendrake looked the Secret Service man in the eye. He spoke softly, but he was near enough the microphones on the podium that his voice was amplified through the chamber. "You may now decide where your loyalties are. Did you ever take an oath to defend the Constitution? Against all enemies? Foreign . . . and domestic?"

The Secret Service man looked back and forth between the cringing figure of the man he was supposed to guard, and the upright, fearless figure of Pendrake.

Then he shrugged, holstered his weapon, and stepped aside. "I didn't vote for this dweeb," he muttered.

Pendrake now turned his gaze on the Vice President,

saying, "Azrael de Gray is my prisoner. All his schemes are at an end."

A murmur of fear and awe rippled through the chamber. Congressmen exchanged guilty glances; White House staff snarled in fear.

Pendrake continued in a clear voice: "The murder of the President took place in front of security cameras installed in the Pentagon, and was watched, not only by Colonel Van Dam, and by the creature impersonating Wentworth, but also by me. You were present, you saw the crime, and later lied, destroyed evidence, and impeded justice. I accuse you of aiding and abetting murder after the fact; this makes you a member of a murder conspiracy and a murderer. I accuse you of conspiring to overthrow the Constitution of these United States by armed rebellion, which is treason. How do you answer these accusations?"

The Vice President looked back and forth wildly, a trapped, haunted look in his eyes. "I—I—It's a lie, of course . . . a falsehood propagated for political reasons by disloyal . . . uh . . . Azrael made me do it! It wasn't my fault! He had magic powers! I had to tell all those lies! Everyone lies! I had to help them cover it up!"

Pendrake held up the magic blade he carried, almost as if raised in a salute, so that the vice president could see himself in its mirrored surface. "What is a fair and just punishment for such crimes?"

The Vice President swayed on his feet. "I resign. I don't want to do this anymore."

Pendrake caught him by the arm and pushed him toward one of the soldiers who stood behind him. "Have the Sergeant-at-Arms place this man under arrest. We have all heard his confession on national television. Mr. Secretary! I believe you are now President. Please rescind all of your predecessor's orders—now."

The secretary of state stood up slowly, uncertainly. Near him sat the chairman of the Federal Reserve Board, who was calmly looking right and left. He and the two men near him, obviously bodyguards, quietly got up and started down the aisle toward the exit.

Pendrake pointed his sword. "Stop that man!"

The chairman of the Federal Reserve turned slowly. He spoke with great dignity. "There's no national television. The satellite feed must have been cut off by now. What we've done, Mr. Pendrake, was meant to preserve the nation from terrorists like you. At least, that is the story we will allow the press to publish. You would be amazed at how fawningly the press plays up to us. Or perhaps you won't be. You won't be around to see it."

The speaker of the House and the chairman of the Ways and Means Committee both stood up. One of them said, "Aye. I reckon there's none but loyal lads in this here room by now, right, lads?"

Raven shouted, "Wendy! They're . . ."

She said in a cross voice, "I know! I know!"

Roughly a quarter of the congressmen, and all of the cabinet, fell down, shed their skins, and flopped helplessly in the aisles, or were caught painfully atop the arms or backs of seats.

The sight seemed to improve Wendy's mood. She fluttered down out of midair, and hung near Raven. "Well! That explains a lot about politics I didn't understand! Aren't they sort of cute?"

Raven snorted. "I make you rug of some of them, eh?"

Pendrake stood at the podium, looking back at forth at the squirming mass of seals who now filled the chamber, rolling underfoot and nipping at the ankles of those who were human. There were several minutes of chaotic noise.

Pendrake said sharply to his daughter, "Gwen, hush! Those men were killed and flayed and replaced; members of their family and staff as well, no doubt. They died in the service of this country no less than any soldier. Don't make light of this!"

The number of seals astonished him. So many people had been killed, so much of the government had been taken over, without any word or alarm given.

Pendrake was further disconcerted when he saw that the chairman of the Federal Reserve was, in fact, a man.

Raven whistled for silence, and a thunderclap followed that whistle, shattering glass overhead.

Raven said, "Quiet! I want to hear Pendrake talk!"

Wendy flourished her wand; and perhaps she was hoping she could make people realize when they heard the truth.

Pendrake stared up at the camera. "I address my words to my fellow free men of America. Your government has fallen into the hands of a corrupt group of criminals. Their ringleaders were not even human beings, but horrible imposters. These creatures possessed a parapsychological science far in advance of ours, so far in advance that we might as well call it magic. By that magic, they established a beachhead on earth and landed troops in such numbers and armed with such weapons that they certainly would have conquered the earth, with ease, had not I, and a group of private citizens acting with me, directed an atomic weapon at the enemy location in the Pacific. No act of aggression against any nation of the Earth has been intended or has been performed. The operation was concluded successfully; the enemy has withdrawn. Withdrawn, I say, not destroyed. We must be eternally vigilant against their return.

"We must be eternally vigilant as well against those domestic enemies who seek to undermine our freedoms and establish, by slow corruption, a tyranny over our lives. Arm yourselves, my fellow free men; do not obey any order that infringes on your rights to free speech, free assembly, free press; do not permit any searches without warrant of your property.

"Finally, to all members of the armed forces operat-

ing within the boundaries of the United States! You are
in violation of the Posse Comitatus Act of 1878, and
you may not carry out any operation of police powers
on domestic soil. Your President and Commander in
Chief has just resigned; the Secretaries of State and of
Defense were imposters disguised as human beings.
The Speaker of the House is now your Commander in
Chief. In a few moments, he will address you and give
you the order to report back to your posts." Pendrake
turned his gaze, hawklike, toward the Speaker: this
man stood, a horrified look on his face, barking seals
to his left and right. On the floor, beneath the bellies of
the seals, he was staring at the limp and distorted skin.
Here were the dead faces of his friends, coworkers,
and comrades. He brought his eyes up and nodded to
Pendrake.

Pendrake continued: "To the gentlemen and ladies
of the Congress: those of you who were not selkie imposters must have been helping the conspirators. These
treasonous acts were far too blatant, far too widespread, for you to have been in ignorance of them. Yet
none of you warned the American public about this
monstrous conspiracy to seize and destroy their liber-
ties; indeed, you cooperated in the most fawning and
cowardly fashion, abusing the trust given you, and
bending all your efforts to persuade your constituen-
cies to accept their coming slavery.

"If I have correctly judged the mood of the country,
those of you who do not feel honor bound to resign,
will no doubt face investigation. There are lampposts
in Washington enough to hang all traitors. I respect-
fully suggest that you call for special elections to be
held immediately in your jurisdictions, before the call
for a reckoning becomes immoderate.

"And, finally, to those criminals taking advantage of
the civil discord to strike! Know that I soon shall have
at my disposal certain magical means of discovering
the perpetrators of any crime committed at any time

anywhere in the world. This valuable service I intend to sell to private detective agencies and to lawful police organizations. If you do evil, I will know! You will not escape. The fruit bourn by the weed of crime is death."

The chairman of the Federal Reserve Board was now near the second door to the chamber, almost opposite the one where Raven and Wendy stood.

Pendrake called out from the podium, ordering him to halt, and placing him under citizen's arrest.

At this last, the chairman of the Federal Reserve turned. He said smoothly, "I'm afraid you don't have the authority for that. I've done nothing, and you have no proof. Furthermore, your pretty speech went no farther than this room."

The door behind him silently opened, and a wash of black smoke rose up from the doorframe. Three men, and then four, and then more, dressed in all black, wearing wide black hats, emerged from the black smoke and entered the chamber, coming up silently behind the chairman while he was talking. In their hands they carried double-barreled weapons of sophisticated design, able to shoot either bullets or nonlethal darts. Their eyes were hidden behind goggles.

The chairman's two bodyguards, standing behind him, made little or no noise as they fell, darts in their necks. Black-cloaked men stepped silently into their places while the chairman was talking.

One of the men in black grabbed the chairman's right arm; another took his left. This man brushed away his hat and goggles, revealing a stern, young face. "Citizen's arrests are still good in this country, Mr. Chairman," he said, "even when issued by men you tried to have Azrael destroy!"

"No . . ." whispered the chairman.

Pendrake asked, "Vincent! Did Titania's people acquire the all-seeing pool while Oberon was here on Earth?"

One of the black-garbed figures doffed his hat, "All went according to plan, Mr. Pendrake."

"Burbank! What about the pirate satellite feed?"

Another figure doffed his hat, revealing a grizzled, old man's face, one eye squinting in mirth. "Don't worry none about that one, boss. Every word what was said here went out on all channels!"

Another of the figures in black called out, "We've secured all these outer corridors; the resistance just melted away. The White House and the Treasury building are ours! We've won!"

The chairman snarled, writhing in the iron grip that pinned his arms. "You cannot prevail! One word from me, one word, and all the world banks will foreclose on your federal debts! This country will go bankrupt within the hour, and your paper money will be worth nothing! Nothing! It will be a worldwide depression!"

Pendrake smiled thinly, leaning forward across the podium. "Do you honestly think men like me need parasites like you to make their fortunes?"

Then Pendrake straightened up. He saw small windows high up, pass from dark twilight into brightest day. From outside, he heard birdsong.

Wendy cried out, "Mommy did it! Merlin let Oberon bring back the Sun! Apollo's alive again!"

Pendrake permitted himself a grim smile. He called to his men, "Then I guess it's time to celebrate, boys! Welcome back to the land of the living! Vincent! Make sure that weasel there doesn't get away."

And he strode away from the podium with a jaunty step. "Where you off to, boss?" called out one of the men.

"Go visit your wife, Shrevvy! Me? I'm going to the patent office. I've got a design for an infinite energy circuit I'm going to sell; and we'll see how deep this depression will bite once there is a practically free, clean, and endless source of power on the market!"

24

The Last Guardian

I

Van Dam found Pendrake in the corridors immediately outside the congressional chamber only minutes after Pendrake's speech. Pendrake was staring out the doors at where Virginia militiamen were disarming federal troops; and the sunlight streamed through the great doors and reflected off the marble floors to either side of him.

Van Dam walked up beside him, smiling a sort of pleading smile, and he sidled up to the edge of the door, so that he was out of the sunlight and could not be seen from outside.

"Mr. Pendrake! You can't leave yet. There are members of the press waiting . . ."

Pendrake turned his head, his eyes narrowed in puzzlement. Pendrake could see that Van Dam was terribly afraid; it was not clear what he feared.

Just a moment ago, Van Dam had faced armed men

and defied his superior officers without flinching. Just an hour ago, he had been aboard an aircraft carrier fighting the fallen angels of Acheron. He had not shown fear then. What did he fear now?

Pendrake asked, "Tell me what you want from me."

Van Dam spoke in a careful tone of voice, "We want to help you. We can make certain you win the next election. After that speech, we can sell you to the American public . . ."

"What is it you want?"

"To help you!"

Pendrake gave him a skeptical look, and started to turn away. "Wait!" said Van Dam. "We need you! I admit we need you—to lead the country!"

Pendrake looked back. Surprise was on his features. "But why in the world should I want to?"

Van Dam said, "I'm offering you power! Absolute, unstoppable power! If you don't want an elected position, if you don't want to be in the public eye, we can get you an appointed position. Appointees don't answer to anyone except to the administration, which we control. I've seen your charisma; this country is going to go through a long and hard period to recover from this disaster. The people need strong leadership for that period. Not many men could lead us through. Maybe only one—you."

Pendrake drew his magic sword and held it up. "Let me explain the nature of power. Look at the wording on this blade. What does it say on this side?"

"Uh . . . it says 'Take me up.' That's what I'm asking you to do, Mr. Pendrake. No matter who you run against, we can have the IRS investigate their tax returns near election time . . ."

Pendrake turned the blade over. "And on the other side?"

Van Dam stared at the letters, but did not answer.

The words said, CAST ME AWAY.

Pendrake said, "When I was in the dream universe, a

spirit who looked like George Washington came and asked me if I knew who Cincinnatus was."

Pendrake looked at Van Dam. Van Dam said, "I don't know who that was."

"You should read your classics. Lucius Quinctius Cincinnatus was working on his small farm when the Roman Senate came and made him dictator, because their consular army had been surrounded by the enemy on Mount Algidus. He was given absolute power over one of the most powerful city-states, at that time, in the world. He led the Roman armies to victory in a single day, and then he retired back to his small farm. Not many people in history give up being dictator.

"In any case, the spirit of Washington asked me, and I said, yes, I knew who Cincinnatus was. I think he is you, sir, I said.

"He said, they wanted to make me king, some of them, did you know that?

"I said that I had studied history, yes. There had never been a form of government ever before in the world like our Constitution; and I had heard that some people were frightened, and preferred the old ways, the ways they knew. And I asked him, when they came to make you king, why didn't you take it? The Continental Army was loyal to you.

"He had sort of a hard-bitten smile, and he stood with his hands clasped behind him. He just looked at me for time, and said nothing.

"Then he said, 'Ben told me that an old woman found him outside of Independence Hall the day Congress voted ratification of the Constitution. She asked him, What's it to be then, a monarchy or a republic? And Ben replied (of course, old Ben would not have told me the story if it did not contain one of his little witticisms) a Republic, madame, if you can keep it!' "

Pendrake could see the blank look of incomprehension in Van Dam's eyes.

Pendrake said, "Let me use an example. My first act

if you made me president would be to put the nation back on the gold standard and shut down the Federal Reserve system."

"That would not be fiscally sound, Mr. Pendrake. The government needs to be able to inflate the currency to pay for its programs! Inflation allows us to destroy our public debts. Money is power, we need to control the money supply in order to control the economy."

"We cannot let free men control their own money supply? My second act would be to repeal the Sixteenth Amendment, eliminate personal income tax, and declare April Fifteenth a national holiday."

"That would weaken the national government considerably."

"That's my point."

Van Dam said softly, "We must have a leader, a figure who can hold the country together for the duration of the emergency."

"A figurehead, do you mean? I will not serve in that capacity. And, forgive me, what emergency? That just ended."

"Our financial system was destroyed during the war, Mr. Pendrake! Communication networks down, the federal government halted, certain areas up in arms against us. The services of the government cannot be resumed immediately, and the international monetary fund . . ."

"The emergency will end once the federal government returns to its constitutionally permitted business. The state and local authorities can handle local disturbances."

"No. We need central control. Martial law must be enforced until things are put back in order. Someone who understands the new state of things—someone who has the magic on his side—must lead us. One man."

"Colonel Van Dam, you have missed the whole point of what's happened, haven't you? A warlock from our past, from the age of monarchy, slew the man he thought was our monarch, and he killed and replaced what he took to be his ministers and barons, our Congress, with his creatures. Yet, somehow, this country did not fall. And why is that?"

"Now you are being ridiculous, Mr. Pendrake! I am offering you power, power over your fellow men, and all you are talking about is how to dissolve and abolish that power. It was not the common people who saved this country, it was a hero. You, yourself, acting alone. The citizens had nothing to do with it. . . . Without strong leadership now, we will have anarchy . . ."

Pendrake now understood what Van Dam feared.

He smiled a cold smile. "So that is it. Azrael actually convinced you, did he? A dead doctrine, long ago forgotten, that one man can be anointed by supernatural mumbo jumbo to rule his ordained subjects. He told you that some men are born with spurs on their heels, and others born with saddles on their backs. Azrael told you Heaven appointed me to lead, didn't he?"

"You've *been* leading. All I ask is that you continue. It's your duty. The common citizens are not able to govern themselves, not able to save this country, not able to drive back archangels. No one else has a magic sword. . . ."

Pendrake threw back his head and laughed. "Am I not a citizen? Am I not a common man, of rank no higher than any other? I will ask you what I was asked: 'What's it to be, then? A monarchy or a republic?' I've already made my choice, Colonel Van Dam; and I am not tempted at all by yours. As for you, you should turn yourself in before the investigators come to arrest you for your part in this. The court may be lenient."

Van Dam, sullen, slunk back into the shadows. Pendrake, head erect, footstep firm, walked out into the sunlight, out into the wreckage of the streets. And, every-where he looked, he saw the opportunity to rebuild.

II

Wendy had a mischievous smile on her lips, and she tugged on Raven's hand. "Come on! Come on! I've always wanted to do this!"

"Really, should not be here, in this building, I think . . . ," said Raven, frowning, looking up and down the corridors.

"Oh, come on! No one is around, or almost no one." Wendy laughed. Even as she said that, a man came out a door down the corridor, saw them, turned and fled. Wendy waved the Moly Wand toward him; he became a seal, and fell. Raven and Wendy stepped over the seal, and kept walking.

Wendy said, "Haven't you ever been here, like on a tour or something?"

"No," said Raven, looking around.

"Besides! Don't get nervous! Otherwise the Storm-Princes will get loose! Here we are!"

Raven opened the door. "It looks lot bigger on TV. So this is the Oval Office, eh?"

Wendy climbed over the Presidential desk. On her hands and knees, she looked back over her shoulder at Raven, smiled languidly, and waggled her hips back and forth. "Hello there, handsome husband. How many people can say they did this?"

"Did what?"

Wendy collapsed into the President's chair, giggled, and started unbuttoning her blouse.

"Wendy! What are you doing?" Raven moved past the desk, trying to get to the sunlit windows to close the blinds; but as he passed near the chair, Wendy's skirt was kicked up into the air and fell over Raven's head. During the confused moment while he was blinded, Raven found himself tackled by his wife, and pushed backward into the President's chair.

When he threw the skirts aside in a flutter of cotton flowers, he found Wendy, naked as a jaybird, sitting in his lap, legs crossed, toes pointed, arching her back, and running her fingers through her long, black hair. She was smiling, and her eyes were hidden beneath her lashes.

She looked up in mock surprise, and gave a little squeal, drawing her tresses before her breasts. "Oh, Mr. President Raven, sir! I didn't see you there! Please don't tell anyone! I'll do . . ." and her voice dropped to a throbbing, husky whisper, ". . . *anything* . . . !" She batted her eyelashes at him.

Raven reached out and took her naked shoulders in his strong hands. She laughed happily and writhed in his grip. Then she looked up suddenly, "What's wrong? Why haven't you ravished me yet?"

He said, "I am worried about Storm-Princes. What if, you know, during moments of passion, they are getting loose? What if I must be like a monk from now on, eh? This worries me."

Wendy said, "I've got a plan! A great plan!"

Raven said, "What is this plan?"

She leaned forward, caressing her fingertips along his beard and the corded muscles in his neck, pressing her rounded body up against his, and she nibbled on his ear, whispering, "Well, stop worrying, silly boy!"

Raven looked philosophical for a moment, frowning and nodding in thought. Then, grasping his nude wife in one hand, he leaned forward and roughly brushed off the deck with the other. Red and white phones, historically significant pen-sets, important documents, bills awaiting signature, and treaties with foreign nations were swept to the floor. He pushed his wife back onto the green blotter, and, while she squealed and struggled enthusiastically, he had his way with her.

Later, they sat naked in the Presidential chair, her on his lap, with his voluminous cape wrapped around them, looking out at the rain. She said, "Let's see if we can do this while floating!"

And she began to lift up a little ways into the air.

"Eh, darling, what are we doing if someone walks in?"

"I don't know. Charge admission? Here; hold on!" They kissed.

Raven said, "Mm. Did I tell you that I love you, my little bird, eh?"

"I love you, too. And you know what else?"

"Mm? What else?"

"I love it that there will be fairy-tales running loose in the world again! Things are just going to be so weird from now on! It'll be great!"

III

Galen Waylock had taken a nap, and when he woke, he found himself garbed in a robe of white samite, with a garland of bay leaves on his head. He looked up at his grandfather, who sat nearby, staring into the bowel of the Chalice.

The unicorn horn stood, point in earth, upright between them.

It was dusk, and Galen's bow was beginning to glow more brightly against the darkening background.

To their left and right were the scattered ruins of Everness, rain-drenched tapestries and paintings beaten into the dirt, fragments of marble statues, broken faces and arms strewn across warped and shattered floorboards. Some rooms in the north and south wings were still standing.

In between the walls had been toppled, and burning footprints, larger than any footprint of man or titan, had smashed, smoldering, through the center of the tower, breaking it and scattering the stones. A path of devastation led to the broken seawall. The statue of the winged horse, which once had been atop the central tower, was lost.

Lemuel asked, "What did they say?"

Galen sighed. "The gods who dwell on Kadath will not aid us to rebuild; they wish never to become involved in any wars on either side, either of Mommur or of Acheron. But they treated me with grace, and gave me this robe to wear." He sighed again and plucked the bay-leaf crown from his head, and held it, staring down. Then he said, "There are no powers to aid us. Can we reestablish the wards merely with human effort, and with the magic at our command, Grandfather?"

"We shall see. Do you remember the central tower?"

"It's the first thing I memorized, Grandfather. Earth moon, heavenly moon, fiery moon, weeping moon."

"And all the details of the scrollwork in the doorframes? The signs on the scales of the white-and-scarlet dragons intertwined about the foundation?"

"Four gates for the seasons, twelve arches for the hours of daylight; three hundred and sixty-five bricks, each named after a saint on the calendar of saints. Of course I remember the towers. What are we going to do about the books?"

Lemuel smiled. "I had a long time, and I was very bored, when I was fifty. You probably don't remember when I had that photographer come in. He took pictures of everything. Everything. Originally I meant it to show that I hadn't moved anything, in case the Royal Historical Trust ever questioned me. I also had the books microfilmed. It will take some time to have those records shipped here from England." And his smile was good to see. More briskly, he said, "But for now. We have to create the tower tonight. Men die without their dreams."

Galen lay down in the grass.

"There was one other thing, Grandfather . . ."

"Yes?"

"The dream-colts wouldn't come when I called." He spoke in a quiet, sad, small voice.

"Well. Things change," said Lemuel. But he was thinking of when he had seen his first dream-colt as a child.

"I just wish . . ."

"Yes, Galen?"

"I just wish Dad was here."

"Well. He'll come around."

"How come he got so upset when I shot him?"

"Well. He and I had an argument about that once."

"Grandpa? How come it didn't work? What's wrong with his legs?"

Lemuel said, "Go to sleep now, Grandson. Remember the tower."

Galen shut his eyes, and said, "Morpheus, escort me to your wide kingdom . . ." And he was asleep before he finished the sentence.

Carefully, Lemuel poured some of the living energy from the Chalice of Hope into the mouth of the unicorn horn; and a drop of living light soaked from the buried tip into the earth of Everness. "I know what is past shall live again in time . . . ," he whispered.

A part of the twilight sunset came down out of the sky, the color of deep purple clouds, and became a tall figure robed in dusk and shadow. His crown was two black swan wings, a star of light burned within the diamonds of the necklace he wore, the toes of his boots did not quite brush the grass tips. In his hand floated a slender wand of heavy gold. His right eye was covered by a patch; his left eye burned gray and clear.

He cast no shadow.

Behind him, her silky white coat shimmering with captured glints of lambent light, stepping with fawnlike step, more graceful than grace herself, came the Unicorn, mother of the dream-colts. A pleasant scent came from her, like springtime grass. She looked at Lemuel with lavender eyes, so that he forgot who he was for the moment.

A timeless time passed while Lemuel stared.

Eventually he spoke, "Oberon, I offer you the guest-courtesy which is your foremost law, neither to strike nor slander nor carry away; nor, as my guest, can you do anything to work my harm or discomfort, nor over-stay your welcome. The Earth has witnessed my words."

"I accept the invitation," came the solemn, kingly voice, "Nor have I given you cause to fear me, dear Bedevere."

"Why these long generations of deception, sky-father?"

" 'Deception'?"

"I was taught you gave the Key to us, to keep in trust; in fact, Merlin stole it, corrupted your champion, and founded a kingdom on Earth of peace and justice. In fact, you need us to wield the Key. I saw what happened to you when Azrael directed it at you."

"Where is the deception in any of this? Merlin would not have valued any freely given gift; he is a scavenger-bird, and will only treasure what he steals. Does it offend you that I need your house to serve me? Dreams need the hands of men to make them real, even as kings need patient and faithful knights to make their kingdoms. Kingdoms fall when dreams die; Lancelot proved that. Anton Pendrake, even now, seeks to restore the dreams of this land. Are you offended that your ancestors were ordered never to use that Key? Truly, truly, I tell you, there are deep, dread powers who walk the nightmare-world, and men are not wise enough to traffic with them. Your race could not even banish war when war was no more than the enmity of man for man. Now War is a living creature, a god, and walks in flesh among you. How many years before Pendrake can banish him this time? Remember, pride was what tempted Morningstar to fall, and now he is quenched in the depth of the sea."

"And I wonder, Oberon, to hear the same contempt for mankind that came from his lips come from yours!"

"If a father will not let his children play with matches, is this contempt?" Oberon's voice was soft, but there was an echo of ancient strength in it; and Lemuel wondered how old this being was to whom he spoke. Lemuel really had no idea from whence Oberon had come, nor, truly, what he was.

"What have you come for, Oberon?"

"To forgive you."

Lemuel was astonished. "What?"

"You failed to wake the sleepers when duty required; for that failure you are forgiven, for Morningstar, frightened, was defeated merely by the name and rumor of the heavenly knights I have sleeping in the Autumn Stars. But do not be deceived by Anton Pendrake's overweening vainglory. It was not he, but you, who conquered; and your only weapon, the weapon you carried in your heart, your patience, your faithfulness, and, yes, your loyalty to me. Your chief weapon, one even angels could not face, was your willingness to end this Earth that a better world be born."

Lemuel was silent, staring up at that half-hidden, twilight-shadowed, and kingly face. "I accept your forgiveness. Why do the powers of the dream-world no longer bow to the seven sigils? Why do the dream-colts no longer come when called?"

"You know why. My servants are my own. Until you renew your fealty to me, they will not obey."

Lemuel was silent. Then he said, "I need to learn more of you before I can take such an oath."

"I have brought the mother of all dream-colts here to speak with you."

The Unicorn stepped shyly around Oberon, who had draped his hand across her mane. She spoke in a voice like a woodwind: "Beloved, in your hand is the relic of my dead husband; it is the only part of him which still abides on earth. I ask, in pity's name, that you restore it to me, for it is mine."

"What shall you do with it, great lady, if I give it to you?"

Oberon spoke up, "I would unlock the gates of paradise."

Lemuel said, "And I cannot?"

Oberon said, "What spirits will make your works in dream's high kingdom? I have ten thousand times ten thousand angels and lios-alfar at my command. Enough to remake the world entire. Have you spirit enough to raise even a single tower?"

Lemuel did not know how to answer.

The Unicorn said, "If you seek to keep my husband's horn, I charge you to use it with all wisdom, all compassion, all mercy." Oberon looked surprised, and took his hand slowly from her mane.

She said, "There are creatures in the deep which can overwhelm the earth; and so they shall, if the ways are opened in the mist between this Earth and that other world. Your protection, heretofore, was that the mists of Everness made men forgetful to the dangerous wonders around them. Will you now raise the mists, and call on men to forget these dreadful happenings? When they wake to-morrow, all will seem no more than a fading dream."

Lemuel said, "Will the dead be made alive again, or will the widows of all the men who died fighting Acheron simply forget why they weep?"

Oberon said, "The Cauldron of Rebirth is mine. Have I not already promised to restore to pure and uncorrupted flesh those who bow to me?"

Lemuel said, "What need I do to raise this mist?"

The Unicorn said, "Only Oberon knows the names that compel Forgetfulness."

Lemuel shook his head. "Pendrake would never agree."

Oberon said sternly, "I do not ask him."

Lemuel looked up, drawing a deep breath. "But you must. Yes, I have served with great patience and faithfulness all these years. But you forget that I do not owe my fealty to you, Lord of the Autumn Stars, but to the original founder from whom our grant comes. Only Arthur or his heir can revoke my powers. The heir of Arthur is Anton Pendrake; he bears the sword. I have been charged by him to restore the House of Everness; look; here is my mark."

And he opened the throat of his shirt, and exposed his shoulder. Where the flat of the magic blade had touched him, a golden stroke of light seemed to gleam from his flesh. He touched his shoulders with his two fingers, and touched his fingers to the earth. "I call upon the world to witness."

The Unicorn said, "Beloved, I see you still work heaven's will with your heart, even if you say with your lips you do not. Henceforward, for as long as your are faithful, I say to you, my children shall come when you call."

Oberon bowed. "I forgive this, your lack of courtesy as well. Like Merlin, you would not return the stolen horn; but, like Merlin, you may yet do my will, whether you will or no; for they say that all spirits do my works, those who rebel no less than those who obey."

Oberon turned and walked away up the hill. The Unicorn followed, and where she stepped, leaves and flowers came forth from the burnt earth.

At the top of the hill Var was waiting for them.

Oberon said to Var, "Come. Your wife is waiting. A place had been made ready for you at my table, and you will be given white raiment after you bathe in my Cauldron, and wash your years and tears away."

A light like that a silvery lamp might shed, or a low-flying star, appeared through the tree-boles, glinting in the darkening gloom; and Var set off toward it down a path which had not been there a moment ago.

Oberon turned and looked back down into the twilight at the ruins of Everness, the toppled brick, the destroyed beauty.

In some places the shattered beams of wood still smoldered.

He asked, "Eurynome, why did you so suddenly speak to allow him keep your horn? Why did you offer your children again to bear him aloft?"

She said, "It is not your place to question me, young one. Yet for the sake of the Demiurge who first wore your crown, I will answer: I saw a deeper power in the blood of Everness than we had guessed, and I foresaw that he would call upon the Pendragon for aid. They can do little without the spirit-world to do their work; and yet, great Oberon, how many spirits, in this land, are loyal to your dream rather than to the Pendragon's?"

"That remains to be seen."

"Then see; for I foresaw this." A nod of her head, a sway of her horn, drew his one-eyed gaze back toward the ruins.

Softly and gently as a dream, a tower came into view above the ruins, with four great gates looking toward the four quarters of the earth. Runes of power were written on the doors, and on the crown, the statue of a winged horse reared.

Even as they watched, the tower seemed to grow solid against the setting sun, and then it cast a shadow.

"The tower is still surrounded by ruins and rubble," said Oberon.

"But it is a beginning, and Galen has recalled his home in loving detail," said the Unicorn in the soft music of her voice.

"I see now what made us bow," said Oberon, "but I will not ponder it. If not Lemuel, and if not Galen, then the Guardians to come will one day swear fealty to me, recall their oaths, and wake the sleepers. Go ahead then, with my courtesy and thanks return to the One Unicorn, whose image you bear, and carry her this message for me: I ask that the Unicorn's third race of children, the dream-colts of Celebradon, may continue their services to Everness, so that the Guardians will regard us with favor and gratitude. And one day they will forget their pride, remember me, and the horn shall be mine once more, as it was in the age when I overcame Ouranos. But for me, now it is my turn to practice patience."

And, putting his hand once more on the mane of the Unicorn, the King of Dreaming drifted away down the paths toward the twilight, and faded into shadow. A haunting music hung for a time in the air where he had passed.

IV

A haggard man dressed in a cloak of feathers with a blue hood paused on the ridge, leaning on what looked like a walking stick, but was not.

In the valley were smokestacks. The blaze from the foundry, even during the day, flickered like white petals around the upper edge of the blast furnaces. Here were streams of molten iron pouring from spouts in sprays of sparks, and gushes of black smoke rose up like ghosts toward the blue sky.

He walked down to the foundry. When he came to the locked gate, he stared in horrified distaste at the chains, the lock, as if these all reminded him of some terrible thing. Then he raised his staff and spoke a spell; the lock came undone, and the chain rattled and slid aside.

Closer, the stink of molten metal and fire hung in the air, and he heard the endless throb and roaring of machinery, of wheels turning, pistons driving, restlessly.

It was quieter when he walked into the huge ware-house-space standing to one side of the iron works. Here was Prometheus, sitting cross-legged on the concrete floor with pieces of disassembled machinery strewn to his left, papers covered with drawings and diagrams before him on the floor, and several computers, built with an oversized keyboard and mouse, stacked on shelves to this right. All the wall behind him was composed of angled planes of dusty windows. Sunlight in dusty beams made bright rectangles on the floor.

Prometheus was dressed in a blue pinstripe suit, vaster than ship's sails, which some tailor, in return for the publicity, had made for him. On his finger was a ring of black adamantium, which he had forged from the severed links he once wore.

The Titan spoke without looking away from his work, "Hello, Merlin. I was expecting you." An alarm clock went off as he was speaking, and he reached over, and clumsily (for his fingers were too large for the switch) silenced the ringing bell.

The Warlock said in voice of studied casualness. "I've come to talk . . ."

Prometheus smiled disdainfully. "Is that the truth?" Now he turned and looked down at the Warlock, and the Warlock saw the perceptive humor twinkling in the Titan's eye.

The man once called Azreal looked down sullenly. "You know, then, Titan, how this conversation will spin itself out."

"Do I? You may surprise me."

"And if I do not? Come, tell me what I will say."

"I don't know in detail. You, for a time, will talk of trivial things, mentioning how men now know of magic; and you will seek to know my mind in this, whether it is good or ill that the Paradise of Oberon has been denied to them. But you will try to discover my thoughts without asking me directly, for your fear will impede you."

"What fear?" he asked quietly.

"You are afraid that, after all, you are not so much like me as you would like to be."

"And are we not?" asked the Warlock loudly, raising his chin, a sneer of pride on his face. "Have we not both stolen from heaven, and sought to render men superior to gods?"

"You stole; I did not. One cannot steal one's own property. Gods are younger than men by far, though they pretend otherwise. I deserved praise, yet was punished. You deserve punishment, child-killer, yet won the praises of a thousand generations."

The Warlock looked down, crossed his arms, and the lines around his mouth and eyes grew deeper as his face darkened. Eventually he said, "Do none revile you? Is it not a sign of greatness to be loathed?"

Prometheus uttered a brief, deep laugh. "Peter Waylock, from your family, came by not long after the Sun was reborn. He complained quite a bit about how hard it was to get his wheelchair up the stairs. At one point he asked me, and quite bitterly, why I hadn't made men out of something unbreakable, like iron or steel? Why were they so easy to break? And I told him that, of all my creations, only man has no cause to complain about his shape."

"Why?"

"For I have made him out of clay, you see, and clay is malleable. And I never fired mankind in my kiln; instead I gave the fire to him. Are you discontent? Reshape your soul according to your own liking."

Merlin Waylock continued to stand with his gaze harsh, his arms folded. Eventually he said, "And to what shape should we mold ourselves, O Titan?"

Prometheus smiled, "You might as well ask me, and what is goodness? What is virtue?"

Merlin Waylock clasped his hands behind his back, and stared broodingly out the windows. Eventually the Warlock asked, "And how did your conversation with my descendant conclude itself?"

"I told him there were no limits to what men might do to improve themselves. He seemed dissatisfied with the answer, and wheeled away."

The Warlock stood in a pose of black abstraction, and again he was silent for a time. He said sharply, "I saw the Sephiroth of Kether in the clouds over the right shoulder of Raven, son of Raven; nor is that his true name. Had I known his true name, he would not have so easily escaped this land's jail. But I ask, O Titan, what this sign means."

"You know."

"Do I read the signs wrongly? The children of Raven will be kings of the Earth. How can this be, in this land where there are no kings?"

"The estranged bloodlines of titans, gods, and men will be reunited in the children of Gwendolyn Pendrake and Raven Varovitch. Do you know your Scripture, wizard?"

"I know it well, and know as well what hands wrote it; a fact long hidden from mankind."

"The sixth chapter of Genesis reports that there were giants on the Earth in those days, when the sons of god came in unto the daughters of men, and they bore children to them. These same became mighty men, which were of old, men of renown."

"The heroes of ancient Greece, as well, had divine blood in them. What does this mean?"

"You know what it means."

"Only those of immortal blood can command the Night World. Your grandchildren will be magicians and heroes."

"In ten generations, my bloodline will encompass the greater part of mankind. Once, only the spirits and fairies could command the powers of magic; that time is past. I have given my children a second type of divine fire, now."

Merlin Waylock showed no change of his hard expression; but his face grew pale. "Then all my efforts were but child's play. You have more than accomplished everything I dreamed to do."

Prometheus uttered a bass laugh. "You have accomplished precisely what you set out to do! You thought to use the force of Acheron to seize the Key of Everness, and then to use the Key to betray the forces of Darkness, and prevent the rise of Acheron. All this, allegedly, to aid the return of the Pendragon. Now behold! Acheron was unleashed; the Acheron was halted; thousands died; Everness was destroyed; the Pendragon has returned to restore the land. And you, who sought to use treachery for your ends, you have become a traitor. All is accomplished. How can you doubt the power of men to mold of themselves into what they will? You are exactly the type of . . . thing . . . you set out to make yourself into."

Merlin Waylock turned, without a word of farewell or departure, and began to walk away across the echoing, vast concrete floor.

When he came to the huge garage door, which was open to the heat and sunlight, he stiffened, looking down at something just outside the door.

Prometheus, bent over his machinery, pretending to be occupied, smiling to himself.

Merlin Waylock turned. "I shall go to the Pendragon before his hunters find me. It would, after all, only be a matter of time until the planetarium of Everness is restored. I have no doubt he will send me back to Tirion; no prison of earth can hold me against my will . . ."

His voice trailed into silence. Then he drew a breath, gathered his courage, and spoke.

"Titan! What was it you thought, all those years as you hung in chains on the mountainside? What was it that sustained your courage to endure?"

Prometheus spoke without looking up from his busy hands, "Me? I never think much about my present circumstance; I always look ahead. But, if I had to name one thought, it was the one I told to you. That even suffering can be used for the improvement of one's state. Men can change their lives for the better, even those who are very much afraid to change."

"I wish to see Peter before I go. Where is he now?"

Prometheus looked thoughtful. "You will find him in a ski chalet in the Catskills, where interstate highway 287 meets the . . . ah. Excuse me. Look to sea where the ley-line from the old Indian burial grounds overlaps the way of air used by the swan-maidens. He will be dancing with girls far too young for him, and waiting for the slopes to open."

Merlin Waylock stepped out the door and jumped the little way to the ground. In the weeds in the ditch by the roadside, he saw the crumpled heap of a wheelchair, flattened as if by a hammer blow. Leading away were a few footprints in the dirt, unsteady at first, and then lengthening in stride, as if the feet had been running and running.

The magician drew on a heavy leather gauntlet, put out his hand, and called out his name. There was a scream from the sky near the sun, and a small, fierce bird of prey fell down from heaven, landed. His sharp talons cut into the leather glove, and he cocked his head, looking up at the wizard with eyes as proud and predatory as his own.

"I go to do penance for my crimes. I will be caged again, I fear, in Tirion. I will release you to fly the airs alone."

The bird cocked his head the other way, and opened his sharp, cruel beak. "No! I shall not leave you. You shall not go alone this time to your torment."

"I thank you; you cause me joy. And perhaps the sentence will be lighter to bear for your company. Come! I will see my family once more before I return to the world of dreams."

The two of them began to walk down the road, the Warlock carrying the merlin proudly on his fist.

Appendix
The List of the Wardens

*The Ancient
and Honorable Order of
the Watchmen of the Tower
of Time Unchanging,
Called Everness*

This is the traditional list as memorized by the librarians of Everness, and memorialized within the ornaments and images of their archives. Recent scholarship has shown that the list is questionable concerning certain dates and events, and that the Order springs from roots different and older than what is given here:

	YEAR	WARDEN
1.	500	MERLIN
2.	523	DONBLEYS LE FAY, his student
3.	546	ALFCYNNIG
4.	550	LOHORT
5.	574	NENNING
6.	575	NIMBLING
7.	599	CORBENEC OF CARABAS

Glastonbury Line

8.	625	MORS OF YNYS WITRIN. First Warden of the Glastonbury Line.
9.	640	BERTILAK THE GREEN. Declares the Wardenship to be hereditary.
10.	674	ST. CYNWULF. End of Glastonbury Line. First Northumbrian Warden.

Northumbrian Line

11.	684	UTHLAC I. At this time, certain paths and sections of the Forest of Brocillinde are enchanted, and removed from the limits of time and space in order to preserve the corpse of the First Warden from despoliation.
12.	701	CAEDMON OF FAY LAKE
13.	723	NENNIUS THE DECEIVER. Warden is replaced by a selkie, and does much harm before being slain by Adlhelm.
14.	724	ADLHELM THE ACCURSED
15.	730	ANDREAS I
16.	780	UTHLAC II
17.	798	ANDREAS II
18.	813	CYNNINGALF I. End of the Northumbrian Line. Start of the Anglo-Saxon line.

Anglo-Saxon Line — Wardens of Wessex

19.	827	CYNNINGBERT THE DRUNKARD
20.	839	CYNNINGALF II
21.	857	CWENOBALD
22.	860	CYNNINGALF III
23.	866	CYNNINGRED I
24.	871	ALFWISE THE GREAT
25.	899	ALFWARD THE ELDER
26.	925	ATHELSTONE

27.	940	ADMUND
28.	946	ADRED
29.	955	ADWY
30.	959	ADGAR
31.	975	ALFWARD THE FOULLY SLAIN. First Selkie irruption.
32.	978	CYNNINGRED II
33.	1016	ALFWARD COLD IRON

	Danish Captivity	**Wyrdabrunnr**
34.	1017	BEORN OF WYRDABRUNNR
35.	1035	AEGIRBEORN THE NAVIGATOR. Discovers the Americas in a dream. Begins the carving of the Great Globe.
36.	1040	ODBEORN WYRDABRUNNR

	Saxon Line	**Doomsmere**
37.	1042	EDWARD THE UNWISE. Pays the Necromancer to trouble him no longer.
38.	1071	MANDRAGORE THE BLACK. Continues the Dreamgeld payments; eventually bows to and serves the Necromancer.

	Norman Line	**Whitingwell**
39.	1079	WILLIAM WHITINGWELL. He is granted the Guardianship after the Guardian of Tirion hales Mandragore to Wailing Blood.
40.	1087	WILLIAM II
41.	1100	HENRY WHITINGWELL
42.	1135	SYLVESTER TOURDEFAUX. Erects an image of the Tower of the Tor while the true Tower is occupied by plagues.

	First English Line	Wyrdloch
43.	1154	ALBERIC THE WISE. Wrote "De Insomniis" part of the larger *Oneirocritica*.
44.	1189	ARCHIMAGO. Hinders the ambition of the Elfinqueen.
45.	1199	MALAGAUNT. Establishes the planetary motions. Travels in astral body to Malacand and Perelend.
46.	1216	SIMONUS; called Simon Victor. Coquers Nastrond, drives the Kelpie out of Uhnuman. This is the first extradimensional conquest by human kind into the dream-lands.
47.	1272	MANFRED THE MAGICIAN. Expands the human-controlled dream-lands. Titans bow to him.
48.	1307	MALAGIGUS. Human colonies established at Dylath-Leen and Ulthar in the dream-lands.
49.	1327	SIMONDEMAGUS. Humans establish the great city of Baharna on the Island of Oreb.
50.	1377	MERLINDORE. Slain by the gods while attempting to scale the dreaming mountain of Hathegkla. Oberon the Faery King holds the Wardenship during the Rising of the Mist. Dream-lands cut off from Waking world. The Mountains of Oreb destroy the human city: the cats of Ulthar wipe out those humans who treat them with less than perfect esteem. Oberon invests the Wardenship to the Wyscraft of Gaunt.

Second English Line	Wayscraft
51. 1399	WYSCRAFT CADELLIN. Slain in his sleep by Turkish Wizards.
52. 1413	WYSCRAFT EMRYS. Slain in his sleep by Turkish Wizards.
53. 1422	WYSCRAEFT CENNETH. Discovers a second Tower of Time in Byzantium. Marries Irene the Blessed, founds Greek Line.

Greek Line	Thyrewaylock
54. 1461	CONSTANTINE THYREROS
55. 1483	BELISARIUS THYREROS
56. 1483	PHORCUS GRAEAE THIREWAYLOCK

First Younger Line	De Gray
57. 1485	WILLIAM DE GRAY
58. 1509	MARGARET THE MAIDEN DE GRAY, First Wardeness
59. 1547	LOUIS DE GRAY. Resurrects the Founder from the Dead that he might avenge the rape of Margaret de Gray by Selkie. Azrael takes the surname de Gray.
60. 1553	JOHN DE GRAY; also known as John Dee. Azrael is captured and reimprisoned.
61. 1558	SYLVANIUS WAYLOCK. Everness removed to the Americas.

New World Line	Waylock
62. 1603	SYLVIE WAYLOCK, Second Wardeness
63. 1625	MELPOMIDES WAYLOCK. Introduced the cryptic symbolism into the House, built the portico.

64.	1649	JEREMIAH WAYLOCK THE RESTORER. Tore down the portico, built the Old Wing. Second Selkie irruption.
65.	1658	VIRGILLUS MAGUS: Virgil the Magician is recalled from Celebradon to stand the Watch. Virgil creates the Talking Stones of Everness, to warn of coming dangers.
66.	1660	ARCHIMEDES WAYLOCK. Built the Planetarium, restored the Icons. Archimedes does not die, but is taken alive to a realm by one of the Pleiades.
67.	1685	AESCHYLUS WAYLOCK. Restored the lost wing of Melpomides.
68.	1689	PENTHEUS WAYLOCK. Organized the Library.
69.	1689	ARTIMESIA WAYLOCK. Third Wardeness. Married Robin Quicksilver of Elfhome.
70.	1702	CALIBAN WAYLOCK THE BLENTLING. Dies without issue.
	Reid Family	**Red (Reid) Branch**
71.	1714	ORESTES WAYLOCK. Descended from the youngest sister of Pentheus, Britomart Reid nee Waylock.
72.	1727	ORPHEUS WAYLOCK
73.	1760	ALBERTUS WAYLOCK
74.	1820	LAZARUS WAYLOCK
75.	1830	CADELLIN II WAYLOCK. Builds and restores the House and the Tower to its current form.
76.	1837	MINERVA WAYLOCK. Fourth Wardeness. Completed the building of the High House, established the Wards of the Earth, abolished the

Theosophists, drove the Edgewood-
wives into fairy-land. Dies without
issue. Titiania the Elfinqueen
searches for the lost cousin of the
Gordon family, Jason. His son Jere-
miah marries Beth, daughter of
Cadellin II, and takes her name.

	Gordon Family	Gold (Gordon) Branch
77.	1901	RODERICK GORDON WAYLOCK
78.	1910	WILBUR WAYLOCK
79.	1936	PHINEAS WAYLOCK
80.	1966	ANDREW WAYLOCK
81.	1972	LEMUEL WAYLOCK